HOT PLANET

MICHAEL BURNS

COVER ILLUSTRATION AND DESIGN BY JIM WILLIAMS

ISBN   0-9639345-0-3

PUBLISHED BY PLANET PRESS
TUBAC, ARIZONA

PRINTED IN THE USA BY GRIFFIN PRINTING

This novel is for my children, Amy and Sarah, and for all the children of the earth who will grow up on a planet with a damaged atmosphere. My generation hasn't made this world better — we're leaving it to our children in a far worse condition than we can possibly know.

We've cut down most of the world's big trees, we've filled the air with ozone depleting chemicals, and we've promiscuously burned fossil fuels and sent billions of tons of pollutants into the sky, perhaps wishing they would just go away. They haven't.

Carbon dioxide is an invisible gas, but in this case, out of sight, out of mind does not apply. We will see the results of too much carbon dioxide in our atmosphere throughout the nineties, and even more in the next century.

Still, it's not too late. I hope the next generation will take the courageous steps necessary to do what we failed to do.

Great distress shall be upon the earth...
Nations in perplexity at the roaring of
the sea and the waves...
Men fainting with fear and with foreboding
of what is coming on the world.

LUKE 21:23-26

PROLOGUE

Early on a sunny morning in the summer of 1926, Katie Harlowe knew it was going to be a beautiful day. The signs were everywhere; the air was clear and already pleasantly warm, dozens of birds greeted her every step with their cheerful morning songs, and the pungent perfume of magnolia blossoms wafted up and down the street. To Katie, the earth seemed vibrantly alive and it energized her, penetrating to the very core of her soul. What a lovely morning, she thought.

She carried her purse in one hand and part of the Sunday edition of the *Los Angeles Examiner* in the other. She would have time to read it once she got on the train to the downtown area. She wore her walking shoes and carried her dress shoes in a bag inside her purse. She would wear these once she got to her office. For now, comfort was more important than appearances.

Anyone who saw her would have noticed a lively bounce to her step. She appeared truly happy. Summer in Monrovia was her favorite time of the year and, on a day like today, she felt glad to be alive.

Katie walked down Magnolia Avenue in Monrovia, a city in the foothills of the San Gabriel Valley eighteen miles east of Los Angeles. When she reached Foothill Boulevard, she turned east and went four blocks to Myrtle Avenue, the main street of the city. At the intersection, she caught the city trolley, taking it south to the Pacific Electric Railway station on the southeast corner of Olive and Myrtle. At the station, Katie hopped off the little trolley and boarded a waiting big red car for the forty-seven minute ride into Los Angeles. As she entered the car, she smiled and waved to the motorman who stood at the car's front.

"Good morning, Hank," she greeted him.

"Good morning, Katie," he answered jovially. "Isn't it a wonderful day?"

"Yes," she agreed. "It's a grand day!" She took her customary seat aboard the car and waited as several fellow Monrovians boarded the trolley. A minute passed and, seeing that no one else was boarding, the motorman closed the trolley's door and looked back at his passengers.

"All aboard for Los Angeles!" he called out. Then he sounded the car's booming horn and the electric railway car slowly moved down the tracks toward the west. As the car picked up speed, Katie settled back into her cushioned seat. The big red car rolled westward, reaching a speed of nearly fifty miles an hour. The run into Los Angeles would be a fast one, with only a few stops along the way. This was her favorite part of the day, a time of relaxation just before the demands of another hectic work day.

On the inbound trip downtown, she always sat on the right side of the car so she could gaze upon the San Gabriel mountains several miles to the north, their ridges running roughly parallel to the railway tracks. The steep, rugged terrain of these mountains dominated the entire northern horizon and, as always, the bright white dome of the Mount Wilson Observatory was clearly visible atop Mount Wilson's evergreen peak. At 5,710 feet above sea level, the observatory stood out majestically, as if it were some silent guardian, forever watching over all of Southern California.

Two weeks earlier, Katie and several friends had taken the trolley on a Sunday excursion up to Mount Lowe, a few miles west of Mount Wilson and just as high. The ride up the steep grade had been exciting and was a thrill in itself, but the views from the top were so breathtaking, Katie and her friends decided to make it an annual outing.

From Mount Lowe, they could see most of the Los Angeles basin, including much of Southern California's shoreline and the Pacific Ocean beyond. Looking down on California, they beheld a land of dazzling beauty. The dusty brown foothills just below were dotted with chaparral, but in the distance lush green orchards filled the valleys. Just off the coast, Santa Catalina Island jutted up from the shiny blue waters of the Pacific Ocean.

Katie could still visualize in her mind the pristine views from the mountains, and she looked forward to going up there again next year. She smiled happily, knowing she was fortunate to live in such a wonderful area as Southern California, with its clean air and marvelous climate.

Five years earlier, she had moved from Pittsburgh, a dirty city of smokestacks and soot, desiring a healthier place to live and a better lifestyle. Long before she made the move west, a friend had written to her, urging her to come out to the west coast and see it for herself, to see how much better she'd like it here. Katie thought about it for nearly three years until, after one particularly long and depressing winter, she made the decision to leave, and she bought train tickets to Los Angeles.

Fortunately, she found a job within days after her arrival, and for the first few months she rented an apartment in the downtown area. Although she liked Los Angeles, one weekend she took a big red car traveling east, merely out of curiosity to see other parts of Southern California, and she discovered Monrovia.

Here, in this lovely little town nestled in the mountains well away from the hubbub of Los Angeles, she instinctively knew that she had found her permanent home. She used her inheritance to buy a two-story house on Magnolia Avenue north of Grand and immediately became an active member of the community, attending the nearby Methodist church, becoming a member of the Monrovia Women's Club, and donating money and time to local charities such as the Salvation Army and the Red Cross.

Katie Harlowe was a happy woman whose dream had come true. She had come west to a paradise called Southern California, a place with the most temperate climate in all of America. The summers in the San Gabriel Valley were wonderfully hot, but never humid. Fresh ocean breezes provided cool air to the entire valley in mid-afternoon. In the winter, the nearby mountains were frequently blanketed with snow, though it rarely snowed in the valley. For Katie, Monrovia was the perfect place to live. She had no desire to go back to Pennsylvania, even to visit.

Katie worked as a fashion buyer for a major clothier. It had been her goal to start her own apparel business but, after buying her house, her funds had run out, and she decided to take her career in the fashion industry one day at a time. Her employer was good to her and, for a woman in her day, she earned a fine salary. So for the time being she intended to stay at her job and not take any unnecessary risks.

She sensed that there was economic trouble ahead. In her mind, the Roaring Twenties were entirely too promiscuous, and people were acting as if tomorrow didn't matter, speculating on unsound investments when they should have been saving their money for the future.

Katie was currently banking nearly four thousand dollars a year. When she had thirty-five thousand in her savings account, then, and only then, did she intend to quit her job and open a dress shop in Monrovia. But that was still five years away. For now, it was another workday in Los Angeles, another day of commuting into the city.

She turned her attention away from the mountains and opened the *Examiner* on her lap and began to read. As she unfolded the paper, her eyes fell on the photo and accompanying story in the lower right corner of page one. It was about an accident.

A Big Red Car had derailed in Hollywood after hitting an automobile at a street crossing. The two occupants of the automobile were both crushed to death and several passengers aboard the trolley had been seriously injured. Witnesses said they thought the motorman in the trolley was at fault, that he had been going too fast for safety. Katie looked up from the paper, her eyes focusing on the scenes going by her window. How could such an accident be allowed to happen? she asked herself. Such a shame, Katie thought.

The world was changing rapidly. With the coming of the automobile, a new method of transportation had been created, and every day that went by there were more and more autos being built and purchased. People liked the idea of driving to almost anywhere a road could take them. Autos represented ultimate freedom, unlike the ungainly electric railway system, forever confined to the tracks it ran upon. Katie wondered if perhaps the electric railway was becoming obsolete. She set her paper down beside her and continued to stare out the window of her railway car, thinking about what the future might bring.

But, unknown to her, there were forces already at work that would change Los Angeles and the world forever; forces whose main objective was the demise of the big red cars and the very trolley she was now riding on.

Several hours later that morning, eight lawyers met in an office in downtown Los Angeles. The subject of their meeting was transportation. Yet, the gathering of lawyers was about much more than merely transportation.

"This is what we're up against," said attorney Jack Steinig, pointing to a blueprint-size poster hanging on one wall of his office. Steinig stood cockily with his back to the wall, his feet spread to shoulder width and his weight evenly balanced on both feet. He pulled an unfiltered Camel cigarette from his shirt pocket and tapped it against his left wrist. Then, he lazily stuck it in his mouth and from seemingly out of nowhere produced a match, igniting it one-handed, using his thumbnail. He held the match up to the cigarette in his mouth and took a deep drag.

"This is our competition," Steinig went on, "and it's not going to be an easy fight. It's going to take time and money. Lots of money." Steinig smiled effusively at the group of men sitting before him, sticking both thumbs into his suspenders, his cigarette dangling from his lips. "Gentlemen, I have no intention of losing to these bastards." He jangled his thumb toward the poster. "We're gonna beat their asses."

The poster showed a map of the Los Angeles basin, detailing the lines of the Pacific Electric Railway as they crisscrossed the Southern California geography. In the lower right corner of the poster, a boxed advertisement touted the railway's main features: "WORLD'S GREATEST ELECTRIC RAILWAY SYSTEM. 1000 Miles of Standard Trolley Lines To All Points of Greatest Interest in the Heart of Southern California and Traversed by 2,700 SCHEDULED TRAINS DAILY."

The hub of the Pacific Electric Railway was its huge, busy terminal at Sixth and Main in downtown Los Angeles. Trolleys left the terminal at the rate of almost one per minute, heading to destinations all over Southern California. From Sixth and Main, the trolley line went east into the San Gabriel Valley to the cities of San Marino, Arcadia, Monrovia, Duarte, and Glendora. It went northeast into Pasadena and Altadena, north into Glendale and Burbank, northwest into Hollywood and into the San Fernando Valley beyond, west into Santa Monica, and south into Long Beach.

At various switching points, the line branched off into many other areas. In north Long Beach, it turned south and went along the coast all the way to Newport Beach. From Santa Monica, the line went south along the coast into Venice and Redondo Beach. At the Valley Junction, just east of Los Angeles, the track branched east through Covina going all the way to San Bernardino and beyond to Redlands. At the Slauson Junction, the line went down into Whittier and beyond into the city of Fullerton. In short, the Pacific Electric Railway effectively covered most of Southern California.

"This really is the world's greatest electric railway system," Steinig stated unequivocally. "Some people call it the Red Line. *Ride The Big Red Cars.* That's what they advertise. Their 1200 Class trolley car can go sixty miles an hour. That's the one they use on their long trips, like out to San Bernardino. Right now, they're logging over one hundred million passengers per year and their fares are cheap by any standards.

"But the end of the trolley system is only a matter of time. The age of the automobile is dawning." Steinig laughed loudly. "Yes, the age of the automobile, powered by the internal combustion engine. I intend to make these people realize what the future will bring. We will whittle down the Pacific Electric Railway bit by bit. Gentlemen, we will win this fight!"

Steinig was president of the Association of Southern Californians for Efficient Transportation in the Twentieth Century, though he wasn't a California resident; he had recently come to Los Angeles from New Jersey. His "association" was in reality a lobbying group that promoted the automobile exclusively. Today, Steinig was discussing his progress with a group of lawyers who had just flown in from the East Coast. Each of them, including Steinig, represented large corporations, all oil and car companies.

They spent the better part of this summer day discussing future strategies on how to best accomplish their aims, how to destroy the Pacific Electric Railway and make the automobile the standard method of transportation in Southern California. For these particular attorneys, this was business as usual.

Later that night, when most of them had gone to their respective hotel rooms and to bed, Steinig and Bart James, a lawyer for a fledgling oil company, went to a bar in Santa Monica, drinking and talking into the wee hours of the morning, going over their surreptitious agenda for winning their fight with the Pacific Electric Railway.

"How much more cash do you think it will take?" James asked Steinig.

"Probably several million," Steinig replied. "Don't forget, I'm not merely buying off local mayors and city council members. There are also state organizations like the State Railroad Commission, and people in the governor's office. And there are a few local attorneys I use to sue Pacific Electric whenever one of their trains gets in an accident. Then you've got newspaper reporters. After all, the more bad press the Pacific Electric gets, the more people will want to buy cars.

"I'm telling you, it takes lots of money. But in the end it will be worth it. Southern California is a natural for the auto market. We'll have gas stations on every street corner."

"Yes," Bart said, "but you have to understand, my boss wants results, and he wants them soon. Our stockholders want results."

Steinig nodded his head sideways, pulling out a cigarette and lighting up. "Your boss needs to have patience," he said. "And so do the stockholders. The Pacific Electric Railway is an entrenched system. And, as I've told you, they're good at what they do. We won't win this fight overnight. But don't worry. We will win. It may take us twenty years but, in the end, it'll be worth it. We'll have a monopoly on the whole system."

"You really think it'll take twenty years?"

"Probably," Steinig replied, "although nothing is certain."

"So what do I tell my boss? And the others?"

Steinig looked at him with a sneering grin. He took a deep drag from his cigarette and blew the smoke out forcefully. "Bart, tell them we've got to look at the big picture. This is going to be a long haul, okay? But, believe me, by the time we're through, we'll change the entire transportation system of Los Angeles. Shit! This whole state. Maybe the whole country.

"What we do here will affect the future for generations to come. We'll make the automobile the cheapest, most effective way to go from point A to point B. We'll build highways and roads everywhere. I can just see it now. Everyone will own a car and they'll be forced to buy our gasoline. Hell, they won't have any choice. And our stockholders, including us, will all become filthy rich. Bart, mark my words. Once we get rid of the Pacific Electric Railway, it won't be long until the automobile will take over."

"You seem pretty sure about this."

"Damn right!" Steinig said, laughing wildly. "Someday, this whole place will be crawling with cars!"

Eighty years later, in the year 2006, in January, a blizzard descended upon the Black Hills of South Dakota. It snowed furiously for two and a half days. On the afternoon of the third day, the snowstorm began to move to the east.

Early the next morning, Timid Eagle walked outside his small house on the Pine Ridge Indian Reservation. The sky was clear and the air was cold. A morning star hung low on the eastern horizon, shining brightly against the purple and blue hues of a frigid winter sky. The star beckoned him, and he interpreted it to be an omen.

As he gazed about, Timid Eagle sensed that something was wrong. He felt an inner pang, deep within his soul, and then he realized what was troubling him. Today, he would receive a vision. He went back inside his house and made his breakfast, a gruel of oats and barley.

When the sun came up, he took his blanket and smoke-making materials and trekked up the hill behind his house. The going was difficult because there was nearly two feet of fresh snow on the ground. Timid Eagle was an elderly man, in the eightieth year of his life, and by the time he reached the crest of the hill he was breathing hard.

He looked around, carefully choosing a spot where he could spread his blanket. He cleared a place in the snow and laid the blanket down, orienting it so that the corners matched the four corners of the earth. On the northeast corner of the blanket, he placed a large seashell and filled it with sweetgrass and dried sage. He knelt down and set the mixture on fire, blowing into the shell until a small plume of smoke began to rise from within. Satisfied it would remain lit, he sat in the middle of the blanket.

On the southeast corner of the blanket, Timid Eagle placed a medium sized quartz crystal on its end. The crystal immediately began to broadcast the sun's light back onto a small area of the blanket. Next, he took his large eagle feather and waved it over the smoke, forcing the smoke back into his face, smudging himself. He crossed his legs and cupped his hands onto his lap, closed his eyes and began to open his mind.

Timid Eagle was a Lakota Sioux medicine man. He was recognized among the Sioux tribes as being the best of all their medicine men. No other matched his power. No one had his insight.

He sat quietly, outwardly serene and at peace, but his mind was troubled. It took him a full hour to relax, taking slow, purposeful breaths. Eventually, a vision of the earth formed in front of his closed eyes. When he recognized what it was, he knew this would be an important vision. As it grew stronger, Timid Eagle became afraid for the first time in his adult life, not for himself, but for the people of the earth.

He saw the entire planet bathed in a harsh, glaring yellow light. He began to feel warm, in spite of the snow and the cold around him and a chilly wind blowing from the northwest. As the vision grew stronger, he felt hot and began to sweat, small beads of perspiration forming on his forehead and above his lips.

Timid Eagle sat for another hour, but the vision would not go away. If anything, the yellow glaring light only became more intense. After seeing and feeling the vision for such a long time, Timid Eagle became soaked in sweat. As if with a fever, he began to tremble. His head felt like it was burning and his body felt on fire. His mouth was dry and he thirsted for water. Large drops of sweat rolled down his chest and his back. The vision overwhelmed his senses.

He saw the earth turn yellow and he could no longer see the normal colors of the oceans or the land. Clouds hissed and turned to steam, then disappeared. The sky changed from yellow to orange and then Timid Eagle began to soar over the earth, flying high above the ground. He saw that the forests were gone and the mountains were lifeless. He heard no birds and he saw no creatures moving about anywhere. The barren ground was cast in the orange light, parched and dry.

Ahead, he saw a river, its orange water running fast. A young deer approached the water to drink and, as it neared the banks of the river, the water suddenly evaporated. The deer became afraid and ran out into the riverbed. When it reached the middle, its entire body burst into flames and it vanished.

He looked above him and saw three crows flying together, and suddenly they all burst into flames, their bodies becoming black smoke against the orange sky.

He looked back down and saw a snake on the ground and watched as it crawled into its hole. He flew down and called upon the snake to come out, but it would not, for the ground was too hot for the snake. Timid Eagle knew that it had died inside its hole, and so he flew on. Soon he was over a high mountain and saw an owl perched on the very tip of the mountain peak. He flew near the owl, circling low over it, and he could see its big, sad eyes.

"Why have you destroyed the earth?" the owl cried out.

"This cannot be!" Timid Eagle replied.

"Yes, it is destroyed. But why? It was your earth, too," the owl said. "Now look what you have done."

"I'm sorry," Timid Eagle said, knowing that the owl was speaking the truth.

"There is no place left for me," the owl said. "You have destroyed my home and I have nowhere to go. I will die."

"I'm sorry," Timid Eagle said.

The owl suddenly jumped up and disappeared in a bright flame of fire, and black smoke rose from its body. Timid Eagle felt badly about the owl, and he circled the peak for awhile, hoping its spirit would talk to him, but it would not.

Timid Eagle flew on toward a nearby mountain range. He flew high over it and saw that a large ocean loomed beyond. The ocean was blue and vast and as he flew over it, he saw millions of white flecks bobbing on the surface. He flew lower and he saw *that they were fish, but they were all dead, bobbing on the surface, their lifeless eyes looking, but not seeing. He turned and flew back to land.*

The sky turned back to yellow and became blue again, though the surface of the earth remained desolate and barren. The earth was dead, and all life had been destroyed.

The vision was over, and Timid Eagle opened his eyes. The sweetgrass and dried sage in the shell had completely burned, the last wisp of smoke still rising into the air. As he looked about, he had to squint against the blinding sun reflecting off the bright white snow. His clothes were wet with his own sweat. He felt weak, on the verge of collapsing.

Hands shaking, he reached out and grabbed some snow, hurriedly placing it into his mouth. The snow was pure and it tasted good, and wet. He grabbed more, eating the snow until his thirst was quenched. Timid Eagle sat there for a while, letting the wind blow his clothes dry. He still felt warm, and the wind upon his wet clothes felt good.

After some time passed, Timid Eagle stood up and began to gather his belongings. He felt very weak. He folded his blanket and carried his smoke-making materials in both hands, walking downhill on the trail he had made through the snow.

Timid Eagle knew he was going to die. He realized this would happen soon, within a day or two. But, knowing the vision was a true one, and that Grandmother Earth was in great trouble, he wanted to die anyway. He would readily accept death.

As he walked back to his house, he decided he would die in the Black Hills, the homeland of his people. He would not die on the white man's reservation. Deep inside, he was angry. The white men had caused all this.

When he reached his house, he made a hot lunch and rested for several hours. In mid-afternoon, he began to pack what few belongings he would need. When he was finished, he called his grandson to drive him to the Black Hills, well to the west of the Pine Ridge reservation.

"Why?" his grandson asked.

"It is my time," Timid Eagle said. "I have received a vision. But I don't want to die here in this house. I will die in the forests of the Black Hills. After I am dead, I want you to bury my body there. Do not bring me back here."

"It's getting late in the day, grandfather," John said.

"Yes, I know. Come early tomorrow morning. It will take some time to climb up the mountains."

Timid Eagle's grandson, John Flying Hawk, knew better than to question him. The next morning he drove over to Timid Eagle's house, bringing both his own sons, Sam and Pete, who were ten and eight years old. When they arrived, they saw Timid Eagle waiting for them on his front porch. The three of them got out of their car and walked quickly to the porch, taking standing positions all around Timid Eagle. The boys were wearing heavy coats, but still they were cold, and they shuffled their feet to keep their blood flowing. None of them said anything, but Timid Eagle could see the love in their faces.

"Are you ready, grandfather?" John asked.

"Yes," he answered. "My things are in the house."

"Where are you going, grandfather?" Pete asked.

"To another place," Timid Eagle answered.

"Is it time for you to die?" the boy asked.

"Yes," he replied. He took the boy by the waist and pulled him closer. "But it is not death. It is only sleep. My spirit will soon be soaring above the Black Hills. I will be happy. I will be with Wakan-tanka."

"We will need snowshoes, grandfather," John said. "I've brought some for you."

"Good thinking, John. I knew I could depend on you," he said, smiling at his grandson and gazing at him fondly. In looking at his face, he could see his own son, John's father, killed years before when in an alcoholic stupor he drove his car off a reservation road at ninety miles an hour. John Flying Hawk had his father's features, but not his disposition.

Timid Eagle rose from the chair and went inside to get his belongings. He came back out and the four of them walked to the car, Timid Eagle sitting in the front passenger's seat.

John started the engine, then looked questioningly at his grandfather. "Where do you want to go?" he asked.

"To the southern part, near Burdock."

"Grandfather, that's national forest. They won't let us go up there..."

"What they don't know won't hurt them," Timid Eagle replied. "Besides, they will not find us."

John nodded and put the car in gear and drove off. Timid Eagle did not look back at the house he had lived in for the last forty years. He kept his eyes straight ahead, glad in his heart that he would not die on the reservation.

They drove for several hours, taking the interstate through Oglala, heading west off the reservation toward Oelrichs. There, the highway turned north and started climbing up into the Black Hills. The road took them to Hot Springs, then west again to Minnekahta and finally to Edgemont, where they took a snow covered gravel road north into the pine forests of the Black Hills. The road had been recently plowed, but they only went four miles before they came upon a snowplow and had to stop. Ahead, the freshly fallen snow was over two feet deep, impossible for the car to drive through.

"It's okay, John," Timid Eagle said. "This will do."

John pulled over and turned off the engine. He looked at his grandfather in wonderment. John Flying Hawk realized it was going to be a very long day. He thought that perhaps he could talk his grandfather out of this, but how?

They got out and began putting on their snowshoes. They were in the mountains, but not as far in as Timid Eagle had hoped. John took his grandfather's belongings to carry, and they began walking up the nearest slope, which got progressively steeper.

They walked for three hours, then rested, then walked a bit more, until they came upon a low-lying peak. They stopped and gazed upon the mountain.

"That is where I will die," Timid Eagle said, pointing up to the peak. They rested for nearly half an hour, then began the climb up the mountain, reaching the top after a steep hike that took nearly two hours. John was amazed that his grandfather could keep up such a strong pace. It was a difficult climb.

When they reached the top, Timid Eagle looked about and found some shelter between two large granite boulders. Here, he laid his blanket in the snow. He felt bone-weary and it showed upon his face. John and his sons looked at each other, but said nothing. What could they do to help him?

"You should go now. Come back for me in a day or two," Timid Eagle said, sitting down heavily on the blanket.

John took the bag he had been carrying and set it next to him. "Are you sure about this?" he asked.

"Yes," Timid Eagle said. "When you come back, I will be dead. My spirit will be here, though. It will always be here."

John Flying Hawk looked down at his grandfather, realizing it was now or never to try to talk him back down the mountain. "Grandfather, this doesn't seem right. Why don't you come back with us? I don't want to leave you alone here."

"You must. Go now. Come back tomorrow, or the next day."

"Grandfather..."

Timid Eagle looked directly into his grandson's eyes. "I had a vision. This has all been foretold. Grandmother Earth is in great trouble. The planet will soon begin to get very hot."

John was perplexed at this. "It is?" he asked. "But when?"

"It has already begun."

John Flying Hawk looked around. The snow was deep and the air was cold. The boughs of the pine trees were bent down, such was the weight of the fresh, wet snow upon them. It seemed as if this winter would be a cold one.

"But, Grandfather, we've just had a blizzard. And more cold weather is on the way..."

Timid Eagle raised his hand, silencing his grandson. "Go now, John. Come back in a day or two to bury my body. And tell our people of my vision. They should know the truth."

"Let me take you back now."

"No," Timid Eagle said sternly. "I will not die on the white man's reservation. They are responsible for what is about to happen. It is they who are destroying Grandmother Earth. Tell our people that also."

"What should I say?"

"Tell them that the earth is in great trouble. Tell them it is because the white men haven't cared for the land and they haven't loved the land, not the way our people did. First they killed the buffalo and forced us out of our beloved Black Hills. Then they made treaties that they forsook, so they could search for their precious gold. They didn't care about the earth. They just took what they wanted.

"After they stole our land and we resisted, they killed us at Wounded Knee. Then, they put us on reservations, and now they are destroying Grandmother Earth. It is their final insult against us."

He put out his arms, waving Pete and Sam to hug him. He embraced both of them. "I will be all right," he said. "Don't worry about me. Soon, I'm going to be with Wakan-tanka."

"Goodbye, Grandfather," the boys said.

"Goodbye," Timid Eagle said. "You must be brave Lakota, no matter what the future brings."

Both boys nodded solemnly, and Timid Eagle released his grip on them. He looked up. "Go now, John Flying Hawk."

John knelt down and hugged his grandfather, tears beginning to stream down his face. "Grandfather, I love you," he said.

"I love you, too. After you leave, I will ask Wakan-tanka and his helpers to watch over you and all our people. I think you will be okay, at least for another year or two. I don't envy you, though. When it begins to get hot, remember what I have said."

John nodded, then he stood up and looked up at the sky. It was beginning to get late, and they would have to be going if they expected to get back to the car before dark. He knew it would do no good to argue further with his grandfather, so he turned away from the old man and nodded at his boys. They began to retrace their steps through the snow. When they were fifty yards distant, they waved their final goodbye.

Timid Eagle waved back at them, watching as they turned and disappeared into the trees. He looked at the blue sky, the white snow, and the pine trees. He was utterly alone now, but he felt at peace, glad in his heart that he was here.

The wind began to gust strongly, whistling mysteriously through the pine trees. He listened to the sound of it, and he realized that life itself was mysterious, and that men would never fully understand its meaning.

High above him, a golden eagle began to circle. He watched as it soared on the wind, happy and free, its mighty wings catching the currents with ease. The sight of it made him realize just how much he loved the earth and all the living creatures upon it. God had made the earth a perfect place, an abode for life, but now, he knew the white men had ruined it. He grimaced, his jaw tightening. He felt as one with the earth, but he knew he could not undo what had already been done, and he felt sad about the future.

He closed his eyes, opening them a few minutes later. He looked up, searching the sky for the soaring eagle, but it was gone. He sighed, feeling tired and very weary, and he welcomed the prospect of the long sleep that was about to befall him. Then, for the first time, he felt a pain in his chest, and his arms began to tingle ever so slightly. He smiled, knowing his vision had been a true one. The pain began to grow worse. Soon, he knew, he would sleep with his fathers.

ONE

They were camped on a high mesa seventy miles northeast of Yuma, Arizona, near the Little Horn Mountains. In mid-afternoon, a wind had come up and in the heat of the day the sky above the mesa had begun to cloud over. An isolated thunderstorm was approaching from the north, moving south toward Mexico, bright white bolts of lightning sporadically flashing all along the edge of the advancing storm, occasionally from among the dark black clouds in its midst. The storm advanced inexorably toward them, the distant rumble of thunder rolling through the sky and over the earth.

As he stood watching the oncoming storm, Dr. Jonathan Holmes realized that the thunderbolts were an evincive display of nature's violence and wonder, tremendous bursts of energy that could kill a human being in a split second, yet so incredibly beautiful, they could dazzle the senses for hours on end.

He figured that there was enough energy within the storm to power the nearby city of Yuma for the next year. Too bad, he thought, we don't fully comprehend it. If we did, we would know how to harness the billions of volts of electricity now striking the ground, being wasted. We are so arrogant, he said to himself, yet so ignorant!

Far off on the northern horizon, a huge bolt of lightning zigzagged and arced from the clouds and Holmes began counting silently to himself: one thousand one, one thousand two, one thousand three... When he reached "one thousand twenty," a series of loud thunderclaps burst across the mesa. Holmes instinctively tightened his jaw muscles. The storm was four miles away. The last time he had tried counting, it had been five miles away, and that was just a few minutes ago. It was moving in fast.

"Thank God," Jamie Holmes said as she looked toward the approaching storm. "It's going to hit us."

"I don't know if I'd care to thank Him yet," Holmes told his daughter. "That's one of the ugliest-looking storm systems I've ever seen."

"At least it will be wet," Matt Farr said. "But you're right, Dr. Holmes. It looks like a really humongous system."

"A winter thunderstorm," Holmes said, "and very abnormal for this time of the year in the Southwestern United States. And look how high those clouds are. It's almost..." he searched his mind for the right word, "...primal."

"It's strange-looking, all right," Matt agreed.

The bottoms of the thunderclouds were at 20,000 feet and, though they couldn't see through the clouds, the storm topped out at over 70,000 feet. More lightning jolted down, powerful electric charges that seemed unusually strong.

Ominously, the thunder grew louder and a steady wind began to blow. All along the front of the system, they could see rain falling from the clouds.

"It'll hit hard," Matt Farr said. "We'll probably take some lightning strikes here on this mesa."

"Perhaps we should head for cover."

"Oh, Father," Jamie protested. "You're sure getting soft in your old age. We can stay here longer. It's still miles away."

"Yes," Holmes said, testily. "Four miles to be exact. But Matt's right. Lightning will probably start striking here, and it could happen at any second now. Lightning is unpredictable."

He stood between Jamie and Matthew and did a three hundred and sixty degree turn, surveying the scene all around them. They were standing close to the north edge of the mesa, where a three hundred-foot cliff dropped dramatically to the desert below, the desert floor flowing in all directions, giving way to occasional hills and other mesas. To the west, south, and east, the skies were unaffected by the approaching harsh weather, still vivid blue and dotted with white fluffy clouds with flat bottoms. From the mesa, the view was a spectacular southwestern panorama.

"Matthew, what was your last temperature reading this afternoon?" Holmes asked.

"One hundred degrees. Both instruments recorded the same temperature."

"Incredible," Holmes said. Though late in the afternoon, it was still over ninety degrees. He removed his UV-coated sunglasses and wiped the sweat from his forehead with a handkerchief. He was a tall, lean man, with longish sandy hair and bright blue eyes. Born in Australia fifty-six years earlier, the rugged lines around his eyes reflected his age, giving him a look of gentle wisdom.

"The state of Arizona must have set some new records for this day of the year," Holmes pronounced. "Indeed, probably there were records set all over the Northern Hemisphere," he added.

"Yes, probably so," Matt said. "It's hard to believe that Christmas is only four days away."

"No," Holmes agreed. "It certainly doesn't seem like it's Christmastime, especially here in the Southwest."

"You think this heat wave will last, Dr. Holmes?" Matt asked.

"Difficult to say," Holmes responded. He turned and smiled at the young American. "Matt, if I had all the answers, I'd be making the weather, not merely studying it."

Matt smiled back, realizing what Holmes meant, and that's why he liked him. In spite of his tremendous knowledge, Matt had found Jonathan Holmes to be a modest, unassuming man.

"However," Holmes continued, "I do enjoy being out here like this. What is life without a little adventure?" He chuckled at his little joke, but quickly became serious again. "Have either of you heard a recent weather report?"

"I was listening to the shortwave awhile ago," Jamie said. "Continued hot weather from the east coast to the west coast. The

U.S. Weather Service reported Las Vegas to be the high in America. It was one hundred two degrees there."

"The heat seems like it's building, Dr. Holmes," Matt said. "It just doesn't want to stop."

"This isn't a normal heat wave. If it were, it would be isolated, but this is worldwide, and it's quite sudden."

"The United Nations should do something," Jamie said. "They can't pretend that this isn't happening and just ignore the facts. It's as if they're trying to cover it up." Her lilting Australian accent nearly masked the seriousness of her statement.

"The truth will eventually be known. Governments can cover up many things, but they can't hide from the weather."

"None of us will be able to hide," Jamie said.

Holmes shrugged. "Perhaps, my dear, this heat is just an aberration."

"This *isn't* an aberration!" she stated forcefully.

The wind began to gust, and they smelled the moisture and the promise of rain to come. They stood there for another minute, watching the approaching storm. The wind grew stronger, and there was no doubt that the thunderstorm would soon be over the mesa.

"Look at that!" Matt exclaimed. "It's really bad looking. I think it's going to pour."

Holmes turned away from the cliff and toward their encampment several hundred yards away. "Come on," he said, noticing the movement near their colorful dome tents. "We'd better help Chris and Gail secure the camp. This storm may do some damage."

Jamie and Matt nodded their agreement, and the three scientists began walking briskly back to their camp. Their helicopter wasn't due to take them off the mesa for two more days, so they would have to endure whatever weather nature provided, including rain, wind, thunder and lightning.

Jonathan Holmes and Jamie were part of Save Our World (SOW), an international environmental group headquartered in New York, and they had come to Arizona to set up a remote weather station that could be monitored continuously in real time by satellite. Matt, Chris, and Gail, three young scientists from Phoenix, had volunteered to help set up the Arizona location.

The remote weather station was part of a project SOW had undertaken to study global warming, and the organization had placed Holmes in charge of the fieldwork for the project. This site was selected because it was far away from prying eyes and curious onlookers, not to mention vandals and thieves. It would make a perfect addition to SOW's global network of weather stations. Their instruments would measure air temperature, air pressure, relative humidity, wind speed and direction, and rainfall, transmitting the data to a satellite in geosynchronous orbit, later to be downlinked to New York.

The station was powered by highly efficient photovoltaic solar panels, and all the equipment was of extremely rugged design because it would have to endure the harshest elements. And, thought Holmes, as he hurried back to their camp, it's about to receive its first big test.

Chris Hatcher and Gail Thompson were hurriedly tossing camping gear into the tents and, when Holmes, Jamie and Matt reached the camp, they began to do the same. Cooking stoves, folding chairs, beach umbrellas, and anything that could suffer rain damage or be blown away was placed into the relative safety of the domed tents.

As the wind started gusting to twenty mile an hour bursts, they all began to work in earnest. Sand and dust were blown up by the wind, driven into the faces of the five scientists. Then it started to rain. It quickly became a driving downpour.

"Better get inside," Holmes shouted to the others. "Your safety is more important than a few odds and ends. And stay on your cots in case of a lightning strike." He watched as they all ducked into the tents and zipped them closed. Properly secured to the ground, the tents seemed able to withstand the wind now driving against them.

Satisfied the camp would survive the storm, Holmes walked over to the entrance of his own tent. He stood there for a minute as the storm released its water. The raindrops were cool and heavy, and they plopped down on him with a delightful intensity, providing a welcome relief from the heat that had plagued them over the past few days. He took off his hat and held his face to the sky as the rain fell upon his skin.

Without warning, the storm suddenly became a tempest. The rain started coming down so hard the dry surface of the ground was unable to soak it up and huge puddles began forming all over the mesa. Holmes quickly retreated into his tent. He took off his wet clothes and boots and lay on his cot, on top of his sleeping bag and air mattress, listening to the rain ferociously pelt the tent's fabric. Good thing, he thought. The wooden cot was two feet off the ground, and would probably protect him if a lightning bolt hit his tent.

The storm grew even stronger, and Holmes wondered if his little structure would withstand the driving wind and rain. The violent weather was harshly attacking the tent. He had traveled the world, but this was one of the worst storms he'd ever witnessed. The wind was whirling about from many directions, lashing down on the mesa with howling fury.

Suddenly there was a tremendous explosion nearby, and Holmes realized the mesa had taken its first strike of lightning. The shock of it riveted him to his cot, and he didn't dare move off it, sure that more strikes would follow.

He lay there, analyzing the physics of lightning: the clouds had somehow ionized themselves, separating into positive charges at their tops, negative charges at their bottoms. The ionizing effect was so powerful that, as the clouds passed overhead, they forced the surface of the earth for miles around to become positively charged. Eventually, these massive electrical fields became quite distinct and, since unlike charges attract each other, electricity in the form of lightning was created, trillions upon trillions of electrons moving through the air at the speed of light. As the flow of electrons shot through the atmosphere, the dense molecules of air around the flow were superheated to over 60,000 degrees, instantly expanding, then smashing against each other with great force, resulting in a violent explosion of thunder.

Scientists had studied lightning and thunder for decades, but even with the advent of supercomputers had still not found a way to take the energy from the sky and utilize its mind-boggling power. Each electrical discharge generated more kinetic energy than a heavy bomber dropping an entire load of fifty one-thousand-pound bombs. Indeed, Holmes thought, the entire storm system probably contained the energy equivalent of a dozen hydrogen bombs.

The maelstrom continued unabated for the next two hours. When it was over, they all came out of their tents, assembling in the spot where they did their cooking. The rain had turned the previously rock-hard earth of the mesa into a muddy mess. Amazingly, as the storm moved toward the south, the air began to get hot again, though with more humidity than before. They all felt it, and they knew it wasn't normal.

"What do you make of it, Dr. Holmes?" Chris Hatcher asked, her worried eyes gazing upon the dark thunderclouds now moving away to the south.

"I don't know quite what to make of it," he answered. "It was definitely an isolated storm system and a very powerful one. But it really didn't cool us down, did it? I'm not sure I've ever seen anything like this."

"I've lived in Arizona all my life," Matt said. "I've never seen a storm like that. Not even during the monsoon season in July or August. I was sure my tent would be blown away."

"I was so afraid." volunteered Gail Thompson. She suddenly laughed. "I was shivering inside my sleeping bag."

"Well," Holmes said, smiling broadly, "don't worry. It's gone now, and I'm starving. Let's cook dinner, and afterwards we'll check our equipment to make sure it wasn't damaged."

They began to make ready for the evening, though the mood of the camp had changed dramatically. As they prepared their dinner, each one of them occasionally glanced upward, their eyes looking to the south, following the thunderstorm's progress.

That night, for the first time since coming here, they built a fire after scouring the area of all the large pieces of wood they could find. With the passing of the storm, there was now no chance of starting a brush fire on the mesa, even though in places it was thick with dense chaparral.

They lit the campfire well after dusk. On the ground where it burned, it turned a completely pitch-black night into a thirty-foot circle of radiant yellow light. Beyond the circle, the fire's flickering glow faded quickly into total darkness, the night recapturing its dark grip on the desert. Out of habit, they all kept their flashlights by their side.

Above them, the stars shone with incredible clarity, the storm taking every bit of dust out of the atmosphere, cleansing it to reveal the beauty of the night sky. It was so clear it seemed there could easily have been a billion stars visible to the naked eye.

Although night had fallen, it was still hot, at least eighty degrees, though none of them bothered checking to be sure. It was the unrelenting heat this late in December, which gave them a sense of foreboding. It had started in November, when the climate of the planet had inexplicably begun to heat up after a wetter, warmer than normal summer. The rise in air temperature was gradual, yet constant. By mid-December, the daytime temperatures throughout much of the Northern Hemisphere were reaching highs, depending on location, in the mid-eighties to low nineties. The nighttime lows were going down into the sixties. Only in the most northerly latitudes was there any nighttime freezing occurring, in places like Stockholm and Anchorage. For the past few days, the midday air temperature regularly exceeded ninety degrees in most cities south of forty degrees north latitude. The steady climb in temperature had continued unabated.

For a while, as they sat around the campfire, they talked about the storm and its strange appearance. Then, as they all knew they would, they began to discuss the weather and the earth's climate.

"Dr. Holmes," Gail Thompson asked, "what do you think is going to happen? What will it be like by spring or summer?"

Holmes smiled and shrugged. In the firelight, the wrinkles around his eyes were highlighted, and he looked older and wiser than he normally did. "I dunno," he said, his Australian accent slightly thicker after two glasses of wine. "It's anybody's guess."

"Dr. Holmes," Chris protested. "Surely you have an opinion. Please tell us, okay?"

Holmes frowned. How would he approach this? He had never wanted to be categorized as a prophet of doom but now, knowing all that he knew, his outlook was a dismal one. Should he tell these young people what he really thought?

"Okay," he said. "If you want to know the truth, I think that global warming is beginning to occur. These weather patterns are simply too abnormal. Where it will stop, I couldn't say. But, I think we're seeing the beginning phases."

Jamie looked surprised. "Father!" she said. "I'm shocked. You finally agree with me about this."

"Now, Jamie," he said. "You know I've always valued your opinions and I've always given you plenty of rein, just like I would any strong-minded woman. Especially someone with a Ph.D. like you. At least we can debate on an equal level." At this, he laughed loudly, and everybody else laughed too.

"Well, it doesn't sound like we'll be debating this issue," she retorted. "I knew it back in November. It was just too hot. At night, I could feel it."

"I'm not as quick to formulate my opinions as you, my dear, and we still need to do a lot more work. Right now, I couldn't prove that global warming has begun. It's only my opinion."

"And it's a damned good one," Matthew said. "The chickens have come home to roost. Now we're going to pay for all our past sins."

"Yes, well," Holmes said, "it was probably inevitable. But none of us thought it would be this quick. I fear that the climate of earth is undergoing a rapid change."

"But, Dr. Holmes," Gail insisted. "What will happen?"

"There are several possible scenarios, and none of them are good. The Venus scenario is probably the most likely possibility.

Earth is a water planet, so if the greenhouse effect becomes too strong, this whole place will become one big steambath. The temperature of the atmosphere could eventually reach several hundred degrees, similar to conditions on the planet Venus. Of course, long before that happens, we will have all died. Us and every other form of life on the planet. It's not a very pleasant thought. Unfortunately, the other scenarios aren't much better."

No, they all silently agreed. The ultimate outcome of this situation might not be pleasant. Would the heat continue, or would it stop and then everything go back to normal?

Long into the night, as the campfire withered into hot embers and coals, the five of them sat under the stars and talked about the science involved in global warming: the sun, the earth, the greenhouse effect, the composition of the atmosphere, the pollution by greenhouse gases, and the hydrologic cycle. It was a night none of them would soon forget.

TWO

The next day, three men were hiding in a narrow canyon on the sprawling Navajo Indian Reservation in Northern Arizona. They had been hiking for nearly two days, and now were waiting for the onset of dusk. They did not have permission to be on the reservation, and all three of them were heavily armed and packing dynamite.

James Flynn tipped his canteen to his mouth and slowly took a mouthful of water, holding it for several seconds before he swallowed. He figured it was around ninety degrees, even in the shade. For Northern Arizona in late December, it was unusually hot. At this time of year, there should be snow on the ground. Damned strange, he thought. With the year 2007 just days away, it seemed to be getting hotter, not cooler. Most people said this was just a temporary heat wave, that things would soon go back to normal. Flynn wasn't so sure.

"Four hours until sunset," he said to Stu Smith, "and it's still awfully hot. I don't think we'll be seeing a white Christmas, do you?"

"No, not with this kind of weather. Anyway, it's not Christmas that I'm worried about. If this heat continues, next summer's gonna be a real killer."

"Yeah," Flynn said. "I've been thinking about that, too." He looked over at the third member of their team, Jeff Walker, who was lying ten yards away in a soft spot of sand on the canyon floor. Flynn smiled at his form. Jeff was lying on his poncho flat on his back, his hat pulled over his face, the toes of his boots pointing up at the sky.

"I'm afraid they've really screwed things up," Stu said, taking off his neckerchief and wiping the sweat from his forehead. He looked up at the sky, as if he were looking for something. "This weather we're having is weird, man," he said.

"Yeah, it's pretty weird," Flynn agreed, "but at least we're trying to do something about it."

"I know. And we'll keep on doing something," Stu said firmly. "There's too much at stake not to. You and me, James, against the world."

Flynn nodded. "The world is totally screwed up right now, and nobody gives a damn. No one except us."

Stu looked up at the sky again. "It's getting worse, don't you think?"

Flynn took another swallow of water, swishing it slowly around in his mouth. He looked at Stu and said, "Yeah, I think so. It makes me feel like killing someone."

Flynn said it casually, but there was a hint of anger in his voice. Stu didn't respond to Flynn's improbable statement. Sometimes, he knew, Flynn was like that, displaying sudden flashes of cold anger.

When each had joined the Defenders of the Planet, they had taken an oath to avoid killing at all costs, but both knew that in his regular line of work Flynn had already killed several men. They also both knew that if he had to, he was quite capable of killing again.

Flynn was a cop, a lieutenant in the Phoenix police department. Several years earlier, when Flynn had been promoted to detective and placed in homicide, he and three other detectives had gone to arrest a murder suspect, a gang member, when they were ambushed by a dozen members of the suspect's gang. The three cops with him were shot immediately, but the volley of gunfire somehow missed him. Armed with only a Smith & Wesson nine millimeter automatic, he killed three of his attackers and wounded three others. One of those he killed was the murder suspect they had gone to arrest, a young thug named Julio Lopez.

Though his fellow officers had declared him a hero, the incident created a crack in Flynn's psyche. After the gunfight, he realized he was still searching for some meaning to his life, that he wasn't satisfied with who he was and what he was doing.

Why, he wondered, was he spending so much of his time fighting with men like Lopez? He had always wanted to accomplish something significant in his chosen career, not chase after small-time, brutal criminals who didn't value human life — their life, or anybody else's.

Two years ago, when his friend Stu recruited him into the Defenders of the Planet, Flynn finally had the answer. It was then that he knew what he was meant to do with his life. After his first mission, he felt as if he had done something good. Better yet, he felt truly alive, a feeling he hadn't ever experienced before. After that mission, Flynn realized he had found his reason for being. In mind, body and soul, Flynn came to fervently believe in fighting for the environment.

Now, as he sat in the sweltering heat of the canyon, he was positive he'd made the right choice. He looked over at the black man sitting a few yards to his right, his longtime friend, Dr. Stuart Smith.

The two had been best friends since their high school days in Tucson, where they had met on the track team. After high school, they both went on to the University of Arizona in Tucson. Flynn had majored in criminology. Stu was a pre-med student who went on to attend the U of A's excellent medical school. While Stu studied to become a doctor, Flynn graduated and moved to Phoenix. Nearly five years later, after getting his medical degree and passing his internship, Stu also moved to Phoenix, joining an established office of pediatricians.

As adults, the two remained best friends. Regardless of their long hours at work, they made it a practice to work out together three times a week at a local gym. After several years of this, they both looked like bronzed Olympians.

One Saturday morning at the gym, Stu suggested to Flynn that he should join the Defenders of the Planet and do something about the real criminals of society. At first, Flynn thought he was joking. When he realized his friend was deadly serious, an intense argument ensued.

Stu told him that he could prove that the damage to the environment was real. The next week, he brought Flynn into his office. Stu had arranged to have some of his young patients come in for a checkup on this day, and he made Flynn wear doctors' whites and pretend to be his assistant. Flynn watched in horror as, one by one, Stu showed him six children with the beginning stages of skin cancer. None of the kids was older than ten.

When the last young patient was gone, Stu turned to Flynn and said simply, "There you see, my friend, just what is really going on. Even for an area like Phoenix, with all the sunshine we get, this is unheard of in our medical history. These kids are suffering because of what the chemical companies have done."

"Are they going to be okay?" Flynn had asked.

"We can probably save most of them. All of the kids you saw are going in for surgery within the next few days, but whether we've caught it in time is questionable. Right now, we're losing about ten to fifteen percent of them."

"This is crazy!" Flynn had said.

"No," Stu said. "It's criminal. There is no doubt in my mind that we have seriously damaged our atmosphere. And nobody is really doing much about it except the Defenders of the Planet."

Flynn realized he couldn't turn down his friend. He looked carefully at Stu and said, "Okay, I'll help you."

"Good," Stu smiled at him, grasping him by his shoulders. "We need good people to help with the fight." Later, Stu gave his friend the oath all recruits must take.

To some, the Defenders were heroes, out to save the earth from greedy industrialists who didn't care about the planet or its environment. To others, the Defenders were a gang of criminals who had committed various felonies, including arson, bombing, murder, and attempted murder, as well as numerous lesser crimes. As far as the U.S. Government was concerned, the Defenders of the Planet was a terrorist organization, and the FBI had been hunting them relentlessly, ever since they had burst upon the scene by bombing and seriously damaging a utility plant in North Carolina in the year 2000, publicizing their feat to the entire world.

The Defenders were a diverse group, spread out all across America. Time after time, they struck against the establishment and, thus far, the FBI had been unable to penetrate the organization, now matter how hard it tried.

Now the Arizona team, in the persons of Flynn, Stu, and Jeff, was preparing to strike again, their fourth mission together, and one they had been planning for several months. It would be their boldest yet.

Flynn looked up into the sky, momentarily studying the position of the sun. "Why don't we get moving?" he said, his eyes squinting as he looked upward.

"Yeah," said Stu. "I'd say we'd better be going. It's still four or five miles to the line. Over rough country."

"I'd better see if Jeff is awake," Flynn said, but before he could get to his feet, Stu suddenly stood up.

"I'll do it," Stu said, and he walked over to the place where Jeff was lying in the sand. He gently kicked the bottom of his right boot.

"Is it time?" Jeff asked, talking through his hat.

"Yeah," Stu said. "It's time."

"It's still too hot."

"We have to be there before it gets dark."

"Yeah, I know." Jeff sat up and flipped his hat back onto his head, looking up at Stu with a half-smile. He got up on one knee and began to roll up his gear, stuffing it into his backpack. The pack was filled to capacity, and weighed nearly sixty pounds.

When he was ready, Jeff propped up his backpack on the ground and sat down in front of it, leaning back into it. He pulled the straps over his shoulders and cinched his lap belt.

"Hey," he called out. "How about a hand?" Stu and Flynn were busy with their own gear, but Stu came back over and stood in front of him. The two clasped hands and Stu hauled him to his feet.

"Thanks, Dr. Smith," Jeff said.

"Any time," Stu smiled.

For a moment, the two of them stood face to face, a marked contrast between them. Jeff, a Phoenix fireman, was blonde, tall and athletic, wearing a green T-shirt and worn bluejeans. Stu was slightly shorter and leaner than Jeff, and he wore a cotton long-sleeved shirt and khaki pants. They both wore dark sunglasses, broad-brimmed hats, and heavy hiking boots.

"You got sun-screen on those lily white arms of yours?"

"Yeah, Doc," Jeff responded. "Eight. Is that good enough?"

"A blue-eyed blonde should have forty or fifty," Stu said.

Jeff shrugged. "We all have to die sometime," he said. "We could get killed tonight, you know?"

"Not me," Stu said, smiling. "I'm going to live forever!"

"Yeah, right, Doc!" Jeff laughed. "Come on, let's get your pack on. We've got things to do."

Flynn and Stu put on their heavy backpacks just the way Jeff had, and Jeff helped them both to their feet just as Stu had done for him. They stood there together, adjusting their packs, cinching straps and making sure the loads were evenly balanced. Of the three, Flynn was in the best physical condition, but since he worked out or ran nearly every day, that was to be expected.

James Flynn was thirty-three years old, stood five feet, eleven inches tall, and weighed one hundred and ninety pounds, with brown hair and blue eyes. His physique was nearly perfect. He had strong shoulders and a trim waist. His jaw jutted out, and he carried himself with an air of near total confidence. His expression seemed to suggest that he knew he could handle anything. He gave his backpack one final tug, then looked up at his friends.

"You ready?" he asked.

Stu and Jeff nodded, and all three of them walked over to the canyon wall, where three assault rifles leaned against the granite face of a large boulder.

"Better lock and load," Flynn commanded. "We might run into Navajo police."

"Right," Stu said calmly, picking up his rifle and chambering a round, then flicking the safety on. Flynn and Jeff did the same, and the sharp clicks of their rifle bolts snapping shut echoed loudly in the confines of the canyon. They set the safety catches of the rifles on, taking care to point the weapons away from their bodies.

"Remember," Flynn reminded them, "we cannot allow ourselves to be jeopardized. This mission must go off without a hitch. If we have to... well, we have to. Let's hit it."

They began a quick walk toward the north, their weapons at the ready. As they came out of the mouth of the canyon, the terrain turned into a series of low lying hills. In this part of Arizona there had been no thunderstorms, and the sun, though low on the winter horizon, beat down relentlessly. They moved at a rapid pace in spite of the heat.

The three of them had covered this terrain months before. That had been a reconnaissance mission. Now they were doing it for real and they felt a sense of urgency.

Flynn walked the point position, his eyes wary for any movement within his field of vision. Stu walked five meters behind Flynn, and Jeff brought up the rear, a good ten meters behind Stu. If they encountered anyone, Jeff's job would be to quickly circle to one flank or the other, to enable them to have crossfire ability. On this afternoon, they were alone. They saw no one.

They followed the creek bed for nearly an hour, then Flynn abruptly changed course, and they began a slow climb up a hill. For the next few hours, they alternately climbed and descended one hill after another. Just as dusk fell upon Northern Arizona, they came to the last hill. After ten minutes, they crested it and looked down upon a low valley.

"There's the line," Stu said, pointing with his weapon.

"Right where it's supposed to be," Flynn said.

Jeff came up to them and he, too, looked down into the canyon. When he saw the line, he grinned broadly. The "line" was a high voltage power line, transmitting electricity from the

2,250-megawatt coal-fed Navajo Generating Station toward the city of Phoenix. Spaced at two hundred meter intervals, steel towers resembling giant gray robots rose into the sky, supporting the electric lines.

The Navajo Generating Station was located near the Utah border, fifty miles north and east of the Grand Canyon, where it had been spewing millions of tons of sulfur dioxide gas into the atmosphere for decades. It had three smokestacks, each seven hundred fifty feet high, that together threw thirteen tons of gas per hour high into the atmosphere. The giant facility burned 24,000 tons of coal per day, so much that a special railroad track had been built to transport entire trainloads of the black stuff from the primary loading site on Black Mesa, one hundred and twelve miles north of Winslow.

To the Defenders of the Planet, the Navajo Generating Station was a scourge upon the earth. Ever since it had been made operational, a constant haze had settled over the Grand Canyon. Smog also drifted northeast into Utah's nearby national parks, Zion and Bryce Canyon.

They began walking down the hill and, as night began to fall, they got ever closer to the line. They crested a small ridge, and Stu took out his binoculars and scanned the entire area. An access road ran parallel to the power line, but there were no people or vehicles anywhere in sight.

"Nothing out there," he said after a minute.

"We'd better move out," Flynn said.

They began a slow run toward the nearest tower. When they reached it, Flynn took off his pack and began working at a frantic pace. Jeff continued running down the access road toward the next tower to the left, while Stu ran in the opposite direction toward the nearest tower to the right.

Flynn took eight sticks of dynamite out of his pack and placed two sticks next to the base of each of the tower's four main posts, quickly wiring them together. At the other two towers, Stu and Jeff were soon doing the same. Each man had his own wire and detonator, and after working for only ten minutes, the three towers were ready to be blown.

Flynn put his pack back on, took his rifle, and began walking away from the tower, a reel of detonating wire trailing behind him. The reel of wire was two hundred meters long, and Flynn used the entire length to get as far away from the tower as possible. Stu and Jeff were also moving back and away from their towers, angling toward him.

When his wire played out, Flynn took off his pack and pulled out a detonator, quickly wiring both leads of the wire to its posts. He then set the detonator on top of his pack and knelt down. He took a deep breath and let it out slowly. He was ready.

It was getting dark now, and though he couldn't see Stu or Jeff, he assumed they should be ready, too. He pulled the detonator's handle upward.

"Fire in the hole!" he shouted. He waited a few seconds until he heard them also yell out the same warning, and then he pressed down hard on the handle of the detonator.

There were three near-simultaneous explosions. The sound was absolutely deafening, and Flynn felt the concussion and roar of the blast roll past his body and into the surrounding hills. All three towers' posts were blown off their foundations, and the tall steel structures began to crumple to the ground.

As the high power lines grounded themselves, a series of secondary explosions occurred and giant sparks surged high up into the air. With each shower of sparks, the area was flooded in intense, bright white light. It was an amazing display, though the noise and cascade of sparks soon ended and it became dark again.

Flynn began to back away from the now-crippled line, using a flashlight as a beacon to draw his friends to him. In the dark, they found him a few minutes later. Both of them were out of breath.

"We did it!" Stu said excitedly.

"Score another one for our side," Jeff said.

"We've gotta move fast," Flynn said. "They'll be looking for whoever did this. And that's us."

"To hell with them," Jeff said, exhilaration in his voice.

"We've still got the other half of our mission," Stu said. "Then they'll really be after us!"

Flynn said, "Yeah, they'll be out for blood... helicopters, dogs, four-wheel vehicles. But they won't be expecting our next move. Let's go. We've got to cover lots of ground before morning, and it looks like a good night for hiking."

With that, they moved out into the night. Flynn walked at a steady rate and, after three hours, a half moon rose into the eastern sky.

During the night, they moved north and east, through the high country of Northern Arizona across the Kaibito Plateau. Flynn used the stars to navigate by, and under the clear night sky the stars fairly jumped out at them. They had no trouble staying on their course.

By daybreak, they had traveled over twenty miles from the downed power line and were close to reaching their second objective. Tired but alert, they walked single file, ten-meter intervals between them, their rifles at the ready. As the first rays of sunlight streamed through the skies, it looked like it would be another hot day.

An hour past sunrise, Flynn raised his right hand into a fist, then knelt down. Stu and Jeff rushed forward, kneeling down next to him. It was obvious to Flynn that they were both tired, but they seemed up for what they were about to do.

Flynn pointed to their front with his rifle and said, "Railroad tracks. We're almost there."

"Damn!" Stu said. "There they are!"

"We made it," Jeff said, his face breaking out into a big grin.

"Yeah," Flynn agreed. "It's showtime once again. We'll blow the train and then get back to Phoenix, muy pronto! It'll take them a long time to recover from this!" Flynn felt his adrenaline start to flow again. He pulled off his canteen and took a few swallows, offering some to both Stu and Jeff. When they had also drunk from it, he slung the canteen's strap back over his shoulder.

"Too bad we don't have time for breakfast," Jeff said. "I'm starving."

"There's no time," Flynn said. "The train will be coming soon."

Jeff nodded his understanding.

"Let's go do it," Flynn said.

They got up and began a slow run across uneven terrain dotted with scrub oak and pine trees. When they reached the rail line, they turned right toward the south, jogging parallel to the tracks for nearly a mile.

Eventually, the tracks meandered along the slope of a hill, the slope becoming gradually steeper and falling away to the right. The shiny steel rails curved around the hill and over a small bridge that spanned a shallow stream. This bridge was their second objective.

Flynn sprinted forward, running beneath it and throwing himself down on the bank just above the stream, Stu and Jeff right behind him. All three of them were breathing hard, their clothes soaked in sweat, and they lay there for nearly ten minutes, unmoving except for the heaving of their chests.

"Man, that nearly killed me," Stu spoke first.

"Good thing we trained for this," Jeff said. "But this one's gonna be my last mission for a while. This is too much damned work."

"You can say that again," Stu agreed.

Suddenly, Flynn sat up, his ears straining to detect a sound. "Do you hear that?" he asked.

"What?" Jeff asked.

"There's a train coming," Flynn replied.

"I don't hear anything," Stu said.

"I can feel the vibrations," Flynn said. "Come on! Let's get this bridge wired." He took off his pack and started pulling out his remaining dynamite.

For this job, they each carried four bundles of eight sticks of dynamite each, which they began placing high up beneath the bridge's main supports. Since the bridge was only thirty-four feet long, it took just a few minutes to place the dynamite bundles and wire them in sequence to a main lead.

Flynn took the lead in his hand and began walking downhill away from the bridge and toward open terrain. After he had gone twenty meters, it played out and he dropped it to the ground, running back to the bridge and grabbing his pack and rifle. He saw that Stu and Jeff were still up in the bridge supports, double-checking their wiring job.

"Let's go," Flynn shouted up at them. "That train will be here any minute now."

"Almost through," Stu said.

"Yeah," Jeff said through clenched teeth. "They look pretty good. They should blow."

"Well, hurry up," Flynn commanded. He shouldered his pack and ran back to the spot where he had dropped his lead wire on the ground. From his pack, he pulled out a new reel of detonating wire and hurriedly spliced the end to the lead wire. Then he pulled some electrical tape from his pack and heavily taped his splices so they could not be pulled apart. He put on his pack and began to walk away from the bridge, unreeling the detonating wire as he went. Stu and Jeff soon caught up to him, and they walked three abreast as far away from the bridge as the four-hundred-foot reel would permit. When the wire played out, they took cover behind a fallen dead pine.

"Just in time," Stu said. "Here it comes!"

In the distance, they saw a plume of dense black smoke rising above the tracks. Three diesel engines were creating the smoke as they pulled open carloads of coal. The train was long, over a hundred and fifty cars. It was a robot train, unmanned.

Flynn took his detonator from his pack and attached the wire to the two posts, pulling the detonator's handle up and gingerly setting it in front of him. He looked up at the approaching train. "Ready!" he told the others.

Slowly, the long train clamored along the tracks. After several agonizing minutes it reached the bridge. Flynn put his right hand on the detonator's handle and, as the first engine passed over the bridge, he pushed the handle down hard.

The bridge blew up and the lead engine rose nearly ten feet into the air, then came tumbling down in slow motion, falling onto its side into the ravine. The other two engines also fell into the ravine, followed by a dozen carloads of coal. Other cars began to derail and pile up behind the heap that had gone into the ravine, and the rest of the train came to a screeching halt. The horrendous sound of metal scraping against metal filled the air.

"Jesus Christ!" Jeff swore. "What a mess!"

"Amen," Stu said. "I think we just put the Navajo Generating Station out of business for a long time."

"Let's hit it," Flynn said. "No use hanging around." He quickly detached his detonator and threw it back into his pack. He leaned into the pack's shoulder straps and got up, cinching them tight. Stu and Jeff did the same and, when they were ready, took their rifles and began moving rapidly to the southwest. They wanted to put as much ground between them and the train as they could. Though their muscles ached, they walked at a torturous pace.

As the morning wore on and the sun rose higher over the southern horizon, the air temperature shot up into the low eighties. On this day it would reach ninety-three degrees on the Kaibito Plateau.

By mid-afternoon, the men were exhausted. When they were nearly twenty-five miles away from the fallen bridge and the wrecked train, they finally stopped to rest. They plopped down in the shade of a grove of scrub pines.

"I don't think I can walk another mile," Stu said.

"Me neither," Jeff said. "Not even an inch further."

Flynn looked at both of them and said, "We'll rest here for half an hour. Then we'll move on. We need to put five more miles between that train and us before dark."

"You're crazy, James," Stu said. "There's no way."

Flynn tossed his hat aside and settled back on his pack and closed his eyes. "You can do it, Doc. You just have to put your mind to it."

"This heat is killer stuff," Jeff reminded him. "We never expected it to be like this."

"Yeah, but we can take it," Flynn said. "So far, everything is going as planned. I don't want to take any chances. They're probably stopping every vehicle going in or out of this area. They won't expect us to be on foot, but they might suddenly get smart. We'll set up our camp just before dark."

Stu and Jeff looked at each other in amazement. They both knew Flynn was leading the mission, so there was little they could do or say, even though both of them were dead tired, more tired than they had ever been in their lives.

They settled back against their backpacks just as Flynn had done, determined to take advantage of this break. Around them, Northern Arizona sweltered in the unusual December heat.

THREE

Something strange was happening in Antarctica, and all the men on the *U.S.S. Tawney* knew it. On Saturday, December twenty-third, the ship was sailing just off the coast of the world's fifth largest continent, near the huge Ross Ice Shelf, when her captain noticed more movement off the port side of the ship.

"There goes another one!" he bellowed.

Everyone on the bridge of the huge U.S. naval supply vessel looked over to see another large chunk of ice breaking off the shelf. A minute later, a swell struck them broadside, causing the entire ship to list sharply as it rode over the wave.

"I've never seen it this bad," Captain Munson said, a frown on his face. "I want regular radar readings. The last thing we need to do is run into one of those monsters."

"Aye, aye, sir."

"Lookouts are posted, sir," an ensign reported.

"Tell them to keep a sharp eye out. I don't like the look of this," Munson said.

It was summer in the Southern Hemisphere, and the sun struck full force upon the continent of Antarctica, bouncing off the water and the ice in an unrelenting glare. Everyone on the bridge of the *Tawney* was wearing UV-coated dark sunglasses.

"Sir," an enlisted man said excitedly, "radar reports ice floes ahead. They're all over the place."

"Radio McMurdo," Munson ordered. "Tell them we're still encountering large icebergs."

"Aye, aye, sir," the enlisted man responded.

Munson watched as another huge chunk of ice fell away from the ice shelf. Already his ship was ten hours late due to icebergs floating all around the Antarctic Circle, causing the *Tawney* to have to zigzag around them. There was no way to avoid the ice.

The *Tawney* was carrying several thousand tons of supplies and equipment destined for the American scientific base at McMurdo Naval Air Station. But, first, the ship would have to get into McMurdo Sound, and Munson wasn't sure if that would be possible, given the current conditions.

"Iceberg dead ahead," the helmsman reported, as he studied a radar screen. "Distance, six hundred meters."

"Come right twenty degrees," Munson ordered.

"Aye, aye, sir," and a moment later the *Tawney* began to turn away from the shore.

Just then, a young lieutenant came into the bridge. "Sir," he said excitedly, "You're not going to believe this."

"Believe what?" Munson asked.

"We're recording an air temperature of seventy-four degrees. No wonder all this ice is breaking apart."

"Seventy-four degrees?" Munson asked. "You sure about that?"

"Positive, sir."

Munson frowned again. Damn it, he thought. It never got much above 32F, not even in December or January, the summer months for the South Pole. Seventy-four degrees was unheard of.

"Radio that to Pearl Harbor ASAP," Munson ordered. "Code the communication."

"Right away, sir." The lieutenant left the bridge.

"More ice ahead. Radar is picking up at least a dozen icebergs dead ahead. They're on our present course."

Captain Munson grimaced. More icebergs! he thought. Well, he'd had enough. He quickly made up his mind. "Come hard about," he ordered. "We're not losing this ship to a bunch of damned icebergs! We'll set a course for New Zealand. And radio McMurdo Station. Tell them we're leaving the area."

The *Tawney* began a sharp turn away from Antarctica. Munson figured that, if necessary, they could harbor in New Zealand and wait until the unseasonable warmth subsided and the ice stopped breaking up. As the ship turned, Munson took one last look at the ice shelf. It was pristine white, the purest white he had ever seen. The shelf was a magnificent formation of frozen water, towering high above the ocean. Now the ice was coming apart, posing a serious danger to his ship. *What the hell is going on?* he wondered.

A few hours later, several senior naval officers at the Pentagon gathered around a flat panel screen. They were carefully studying the latest satellite photos taken of Antarctica. A naval intelligence officer and photo-analyst, Lieutenant Steve Russell, sat at the computer controlling the screen's images.

"The ice shelf is breaking off all along the perimeter of the continent," Russell said. "It's no wonder the *Tawney* had to turn back. The hazards are simply too great. Look at these photos," he said. "These are the most recent we have. They were taken twenty minutes ago from two hundred and seventy-eight miles above Antarctica by one of our KH-15s." He pressed a few keys on his keyboard, and the screen flashed various photos taken by the latest high-tech American reconnaissance satellite. Some were close-up views and some were wide angle shots of the entire continent.

Navy Captain Rob Jones carefully studied the computer screen. It had been his decision to call Admiral Hart and ask him to come view the graphic evidence, evidence he was sure would be convincing.

"Go to enhanced infrared," Jones said.

"Okay, sir," Russell said, tapping fingers on the keyboard. A fantastic array of colors filled the flat panel screen.

"Admiral," Jones said, "this is an infrared scan that's been computer enhanced. This is a scan of the coastline near the Ross Ice Shelf. Do you see the purple color all along the edge of the ice shelf?" he asked, pointing to part of the screen. "The color of the water would normally be a bit lighter. The infrared shows the water temperature all along the coast is slightly colder than the surrounding water. This is due to melting ice. Just a few weeks ago, things were still normal."

"Friggin' damned weather!" exclaimed Admiral James Hart, Chief of Naval Operations. "This can't be happening this fast! What the hell is going on? Rob, what do you make of it?"

Jones nodded grimly. "It's bad, sir," he said. "This satellite confirms it, Admiral. The Antarctic ice cap is melting, and it is melting fast. It doesn't look like it will reverse any time soon. We should consider that we'll have to prepare for the worst. I would advise that we initiate Operation Safeharbor."

"Jesus Christ!" Hart swore. "Are you sure?" he asked.

"No, sir," Jones admitted. "I'm not sure about any of this. Then again, neither is anybody else. This sudden hot weather is a worldwide phenomenon. When it will stop, if it will stop, is unknown. But, based on what we're seeing, and the reports we're getting from McMurdo, it's my opinion that we've got to begin the operation. Seventy-four degree temperatures will cause the ice to completely melt. It's only a matter of time."

"How unusual is that reading?" Hart asked.

"Sir, it's an all-time record high temperature. What bothers me is that it's the beginning of summer down there. The probability is that the situation will get worse. We have to take immediate action."

Admiral Mark Simmons nodded in agreement, his expression one of total seriousness. Simmons had responsibility over every U.S. naval facility in the world. "If we don't," Simmons said, "we might get caught with our pants down, and then there would be a lot of questions to answer. On the other hand, if the weather cools down, we can always move everything back."

"And look like goddamned fools," Hart said.

"Yes, sir," Simmons said. "Except I think we're going to look foolish no matter what we do." He frowned, deeply concerned about the job he would have to undertake.

"This is incredible," Hart fumed. "You're both right, of course. As of now, consider this information ultra top secret. It's not to be discussed with anybody else, at least until I decide otherwise."

Both Simmons and Jones nodded. Both men realized exactly what Admiral Hart was implying. The last thing the Pentagon wanted was to create a panic.

"Rob, I want you to brief Albert Mills. Maybe the JCS and the Secretary, too. Today."

"Yes, sir," Jones said.

"So start getting ready. I'll get back to you when I've got it set up." Then, in his customary fashion, Admiral Hart whirled around and strode briskly out of the room.

FOUR

"It's an urgent call from Admiral Hart," Betty's voice boomed over the intercom. It was nearing 3:30 p.m. and the Secretary of the Navy was about to leave the Pentagon for the day when Betty informed him of the call from Admiral Hart.

Albert Mills was scheduled to leave for his annual winter vacation and he was anticipating the trip to Aspen, Colorado, even though the skiing was nonexistent. Maybe, he and his family hoped, it would still snow in time for Christmas. After all, they figured, the sudden onset of hot weather could just as easily go away.

At 1:00 p.m. he had told his secretary to hold his calls so he could clear his desk, and so it was with some annoyance that he took Admiral Hart's call.

"Yes, Admiral, what is it?" Mills asked gruffly.

"Mr. Secretary," Hart began. "Something's come up. I'm afraid it's a matter of national security."

"What's happened?" Mills asked.

"One of our ships, the *Tawney*, had to cancel a supply mission, one that's been planned for over six months. I personally know the captain, and I can vouch for his ability. The *Tawney* was going to resupply McMurdo in Antarctica. She had to turn back because of icebergs."

"Icebergs?" Mills queried. What's so important about that? he wondered.

"I'd like to show you some satellite photos of the area and I've prepared a briefing. It's very important that you see this."

"Damn it, Admiral Hart, I don't think I need to worry about icebergs, do I?"

"It's bigger than that. It looks like the ice shelf of Antarctica is breaking up, and it's happening very quickly. My people think we should initiate Operation Safeharbor."

Jesus Christ! Mills thought, there goes my vacation. The Secretary of the Navy stared across his office at a huge map that hung on the far wall. His mind began to race. Admiral Hart was a man of nearly forty years' experience. There could be no doubting him, even though he didn't want to believe it.

"Are you absolutely sure about this?" Mills asked.

"Our people have been studying it for nearly a week. The call from the *Tawney* was the final straw. We're sure as to the physical evidence, but any decision will have to be made at the highest levels," Hart said.

"Yes, of course," Mills said, feeling his adrenaline began to flow. "All right, then. I need to make a phone call. I'll call you back in a few minutes."

Secretary Mills hit another line on his phone and immediately placed a call to the Secretary of Defense. Within the hour, phones began ringing throughout the highest levels of the Pentagon. There was an urgency in these calls that the Defense Department hadn't witnessed in years.

At 17:00 hours in a conference room on the third floor of the E Ring, Admiral Hart began a briefing as important as any ever given at the Pentagon. Sitting around the conference table were the Secretary of Defense, the Deputy Secretary of Defense, all the secretaries of the branches, and the Joint Chiefs of Staff.

The conference room overlooked the Potomac River and, beyond that, the Capitol. Often at this time of year, the Potomac was frozen over and a blanket of snow covered Washington, but on this day the river was ice free and the nation's Capitol looked like it would in early spring. In fact, some trees had begun to leaf out, tricked by the unseasonable warmth.

Against this backdrop, Admiral Hart began the briefing by introducing Captain Jones, who came forward with slides in hand, quickly inserting them all into a computer projector.

"Although most of you don't know him, Captain Rob Jones is one of our top oceanographers. He received his doctorate from La Jolla's Scripps Institution of Oceanography after graduating from USC. He joined the Navy in 1983. Recently, he was attached to my staff, where he's been researching climate affects upon the ocean and how it might concern us here at the Pentagon.

"It was Captain Jones who brought this whole matter to my attention. I believe this is an extremely serious situation, as he will explain. Captain Jones, you have the floor."

"Thank you, sir," Jones said, suddenly feeling alone at the lectern as he watched Admiral Hart walk back to his chair. Rob Jones stood six feet, four inches tall, with dark, thick hair and rugged good looks. He had been a swimming champ in college, and the physique he obtained from long hours in the water had stayed with him into his adult life. He had broad shoulders and a strong muscular chest but, in spite of his imposing physical presence, Jones spoke in a soft, low voice.

"I'd like to show all of you some recent satellite photos, some of which are enhanced, of the Antarctic region." Jones flipped a switch built into the lectern, the curtains were automatically drawn and the lights turned off. Jones hit another switch and picked up the remote control for the computer projector. Walking away from the lectern, he used the remote to bring up the first of the satellite photos from the KH-15, displayed on a large, flat panel screen hanging at one end of the conference room. The screen measured six feet wide by eight feet long and had exceptionally clear resolution. The first photo showed icebergs floating all around the Antarctic Ocean.

"Earlier today," he said, "the *U.S.S. Tawney* had to break off a resupply mission to our base in the Antarctic due to a large number of icebergs in the area. This is very unusual," he said. "We have never, ever seen this many icebergs in the Antarctic. There are literally thousands of them.

"It's an indication that something very strange is occurring. As you all know, for the past six weeks there has been a series of heat waves all over the earth, including Antarctica. We're not just experiencing hot weather here in the States. It's all over. Of course, in the Southern Hemisphere it's summer, so the hot weather in Antarctica is relatively worse than here in the U.S."

He flipped to the next shot, a close-up view of the Ross Ice Shelf taken by the KH-15 as it made its pass over Antarctica. He stepped forward, picked up a pointer and placed its tip against the screen, on a thin black line in the white ice, one of many such lines.

"This line is a crack in the ice shelf," he said. "You can see that there are numerous cracks, which indicate the amount of fragmentation of the ice," he explained. "This is another serious consequence of abnormal weather conditions, because this has never happened before. These cracks extend deep into the interior of the continent, so this is not an isolated phenomenon. The fragmentation of the ice is occurring all over Antarctica."

"Do you have a trend on this? Will it stop of its own accord?" the Secretary of Defense, William Wilson, asked.

"As of twenty minutes ago, Mr. Secretary, the air temperature at McMurdo Naval Air Station was holding steady at seventy-four degrees. The temperature at 10,000 feet above the air base is holding steady at sixty degrees. Barometric pressure at sea level is 1020 millibars and rising. Our weather experts at McMurdo are forecasting no changes in this pattern over the next week. If there is a change, it will be for the worse, since high pressure in the area seems to be building. There are precious few clouds over the continent at the present time. Without any cloud cover, the sun will continue to strike the ice."

"Just how abnormal is this situation?" Wilson asked.

"It's totally abnormal," Jones stated. "In all the years we've been recording temperatures in the Antarctic, we have never recorded temperatures this high. It's so high above normal, we don't know what to make of it. And it's happened so fast we've been caught completely off guard."

There was a sudden silence in the conference room as the ominous implications of this information began to sink in. Jones' statement was a tacit admission as to just how powerless they all really were.

Admiral Hart cleared his throat. "We're now monitoring the weather all over the earth," he said, "in order to try to make a forecast. However, the situation is highly unpredictable."

"Well," Wilson asked, directing his question toward Rob Jones, "If you were to make a prediction, what would it be?"

"I don't think this weather pattern is going to change. Based on the data we're now getting, it's my opinion that we should immediately begin Operation Safeharbor."

"You realize what you're asking?" Wilson stated.

"Yes, sir, but I don't believe we have any choice."

Wilson sat back in his chair, absorbing this information. He looked up at the screen, carefully studying it. "Go on, Captain," he urged. "Please tell us what all this means."

Jones nodded. "If the situation at the South Pole continues, the consequences will become serious," he said. "Our computer projections tell us that at the present rate, the ice in Antarctica will completely melt by about the end of May. However, that's a rough extrapolation of current data. We're going to do a much more thorough analysis on a supercomputer within the next twenty-four hours. Then we can give you a more precise forecast." He flipped to the next satellite photo, an infrared computer enhanced image, which showed the colder water temperatures all along the edge of the continent.

"Let me tell you why we believe the ice is going to melt. Here, we see an infrared view of part of the coastline around Ross Island, where McMurdo Station is located. This little band of dark purple shows a slightly colder water temperature. It's darker in color than the water further out from the continent and, as you can see, it's coming from everywhere. It means there is a lot of freshly melted ice water flowing into the ocean. The base commander at McMurdo, Admiral Fletcher, said that the streams in the dry valleys near the Sound are running at flood level. Admiral Fletcher has been in contact with the other Antarctic bases, and they're also seeing large amounts of melting ice."

Jones flipped to another shot, this one a view of the entire continent.

"Here's another piece of evidence. December is the beginning of summer in the Antarctic. Normally, at this time of year, the sea ice all around the continent begins to unfreeze. Looking at it from space, the continent would appear to be contracting as the ice pack around it melts, but it doesn't reach its maximum contraction until February."

Jones switched to another slide. "This wide angle shot shows that all the sea ice has melted and the appearance of contraction has already reached its maximum. To me, this is one of the most disturbing aspects of the whole situation. You see, the hottest months down there are still ahead.

"Let me explain. Sea water normally freezes at 28.8 degrees Fahrenheit. Above this temperature, sea ice reverts to sea water. The temperature changes in the water are slight and take place rather slowly. The buildup of the ice pack around Antarctica takes months to achieve and, likewise, it takes months to melt. Well, we've just witnessed the complete melting of the icepack around the entire continent. *It only took six weeks.* Today, it looks just like it would in late February. This is absolute proof that something highly unusual is occurring."

"Incredible!" Secretary Wilson exclaimed. "This is amazing."

"I couldn't agree more, sir," Jones said. "The ice cap at the South Pole is over two miles thick. If it all melts, there is enough water there to raise the world's sea level by two hundred feet. Every naval base in the world will go underwater."

These words were met with total silence. Jones wondered if he should bother them with the next bit of information, but he decided he should. They should know the truth, he thought.

"If this hot weather continues, the North Pole will also begin melting. This, however, will have no effect upon the sea level, since the North Pole is just one big floating iceberg and it's already displacing surrounding sea water. However, there is glacial ice in Alaska, Canada, and Greenland which will melt and flow out to sea. This will cause severe problems, but in comparison to the amount of ice at the South Pole it's not as great a worry. It's really Antarctica that will cause most of our problems.

"We have done numerous studies of how the melting of the South Pole would affect the world but, to be succinct, if this heat doesn't subside by early summer, every major coastal city will go underwater. It will be a global disaster. And many inland cities and areas will be affected due to the expected backup and overflow of major rivers."

"That won't happen," said General John Hershey, Air Force Chief of Staff. "The hot weather can't possibly go on that long."

"We can't make a prediction as to what the weather might do," Captain Jones retorted. "Anything is possible."

"What is your best guess?" Secretary Wilson asked.

Jones frowned. This was an area he had hoped to avoid. He wanted to be truthful, but he knew his remarks would be controversial. He decided to choose his words carefully.

"Some prominent scientists have said that under the right conditions global warming could occur very rapidly in a phenomenon known as the runaway greenhouse effect. I believe we are now seeing the beginning of a runaway greenhouse effect."

"What, exactly, is a runaway greenhouse effect?" Wilson asked.

"Too much water vapor and carbon dioxide gas in the atmosphere trapping the sun's infrared rays," Jones answered. "Under the runaway greenhouse scenario, a certain threshold is reached, a point where the vapor and gas successfully trap most, if not all, of the infrared rays, just like the windshield of an automobile on a hot summer day."

Jones paused and looked around the room. Now, he felt as if he were lecturing students who had little knowledge of the subject. He realized he'd better preface his remarks.

"Ever since the beginning of Earth and the creation of Earth's atmosphere, there has always been a slight greenhouse effect. This is because carbon dioxide and water vapor have always been present in the atmosphere. The characteristics of water vapor and carbon dioxide are such that both are completely transparent to visible light, but both are capable of retaining infrared energy, the heat part of the spectrum.

"Because of this slight greenhouse effect, the earth has always been a warm planet. Let me emphasize that. We have not had a warm planet just because of sunlight; it's due to the earth's atmosphere *in combination with* the sun.

"We know that the sun by itself does not create enough heat to keep the planet as warm as the earth is. For example, if the earth were to rely solely upon sunlight, all of the earth's oceans would have frozen billions of years ago. You see, the composition of the planet just doesn't allow it to totally absorb and retain the infrared part of the sun's spectrum.

"But the earth's atmosphere absorbs the infrared rays, and it holds onto them for long periods of time. If it weren't for the atmosphere, with its water vapor and carbon dioxide, the heat from the sun would just strike the earth and then escape back into space. The earth would be a cold, frozen planet.

"So a partial greenhouse effect is desirable, and that's just what we've had throughout the history of modern man. As long as we can remember, our climate has been temperate.

"However, the earth is walking a fine line; too much water vapor and carbon dioxide gas in the atmosphere and we get a very strong greenhouse effect; not enough water vapor and carbon dioxide and we get no greenhouse effect. For thousands of years, everything's been in balance and the earth has experienced comfortable temperatures.

"Now we're suddenly seeing temperatures in Antarctica that are record highs, and the ice is beginning to melt. With temperatures down there in the seventies, there can be no doubt that all of Antarctica's ice will melt. Unfortunately, this will only increase the amount of water vapor present in the atmosphere, which will increase the greenhouse effect.

"Why is the earth suddenly seeing these high temperatures? Well, we've known for years that carbon dioxide has been building up in the atmosphere in very large amounts, billions of tons per year for the past seventy years or so. It's just possible that, once the atmosphere reached a certain volume of carbon dioxide gas, the greenhouse effect started to build upon itself. In my opinion, that's the most likely possibility. Our atmosphere has suddenly become too efficient at trapping infrared energy.

"The reason I don't think it will reverse itself is that it's happening everywhere. Both hemispheres are seeing very high temperature increases, which leads me to believe that the whole atmosphere is involved.

"My conclusion is we're starting to see a runaway greenhouse effect. This is all happening too fast to be anything else. As I said before, it's caught us completely by surprise."

"How could we be caught so unaware?" Wilson asked.

"Sir, I can't really answer that. Most of the experts said that global warming would take 100 or 200 years. But no one has ever had an accurate forecasting model of the whole earth. The dynamics involved are simply too complex. I can only assume that the carbon dioxide levels finally reached a saturation point.

"I should say that there might be other factors at play. For instance, about fifteen years ago, there were several volcanic eruptions in the Philippines which threw thousands of tons of ash into the high atmosphere. This ash acted like a giant shadecloth over the earth. By now, this ash has probably all fallen back to earth but, while it was up there, it may have had a mitigating effect on global warming. Now that the ash is gone, its disappearance might be involved in this sudden warmup."

"You don't sound too sure about that," Wilson said.

"No sir, I'm not. That's just a possibility. I would rather believe that our hot weather is due to a saturation of carbon dioxide. Recently, at some point in time, we crossed over the threshold and we suddenly started getting hot weather. It's as if someone came along and placed a mile thick layer of glass high in the atmosphere all around the earth."

"This is preposterous!" General Hershey said. "The Air Force has no data to confirm that. Mr. Secretary, I'd like to have time to have my people prepare a rebuttal to all this. I'm sure the Air Force weather experts will have a different opinion. Just because we've had six weeks of hot weather, we can't go jumping off the deep end."

"With all due respect, sir," Captain Jones said, "the Air Force is not in charge of McMurdo Naval Air Station in Antarctica. The U.S. Navy is. And it's in Antarctica that we're witnessing the very first effects of a runaway greenhouse effect. We believe the situation is critical. Operation Safeharbor needs to be implemented."

"You're talking about the potential destruction of the whole planet," Hershey fumed. "It's a gloom and doom forecast, and I'm not going to buy it."

Jones began to feel his forehead turn red. He did not want to get into an argument with a senior officer, but he felt he must defend his position. "Sir," he began, "at this point, we are not talking about the destruction of the whole planet. However, losing our coastal areas and most of our major cities will be a catastrophe."

"You have no proof as to this wild theory of yours," Hershey argued.

"We have hard physical evidence based on modern satellite photography that Antarctica is melting — and melting fast. Further, we have people on the ground who are confirming this fact. I believe we will see the effects of all this very quickly."

"What would these effects be?" Wilson asked.

Jones switched photos on the screen, to a map of the entire Southern Hemisphere. He had prepared for this very question. "The islands in the South Pacific will see it first. The low-lying atolls in the Pacific archipelagoes will be most susceptible. They will start to see major flooding in just a matter of weeks. Then, other islands around the Pacific will start losing their harbors. Places like French Polynesia, Samoa, the Fiji group, and Vanuatu. Closer to home, we'll probably notice it first at Pearl Harbor."

"In just a matter of weeks?" Wilson asked.

"Yes, sir. Once it starts, it will happen very quickly. The beaches and inlets will be lost to the sea, then eventually our docks. It all really boils down to the docks. Once those go underwater, the harbor is as good as gone. Even though most of the waterway will still be usable, the ships will have nowhere to dock. For the Navy, for all intents and purposes, that's the ballgame."

Secretary Wilson suddenly stood up. He had heard enough. He walked around the conference table to the podium where Jones was standing. "Thank you, Captain Jones," he said. "I think we've got the message." Jones nodded and sat down near Admiral Hart.

"Gentlemen," Wilson began, "I believe this is a matter of utmost national security. It looks like a crisis situation to me." He paused, gazing steadily at the men assembled around the conference table. "I'm going to recommend to the President that we begin Operation Safeharbor. Since just the initiation of Safeharbor will take several days, the Air Force and others will have time to prepare other briefings. General Hershey, I'd like to hear if your people feel the situation is as severe as the Navy seems to think. Nonetheless, based on what we already know, I don't think we can sit around. I must brief the President."

Wilson looked directly at Admiral Hart. "I want the Navy to immediately send several teams into the South Pacific. I know our satellites can do measurements, but I want people on the ground. Experts! If Captain Jones is right, I want corroboration on all of this, and we need to start right away. We've got to measure the sea level around these islands."

Wilson looked around the room. "That's my first recommendation, but I'm open to suggestions. Is there anything else we can do in the short term concerning this crisis?"

"Yes, sir," Secretary of the Air Force, Roger Matthieson, spoke up. He didn't like what he'd heard, but he was a team player, and he realized that Wilson had already made up his mind. Besides, he too was more than a little concerned about what was happening in Antarctica. "We can scrub the upcoming

DOD mission on the shuttle," he said, "and lay on a special mission. NASA has special laser devices that can measure topography, including water level. Also, we can detect any increase in water vapor levels in the atmosphere. We can fly the mission with the most able scientists we can get. We can control the mission through the Pentagon."

"Excellent," Wilson agreed. "You have my permission to go ahead. Whatever money you need we'll take out of our special fund. How long before you can launch?"

"It was scheduled for February twentieth," Matthieson replied. "But we can try to move it up. I'll get a team working on it."

"Good. Any other ideas?"

The Secretary of the Army, retired general Terence Bennett, quickly spoke up. "I think we'd better prepare for a major invasion," he said.

"What do you mean, Terence?" Secretary Wilson asked.

"I'm talking about refugees," Bennett warned. "Millions of them." He paused and looked around at the assembled group. "We're going to have millions of people, foreigners, trying to get to the United States. And they're going to want us to help them."

Admiral Hart nodded his agreement. "The Coast Guard and the Navy will mobilize our ships for that contingency."

Bennett shook his head. "I've read the planning for Operation Safeharbor. It was written by a bunch of cluckheads who really didn't believe this would ever happen. It doesn't go far enough." Bennett was the oldest man in the room, at sixty-five, and his voice suddenly rose an octave. "The Navy doesn't have enough ships to carry tens of millions of people to safety. We're going to have to begin the most massive airlift in the history of man. The Pacific island nations will be counting on us."

Wilson's eyes narrowed as he thought about Bennett's words. "What about that?" he asked of Admiral Hart.

Hart nodded perfunctorily. "It is the weakest part of Safeharbor," he admitted. "The Navy will be hard pressed, so the plan has designated priorities very carefully. Our own assets come first, civilians second. Naturally, we will try to save as many people as possible."

"I'm sorry, Admiral Hart, but that's not good enough," Wilson scolded. "Update your plans. We will enlist the entire merchant marine fleet for this operation, if necessary. We simply can't let millions of people around the world be drowned!"

"Sir, may I say something?" Captain Jones asked.

"Of course, Captain," Wilson said. "What is it?"

"I honestly believe we can't wait on this. Secretary Bennett is correct in his assessment. The people on those islands don't have much time. Every minute from here on will count. If you wait until we can absolutely confirm that the sea level is rising, we will run out of time. And so will they. I urge you to begin the airlift right away."

"That would be pushing it quite a bit," General Hershey complained. "I can't risk the lives of thousands of airmen until we're sure about this."

"If we wait, millions of people could drown," Jones said. "And not just in the Pacific. Near our shores are countries that will present logistical nightmares. All the Caribbean countries have major cities which are right on the coast. Kingston, Jamaica. San Juan, Puerto Rico. Santo Domingo in the Dominican Republic. Havana, Cuba. These cities all have major airports that are practically at sea level and could soon be underwater, maybe as soon as February. To airlift millions of people from the Caribbean is only feasible in the near term. Once we lose the airport runways, things will become very difficult.

"When our own ports and harbors start to flood out, the Navy will have limited ability to evacuate refugees because the ships trying to carry the refugees will have no place to effectively dock. When that happens, we'll have to rely strictly upon helicopters. And we just don't have enough choppers to carry tens of millions of people in such a short period of time."

"And we'll have our own people to worry about," Secretary Bennett added. "About half the population of America lives within fifty miles of the coast. They will be forced to move inland when the oceans begin to rise. This sounds to me like a major disaster in the making." Bennett pointed his finger at Wilson. "William," he said, "you must convince the President to commit our forces to action immediately!"

Secretary Wilson nodded dramatically, his face somber.

"We shouldn't get ahead of ourselves. So far," General Hershey said, "nobody has drowned, and nothing has flooded out. I admit, this is a serious matter which requires careful study, but we should not act unwisely. Antarctica has not melted yet."

"Yes," Rob Jones agreed. "Antarctica has not melted yet. However, we project it will melt by the end of May, and that's not too far away. If people are not moved out of the coastal areas well before then, there will be widespread panic, not to mention violence and tremendous loss of life."

"If this thing doesn't play out as you say," Hershey said, "we're all going to look like idiots."

"Yes, John," Admiral Hart said, "we already know that. This is a situation where we're damned if we do, damned if we don't. Before this is over, there will be no winners."

"I just don't think we should move too fast," Hershey said, his body language expressing disdain.

"We won't be able to move fast enough," Secretary Bennett countered. "We have a serious problem. Hell and damnation! We'll be hard pressed just to help our own people. I was born in Florida. I know that whole area like the back of my hand. Most of the entire state is just barely above sea level. What about all those people, General Hershey?"

"The hot weather could easily revert to normal, and we all know that. We shouldn't commit our forces too soon," Hershey said.

Secretary Wilson held up his hands, not wanting this meeting to develop into a debate or, worse, a heated argument. "We're not committing ourselves until the President says so. This will be his decision." Wilson looked around at his assembled subordinates and they all fell silent, waiting for his next statement. "But my guess is that, based on the available evidence, the President will order Operation Safeharbor to begin. Therefore, I can only tell you to be prepared to move and to move fast.

"Now, then, any data leaving the Pentagon concerning Safeharbor will be classified ultra top secret. There can be no deviation from this. The public must not find out about what we're doing, or we'll have panic in the streets. I will meet with the President this evening. I suggest you stay here tonight and get your staffs up to speed on this situation. That's all for now..."

Everyone rose from the table and started to leave the conference room. Wilson's "suggestion" was nothing less than an order to prepare for action, and they all knew it. As they filed out of the conference room, the expressions on their faces were somber.

Secretary Wilson looked directly at Jones. "Captain Jones," he said, "could I have a word with you? Admiral Hart, if you would also stay..."

Jones and Hart exchanged glances, and dutifully remained behind as the others exited. Wilson waited until the room was empty and the door had been closed.

"Captain, I must say, that was some briefing," he began. "You may not have convinced everyone, but you certainly convinced me. Would you repeat the briefing for the President?"

"Yes, sir," Jones said resolutely.

"Good," Wilson said. "Bring your slides to the White House. Admiral Hart knows the way. We will meet there in exactly one hour. As you say, every minute counts."

FIVE

"Look at that," said the President of the United States. "It's so unreal. It may as well be summer out there." President Philip Rawlings was in the Oval Office, standing next to the bullet-proof windows that looked out upon the lush, manicured lawns surrounding the White House.

It was Christmas Eve morning in Washington, D.C., a Sunday, and it promised to be another unseasonably hot day. The President had called in his closest advisors to discuss the briefing they had all been given the previous evening. Rawlings had refused to give Secretary Wilson an immediate answer to the Antarctic crisis. Instead, he had said he needed to sleep on it.

Today, he would have to make a decision on whether to begin Operation Safeharbor, which would call up the active reserves, dismantle every major U.S. naval port, take hundreds of ships out of mothballs, move all naval assets either out to sea or inland away from the flooding, and prepare to evacuate possibly tens of millions of people.

"I've never had to make this kind of decision," Rawlings lamented. "I need your advice. What do we do?"

"We don't know for certain there will be flooding," James Sisk, the President's National Security Advisor, cautioned. "I'm certainly not convinced. Nobody knows what the weather will do." Sisk, in his early sixties, was thin and partially bald, with a countenance expressing infinite political savvy. The mere raising of an eyebrow was enough to give his subordinates the jitters. "There are some in the Pentagon who disagree with the Navy," Sisk advised the President.

"Yes, I'm aware of that," President Rawlings said.

"Admiral Hart and Captain Jones did make a good argument," said Malcolm Teale, the President's Chief of Staff.

"Furthermore, Secretary Wilson is on their side. How can we ignore the evidence they presented?"

Teale was one of the most popular men in government and, next to the President, he held more power in the Oval Office than anybody else. A former senator from Georgia, Teale had resigned from the senate when Rawlings became President and had asked Teale to take the important job of Chief of Staff.

"No, Malcolm," the President said. "We cannot ignore it. We have to study it and weigh the consequences."

"The problem is these damned terrorists," growled Jack Roper, the President's press secretary and lifelong friend. "The Defenders of the Planet! Going around bombing and killing innocent people. If we declare a national emergency due to an environmental crisis, we'll make them look like heroes. Besides, there is no telling what they'll do."

"Not to mention a worldwide panic that might follow if our Navy starts moving their ships around," added Sisk. "Those correspondents at the Pentagon will surely pick up on that. And they'll report it. I wouldn't act too hastily, Mr. President. We could get our fingers burned."

"This is the worst thing that could have happened," Rawlings said. "What am I supposed to do, anyway? We can't wage war against Mother Nature. We can only react."

"We could wait for another week or two," advised Roper. Roper stood five feet, ten inches, and weighed two hundred and forty-five pounds. His trademark among the press was a cigar constantly stuck in his mouth. Here in the Oval Office, smoking was strictly forbidden, so Roper mouthed a wet, unlit Havana. "In the meantime, we might come up with some alternatives."

"Both Admiral Hart and Captain Jones stressed that time is of the essence," Teale retorted. "As we speak, the ice is melting, and Safeharbor is a major operation. They're going to need lots of lead time."

"They could be exaggerating," Sisk stated.

"I don't think so," Teale countered. "Besides, what if they're right? Can we continue to just wait around?"

"The President will decide that," Sisk said.

"Goddamn it all! I'm not omnipotent!" Rawlings stated forcefully. He walked over to his desk and sat down heavily. "You're right, Jim. If I order the Navy to start moving their assets around, the press will be onto us. There's no way we could keep it quiet. Then we'll have a worldwide panic on our hands. Civil disobedience on a scale we've never ever witnessed before."

Hearing this, Sisk smiled triumphantly. Now he was sure that the President would hold off on ordering Operation Safeharbor to begin. Waiting, Sisk knew, was the safe play.

"We have to act decisively, Mr. President," Teale continued to argue. "The weather doesn't look like it will get any better. If Antarctica fully melts, there's going to be worldwide panic anyway. Captain Jones said we'll see waters rise in the Pacific in just a matter of weeks. The media and the press will certainly report that, won't they?"

Roper and Sisk became quiet as they pondered the logic of Teale's statement. Teale, even though he was Chief of Staff, was not a yes man, and his careful analysis of any given problem held him in good standing with the President.

"So, what are you getting at, Malcolm?" Rawlings asked.

"Well," Teale began, "we can use all of the power available to us to try our damnedest to keep Safeharbor a secret for as long as possible. The Navy wants to get going on this right away, and I believe they should. The welfare of their ships and bases is at stake. We can hide this from the media for a while, I'm sure. It might be long enough to make a difference."

"No way," Roper disagreed. "In order to get those ships out of mothballs, the Navy has to call up half a million reservists. We just couldn't contain that." Roper nodded his head back and forth in a pronounced fashion. "No. No way will that work," he said. "When we initiate Operation Safeharbor, it'll be like waving a red flag. The sky is falling..."

"Perhaps the weather will reverse itself," Sisk said.

Again, there was a lull in the conversation. Everyone was hoping that the weather would go back to normal, but so far it hadn't. And even these most powerful men couldn't change that.

"We must act with the assumption that the weather will continue to remain warm," President Rawlings said, refusing to use the word "hot" to describe the present predicament. "If it continues, then we have to accept the scientific evidence that the ice at the South Pole will melt. Then, everything will happen as the Navy says it will. We will lose our coasts, including some of our biggest cities. The important question is, how will we present this to the American people?"

"The country could fall apart," Sisk said. "This is too big. I don't think they can take it."

"We can't stick our heads in the sand and pretend this isn't happening," Teale said. "If there is civil unrest, we can call out all military reserves to keep order in the streets. We can declare Marshal Law. Mr. President, our government must be allowed to function. If you give the approval, we're going to be very busy initiating Operation Safeharbor. So will the military, especially our Navy and air force. If we have to face civil unrest at the same time, our armed forces will have a dual crisis to contend with. It will be totally impossible for them. There's just too many goddamned guns around."

"He's right about that," Roper nodded at Rawlings.

"The important thing for them is to get a headstart," Teale continued, "and the only way to do that is to try to maintain secrecy. The services must be allowed to concentrate their efforts in coping with the rising oceans. Once Safeharbor is up and running, then we can deal with telling the public, and the world, the truth. But the military has to have some breathing room. We can't possibly deal with multiple crises at the same time."

The President, his face drawn in a tight grimace, nodded. Teale's logic made perfectly good sense. But could they pull it off? Rawlings ran Teale's idea through his mind, searching for any potential drawbacks. The hazards of following such a course were great, but the hazards of inaction might be even worse. As he sat there thinking, the silence within the Oval Office became overwhelming.

Finally, the President said, "Malcolm, you may be right. Draw up a plan, and I'll back you fully. We must move ahead and try to anticipate the worst."

"Mr. President," James Sisk pleaded. "Can't we wait a few days? Just to give it more time?"

"No. I'm afraid not. The Navy needs as much time as possible. If the world's oceans start to rise, we will need our Navy, maybe more than ever. We can't jeopardize all those ships and equipment. I fully intend to use our military to help as many people as possible from the island nations. It's the least we can do." President Rawlings looked at them earnestly. "Beyond that, we must have *and we will have* law and order."

"Then we initiate Operation Safeharbor?" Roper asked.

"Yes," President Rawlings said. He got up and walked around his desk and sat on its corner, facing the three of them. "I'm compelled to agree with Malcolm. We'll just have to try and keep Safeharbor secret for as long as possible. I'll order the Navy to get moving. For now, we'll call up the active reserves. Later, if we have to, we'll bring in the inactive reserves. Also, until we make a public announcement, this will be a United States operation. Because of the immediate need for secrecy, we won't inform the United Nations of our intentions. However, I'll call Prime Minister Howe and notify him. I'm sure we can trust the British."

"What about the Russian and Ukraine navies?" Teale asked. "They could be a great help."

"Yes, we should probably work with them, too. And I wouldn't be surprised if they probably already know what's going on. But, just in case, I'll talk to their leaders, too. Today."

"This whole thing is getting complicated," Jack Roper commented. "Who else can we trust?"

The President chose to ignore the question. "Malcolm, I'll expect your first draft by four o'clock this afternoon. Get your staff right on it."

"What about the Defenders of the Planet?" James Sisk asked.

"You take care of them, Jim," Rawlings replied. "Double or triple the number of FBI agents on the case. Those people have to be stopped before they cause any more trouble. If, in the final analysis, I have to declare Marshal Law, the FBI can round up all suspects. We can't have them running loose during this crisis. Keep me advised."

"Mr. President," Roper said, realizing he and Sisk had lost the argument to Teale. "I'll try to contain this with the press for as long as I can, but I can't guarantee for how long."

"Just do your best, Jack. Be creative. That's all any of us can do. If we have to, we'll lock some of the press up, too, at least, those who don't cooperate with us." The President got up from his desk and strode back to the windows. As he stared out, he said, "I'm sorry you all have to spend Christmas Eve this way, but we've got a national crisis pending." He turned and nodded toward his three advisors. "Shall we get going?" he asked, signaling that the meeting was over.

With that, Teale and Sisk excused themselves, but Roper stayed with the President. Roper felt he was still needed by his old friend, though he knew better than to make any further argument. The President had obviously made his decision.

"Jack," Rawlings said, after the others had left, "This is the damnedest situation. I never thought when I took this office that I'd ever have to face something like this."

"Who would have ever thought that this would happen?" Roper asked. "I mean, I know that various scientists have been predicting this, but not in our lifetime..."

"The Navy took it seriously. That's why they drew up the plans for Operation Safeharbor."

"Yes," Roper agreed. "The military has contingency plans for everything. Even global warming."

"If we come out of this, it'll be in large part due to the United States Navy," Rawlings said. "Let's hope they know what they're doing. God, I wish this weren't happening!"

Roper decided to change the subject. "Mr. President, what about tonight's Christmas Eve concert?" he asked. "I suggest you go ahead and attend, just to keep up appearances."

"Yes, of course," Rawlings agreed. "We have to act like none of this is happening. We all have to go on with our duties, with our everyday routine, in spite of what we know. We can't falter at a time like this."

Roper nodded glumly. No, we can't, he thought to himself. But his primary concern was the White House press corps and the national media. They were like sharks. They could smell blood in the water, and then they'd be coming in for the kill. The only way to stop them was to lock them up. Was that what they would have to do?

"Jack, do me a favor," Rawlings commanded.

"Yes, sir. What is it?"

"Go out and have them call the British Prime Minister. Put the call through to my desk. I'll take it alone."

Roper nodded, getting to his feet and immediately heading for the door.

"One more thing," the President said.

Roper turned, a questioning look upon his face. "Yes, Mr. President?" he asked.

"Would you call Secretary Wilson for me? Have him come over immediately."

Roper nodded. "Yes, sir, I'll call right away." As he exited the Oval Office, he took one last look at the President. Roper couldn't remember a time when his boss looked so distraught.

SIX

Carrie Cameron was sitting at her desk at four p.m. mountain standard time on Christmas Eve, surrounded by five computers with flat panel screens. With all five systems running, she was able to bring up real time satellite data that almost gave her a global weather picture.

Carrie wore a slight frown, as her fingers clicked rapidly across her computer keyboard. She was having a problem bringing up the picture from the Southern Hemisphere, from the NIMBUS V satellite, and no matter what she tried, nothing seemed to work.

That's funny, she thought, this damned thing just won't come in. She typed in a set of commands to her computer for the eleventh time, somehow thinking that she was making an inputting error, but again the screen remained blank. There was no satellite picture from NIMBUS V.

She had a thought, and reached for her phone, dialing a contact she had at the U.S. Weather Service in Washington.

"Jim Greer, here," said a friendly male voice.

"Hi, Jim," she said. "It's Carrie at DSN."

"Hello, Carrie," he greeted her. "What's up?"

"Jim, I can't get a picture from NIMBUS V."

There was a moment of silence, and then Greer said, "Yeah, it's gone down. It's a NASA responsibility. I'm sure they're trying their best to get it back on line, but so far they haven't got it working."

"Do you know what happened?" Carrie asked.

"I think it's the transmitter, but I'm not sure. I could look into it for you," he said.

"Would you?" she asked. "That would be great."

"OK," he said. "I'll call you right back."

"Thanks, Jim. I really appreciate this."

"No problem, Carrie. Talk to you later."

Carrie hung up the phone and then replayed the conversation in her mind. She frowned as she thought it over. Something was wrong. She concluded that Greer was lying, but why? Why would Jim Greer lie about a stupid satellite?

Carrie immediately made another phone call, this time to a contact within the Pentagon. "NRO," a gruff voice answered.

"Colonel Snowden, please," Carrie said.

"Colonel Snowden has gone for the day," the gruff voice replied. "I suggest you call back tomorrow..."

"Yes, thank you," she said, hanging up her phone. She placed another call to the Pentagon, to DSN's Pentagon bureau.

"DSN," Josh Talbot answered.

"Hi, Josh, it's Carrie. I was hoping you'd still be there."

"Heya, kid. What's cooking?" Talbot offhandedly asked.

"I don't know, but something is up," she replied.

"Yeah? What?" Josh asked.

"Something's going on," Carrie said. "It has to do with our weather. I just tried to call Brent Snowden, you know, over at the NRO, and they told me he's gone home for the day."

"Maybe he has," Josh said. "After all, it is Christmas Eve and it's Sunday night, too."

"I talked to him yesterday, and he said he'd be working tonight. The Air Force has some special study that needed to get done, and they were going to utilize the National Reconnaissance Office's satellites. Suddenly, he's not available..."

"Anything else I should know about?" Josh asked.

"Yes. I just found out that NIMBUS V has gone down. I can't get a picture of the Southern Hemisphere. A friend of mine at the U.S. Weather Service just told me that its transmitter has malfunctioned, but I think he was lying to me. I knew that Brent would know about it, and I wanted to get his confirmation as to why it went down."

"Hmmmmm," Josh mused, thinking about what Carrie had told him. "And you think this has something to do with the funny weather?"

"I know it does," Carrie said. "I suspect they don't want us to see what's happening in Antarctica. And there is something happening down there."

"Antarctica?" Josh exclaimed. "You mean the South Pole is melting or something?"

"Yes," Carrie replied. "It could be. A few hours ago, a scientist friend of mine told me that Antarctica was experiencing abnormally high temperatures. He said he'd heard it was over sixty degrees over the continent. I checked it out with the weather service, and they were reporting temps only in the high thirties. That's a big contradiction, so I've been trying to do some checking. Now I'm suddenly getting stonewalled."

"You think something's going on?" Josh asked.

"Yes," Carrie said. "Anyway, Josh, I suggest you look into it. They're up to something in Washington. I know it."

"Okay," Josh said. "I'll check around and get back to you. Right now, things are pretty quiet around here. I can't promise anything right away."

"I understand. Thanks, Josh. If I don't talk to you again today, have a Merry Christmas!"

"And Merry Christmas to you, and to all a good night!"

Carrie couldn't help but laugh. Josh was forever the comedian. "Good night, Josh. Take care," she said, and with that she hung up her phone.

Carrie sat back in her chair, analyzing the situation. She was due to go on the air in less than ten minutes, so she decided to forget about NIMBUS V for now, and she began concentrating on studying the weather pattern over the continental U.S. The temperatures on this Christmas Eve were still high, although they had dropped within the past twenty-four hours.

Satisfied that she understood the weather around the country, Carrie got up from her desk and headed for the studio. She'd have less than two minutes to summarize the day's weather and give a forecast.

She didn't mind having to work on Christmas Eve. She knew that with the sudden strange weather the world was having, millions more people would be tuned in to watch, and everyone would want to know what Christmas Day would be like.

Carrie walked through DSN's offices with a purposeful stride, mens' heads turning as she made her way to the weather studio. She was a beautiful woman, with high cheekbones, a cute upturned nose, long blonde hair, and deep blue eyes. And, importantly for television, her body movements were lithe and graceful, and her voice was strong, though distinctly feminine.

Carrie was a degreed meteorologist who reported the weather with an acumen few could match. Her broadcasts on the Direct Satellite Network had helped boost their share of the evening television market in the U.S. to over fifty percent. She could have reported any segment of the news, but her main interest was weather.

In college, she had studied meteorology, feeling it was the one important factor that affected peoples' lives every day, a fact of life she had learned from personal experience. Her father had been an Iowa farmer, and their whole existence had depended on having decent weather at just the right time. She had never forgotten her father's worried face when the weather wouldn't cooperate, especially those times when, if only he had had an accurate weather forecast, he might have delayed a planting or hurried a harvest. And she had never forgotten the floods of the early nineties.

When Carrie started college, she vowed to become the best weather reporter in the country, and she worked diligently toward achieving that goal. She majored in meteorology and minored in broadcast journalism. Throughout college, she maintained a 4.0 grade point average, graduating *summa cum laude*.

Her first job out of college was as a weather reporter at a local TV station in Dubuque, where she put in hours of extra work every day to make sure that the local farmers had an accurate and dependable forecast. Her abilities grew in quantum leaps and, after only a year in the business, she accepted a job in Des Moines, receiving a hefty increase in salary. She stayed in Des Moines for four years and was offered a job at a station in a much bigger market, in Chicago. The attendant salary increase was too much for her to ignore, and she readily accepted the position. Two years later, she was discovered by a DSN producer, a job offer soon followed, and shortly thereafter she headed for DSN's Denver headquarters. Overnight, she found she had national exposure, and DSN had a new star weather reporter.

On this Christmas Eve, Carrie knew that about seventy million people would be watching. When she reached the studio, Susan Dahlman, a DSN producer, met her at the entrance.

"The backgrounds are set," Susan announced. "As usual, we took the numbers right from the U.S. Weather Service computer system."

"The weather was a little cooler today," Carrie commented.

"Sure was," Susan said. "I'd like you to work that angle, Carrie. Make everybody feel better on Christmas Eve."

"I'll try," Carrie said. "Things don't look good, though."

"Have we got through this hot spell? Is it starting to end?"

"I don't think so," Carrie said, "but I can highlight the lower temperatures. It's only cooled down a bit. We're still experiencing very hot weather for this time of year. I'd be reluctant to make any premature announcements."

"I understand," Susan said, looking at the studio clock. "You're on in about forty seconds," she said.

Carrie nodded and walked out into the studio past the cameras and stood in front of a huge blank screen. A technician fitted her with a small radio microphone, and almost immediately the camera's red light came on, and in the background she heard the DSN anchor announcing her.

"Good afternoon," Carrie beamed into the main camera. "Well, we finally got some good news, just in time for Christmas. There was a slight drop in temperatures today. The high in the United States was ninety-two out in Death Valley,

California. Elsewhere in the United States, temperatures have also fallen slightly." Behind her, a huge map of the United States was shown in a broad band of color.

"We're still experiencing record hot weather across most of the nation, but not quite as hot as it has been in the past few days. Boston hit seventy-seven, Detroit seventy-four, Dallas eighty and, out in the West, Los Angeles hit eighty-two, San Francisco seventy-six, Phoenix eighty-five. Here in Denver, we reached a high of seventy-four."

Then, the background suddenly changed and the map showed a 3-D relief of the entire North American continent. Carrie went right with it. "As you can see, we have several low pressure systems over parts of the nation.

"Today, there have been heavy rains in the southeast. Little Rock, Arkansas received over twelve inches of rain today. In Miami, it has rained throughout the day and they will be getting heavy rain tonight and into tomorrow. Iowa and Missouri and Southern Illinois can also expect heavy rains this evening. Humidity will remain high."

Carrie turned away from her weather map and smiled into the camera. "It's very much like summer out there, with some areas of the country reporting thunderstorms. Though the nation has cooled down a bit, things are still very unusual.

"Out in the West, a low pressure system is moving through Nevada and Idaho, and they are reporting thunder and lightning, with scattered showers. Near Boise this morning, lightning is responsible for starting a small forest fire which is still out of control.

"It looks like tomorrow's temperatures will be like today's, perhaps one or two degrees cooler." As Carrie looked into the camera, a digital number above it started counting backward from ten down to zero, her signal that they were about to go to commercial. She smiled into the camera. "I'll be back with the forecast for Christmas Day after this..." As the digital number hit zero, the red light on the camera went off.

There would be a full ninety seconds of commercials, but it would go by very quickly. Everyone in the weather studio stayed in position and there was no conversation or banter. When she came back on, Carrie gave the forecast. "Tomorrow's temperatures will be more of the same. Looking ahead, there is a large storm system moving rapidly in the Gulf of Alaska, so I'd say that the Northwest will experience heavy rain probably by next Tuesday. I think the southern edge of this storm will dip as far south as the Central Valley of California and continue to move through parts of Nevada and into Arizona.

"Now, here are the current local temperatures in your area of the country." Carrie looked over at a monitor as the list of cities and their temperatures began to scroll down the screen. For now, she was off. She would be back on the air in half an hour with an expanded version of her weather report.

"That was great! See you in thirty minutes," Susan said.

"Thanks," Carrie said. She smiled at everyone as she removed her microphone, then left the studio and went back to her office. Just as she reached her desk, the phone rang and she picked it up. "Carrie Cameron," she said.

"Carrie, it's Josh."

"That was quick," she said. "What's up?"

"You were right. There's something big going on here. I just found out that the U.S. Navy is calling up its entire active reserves. The order just went out."

"What? What does that mean?" Carrie asked.

"It means something big is going on. My source told me not to report it, or else I'd be put in jail. My source told me it's a matter of utmost national security. So I agreed to keep it under wraps. That goes for you, too. What I'm telling you is just between us. This is top secret stuff. Understood?"

"Understood," Carrie agreed. "But why the secrecy?"

"Because it has something to do with the weather situation. They're scared about this, Carrie. I can tell. I've only got a few clues to go on. Most of my key contacts aren't here right now. The one person who would talk to me told me to keep my mouth shut. I think it's really big, Carrie, you were right about this! Also, I found out that the Secretary of Defense is here working tonight, and all the other Secretaries for that matter. That means for sure there's something important going on."

"What do you think it means?" Carrie asked.

"I'm not sure. I was told not to do any digging, or else. I'm going to have to sit on this story, Carrie. I don't have any choice. I think I'll just go home and forget about it, and I suggest you do the same." There was a finality in Josh's voice. Carrie thought she also sensed uncertainty and fear.

"Okay, I will," she said, "and thanks for calling back."

"Take care. I'll see you, Carrie. Have a merry Christmas."

"Merry Christmas," Carrie said, putting her phone down. That was a strange conversation, she thought.

Suddenly, the phone rang again. It was Greer from the U.S. Weather Service. "Carrie, I just found out about NIMBUS for you."

"I appreciate that, Jim. What happened to it?"

"Its transmitter has definitely malfunctioned. It can no longer send photos back to earth."

"Can they fix it?" she asked.

"No... they've tried everything. NASA is going to have to put up a new system, but it's going to take at least six months, maybe more. They have other priorities right now."

"Well," Carrie said. "I guess that takes care of that. Thank you, Jim, for calling me back."

"Yeah, sorry I couldn't be any more help," Greer said.

"That's okay," Carrie responded. "There's nothing you can do and it's certainly not your fault."

"Well, it will put a crimp in some of our abilities."

"Oh, well," Carrie replied. "Thanks, Jim. And have a great Christmas, okay?"

"Thanks, and merry Christmas to you and everybody at DSN."

She set the phone down, frowning. Greer, she decided, was a very bad liar. It had taken every bit of discipline she could muster not to accuse him outright. To hell with him, she finally thought.

Carrie looked at her computer screen, thinking about the conversation with Josh. Should she take a chance and possibly jeopardize his position? And did she really have any choice? She made a quick decision, and switched programs on her main computer. Then she typed a terse message. It read: Situation at South Pole may be critical. I suspect government is lying about abnormally high temperatures in Antarctica. Coverup! NIMBUS V taken off line. U.S. Navy calling up all reserves. Birddog.

Then, using special software, she encrypted the message so it would be impossible for anyone to decode it, even the most sophisticated agencies of the U.S. Government. She used her modem to transmit the coded message to another computer in New York, where it was automatically routed to yet another computer within the city, one which could be accessed via its electronic bulletin board.

Carrie cleared the computer screen and sat back in her chair, a half-smile on her face. Well, she thought, the day hasn't been completely wasted. In a matter of a few hours, several key members of the Defenders of the Planet would know what she knew.

SEVEN

On the afternoon of Christmas Eve, Jonathan Holmes, his daughter Jamie, and Matt Farr were in Phoenix, standing atop the main building of Babbitt Center, a recently completed skyscraper complex named after Bruce Babbitt, former Arizona governor and Secretary of the Interior, one of the most popular men in the history of Arizona politics. In 2003, Babbitt had been killed in an airplane crash while trying to settle a dispute between environmentalists and ranchers in Wyoming.

The circumstances surrounding Babbitt's death were mysterious. Some said the ranchers had killed him by planting a bomb aboard his plane, while others said the environmentalists had perpetrated the act, though no one knew for certain, and an exhaustive investigation turned up few clues.

Regardless, shortly after his death, construction on the complex began and, since the Center was to house several state offices and was designed to be a model environmental showpiece, the Arizona State Legislature voted to name it after Babbitt.

The main building of the complex, the tallest skyscraper in Phoenix, stood one hundred and two stories tall, completely dominating the desert skyline. Atop the building, there was a small weather station which Matt's company was in charge of maintaining. This station fed weather data to the National Weather Service, all the local Phoenix television and radio stations, and to Arizona State University.

Matt had brought them to the top of the skyscraper to show them the station and the view. It was hot and humid in Phoenix, and the three of them were breathing hard and sweating profusely, having just climbed to the roof via the stairs because the elevators weren't operational.

When Flynn, Smith, and Walker had downed the transmission lines leading from the Navajo Generating Station, the main generators had "tripped," shut down in an unusually severe fashion, and many of the station's circuits and transformers had blown out. The Navajo Generating Station was forced to shut down. Despite a 'round the clock effort, it would be another week before it would be running again. Even with the huge Palo Verde nuclear power plant west of Phoenix running at 100 percent capacity, the interlocking power grid in the southwest had been disrupted, and many areas were experiencing brownouts. To offset these dire effects, Arizona Public Service, Phoenix's local utility company, had ordered key installations to cut their power use to an absolute minimum, and so the main power systems of Babbitt Center were off line, including the elevators.

"That was quite a hike," Matt said. He pulled a water bottle from a small backpack and offered it to Jamie. "Care for some water?" he asked.

"Thanks," Jamie said, smiling at him as she took the bottle.

Holmes looked at the two them, sensing the beginning of a romance. Since their arrival in Phoenix, Jamie had suddenly taken a keen interest in this young American weather scientist, and Holmes wondered if it might become serious. Jamie, he knew, had a habit of leading men on, eventually losing interest in them. Her involvement with Matt, though, seemed different.

Matt pulled out another water bottle. "Water, Dr. Holmes?" he asked.

"Yes, don't mind if I do." Holmes took the bottle, unscrewed the top and drank a fourth of it, then put the top back on. "Thanks," he said, holding onto the bottle. "Matt, I don't think I'd like to do that again, at least not for a day or two. You promised us a workout, and I certainly got one."

"It's the first time I've ever had to use the stairs," Matt said sheepishly. "My legs are like jelly right now. I didn't realize how important elevators are. Are you okay, Dr. Holmes?"

"Yeah, I'm okay," Holmes said, a wry smile on his face.

"Really? Your legs aren't hurting?"

"No, I'm fine. I do work out, you know. I try to stay in shape because my work sometimes takes me to some pretty rugged areas."

"What do you do?" Matt asked, "I mean, when you work out."

"I normally walk or run five or six miles a day. If I'm at home, I like to swim in the ocean, maybe a mile or two at a stretch."

"Do you lift weights?"

"Only if I'm stuck in a big city and I can't do my normal routine. But, I assure you, the weights I use are very light."

"You look like you handled that hike okay. For someone of your age, you're in great shape."

Holmes smiled at Matt's attempt at flattery. "Thank you," he said. "But, like I said, I wouldn't want to do it again."

Matt nodded. "Well, why don't I show you the station, and then we'll go back down to my office. It's right here in the Center on the thirty-second floor."

Suddenly, Jamie took Matt's arm. "Come on, Matt. First show me the view like you promised. Father's seen plenty of weather equipment lately, haven't you, Father?"

Matt hesitated, not sure if Holmes would approve. As Jamie clung to his arm, he looked to Holmes for guidance.

"You two go on," Holmes said. "I'll just kind of nose around up here on my own." He watched as Jamie led Matt away, then he turned and walked in the opposite direction. Checking the sun's position, Holmes began walking toward the east side of Babbitt Center.

As he walked, he noticed dark skies far to the east of Phoenix. He came around the corner of the roof and kept walking until he was in the center of the roof's east side. He stood there, gazing out upon the eastern horizon.

To the east were the suburbs of Tempe and Mesa. In the distance were the Superstition Mountains, and further to the east was an even higher mountain range called the Pinal Mountains.

Above and to the east of these peaks, bright flashes of light in the sky signified lightning, though the storm was too far away for him to hear the thunder. It appeared to be a large storm system.

Over Phoenix, the sky was clear and sunny. With the sun behind him and low on the southern horizon, the west sides of the Superstitions and the Pinals stood out brightly in the yellow rays of sunlight. At the same time, the sky to the east of the Pinals was dark, so much so that it seemed etched in charcoal. As he watched the scene, Holmes saw a rainbow begin to develop between the outskirts of Phoenix and the mountains.

As he studied it, he ran the physics of this phenomenon through his mind. Rainbows always form on the edges of rainstorms when the sun is behind the viewer. As the sun's rays strike and penetrate though the raindrops, the tiny droplets of water act like trillions of tiny prisms, dividing and broadcasting the colors of the spectrum in unison.

Holmes knew that the mountains were some distance away. The brightly colored arc of this rainbow seemed to have formed well to the west of their ridges, indicating that there must be water vapor present in the vicinity of the rainbow. But it did not appear that the vapor was part of the storm itself.

He concluded that the water vapor present in the atmosphere was abnormally high, for the rainbow was gigantic and seemingly removed from the storm itself. Holmes wasn't sure if he'd ever seen anything like it before in his life. He knew that something unusual was occurring.

For several minutes, Holmes was lost in thought, deeply troubled by the signs in the atmosphere. Then Matt and Jamie came around the corner and joined him, the three of them watching the skies to the east. None of them spoke for the next five minutes. The view to the east was at once eerily beautiful and darkly ominous.

"Another storm," Matt said simply.

"And a big one, at that," Holmes replied.

"It looks like it's moving up from the south. That's a summertime pattern. Very strange," Matt said.

"I'd have to agree," Holmes said, his face serious.

"Why don't we go down to my office?" Matt suggested. "We've got a supercomputer tied in to a world network of weather stations, including the one we just set up near Yuma. We've installed some special software that can show us a global weather pattern."

"Excellent idea," Holmes nodded affirmatively. "I'd like to know what is going on in the world."

"Me, too," Jamie said. "I'd like to see what we can expect down in Quito when we set up our next station."

The three of them began walking back to the exit onto the roof. As they turned the corner of the rooftop, Holmes took one last look at the storm. Dark clouds on the horizon, he thought, and he wondered about the future that was awaiting them all.

Later that evening, Holmes and his daughter went out to a Christmas Eve dinner with Bill and Maggie Roosevelt. The Roosevelts were environmental science professors who taught at Arizona State University, and both were longtime supporters of Save Our World.

They had brought Jonathan and Jamie to the posh Phoenician, a luxury resort in nearby Scottsdale, to its famous restaurant on the fifth floor, Mary Elaine's. On this Christmas Eve, the restaurant was full and the mood was festive. From their table, they could look out over the entire Phoenix metropolitan area. Below the restaurant, the grounds were lushly landscaped, hundreds of palm trees standing out against the soft city lights in the distance.

The dinner was splendid, their food sumptuous and exotic; a salad of goat cheese, stuffed vegetables, and roasted eggplant, followed by a main dish of roast turkey with garlic and rosemary, grilled vegetable gratin, artichoke casserole, and celery and potato gratin. Bill Roosevelt ordered a bottle of 1986 Laurel Glenn Cabernet Sauvignon, and they all agreed it was an excellent vintage, so he ordered another bottle.

Holmes, wanting to keep a clear head, limited himself to just two glasses. At eight o'clock he was scheduled to give an environmental speech at Gammage Hall on the campus of the university in nearby Tempe, Arizona, an event arranged by Bill Roosevelt.

After they ate, they all drank coffee. As he sipped from his cup, Holmes gazed fondly at the Roosevelts. To Holmes, the Roosevelts were a perfect match. They were both in their early fifties, but they seemed younger and they had a vitality and enthusiasm for life that was contagious. They were major contributors to half a dozen major environmental organizations, but especially to SOW.

Bill Roosevelt had been born into wealth, and neither he nor Maggie had to work, but he was fond of saying that since he was a distant relative of Teddy Roosevelt he was obliged to carry on the family tradition of protecting the environment. Holmes first met them many years earlier during a European SOW convention in Zurich. They had developed an instant rapport and had remained in close contact over the years.

When they had learned that he would be in Arizona, Bill had asked Holmes if he would speak to a gathering of local Phoenix environmental groups and interested ASU students, and Holmes accepted his invitation without hesitation.

Holmes smiled graciously and said, "That was delicious. I haven't eaten food this good in ages."

Maggie Roosevelt smiled, "Jonathan, you can't expect anything less than the best from a five-star restaurant like Mary Elaine's."

"That's right," Bill added. "The chef here is world class."

"Maggie and Bill," Holmes said, "this is one of the nicest Christmas Eves I've ever spent, at least since my wife Eileen died. Thank you for inviting us out."

"Yes," Jamie agreed. "Thank you! It was a lovely dinner."

"We're the ones who should thank you," Bill Roosevelt said. "It's wonderful of you to stay here in Arizona to give this speech."

Holmes shrugged and said, "Jamie and I probably would have spent this evening unpacking in a hotel down in Quito. I'm sure that would have been a little dreary," he said. "Besides, I view giving speeches as important opportunities. I feel it's important to convince as many people as we can about the dangers facing the environment. Especially right now."

"You're absolutely right," Bill said. "It's so darned important to educate people, especially the younger generation. They may be the last hope for us," he said.

"I know," Holmes said seriously. "I want to make a convincing argument tonight. I hope my speech goes well." Holmes suddenly laughed. "Sometimes I get a little nervous beforehand."

"You shouldn't be nervous, Jonathan," Maggie said. "You'll be among friends. We're all looking forward to it."

"Well, so far it's been a perfect evening. Next Christmas Eve, Jamie and I shall have to return the favor. If this weather situation turns around, you'll both have to come to Sydney."

"Absolutely," Maggie said. "That would be wonderful! We would be honored to come to Australia."

"That is, if we ever get back to Australia," Jamie said jokingly. "My father's work is taking us on a never-ending journey."

"There are only a few more locations to set up," Holmes said. "Then it's back to New York and home to Australia. We'll see," he paused and looked around the room. "I have a strange feeling our future may not go as planned."

"How so?" Bill asked.

"I believe our planet is in serious trouble," Holmes said, "and I've made a few changes to the text of my speech. Tonight, I want to sound the alarm."

"To stir up the pot?" Maggie asked.

"Exactly. And to provoke the powers that be. I mean, look around you. Look at all these people acting as if nothing is going on. Don't they realize the trouble the earth is in?"

"Father, it is Christmas Eve," Jamie said.

"Doesn't matter. These people seem to be blind to the facts. Tonight, I think I'll wake them up a bit. I hope there will be a good turnout."

"Do you think many people will be there, Professor Roosevelt, considering it is Christmas Eve?" Jamie asked.

"Your father is one of the most famous scientists in the world. I expect it will be standing room only, and Gammage Hall can easily hold three thousand people."

"Besides, Jonathan," Maggie said, "I'm sure that, with this unrelenting heat wave throughout both hemispheres, there will be much interest. Not everyone is blind to what's going on."

Holmes looked at her, his eyes appraising. Maggie was not only intelligent, but she was beautiful, too. Bill is a lucky man, Holmes thought.

Maggie Roosevelt was a lovely, green-eyed redhead, with a milky white, supple complexion. Tonight she looked stunning. She was wearing a black evening dress which revealed a lot of cleavage and an hourglass figure. For the first time in a long time, Holmes was reminded of the pleasures of having a good woman at one's side. His wife Eileen had died of cancer nearly five years earlier and, ever since that personal tragedy, he had thrown himself into his work.

"What do you intend to say?" Bill asked.

Holmes nodded, the question causing him to focus his thoughts back on the conversation. "I believe we are experiencing the initial signs of serious global warming," he said. "That's why I've decided to revise my speech a bit. Considering what the Defenders of the Planet have done here in Arizona recently, I intend to add fuel to the fire, so to speak. You see, the more I think about it, the more sure I am about it. Jamie and I spent the afternoon at Matt Farr's office, the three of us analyzing the situation. He's got a computer workstation that processes information at ten billion instruction sets per second, and he's got a weather program that provides a nearly complete global picture. So, though we're not getting complete data input, we're sure that there's a high pressure system over the South Pole that's causing very high temperatures down there. I called New York to see if they could confirm this."

"Did they?"

"Maybe, but we're not sure. Our people at headquarters are convinced that the U.S. Weather Service is purposely reporting lower than actual air temperatures down in Antarctica. The numbers just don't jive with those they've heard about. It looks to me like your government is attempting a coverup. Also, NOAA has suddenly suspended their electronic *Climatological Data* bulletin for reasons unknown."

"What else have you discovered?" Bill asked.

"Well, we know that there are several things occurring which have never happened before. We're seeing some very odd weather systems all over the world."

"What kind of weather systems?" Maggie asked. "Forgive me," she added, "but I've got seven grandchildren, and I've been shopping and wrapping Christmas presents for the past few days. I haven't been following the weather reports."

"For instance, there are large unstable air masses in the equatorial regions and elsewhere," Holmes stated. "Yesterday, there was a huge tropical depression over Sri Lanka. The island got nearly thirty inches of rain in a two-hour period, with thunder and lightning."

"Oh, my," Maggie said. "That is a big storm, unusual for this time of the year."

"Right!" Holmes said. "The low pressure over Sri Lanka yesterday was measured at 945 millibars at sea level. There was a similar storm system out to sea east of Taiwan measured to be 940 millibars of pressure. Looking at the data, my conclusion is that the intertropical convergence zone has shifted north. It's where it should be in July or August."

"Is that significant?" Bill asked. His area of expertise was biology, not meteorology.

"Yes, dear," Maggie said. "It means that the water in the oceans has probably warmed up considerably."

"That's right, Maggie. Also," Holmes went on, "there was a similar system over North Africa two days ago."

"Indeed, Father," Jamie interjected, "don't forget that there was one over Yuma this past week. I know, because I was there. I'm not sure I've ever seen a rain like that! It was a ferocious thunderstorm."

"Yes, it was," Holmes agreed. "And there was a storm to the east of here just today. Now, other than these tropical depressions, there's a large typhoon near the Marianas Islands, with reported wind speeds of 240 miles an hour. We've never seen one this powerful. And there's a huge cyclone in the Indian Ocean, about to go ashore near southern Somalia. It, too, has high wind speeds, around 220 miles an hour. That is the fifth cyclone this year in the Indian Ocean. They started occurring in October, which is very early for the cyclone season. To me, it's one more indication that the water in the oceans has warmed up tremendously."

"I wonder what the spring and summer will be like here in the United States. What do you think, Jonathan?" Maggie asked.

"Most likely it will be quite abnormal," he stated. "If the temperature increase is relative, there will be one large storm after another. Your American hurricane season might be the worst in history. You could see monster hurricanes capable of enormous damage."

"That's quite a dire prediction," Bill Roosevelt said, his expression full of concern.

"That's not the end of it," Holmes went on. "I think there will be unusual tornadoes and abnormal wind conditions popping up all across the continent."

"That doesn't sound good," Bill stated.

"No, it doesn't, but Antarctica is what I'm most concerned about. As I was saying, our headquarters suspects there has been unusually warm weather down there. I was told that several key satellites are no longer accessible. And all radio contact with Antarctica has been inexplicably cut off. We haven't been able to get a decent temperature reading at the South Pole for about three weeks. But the last verifiable air temperature SOW was able to get was forty-eight degrees on November fifth."

"Forty-eight?" Maggie asked incredulously.

"Yes. Remarkable, isn't it?"

"What does that mean?" Bill Roosevelt asked.

"Well, the air temperature all around the world has increased tremendously since November. We know this is a worldwide phenomenon, so I'd say that it's been going up in Antarctica as well. By now, it's most likely in the mid-seventies, all things being relative."

"Jonathan!" Maggie exclaimed. "Do you realize what you're saying?"

"Yes," he said plaintively. "If that is the case, then the ice cap in Antarctica is melting."

There was a dramatic pause in their conversation. They all knew what a melting South Pole portended.

"This really is an incredible situation," Maggie said.

"Is there any way you can confirm that?" Bill asked.

"Unfortunately, no," Jonathan replied. "But, believe me, we're trying desperately to understand the situation down there. It's such a remote place and access is highly controlled by the various governments. SOW was sharing data from the Instituto Antarctico Argentino at their Jubany Base. But that contact is suddenly gone. Rumor has it that the Argentinian Army suddenly took over the base, though we haven't confirmed it."

"So Antarctica may be melting, but the world doesn't know it," Bill said. "This is all news to me."

"I only learned of the I.A.A. situation today. Linda Tanaka, our director of operations, told me. Matt Farr brought the Antarctic situation to my attention with his supercomputer. I've been traveling so much lately, I've been out of touch with this whole developing situation." He paused to take a sip of coffee, his face deep in reflection. "So today I've been calling around, trying to put the pieces together. I called some friends of mine in Australia. It's been very hot there. Sydney hit one hundred and twenty-two degrees today, but even worse, they told me that in the interior deserts of Australia the high was one hundred and forty-five."

"One hundred forty-five!" Maggie exclaimed.

"Yes, a new world record. It was Christmas Day there today, you know," Holmes stated softly.

"This is incredible! No wonder you want to sound the alarm!"

"Tonight, he's going to tell the world," Jamie said proudly. "We won't let them hide the truth any longer."

"Excellent," Bill said. "The truth will get out, because the press will be present. I have a contact at the *Arizona Daily Times,* a reporter named Mike Allen, and he promised to come tonight."

Maggie looked at her watch. "Speaking of which," she said, "we'd better be going, or we'll never get to Tempe on time."

"You're right, dear," Bill said, also looking at his watch. "I'll get the check and we'll be off," and he waved toward their waiter.

At precisely eight that evening, Jonathan Holmes began his speech at Gammage Hall on the campus of Arizona State University. Bill Roosevelt had been right. In spite of it being Christmas Eve, the hall was filled, mostly with students from ASU concerned about the weather and wanting some answers. Holmes intended to give them an earful.

He was not introduced by anyone. At the appropriate time, he simply walked out onto the stage and stepped up to the lectern, notes in hand. As he walked out into the audience's view, the applause was thundering. To environmentalists everywhere, Holmes was a legend who had devoted his entire life to fighting the greedy interests bent on destroying the planet. For many years, he had been part of the ongoing debate about ecology versus business, especially big business. Now, because of the incident at the Navajo Generating Station, the fight over the environment had taken on a new meaning in the Phoenix area.

"As you have all been aware," he told the audience, "the world is in the grip of a giant heat wave. Today, the high in the country was reported by the U.S. Weather Service to be Death Valley, where they said it was eighty-nine degrees. The organization I work for, Save Our World, has a remote weather station set up near Yuma, Arizona. Today, in Yuma it reached eighty-eight degrees. Here in Phoenix it was eighty-seven degrees. Eighty-seven degrees on Christmas Eve! Even for Arizona, these temperatures are totally abnormal. The thing that concerns me is that this is happening all around the world." Holmes paused for dramatic effect. "The truth is, my friends, I believe that global warming has begun in earnest."

At this, there was an outburst from the audience, so loud that Holmes had to stop speaking. He waited until he knew he could be heard again.

"Let me tell you what I believe. Yes, I know that today's temperatures are cooler than they have been in the past few days, but this was to be expected. At this time of the year, the Northern Hemisphere is receiving the least amount of sunlight. As you know, the Northern Hemisphere had its winter solstice just the other day. It is only natural that we start seeing lower temperatures, even during this ongoing heat wave. After all, even with the beginning of global warming, everything is relative.

"Still, today's temperatures in the U.S. and in Europe and Russia are high above normal for this time of the year. Meanwhile, in the Southern Hemisphere, it is the beginning of summer. They've just had their summer solstice, that day of the year down under when the sun's rays strike the Tropic of Capricorn at a perfect ninety degree angle, giving the maximum amount of sunlight.

"I might remind you that this invisible line we call the Tropic of Capricorn runs right through my native country of Australia. I have many friends down under, and today, which is Christmas Day there, it was reported to me that the interior deserts of Australia reached a high temperature of one hundred forty-five degrees Fahrenheit. Ladies and gentlemen, this is a new world record for our planet!"

Again, there was an outburst from the audience, and Holmes had to wait for a moment. It was apparent from their reaction that the people in the audience did not doubt at all what he had just told them. He stood there calmly, taking time to refer to his notes, which were copious.

"I have been told that temperatures around the equator are hotter than ever before in history, around one hundred twenty-five with attendant high humidity. Can you imagine those conditions?

"I have spent this past week working on a SOW project here in Arizona. Tomorrow, I am leaving for Ecuador to continue our project. In Ecuador, I will experience myself just what those temperatures at the equator are really like. From Ecuador, we head for Brazil and then to Argentina, where we hope to complete our work. Argentina is where SOW will install its final remote weather station. Then our organization will have two hundred such stations in place at key locations all around the globe. We started this project six years ago. Our goal was to do an independent, long-term study about what is really happening to the earth's climate. The data from all these weather stations is fed into a supercomputer at our New York offices. We were attempting to determine if the world's climate was changing due to global warming. We expected the study to take twenty or thirty years.

"I now fear that we may be too late."

Holmes' voice boomed deeply over the public address system, and for just a moment he paused and looked out at all those concerned faces. "We may very well be witnessing the beginning of the destruction of all life on this planet as we know it." He paused again, his expression becoming very solemn.

"And what can we do about it at this late date? Can we continue to listen to the leaders of our planet and do nothing? Should we obey politicians who have been in bed with the oil companies for their entire careers? Can we just let the oil companies continue to run everything the way they have for over eighty years? Can we stand by and watch as the earth is slowly destroyed?

"I fear the worst is upon us, and I don't know quite what to tell you. But, based on what I've already seen and know about, I think we're witnessing a runaway greenhouse effect. And that doesn't bode well for any of us.

"Let me tell you what the definition of a runaway greenhouse effect is." For the next twenty minutes, he explained in precise detail the phenomenon of the greenhouse effect on the earth. During that time, Holmes showed slides to help illustrate the principles involved. Although Holmes didn't know it, his presentation was remarkably similar to the one made by Captain Rob Jones at the Pentagon, yet without the sensitive satellite information.

"The earth is more delicate than any of us have imagined," he said. "Our planet is dependent upon many factors for its survival, many of them beyond human control. However, the one thing we can control is the amount of pollutants we spew into the atmosphere. And, of course, we haven't done a good job at preventing this pollution. Every day that goes by, another few million tons of waste gas are pumped into the atmosphere. Each day, more carbon dioxide is added to the atmosphere. It's been going on like this for nearly a century."

The lights came back on, and Holmes stood facing his audience. "I ask again," he said. "What can we do about it?" The silence in the auditorium was overwhelming. What *could* they do about it?

Suddenly Holmes said, "Perhaps, in the face of a world-wide catastrophe, blowing up power lines is not such a bad idea after all, especially from utilities that continue to burn fossil fuels." Some in the large room began to cheer and applaud. Holmes waited until it grew quiet again. "If we don't stop burning fossil fuels, the heat will only get worse, so perhaps blowing up a few oil refineries might also be in order." The applause became louder.

"You see," Holmes explained, "inaction at this time is a sin. To do nothing is morally corrupt. If we go along with the status quo, we are turning our backs on our planet, and we are ignoring a very desperate situation.

"Under normal circumstances, I could never endorse the actions of the Defenders of the Planet. But I must tell you that these are extraordinary times, and I believe they require extraordinary action. I praise the Defenders for their courage. At least they're doing something. We have to stop emitting carbon dioxide into the atmosphere. And we must stop immediately! We can no longer wait for tomorrow. Tomorrow is here. Even if all nations stop emitting all their waste gases today, right this minute, it may still be too late.

"All good people everywhere must find the courage to do what is right. If we don't, we are doomed. Sadly enough, I don't think enough people will try. I am very much afraid for the future of this planet." And with that, Holmes walked off the stage.

That night, news of his speech was broadcast all over the world.

The next morning, he and Jamie were getting ready to board a plane at Skyharbor Airport in Phoenix. Matt was there to see them off, and they were saying goodbyes in the terminal when six men in suits suddenly approached them.

"Dr. Jonathan Holmes?" one of the men asked.

"Yes?" Holmes said with a puzzled expression.

The man immediately produced his identification. "FBI," he said harshly. "I'm Special Agent Kessler. You're under arrest, Dr. Holmes. All of you are under arrest." The agents moved forward and began placing handcuffs on them.

"What?" Holmes asked incredulously. He knew he had broken no law. Who do they think they are? he wondered.

"This is ridiculous!" Jamie said, struggling with the agent who had grabbed her arms, trying to pin them behind her back. Somehow she broke free and punched him squarely in the nose.

The punch knocked him backwards and blood began to flow from his nostrils. Another agent forced her to the floor on her stomach, twisting her arms behind her back.

"Let me go!" she screamed. "Why are you doing this?"

Matthew, two agents on either arm, started to move to help her. As he struggled, a third agent stepped up and punched him with a vicious blow to the stomach, causing him to double up in pain. He sagged forward, his face contorted in agony.

"Don't resist!" Holmes shouted. He turned to Kessler. "There must be some mistake. Why are we being arrested?"

"Domestic terrorism. Conspiracy. Transport of explosives. Destruction of public property. We have reason to believe you were involved in blowing up those utility transmission lines!"

"You must be joking," Holmes said. "We were nowhere near that part of Arizona."

"You were out in the desert when it happened," Kessler said.

"We were near Yuma, not Winslow," Holmes said.

Kessler responded by handcuffing him and telling them their rights, that they had the right to remain silent and that they could have an attorney present during questioning.

"Where are you taking us?" Holmes demanded to know.

"Downtown, to the Metropolitan Correctional Center."

"This is insane!" Holmes said. "We had nothing to do with that incident. I have work to do which I must finish."

"After that little speech of yours last night, it's obvious that you support the environmental terrorists, Dr. Holmes. This nonsense has got to stop. We can't have foreigners like you running around inciting people to destroy our institutions."

The men holding Jamie down hauled her up to her feet. The FBI agents began to hustle the stunned trio out of the airport as dozens of people gathered to watch.

"You can't do this," Holmes protested. "We must get to Ecuador. I have a project to complete."

"Too bad," Kessler said. "You're going to be spending Christmas in jail."

The agents took them outside to a waiting van, putting them inside through a rear door. Once they were locked in, the van sped away toward downtown Phoenix. They sat there helplessly. The back of the van had no windows and they were totally separated from the driver.

"This is humiliating," Jamie said angrily. "We haven't done anything."

"Don't worry," Holmes said. "Everything will be all right. I'll call Martin immediately."

"Damn!" Matt Farr said. "I can't believe I've been arrested by the FBI. This is really crazy."

"I'm sure we can get this cleared up," Holmes said. "It's just a minor setback, Matt. I'll take care of this."

Once they arrived at the M.C.C., they were booked, their photographs taken, and they were led to separate holding cells.

Several hours later, Jonathan Holmes was allowed to make a phone call to his friend and fellow environmentalist, attorney Martin Sherman, who was spending Christmas on his ranch in Montana. Holmes listened as Sherman's wife Angie answered.

"Hello," she said in a warm and friendly voice.

"Angie, it's Jonathan..."

"Jonathan! Merry Christmas," she said cheerfully.

"Merry Christmas, Angie. But I'm afraid I've got bad news. Is Martin there?"

"Yes, I'll get him..." A moment later, he heard Sherman answer. "Hello, Jonathan, what is it?"

"Martin," he quickly said. "I'm only going to have a few minutes. This is urgent!"

Sherman heard the desperation in Holmes' voice. "What's the matter, Jonathan?" he asked.

"I'm in Phoenix. I've been arrested!"

"On what charge?" Sherman asked.

"The charges are numerous. The U.S. Government thinks I had something to do with that big Arizona power plant being shut down. The FBI arrested me this morning. They also arrested my daughter Jamie and a local scientist, Matthew Farr. Something about conspiracy."

"I heard about your speech last night. I think I see what's going on. Okay," Sherman advised him. "Stay calm. I'll fly down to Phoenix first thing tomorrow morning. This may be more serious than you might imagine."

"I know you can help," Holmes told his old friend.

"You're damn right!" Sherman responded. "There's no way I'm going to let them get away with this. Don't talk to them and don't answer any of their questions. I'll see you tomorrow. Goodbye, Jonathan."

"Goodbye, and thanks," Holmes said, hanging up the phone. He looked up to see agent Kessler staring at him.

"What did he say?" Kessler asked.

"He said not to answer any of your questions," Holmes responded. "I think that's good advice."

"Martin Sherman, huh?" Kessler asked.

"You've heard of him?" Holmes asked the agent.

"Who hasn't?" Kessler responded. "He's one of the most famous trial lawyers in the country. How do you happen to know him?"

"I'd rather not say," Holmes stated, looking at Kessler with suspicion.

"I see," Kessler said, a slight frown on his face. "Okay, Dr. Holmes, you've had your phone call. You'll be taken back to your cell now," he said. Kessler nodded toward two of his fellow agents, who stepped forward and led him from the room. When they were gone, Kessler picked up his phone, dialing the FBI Director's home number in Washington.

EIGHT

That night, in Los Angeles, Tom Ramsey received a call from Washington, D.C. and was told that Jonathan Holmes had been arrested. He was also told the specifics of the arrest, and that the press thus far had not been informed.

"We're going to move up our plans," a female voice said. "For Red Sky."

"Operation Red Sky?" Ramsey asked.

"Yes, so check the board right away," and then the voice had hung up. Ramsey put down his phone and went to his computer. When he accessed the New York electronic bulletin board and deciphered the encrypted message that was waiting for him, he called his four top officers. They met an hour later at a Westside coffeehouse, taking a corner booth. A waitress came by, and they all ordered espresso.

Along with Ramsey was Sharon Holt, Kathy Kirchener, Mike Tolliver, and Jake Jurado. In their public lives, all five were respected professionals. In their private lives, they were the Southern California leaders of the Defenders of the Planet. Ramsey was in charge of the entire Southern California operation.

In California, the Defenders were divided into distinct units of fifteen people each. Each unit was further divided into five three-person teams. The units were always kept segregated so that if anyone were captured, they couldn't identify the other units' members. The number of units operating in any given area depended on the size and population of the region. In Los Angeles, the Defenders had five units operating.

Units never worked with other units, and therefore had no knowledge of the personnel in the other local units. For instance, a person in Sharon Holt's unit did know anyone in Mike

Tolliver's unit, and they did not know who Mike Tolliver, the unit leader, was. Even Holt did not know anyone in Tolliver's unit, other than Tolliver himself. Only Ramsey knew every unit member's name, all seventy-five of them.

As the leaders, Ramsey, Holt, Kirchener, Tolliver and Jurado were the key to the entire Los Angeles operation. If any one of them decided to turn on the others, they could completely wreck the operation. But, they had been carefully recruited and, after working together for several years, they all knew they could trust one another.

The Defenders of the Planet had been formed in the United States in the year 2000, the beginning of the new millennium. Their stated goal was to rectify the wrongs of the past, to do whatever was necessary to preserve the planet and all its inhabitants. "Whatever necessary" included use of violent methods. To most Americans, the organization appeared to be a secretive group of radicals who went around the country blowing things up or burning buildings and industrial installations, occasionally killing people who got in their way. In the past seven years, six men had died, all security guards who had confronted unit members during night operations.

The Defenders never bombed office buildings and they never sent letter bombs to individuals. Assassinations of selected individuals were against their stated policies. The Defenders of the Planet wanted to engender public support. If they employed assassination and murder as part of their method of operation, they knew they would never receive that support.

Officially, the Defenders of the Planet created more cause for concern than any American radical group since the famous Weathermen of the 1960s, mainly because they could not be penetrated by the FBI or any other law enforcement agency. Nobody knew what they were going to do next.

To date, the Defenders of the Planet had been extremely successful in their operations. Their favorite tactic was to destroy or cripple installations that burned fossil fuels. Their next favorite tactic was to attack chemical companies that sold ozone-depleting chemicals. In seven years of operations, only four of their members had been captured, and none of them had talked or given away their team members. Three had received lengthy prison sentences. One was sentenced to death and executed, convicted of participating in the killing of a security guard who had been protecting a plant owned by a major chemical company. The Defender, Timothy Holden, died with sealed lips, without identifying any of his fellow members, despite repeated interrogations by FBI agents.

During Holden's trial, it was learned that the chemical company was still producing and selling ozone-depleting chemicals. The trial took place in 2002 and it had created a national stir, the media furiously debating the methods of the Defenders. The whole affair created an intense interest in the group. Because of the publicity, the government wanted a speedy trial and even swifter punishment. Holden was executed only twenty-seven months after his conviction, though he went to his death satisfied that he had done something significant for the planet.

In spite of the publicity, little was really known about the organization calling itself the Defenders of the Planet. The national leader of the Defenders was unknown to anyone save a few select members. It was rumored that he was a computer wizard, a former member of the National Security Agency, or the CIA, or possibly a former member of Congress with a military background, though no one knew for certain. It was also rumored that the leader was really a woman. Whoever he or she was, the person was obviously a fervent environmentalist who believed in violence to achieve his or her goals.

Operation Red Sky was to be their most ambitious planned operation to date. It called for the simultaneous destruction of sixteen oil refineries all around the country. To achieve this objective, the Defenders had smuggled over a thousand pounds of plastic explosive into the country. It had been planned for February fifteenth, right in the dead of winter, but with events moving rapidly, the date had been moved up.

"It looks like everything is happening at once," Ramsey told the others. "And it doesn't look good. Jonathan Holmes getting arrested by the FBI. The U.S. Navy calling up all its reserves." He turned to Sharon, whom he knew had a brother who was a reserve officer in the Navy. "Have you confirmed that the Navy is calling up their reserves?" he asked.

"Yes," she stated. "My brother got a telegram yesterday. He's supposed to report at 0600 hours tomorrow morning. It's top secret and he's not supposed to tell anybody though, of course, he told me and the rest of the family. He said everybody was called in to take an oath of secrecy and no one knows what to make of it. He felt guilty about telling us."

"That's not all," Jake Jurado said. "A friend of mine who's in Greenpeace said one of their ships radioed in from Antarctica. They said the place is hotter than hell and everything is melting. It's only a matter of time before the ocean level starts to rise. We may have a worldwide cataclysm on our hands. That's why the Navy is being called into action."

"Jesus!" Kathy exclaimed. "That means global warming has happened, but they don't want to admit it."

"Yeah," Ramsey agreed. "Why else would the Navy start calling up their reserves? There's no war going on anywhere. Not even a threat of war."

Their waitress came back with five cups of espresso, setting them on the table along with fresh cream and sugar, and their conversation ceased until after she had left.

"So why did you call this meeting?" Jake Jurado asked, sensing the need for action.

Ramsey frowned thoughtfully, and took a sip of espresso. "I've been ordered to move up our plans. Operation Red Sky will take place on January the first. We're going to hit the refineries on New Year's Eve."

"But, we're not ready," said Mike Tolliver. "I don't have all my people trained to use the plastic explosives yet."

"Do it quickly," Ramsey said. "We're going to have to move fast, because I think the government is going to try to keep this whole thing under wraps. Although I can't be sure, I think our national leadership wants to expose them. We can't let them hide this from the American people."

"You're right," Jake Jurado said. "Listen to this: my friend also said that after their transmission about all the ice melting, the Greenpeace ship had radio trouble. Their frequency became full of static, as if their radio transmissions were being jammed. No one has heard a report from them since."

Ramsey said, "You see what's happening? They're going to try to cover everything up. It's all beginning to make sense. Why would they arrest Jonathan Holmes? They know he's not part of us. He's a powerful voice who's not afraid to speak out. I think they want to keep him on ice and keep him quiet. Especially after that speech he gave in Phoenix." Ramsey grimly smiled, knowing that Holmes did not realize just how prophetic his statement about blowing up oil refineries would be.

"It must be true about Antarctica," Sharon Holt said. "Just consider how long this heat wave has been going on. I think Ramsey's right. We've got to expose the government. We've got to take strong action. Besides, if the icecaps start to melt, in a few months it won't make any difference. Wilmington and San Pedro will all be underwater."

"Maybe it's too late, then," Mike stated, still worried about not being ready to take part in Red Sky.

"It's never too late," Sharon said firmly.

"Why New Year's Eve?" Jake asked.

"It will provide a diversion. It's a perfect night," Ramsey said. "We will still have enough time to get our people ready. Most of the planning has already been done. We're just going to have to skip a few steps. Anyway, that's why I called this meeting. We're going to attack the L.A. oil refineries one week from tonight." Ramsey looked around, gauging their reactions. They seemed positive. "Are we agreed on this?" he asked.

They all nodded, then one by one they raised their right thumb up. The decision to go along was unanimous. Everything they did was voluntary. None of them had to go through with Operation Red Sky if they didn't want to.

"Okay, then," Ramsey said. "Let's get moving and prepare our people for New Year's Eve. Mike, you'll just have to get your unit trained. We still want to stick to our original goal, to shut down Los Angeles. So we have to get the major refineries, and I mean all of them.

"Sharon, go ahead and put the message up on our local bulletin board, but I'd like you to constantly monitor it to see if the FBI or CIA or anybody else attempts to break in."

"And if they do?" she asked.

"Then we'll know that we've been penetrated," Ramsey responded. "And we'll have to act accordingly. The operation will go forward and there will probably be a huge firefight, because they will be waiting for us."

"No, they won't," Kathy Kirchener said firmly. "More likely, they'll start making arrests well in advance of New Year's Eve. They won't want bullets flying around all that gasoline."

"Yeah, you're right," Ramsey agreed. Kathy should know, he thought. She was a detective in the Los Angeles police department, and their only contact with law enforcement in all of Southern California. Recruiting her had been a real coup.

"If they penetrate us, they probably won't get all of us," Kathy continued, "But if we've been uncovered, they'll have enough information to screw up the operation. I'll do some special work this week and try to find out if the local FBI is doing anything out of the ordinary. It might be a clue."

Ramsey nodded. "Okay," he said. "But let's not worry too much about it. They haven't penetrated us yet, so they probably won't this next week."

"It's good to be vigilant, though," Sharon said. "After the Arizona thing, I'm sure they're trying their damnedest!"

"They won't take me alive," Jake stated. "I think the FBI and CIA are nothing but storm troopers for the oil and chemical companies. They don't care that they're raping the earth!"

"Be real, Jake," Sharon said. "We just want to make waves, not kill people."

"They'll kill us if they get the chance," Jake retorted.

"That's true," Ramsey said. "Don't worry, Jake. We'll go in fully armed. But we fire back only in self-defense. The most important thing is to carry out our mission.

"What's at stake here is the planet itself, our future and the future of all life on Earth. Remember, we are the Defenders of the Planet. If we don't take action to protect the earth, no one will." Ramsey then put his right hand out in the middle of the table, and immediately the other four placed their right hands firmly on top of his. With eyes flashing and jaws set firmly, for a brief moment in time, they were one.

NINE

The day after Christmas, Martin Sherman arrived in Phoenix on an early morning flight out of Boise, Idaho, anxious to see his old friend. The taxi ride from the airport took over twenty minutes, but once he got downtown, Sherman was immediately led to a conference cell within the Metropolitan Correctional Center, and Jonathan Holmes was there waiting for him. They did not shake hands, instead giving one another a bear hug.

"I've got to tell you," Sherman said. "That speech of yours was something. It was carried on just about every newscast in the country. You've really upset the establishment. Jonathan, I think the government is out to nail you to the wall."

"Yes," Holmes laughed. "It must have been my speech. But, it's no surprise. I knew years ago that the FBI had an extensive file on me."

"You and every other environmentalist who might be connected to the Defenders of the Planet," Sherman said. "You could have picked a better time to come to Arizona."

"I didn't know the power lines were going to be damaged. My work brought me here, and we scheduled the speech around my project. I defend the planet, too, except I do it in my own way."

Sherman nodded grimly, and then they sat at a small desk. Sherman looked carefully at Holmes. "Before we get started, I have to know one thing. Were you involved in blowing up that transmission line and the coal train?"

"Of course, not!" Holmes responded. "I'm a scientist, I'm not a..."

"A terrorist?" Sherman asked.

"I hesitate to use that word," Holmes said. "As of today, I have to ask myself who the real terrorists are."

"Yes," Sherman agreed, "but right now, we don't have time for philosophy. In a few hours you'll be standing before a judge while they read all the charges. I want you to plead not guilty. Don't say anything else. Okay?"

"I understand," Holmes said.

"I don't know what kind of a case the government is building against you. But, no matter what, I'll get you out of this."

"I must be set free," Holmes said. "I have to get to Ecuador to work on my project. SOW is counting on me."

"That's out of the question, Jonathan. Even if we get you out on bail, once you're released from here they won't let you leave the county, let alone the country. You'll be under the jurisdiction of the court."

"Martin, you must get me released. Permanently!"

Sherman nodded. "I will, Jonathan. But this could take weeks, if not months."

Hearing this, Holmes grimaced, his shoulders sagging. He leaned forward, putting his face in his hands. "Martin, I must be free to complete my work. The world needs me. The situation demands it. You may not realize just how serious this is. I think this unusual weather is due to a runaway greenhouse effect. We may be witnessing the beginning of severe global warming."

"I know," Sherman said. "I've been following this like everyone else. I couldn't agree with you more. But, what can one man do? I think it might be too late for all of us."

"It's never too late, Martin. If we can just convince everyone to stop emitting gases from fossil fuels, we might be able to turn this whole thing around. Maybe not quickly, but eventually. There will be flooding and millions will probably die. But we might be able to save the planet."

"And if we don't convince them?"

"Earth is in great jeopardy. Once the average global temperature reaches one hundred and thirty degrees, just about everything will die. It will be slow and miserable. People won't be able to go outside. All plant life will die. Society will grind to a halt as people fight over what little food will be left. Systems will break down. I imagine it will get very chaotic."

"Would the climate ever go back to normal?" Sherman asked.

"I'm not sure," Holmes said. "But that's beyond our lifetime, Martin. It's the near future I'm most worried about. People may not be able to accept this."

"In other words, we don't have a chance?"

"It's very difficult to predict, Martin. I've been studying this for over forty years and I still don't know. We're dealing with a very complicated set of factors. One thing I'm sure about. The greenhouse effect will keep building upon itself. The weather we're witnessing around us is too abnormal."

"I know what you mean," Sherman said. "We've had summer-like rains around Boise for the past week. Thunder and lightning. I mean, it's really out of the ordinary. And the heat! Whew! It's really been hot. And it's wintertime!"

"I know," Holmes said. "Martin, for the first time since I was a child, I've felt afraid. Not just for me, but afraid for everybody. This heat will stop only if mankind takes immediate positive action. I'm convinced of that." Holmes looked straight at Sherman, his eyes pleading. "Now you understand. I must be free to continue my work. I have to convince people how serious this problem really is. I cannot be kept here, isolated from the world."

"Maybe, as this becomes worse, the U.S. government will do something," Sherman suggested. "Perhaps the United Nations will take action."

Holmes shook his head. "I hope so, but your government, all governments, are run by proud, arrogant men. I don't think they want to admit how powerless they really are. As for the United Nations, they've been impotent up to now, and I don't think that will change. After all, the U.N. is just a collective of governments. No, it's really up to the people of the world. What we need is some kind of concerted action. People have to rise up everywhere and just turn everything off. At least for awhile."

"Yes," Sherman agreed. "But that is a slim possibility."

"What is the outside temperature in Phoenix?" Holmes asked.

"It's going to be in the low eighties today," Sherman responded. "They say it's starting to cool down a bit. A cooling trend."

"A cooling trend," Holmes repeated, and chuckled. "That is preposterous."

"What do you mean?"

"It's the lag effect, that's all," Holmes said. "In fact, I even mentioned it in my speech. The Northern Hemisphere hasn't had direct full sunlight for over a month. The winter solstice was a week ago, and from here on we'll be gaining sunlight. From early November through the end of January, the northern half of earth receives less energy from the sun. Right now, the North Pole is dark all day long. So the lag effect is starting to take hold." Holmes looked carefully at his friend, and he noticed a blank look on Martin's face.

"Let me explain more precisely," he said. "The shortest day of the year in the Northern Hemisphere is December twenty-first or December twenty-second, depending. But, you don't see the coldest temperatures until January or February. The planet continues to cool down well into February. We're seeing that cooling trend now.

"You see, the earth retains some of the sun's energy. As this part of the world receives less sunlight and fewer infrared rays, the earth starts to give up much of that retained heat. It's been doing that since early November. It's only natural that the Northern Hemisphere would start to cool down a bit. However, I can assure you, it's quite temporary. This spring and summer will be much hotter than normal.

"The lag effect also works in the summer. Even though the longest day of the year is June twenty-first or June twenty-second, you don't see the hottest temperatures until July or August. Air temperatures are not simply a function of daily hours of sunlight. And water temperatures also hold to the lag effect. That's why you don't see hurricanes on your east coast and the Gulf states until August or September."

"I see," Sherman said. "And what about the rest of the planet?"

"This heat buildup is a worldwide phenomenon. That's why I must get to the equator. I've got to see for myself what is happening there. That's why my work is so important. SOW has been setting up remote monitoring stations in key positions all around the world. We'll be able to get instant readings on worldwide temperatures from two hundred key locations. We can then enter them into our computer model. We can tell the world just how bad it is, without worrying about government interference. We might even be able to make weather predictions."

"What good will that do?" Sherman asked.

Holmes shook his head. "It won't matter that much as far as the physics is concerned. We can only report what is happening and what will happen. Our goal is to convince people to take action. At this point, it appears the U.S. government is not willing to do that. The future looks too bleak, and they won't admit it. Even in the face of disaster, they're not willing to shut whole industries down and put people out of work. They are willing to destroy the planet in order to save peoples' jobs. It's insane!"

Sherman nodded in understanding. "Maybe that's why they want to keep you locked away, Jonathan. You're a pain in the ass. You're upsetting their game plan."

"They don't have a game plan, Martin, other than to retain the status quo."

"I admit, it doesn't look good. Not if this theory of yours about the lag effect is true."

"It's not a theory, old friend. It's a well-known phenomenon that we can actually measure. The scary part is what might be happening in the Southern Hemisphere right now. As we speak, the sun down under is at its zenith. If Antarctica is melting, we're going to have serious trouble, and very quickly. Almost every major city in the world is a port city. My hometown of Sydney will be one of the first affected."

"I'm sorry," Sherman consoled.

"Yes, so am I," Holmes said. "This is a ludicrous situation. It should never have been allowed to happen. There are so many things we could have done. If only we had switched to alternate fuels for our cars back in the 1970s. We might have prevented all this."

"I always knew we should be burning methanol or ethanol."

"No," Holmes said. He smiled, knowing that Sherman was not a scientist. "Those fuels would not have done us much good."

"Oh," Sherman said, rather meekly.

"Methanol comes from coal or oil feedstocks," Holmes explained. "It wouldn't have helped in alleviating carbon dioxide buildup. Besides, it is a toxic substance. One ounce of methanol will make you blind. Two ounces will kill you!

"Ethanol, on the other hand, is pure grain alcohol. You can drink ethanol and it won't hurt you. If it burns clean, it doesn't give off toxic gases, but it's nearly as bad as methanol in terms of greenhouse gases. You see, once either methanol or ethanol has been burned, they give off carbon dioxide and water vapor. And if they haven't burned perfectly clean, they'll also give off carbon monoxide and other toxic gases."

"So alcohol-based fuels weren't the way to go?"

"Not really," Holmes shrugged. "Although they would have helped stop that brownish haze around cities, and that would have been helpful in terms of having clean air to breathe. But the oil companies would never have allowed that to happen. They knew they couldn't control the market and they didn't need the competition. With ethanol, the supply would have come from millions of farmers all around the world. Here in your own country, it would have been the best thing that could have happened to your farmers. But, the oil companies' profits would have suffered. Greedy bastards."

"I know," Sherman agreed. He looked questioningly at Holmes. "So what should we have been using in our cars and trucks?" he asked.

"Liquid hydrogen," Holmes answered. "The only byproduct would have been pure water vapor. In the long run, it would have been a very cheap fuel. Unfortunately, no one went to the effort and expense of developing the technology.

"Burning liquid hydrogen is just one example. I can cite dozens of things we should have been doing. For instance, every major city in the world should have had a rapid transit system working, all powered by electricity. And we should have created fusion energy, but no one wanted to spend the money necessary." Holmes shook his head. "We had our chance and we failed," he said. "Now, look what's happened!" A look of despair came over his face.

"You don't have to worry. I'll do everything I can to get you out of here."

"I know you will," Holmes said.

"Just remember," Martin said. "When we go before the judge, you will stand up and say you're not guilty."

"Of course, I'm not guilty!" Holmes said. "It's so ludicrous, I just can't believe this is being allowed to happen. I always thought I'd be safe here in the United States. Whatever happened to freedom of speech?"

"These appear to be desperate times," Martin said. "And desperate men in positions of power, our so-called leaders in government, can simply rewrite the rules."

"I must get out of here. I've got work to do."

"Look, Jonathan," Sherman said. "Don't worry. I don't care what the government's up to. I'll get you out on bail. I can assure you, it's only a formality." He suddenly stood up. "Now, I've got to meet with Jamie and Matt, and then process some paperwork. I'll see you in court later, okay?"

Holmes nodded and stood up. The two men shook hands and then two deputies came in to take Holmes back to his cell. As they walked along the corridor, one of them turned to him and said, "We're rooting for you, Dr. Holmes."

The statement caught him by surprise. "What do you mean?" he asked, eyeing the man carefully.

"The Feds have a weak case, and everyone knows it. You'll be out before lunchtime. That's the word around here."

"Really?" Holmes said, suddenly smiling. His expression brightened noticeably.

"That's right," the other deputy said. "This is a Federal operation. Just so you know, Dr. Holmes, we locals had nothing to do with your arrest. We all know there's something funny going on. Funnier than the weather. Once you're out of here, give them hell."

Hearing this, Holmes laughed. "Why are you on my side?" he asked.

"Because everyone knows you're telling the truth. The Feds just want to cover this whole thing up. They must think people are really stupid. At least you're standing up and speaking out. I've got to admit, you've got balls."

"Well, thank you," Holmes said sincerely. "Thank you very much."

Two hours later, Holmes was taken to the federal court building. As he walked into the courtroom, he saw that Martin, Matt, and Jamie were already there. Much to his surprise, Chris and Gail were also there. Holmes shook his head, realizing they must have been arrested, too. Holmes looked around and saw that the entire courtroom was packed, filled with reporters. He also saw that FBI Agent Kessler and several of his men were sitting directly behind the Assistant U.S. Attorneys. He ignored them and came forward to hug his daughter.

"Good to see you, Jamie," he said. "Did they treat you properly?"

She nodded. "It hasn't been too bad," she said. "Mr. Sherman says we're going to be released. Is it true?"

"Yes," Holmes said. "I believe we will be. So don't worry." He let go of her and shook hands with Matt. "How are you, Matt?"

"I'm fine, Dr. Holmes. Are you okay?"

"Yes, I'm okay. But I look forward to getting out of jail."

"Me, too," Matt smiled.

Holmes also shook hands with Chris and Gail. "I'm sorry about all this," he said.

"Don't be sorry, Dr. Holmes," Chris said. "It's not your fault."

"Mr. Sherman has agreed to represent all of us," Gail said. "And for free. Isn't that great news?"

"Martin is a good man. I'm sure he'll do his best."

Just then, the judge hearing the case walked into the courtroom and the bailiff cried out, "All rise! The honorable James Huston presiding."

Judge Huston was an elderly man, mostly bald and wearing gold-rimmed glasses, yet he carried himself with dignity. Once he seated himself, everyone else sat down and there was a brief hush over the courtroom. Then Judge Huston looked down from his bench at the man sitting below and to his right. "The clerk will read the charges," Huston ordered.

For nearly five minutes the clerk read the official charges, repeating them for each of the five named in the federal indictment. After they were read, Judge Huston looked at Martin Sherman. "Mr. Sherman, it's obvious your clients have selected competent counsel. Are you representing all of the five so named in the indictment?"

Sherman stood up to address the court. "Yes, Your Honor. I am."

"Do your clients understand the charges against them and are they aware of their rights?" Huston fired the questions rapidly, as if this were a mere formality.

"Yes, sir, they understand everything."

"How do your clients plead?" Huston asked.

Sherman signaled for Holmes and the others to stand. "Your honor, my clients would like to individually respond."

Holmes spoke first. "Not guilty," he said emphatically.

Jamie, Matt, Chris, and Gail also said "Not guilty."

"The court so notes," Huston said, and he immediately began reading from a group of documents before him. Again, a quiet settled over the courtroom.

Sherman nodded at the five defendants and they all sat down. Holmes leaned over and whispered a question in Sherman's ear. "What next?"

"Bail determination," Martin responded.

After nearly two minutes of silence, Judge Huston looked up from his paperwork and spoke to the United States Attorneys. "The government is asking the court that no bail be set and that the defendants be kept incarcerated. Please state your case."

Immediately, one of the government attorneys rose. He was a tall man in his early forties, well-built and exceptionally handsome. The man could have been a movie star. His voice matched his looks in quality. "Your honor," he began in a solemn tone, "the government feels that Jonathan Holmes and Jamie Holmes are flight risks since they are both Australian citizens. It would be very easy for either of them to board a jet and fly directly to Australia. We'd have to extradite them, if the Australian authorities could find them, and the possibility of justice for these crimes would become very remote.

"Further, as far as all five defendants are concerned, they pose an extreme danger to society. The city of Phoenix and the surrounding suburbs have suffered tremendously in recent days due to the incident at the Navajo Generating Station. These people, by their actions, have placed a terrible burden on millions of inhabitants in this area. To release them would place at risk tens of millions of dollars of public property, not to mention possible loss of life or serious injury to the citizens of Arizona. In a recent speech, Jonathan Holmes called for terrorist action against public utilities and even advocated blowing up oil refineries. This should be an indication to all that, even though he may be a famous scientist, he certainly is not a reasonable and prudent individual. The government therefore asks these defendants be kept incarcerated at least until the preliminary hearing and we are able to present the evidence in this case."

"And when does the government feel it will be ready to present the evidence?" Huston asked, sounding skeptical.

"Due to the complexities involved in this case, Your Honor, the government will need at least ten court days to assemble our facts and gather our witnesses."

"I see," Huston said. He looked at Martin Sherman. "Mr. Sherman, how do you respond to the government's argument that your defendants are flight risks and that they may pose a danger to society?"

Sherman stood up. "Your Honor, these people are all scientists, and they do not espouse the use of violence. We will show the court that they were nowhere near the Navajo Generating Station at the time of this incident. They were in the desert near Yuma conducting a scientific mission, and I have documents in my possession to prove that. If it would please the court, I can present these documents at this time."

"Objection, Your Honor," said the government attorney. "This is not a preliminary hearing."

"So noted," said Huston.

"Your honor," Sherman went on, "the government is up to something here. Everyone knows that my client is a scientist. He is not part of the Defenders of the Planet. The government wants to put him on ice, to keep him isolated from speaking out about what's happening to our environment. You must not allow that to happen. We do have freedom of speech in this country, and that speech the U.S. Attorney referred to was mere rhetoric. Dr. Holmes was attempting to dramatize events so that people in this country would wake up. If they are released on bail, I can assure the court they will not flee the country and will fully submit to any conditions.

"The charges against them have no basis in fact. We will prove at the preliminary hearing that the government has no case against them at all. I can personally vouch for Jonathan Holmes. I've known him as a close friend for many years. He's a man of his word and he will do whatever the court wants. So will his daughter, Jamie.

"As for my other clients, they are young scientists who live and work here in Phoenix. To keep them locked up would deprive them of making a living. They have ties to the community and nowhere to go except to stay in the Phoenix area. I can assure the court, Your Honor, they pose no danger to society." With that, Sherman sat down, his statement finished.

Judge Huston nodded perfunctorily and without hesitation rendered his decision. "The court rules that bail be determined as follows: $100,000 each for Dr. Holmes and for Jamie Holmes, and $25,000 each for Matthew Farr, Chris Hatcher, and Gail Thompson. Until the preliminary hearing, none of the defendants shall leave Maricopa County. Hearing date is set for Wednesday, January tenth."

Martin Sherman stood up. "Congratulations, Jonathan," he said. "We've just won round one."

"Are we free?" Holmes asked. Jamie, Matt, Chris, and Gail gathered around Sherman, all waiting for his answer.

"Not quite," Sherman responded. "You'll be taken back to your cells until I do the paperwork necessary to post bail. It should only take an hour or so."

"Thank heaven," Jamie said. She turned and hugged Matt, a happy expression on her face. "We're free, Matt," she said.

"I'm glad this is over," he said. "That jail sucks!"

"You can say that again," Chris agreed.

"That jail sucks!" he repeated, and everyone laughed.

TEN

The big United States C-141 Starlifter touched down at Nandi Airport in the Fiji Islands just after sunrise, after having flown a three-leg flight that took it from Andrews Air Force Base in Washington to Miramar Naval Air Station in San Diego, to Barbers Point Naval Air Station on Oahu, and finally on to Nandi. At each stop along the way, the C-141 picked up more personnel and cargo, the entire flight taking over twenty hours.

The airport at Nandi, on the northwest coast of Fiji's main island of Viti Levu, was the busiest airport in the South Pacific, a key central stopover point used by the planes of many nations. Because of the airport, and because it had several large harbors, the Pentagon had decided that Viti Levu should become the focal point for the possible evacuation of several million Pacific Islanders. From Nandi, the refugees could be flown to Australia and New Zealand.

The United States military had no hangar facility at Nandi but, within the last forty-eight hours, the U.S. Government had arranged to lease a large terminal there. Planes carrying U.S. personnel from the Air Force and Navy immediately began flying into Viti Levu.

The U.S. Navy had a long history of operations in the Fiji Islands. In World War II, Viti Levu had served as a base of operations against the vastly superior Japanese forces who had invaded the nearby Solomon Islands. During the Solomon Island campaign, the naval forces arrayed against each other were immense, and the battle that followed was considered to be the turning point in the war against Japan. Now, as American naval forces began to return to the area, an even greater fight appeared imminent. This time, men would not be fighting other men. The enemy was Mother Nature.

As the C-141 rolled toward the end of the main runway, it was met by a humvee and escorted to the U.S. facility. The big plane rolled to a stop in front of the hangar, and a Navy ground crew immediately went to work to unload the cargo.

When the big transport's rear loading ramp was lowered, a blast of tropical heat and humidity entered the plane. Captain Rob Jones marveled at how hot it was. Damn! he thought. It's still early morning here and it's already hot. How much hotter will it get? He took a slow, deep breath as he walked down the plane's ramp, his senses keen to the knowledge that he was now in a vastly different part of the world. The air smelled of tropical vegetation, a fresh, pungent smell that pervaded everything.

Accompanied by six other naval oceanographers, Jones walked onto the tarmac and stopped to take in his surroundings. Standing near the plane, he looked down the runway toward the nearby Pacific Ocean which, according to his most recent data, would soon be covering the airport, as well as much of the Fiji Islands. A C-5 Galaxy and several C130 Hercules aircraft were parked near the terminal.

"Let's go get some coffee and breakfast," Jones suggested to the others, all subordinate officers, and all handpicked for this assignment. "We've got a big day ahead of us."

They had managed to get some sleep aboard the Starlifter on its long flight, but the trip hadn't been very comfortable. They were tired and needed some coffee. The seven naval officers headed for the hangar, whose doors were fully open. Inside, three large Sea Stallion helicopters were being serviced by a maintenance crew. A lanky, fifty-ish looking maintenance chief sauntered toward the incoming officers, offering a lazy salute.

"Morning, sir," he said nonchalantly to Jones, reading his name from the label on his fatigues. "We've been expecting you, Captain Jones. I'm Taggart, from the *Lincoln*."

"Good morning, chief," Jones responded, returning Taggart's salute. "How are things going?"

"The choppers are one hundred percent, sir. We're just making some last-minute checks. The pilots and crew are having breakfast in the cafeteria. You can leave when your equipment is loaded aboard. Have you had breakfast, sir?"

"No, we haven't eaten since we left Miramar Air Station."

"There's a big breakfast prepared in the cafeteria, sir. It's right over there. All you can eat."

Jones waved the others on by. "Go ahead," he said. "I'll be along in a minute." The six officers, three men and three women, headed for the cafeteria.

"Chief," Jones said earnestly, "make sure to take extra care with those boxes from that C-141. Our equipment is very sensitive. When you put it aboard the Sea Stallions, treat it with kid gloves, okay?"

"No problem, sir," Taggart said. "My orders are to give you whatever you need. My men are the best. You don't need to worry." He looked quizzically at Jones. "I don't know what your mission is, Captain, but I know it must be awfully important. The *Abe* sailed at flank speed for three days to get those choppers here," Taggart said, referring to the nuclear aircraft carrier, the *U.S.S. Abraham Lincoln,* which her men had nicknamed the *"Abe."*

"You're right, chief. We do have an important mission. We're here to help the Pacific Islanders possibly evacuate this area."

"We are?" Taggart looked dumbfounded. "What's going on, sir?"

"I wish I could tell you but, for the time being, it's top secret. I'm sure you'll be told in due course. Just remember, our mission in critical."

"I think I understand, sir," Taggart said. He brushed his forearm across his forehead to wipe away the beads of sweat that had formed above his eyebrows.

"What's the status of the *Abe*?" Jones asked.

"She's A-OK. But she sailed out of Pearl so fast, some of our key people missed the ship. They had to fly them aboard. We were told to make flank speed for the South Pacific, but they didn't tell us why. We got Sea Stallions all over the flight deck.

Except for a few fighters, most of our planes stayed in Pearl. I ain't seen nothing like it in all my years in the Navy."

"Where's the *Abe* now?" Jones asked.

"I'm not sure, sir, but probably still to the northeast," Taggart said. "We flew these choppers down here in the middle of the night, so they'd be here when you and your team arrived. She was really moving out but, you know, she's a Nimitz class carrier. Most of her escorts couldn't keep up with her. Our entire battle group is spread out between the South Pacific and Pearl. They just couldn't get all the ships ready in time."

Jones frowned slightly upon hearing this bit of news. The Navy had been caught off guard, but at least everything was starting to move. He was sure it was happening like this in other parts of the world.

"Stay alert, chief," Jones warned. "This will get a little dicey before it's all over." He started for the cafeteria. "Don't forget what I said about our equipment."

"Aye, aye, sir," Taggart said. As he watched Jones leave the hangar, Taggart took off his cap and scratched his head. "I'll be damned," he mumbled to himself, wondering what the world was coming to.

Just as he got to the cafeteria, Jones was stopped by a seaman wearing the specialty marks of a cryptologic technician.

"Sir," the seaman announced, "You're wanted in the comm center right away."

"Okay," Jones said, "but first, let me grab a cup of coffee. It was a long plane ride."

"We've got coffee brewing at the comm center, sir. And it's the Pentagon calling. You're wanted on the double, sir."

Jones nodded. "Where's it at?" he asked.

"If you'll follow me, sir," the young man said, leading the way to the comm center with a long, quick stride. "How do you like your coffee, sir?" the seaman asked, thinking ahead.

"Cream and sugar," Jones said.

"Yes, sir, coming right up. Just a bit farther."

Jones followed the seaman to a locked room at the end of a long suite of offices near the front of the terminal. Once inside, he was met by a young ensign.

"Good morning, sir. This way, sir," he announced as he led Jones over to a special radio. "You'll have to wear this headset. This message is for you only."

Jones did as he was told and put on the headset, watching as the ensign flipped several switches. The conversation was being scrambled and simultaneously descrambled at this end.

"Go ahead, Captain," he said.

"Jones, here," he spoke into the headset's mike.

"Rob, it's me, and I've got bad news."

Jones recognized the voice of Admiral Hart, Chief of Naval Operations. No wonder they wanted him here on the double.

"What is it, sir?" Jones asked.

"We just got a coded message from McMurdo. The air temperature down there is increasing. I'm afraid your analysis will need to be revamped."

"How much has it increased?"

"Another two friggin' degrees!" Hart said vehemently. "And they're forecasting it will go to seventy-eight degrees by day after tomorrow. The situation is getting worse, not better!"

"I see," Jones said. "It's a good thing we started moving when we did."

"Yes, we were right about this all along," Hart stated. "I can assure you that General Hershey is eating crow right now. Serves that son of a bitch right!

"Now look, Rob. I want you to begin your study there at Fiji and get your people on line, but then take a plane down to McMurdo. I want you to get a firsthand look at the situation. When you see what's going on down there, report back to me immediately."

"Yes, sir," Jones said emphatically.

"I want you to know that your study, and your preliminary findings, will be of paramount importance. President Rawlings notified the Prime Ministers of Australia and New Zealand about our operation, and they're balking. They're not sure they can take in several million refugees from all over the South Pacific."

"That's not good, Admiral," Jones said. "There's no way we can haul that many people back to the U.S."

"We realize that. Besides which, we'll have enough trouble on our hands trying to evacuate the Caribbean nations. The Aussies and Kiwis are also mad as hell because we're jamming all communications out of Antarctica. They can't communicate with their scientific bases at the South Pole, so I can't say I blame them for being upset with us. Our State Department really has its hands full, but we've got to keep a lid on this for as long as we can."

"Yes, sir, but I can understand that they would be very upset about this. They've got large bases in Antarctica."

"Yes, they're quite concerned about their summer expeditions down there. Fortunately, they've got a line of communication via aircraft working out of Christchurch, but they're really pissed off with this whole situation. Not much I can do about it, though.

"Rob, when you go through Christchurch on your way to McMurdo, try to be diplomatic with them. If there is any way you can alleviate tensions, or if there are any problems, let me know immediately."

"Yes, sir," Jones said. "I certainly will."

"Good. By the way, we're sending two more carrier battle groups into the South Pacific, so we should have plenty of manpower in case it's needed. Good luck, Rob. I'll be in touch."

Jones heard a slight click, and he realized that Admiral Hart had ended the transmission. He removed his headset, just as the seaman handed him a cup of coffee. He sipped it, a thoughtful expression on his face, wondering what it was like back at the Pentagon. It must be a madhouse, he decided.

He turned to the ensign. "Can you raise McMurdo for me? I need to talk to them."

"Yes, sir. No problem. We've got a link set up through our MILSTAR system."

Two hours later, the three Sea Stallions had been loaded and were taken out onto the flight line. Their engines coughed to life, the big rotors beginning to spin faster and faster. One by one, they lifted off the runway and flew out over Viti Levu Island, on a southeasterly heading. Beneath the blazing tropical sun, the big, roaring helicopters looked like magnificent blue dragons going out to do battle with a powerful foe.

Jones and his fellow oceanographers had split into three teams, each assigned to a specific destination. Jones' Sea Stallion headed for Matuku Island, just over three hundred kilometers from Nandi. The other two Sea Stallions flew toward the islands of Moala and Totoya. Together, these three islands formed a triangle to the southeast of Viti Levu.

Once their equipment was in place, they would be able to measure the level of the ocean in the middle of the triangle to within a fraction of a centimeter, using the three islands as reliable platforms. Considering the constant motion of the ocean and the rising and falling of the tides, Jones knew that a fraction of a centimeter was exceedingly accurate.

While they flew over the main island of Fiji, the three choppers stayed together, but when they crossed the coastline near Korolevu, they split apart, each taking a different heading. Jones watched for several minutes as the other two Sea Stallions got smaller and smaller, eventually losing sight of them against the dazzling blue sky of the South Pacific.

"Captain, can I ask you a question?"

Jones looked over at Lieutenant Kristin Yates, the young female lieutenant who had nearly shouted the question over the roar of the chopper's engines.

"Of course," Jones replied, also fairly shouting.

"How long will we be on the island?" she asked. The other member of their team, Lieutenant Bruce Pike, looked up from a manual he was reading, also eager to hear the answer. A young crewman standing nearby, wearing a helmet and flight suit, showed little interest in what Jones might have to say, but the crewman's eyes repeatedly looked over his female passenger, who was wearing a loose tropical uniform, including shorts. Kristin was a blue-eyed blonde with long, graceful legs, a slim waist, and a curvaceous upper body.

"I'm not sure," Jones responded to Kristin. "Maybe a month or two. I don't think any longer than that."

Kristin's blue eyes widened at the prospect of spending such a long time on a South Pacific Island, and she grinned widely.

Jones smiled back, reading her mind. "It's not going to be easy," he cautioned, "and both of you better realize this will be no picnic. Lots of long hours, and a great deal of tedious work. Probably, after two or three weeks here, you'll be totally sick of this place."

"No way, Captain," she answered. "I love the ocean! And I couldn't have asked for a better assignment. Thank you, sir, for selecting me."

"You were selected based on your record. And quit calling me sir! From now on, call me Rob. There's no need for protocol out here. That goes for you, too, Bruce."

"Sounds good to me," Pike said, smiling.

Jones leaned forward, making it a little easier to be heard over the drone of the engines. "This mission is probably the most important either of you will ever get," he began. "Our job is to determine beyond any doubt that the level of the ocean is rising. We'll report our findings directly back to the Pentagon and they'll use that information to decide who gets moved where and when. We'll try to save as many people on these islands as we can."

"How much time will we have before it gets critical?" Pike asked.

"Not much, I'm afraid. Our latest computer projections say that the Pacific Ocean will rise about two hundred feet by May twenty-second. Based on the data, these low-lying islands in the South Pacific will be mostly underwater by sometime in March. Nandi Airport could be underwater in just three or four weeks."

"God!" Kristin said. "I didn't stop to think about that."

"Yes," Jones said. "Time is critical. Once we lose our runways, we lose our big jets, and those jets are the best hope for these islanders. The information we send back to the Pentagon, even in the early stages, will be extremely important. I'm sure most of these islanders aren't going to want to leave their homes. We've got to convince them, and we have to do it right away."

The two lieutenants looked perplexed, both realizing the enormity of the problem. "Maybe the situation at the South Pole will reverse itself," Pike suggested.

Jones nodded. "It's not. Back at Nandi, I got a call from Washington, and so I called McMurdo. The temperature yesterday rose to seventy-six degrees and they're forecasting it will go to seventy-seven or seventy-eight. Barometric pressure has risen to over 1028 millibars and it's still rising. If the temperature keeps increasing, our projections will change. If it gets over eighty degrees in Antarctica, the ice could all melt by April."

"Eighty degrees in Antarctica?" Kristin asked. "That's impossible!"

"That's what I thought when it hit seventy," Jones responded. "At this point, nothing seems impossible."

"How long will you be staying with us?" Pike asked.

"Just a few days. I've got to get over to Moala and Totoya and make sure all the laser transits are calibrated properly. Then I go back to Nandi and down to McMurdo for a firsthand look. I'll be back to Matuku Island in about a week."

"Well, I hope you hurry back, Rob. This whole thing seems out of control," Kristin said.

"Don't worry," Jones said, sensing her apprehension, "a nuclear submarine will be on station here in less than two days. Its only responsibility will be to look after our three teams. They'll be resupplying and providing assistance as needed. And pretty soon we'll have a squad of U.S. Marines protecting our backside, just in case any islanders start to give us any trouble."

"I wish the Marines were here right now," she said.

"Sorry, Lieutenant," Jones said, "but we're still in the initial phase of Operation Safeharbor. The entire Navy is scrambling right now. We're all doing the best we can."

"I know," she said. "I'm sure we'll be all right."

An hour later, the pilot notified them they were approaching their destination. Jones stepped up and stood between the two pilots, leaning forward and looking out the cockpit. Ahead, Matuku Island was clearly visible in the distance. The big chopper began descending.

The island had a dogleg shape, a ridge of steep, thousand-foot peaks running down the center of its entire length. Except for a narrow passage into Matuku Harbor on it west side, Matuku Island was completely surrounded by coral reefs which prevented any approach from the sea by large boats.

Jones had been briefed on all three islands while still back at the Pentagon. Matuku Island had seven villages, all built very close to the coast. There were no roads or airports. The villages were connected by a foot trail that ran along the coast all around the island. The center of the island was covered with thick jungle, though the steep mountains made this area totally unusable. There were numerous mangrove forests along the coast, mostly on the northwest side of the island, and elsewhere there was an abundance of coconut groves.

As he looked upon the island from above, Jones thought it looked cool and inviting, a rugged, dark green jewel jutting out of a sparkling blue ocean, looking every bit like an idyllic South Seas tropical paradise. He was anxious to land and look around.

The pilot had been given a precise destination. The chopper would set down on a beach which faced to the northeast, toward Moala and Totoya Islands. The Sea Stallion circled around the north end of the island, approaching its designated landing spot from the northeast.

The beach was white sand and narrow, though the jungle growing along its edge didn't appear to be too dense. There was a point to the right of the beach, and on the other side a huge group of mangrove trees grew right up to the ocean, their tangled roots looking like a maze of brown snakes. To the left, the beach curved around the island, disappearing into the encroaching jungle.

As they came in for the landing, they flew low over the water. From the air, the water around the island was light blue in color and crystal clear. The coral reefs were visible just below the shimmering surface. The pilot put the aircraft down right on the middle of the beach.

"Good landing," Jones exclaimed, glad everything had gone well thus far.

"No sweat," the pilot smiled. He shut down the engines, and everyone exited the chopper, eager to check out the beach. The water was calm and warm. As they moved about, they all noticed that it was very hot, almost stifling. The chopper's crew, wearing their flight suits, were soon soaked in sweat.

"Better get out of those suits," Jones told them. "It's too damn hot to be working with those on."

"Aye, aye, sir," replied the pilot, a warrant officer.

Immediately, the crew of the Sea Stallion changed into shorts and tennis shoes. All three were in great shape, and it was obvious that they worked out quite regularly, judging from the size of their pectorals and other muscles. Rob Jones, at forty-six, also worked out regularly, but he knew he didn't compare to these three young men.

They scouted around for a suitable campsite, which they soon found about fifteen meters inside the tree line. Then everyone began unloading the equipment and supplies, nearly a ton in all. The chopper's crew began earnestly flexing their muscles, their skin glistening wet as they moved the heavy crates and boxes out of the chopper.

Jones made four trips from the chopper to the camp site, and then was out of breath, his legs feeling heavy from walking through the sand. He sat down on a crate to rest. In the shade beneath the trees, the heat was only slightly diminished. Lieutenant Pike, in his mid-thirties, soon joined him. Pike was breathing heavily.

"You okay?" Jones asked.

"I wasn't ready for this, sir. It's hotter than hell and I'm not in the best of shape," Pike replied.

"It's all right," Jones said. "Once we get this camp set up, the hard part will be over. During the heat of day, we can rest here in the shade or go swimming. We'll take readings from our instruments early in the morning and late in the afternoon when it's still cool."

"Yes, sir," Pike said.

"Call me Rob, Lieutenant. That's an order!"

"Sorry, Rob." Pike paused to reflect on the situation. "I wonder how hot it is?" he said.

"I don't know. Why don't we find out?" Jones got up and began inspecting the crates, looking for the one which he knew contained a thermometer. He soon found the right crate.

"Get the tool box, Bruce," he said. "I need a hammer." Pike quickly found it, and Jones pried the crate apart.

Kristin came through the trees with several pieces of equipment in her hands. After she set them down, she came over to see what they were doing. She was younger than both of them, only thirty, and the heat had less effect on her. "What's up?" she asked cheerfully.

"We're checking the temperature," Pike replied.

Jones took the thermometer out of the crate and, using the hammer, he hung it against a nearby tree. The thermometer was a digital type, extremely accurate, with an air probe made of gallium arsenide that hung down ten inches. A computer within the thermometer measured the electrical resistance of the gallium arsenide, which varied depending upon the air temperature. The thermometer could be read in either the Fahrenheit scale or the Celsius scale.

Jones switched it to the F setting and the three of them stood watching the digital display climb upward. Finally, it stopped at the number 124.

"One hundred and twenty-four degrees!" Pike exclaimed. "No wonder I'm having trouble moving around. I don't know if I can take this. This place is a steambath!"

"It'll take us a few days to get acclimated," Jones said, trying to sound as positive as he could. "We'll be all right, here. Just drink plenty of fluids and, if you start to feel too hot, go jump in the water."

"I think I'll have to live in the ocean," Kristin agreed. "The water is only around seventy-six, I'd guess."

"This is only the beginning," Pike stated. "The temperature will be increasing in the days ahead."

Jones nodded, knowing Pike was probably right. For the first time, he felt disheartened. It wasn't even noon yet. Before the day was over, the island would probably see an air temperature of one hundred and twenty-five degrees. Would they be able to take it and perform their mission?

"Come on," he said, seeing the chopper's crew coming through the bush, all carrying more equipment. "Let's help get this chopper unloaded."

ELEVEN

A few days later, Rob Jones left the Fiji Islands and flew down to McMurdo Naval Air Station as ordered by Admiral Hart. McMurdo was located on Ross Island, a volcanic island just off the coast of Antarctica. After a long flight that took him through Christchurch, New Zealand, Jones eagerly stepped down out of the C-130 Hercules to survey the base.

The air temperature was seventy-eight degrees, hot by Antarctic standards, but a welcome relief from the hundred and twenty degree plus temperatures of the Fiji Islands. All around the runway, hundreds of Navy Seabees were working to make it even longer, so that it could land big jets. The scene was one of frenzied construction activity.

Jones noticed the Seabees were wearing pith helmets and long-sleeved shirts. He had been told he would be met at the plane and, as he looked around, he saw someone sitting in a humvee parked fifty yards away, waving at him. The man was wearing a cowboy hat. Could that be Fletcher? Jones wondered.

He picked up his duffel bag and briefcase and began walking down the runway. As he approached the humvee, Jones saw that the commander of McMurdo Station, Rear Admiral Martin Fletcher, was indeed sitting in the passenger's seat. He recognized the insignia, but there was little else about the uniform that looked familiar. Besides the cowboy hat, Fletcher wore a naval flight jacket with the collar up, dark glasses, and his nose and the backs of his hands were covered with bright pink cream. Fletcher's driver was similarly attired and together they looked like characters out of a science fiction movie.

"Welcome to McMurdo, Captain," Fletcher greeted him in a booming voice, hopping out of the humvee. Jones saluted, and Fletcher returned his salute.

"I trust you had a good flight?" Fletcher asked, as the two officers shook hands.

"Yes, sir," Jones said. "The landing was a little rough, though."

Fletcher laughed. "We've lost Williams Field," he said. "The ice shelf is no longer stable. It's fractured and uplifted more than sixteen inches. The ice plows just can't handle it. You're lucky the Seabees have got this much runway finished; otherwise, your landing would have been even rougher. I noticed that Hercules pilot really had to burn his brakes to come to a stop."

Fletcher looked thoughtfully at the construction in progress. "Building this runway has been a bitch of a job," he said. "This island is solid volcanic rock. They've been blasting all week. I just had to order three hundred new windows for the base, to replace the ones that have shattered. Fortunately, the weather hasn't turned cold again. We've been able to survive okay without windows."

"Sorry, sir," Jones said. "I guess I shouldn't have complained. I didn't realize your situation here."

"Where is your hat?" Fletcher asked, concern in his voice.

"I don't have one," Jones replied. "I'm here on short notice."

"Hmmm," Fletcher hummed. "Not good! We'll have to get you outfitted right away. The ozone hole is at an all-time peak. We're getting a tremendous amount of ultraviolet light now, with all this sunlight. Normally, it's no problem here because of cloud cover."

"How bad is it?" Jones asked.

"It's bad. Real bad," Fletcher replied. "Two cases of skin cancer on my last medical report. Mostly we see it on the back of a hand. These people have been told again and again to cover their hands! But they don't listen."

Jones nodded, realizing his own hands were not covered. He looked up toward the cloudless sky. The sunlight was dazzling, and he thought he could feel a slight burning sensation on his skin. Was it just his imagination?

"Get in," Fletcher said, springing easily into the front seat. "We'll go back to my office and I'll bring you up to date. I've prepared a briefing for you."

Jones threw his gear into the back of the humvee and hopped into the backseat. Fletcher nodded to the driver, and the vehicle sped away.

His first impression of McMurdo was a dismal one. The base seemed unusually harsh and ugly, resembling a sprawling, disorganized supply dump. The roads were crooked and unpaved, covered with gritty black volcanic dust. Supplies, vehicles, and equipment were everywhere. Some of the supplies were just lying about on the ground in haphazard fashion, and some were in crates stacked on pallets four or five high. Bulldozers, forklifts, trucks, and humvees were parked at random, and every sort of military equipment was being stored out in the open. The nearby buildings were mostly prefab jobs, gray and dingy.

Jones had expected to see snow, but there was little on Ross Island. Antarctica had been experiencing hot sunny weather for a month now and most of the snow immediately around the station had melted. Normally, the snow covered all the defects of McMurdo but, totally exposed, McMurdo Station stood out for what it was, just a drab little base constructed on the edge of a volcanic island in the most remote part of the world.

When they got to Fletcher's office, Fletcher led Jones inside and offered him a cup of coffee. He also told his driver to go over to the officers' messhall and bring back a dozen ham and cheese sandwiches, half on rye and the other half on whole wheat. "And with lettuce and tomatoes. On the double," Fletcher ordered.

"Just leave your gear over here," Fletcher told Jones, tossing his cowboy hat onto a coat rack and removing his jacket. "We'll get you to your quarters later. Your briefing will begin immediately."

Jones did as he was told, stashing his duffle bag in a corner but holding onto his briefcase. He noticed three other officers in a nearby room, sitting around a long table.

"This way, Captain. This is our conference room," he said, ushering Jones through the door. "Gentlemen, this is Captain Rob Jones, from the Pentagon." The three officers stood up to shake hands with him, all of them wearing serious expressions.

"Captain," Fletcher said, "meet Commander Daryl Thorson, McMurdo's meteorologist, and this is Commander Paul Bowman, our atmospheric specialist, and this is Lieutenant Commander Bill Van Horne, in charge of oceanography."

Like Fletcher, all three officers wore heavy pink sunscreen cream on their noses and the backs of their hands. Jones immediately decided that they simply wore the cream all the time as a convenience. "Nice to meet all of you," Jones said. "I wish it could be under better circumstances."

"Welcome to the end of the world," Commander Thorson said, breaking into a half-smile. "You'll get used to our appearance. It's a lot easier to leave this stuff on all the time, and besides, it's in short supply."

"I figured as much," Jones said, smiling.

"You came from Nandi?" Thorson asked.

"That's right," Jones said. "And I've got to get back ASAP. We've set up instruments on three different islands in the Fiji group to measure the rise in the ocean level. The Secretary of Defense wants absolute proof that the water is rising."

"He should come down here," Van Horne said bitterly. "All he's got to do is fly over a few of the glaciers."

"What were the temperatures in Fiji?" Thorson asked.

"Yesterday, it hit one hundred and twenty-six. Humidity was over eighty percent. The place has become a..." Jones paused searching for the right word. "A hellhole," he finished.

Thorson nodded. "That seems to fit the picture, all right. You and I have a lot to talk about, sir."

"You'll have plenty of time, Daryl," Fletcher said. "First, I've been ordered by Admiral Hart to bring Captain Jones up to date on the situation down here. So let's get started. Shall we all sit down?" He motioned toward the conference table and the five of them proceeded to take their seats.

"Sir, if I could ask a question?" Jones blurted out.

"Yes, Captain?" Fletcher said.

"There are no civilians here. And you've got some very good scientists on base right now..."

Fletcher nodded. "Sorry, Jones, but they're excluded from this briefing. First, they're all pissed off because we've cut off all communication with the outside world, so they don't want to be here." Fletcher emphasized the word *want*. "Second, and most important, I've been ordered by Admiral Hart to maintain absolute secrecy about what's going on down here. There are some facts concerning the situation here that even you are not aware of.

"For one thing, the *U.S.S. Excalibur* is stationed a few hundred miles off the coast, jamming all radio transmissions from Antarctica. That has really got our allies pissed off. Yesterday, I had to have six of our Kiwi buddies from Scott escorted off the base under armed guard.

"And there's a Greenpeace ship in the Bellinghausen Sea that's got a U.S. destroyer and a frigate as an escort. We've had to fire shots across her bow twice to keep her pinned down along the coast. For now, we can't allow them to go back to the world and spread the bad news.

"Also, all satellite information concerning Antarctica is strictly off limits to everybody, even NASA. We're attempting to isolate all information about Antarctica from the rest of the world."

"What about air transport?" Jones asked. "Certainly we can't stop the other nations from flying in or out of here?"

"Yes, that's true," Fletcher said. "But some of them have lost their bases due to the ice melting. South Africa and Norway had to close up shop. In fact, the U.K. had to evacuate Halley Station because of the ice shifting. Germany and Russia have lost most of their bases, too. Of those nations still here, several are cooperating with us. The U.K. is helping with the jamming. They've got a ship in the Weddell Sea that's every bit as powerful as the *Excalibur.* Between the two ships, nothing is getting out of here.

"Russia, Germany and Japan are also cooperating, and to some extent so is Australia and New Zealand, although they're balking. As we speak, the Secretary of State is meeting with the leaders of both countries in Australia. I'm told the President has called their ambassadors into the Oval Office and raked them over the coals about the necessity of preventing a worldwide panic. As for the other nations, well, who cares what they say? If some pilot from Chile or Argentina goes home and says Antarctica is melting, who's going to listen to him? Especially when the major nations are mum on the subject?

"We know we can't prevent some information from leaking out, but the plan is to temporarily contain the situation until we can get all our forces up and running. All this is just a holding action. Unfortunately, we're having to step on quite a few toes."

"I see," Jones said. "I didn't realize..."

"No problem," Fletcher said. "Now you understand what I'm dealing with. I guess we're all having to deal with this. I know you haven't had any picnic up in Fiji."

"No, sir," Jones replied. "We've all had to adapt."

"Well, now that we've got that out of the way, who wants to begin the briefing? Daryl?"

"Yes, sir," Thorson said. He pulled a sheet of paper out from several in front of him. "There are two high pressure areas affecting us, both very close to Antarctica and both expanding. One area is over the South Atlantic. The other area is in the South Indian Ocean. Antarctica is caught in the middle. The immediate forecast calls for a slight increase in barometric pressure at sea level, from thirty-one point five inches of mercury to thirty-one point six, and an increase in sea level air temperature to eighty by tomorrow afternoon. There is no cloud cover in the area, and it doesn't look like we'll see any.

"In the longer term, I predict the temperature will reach eighty-one degrees by the end of the week, ultimately reaching the nineties by midsummer. I'm guessing the air pressure will soon reach thirty-two inches or more because the two high pressure areas are not showing any signs of movement. They're simply getting bigger. This will create high temperatures for at least the next three weeks."

"You're sure about these high pressure systems?" Jones asked. He didn't want to doubt Thorson but, considering the numbers being discussed, he felt the question was warranted.

"Positive," Thorson replied. "We've been tracking them for over a month. I am certain about this. I would go out on a limb and say that barometric pressure at sea level will definitely go over thirty-two inches of mercury, except I've never seen that happen before. Now, nothing would surprise me. Based on your temperature readings at Nandi, I can only surmise that the air pressure at the equator is extremely low due to really hot temperatures. That loose air has to go somewhere, so we should start seeing some very significant air movements.

"We've been taking hourly balloon readings here at McMurdo. They've been taking hourly readings at Palmer Station, too. In addition, we've got a weather plane in the air eight hours a day, flying different routes." Thorson attempted a strained smile. "I don't know what else we can do."

"It looks like you're on top of it," Jones said. "Have you noticed any unusual wind patterns?" he asked.

"Not locally," Thorson replied. "And we've got state-of-the-art anemometers set up all over the continent."

"Over thirty-two inches!" Jones said, shaking his head. "That's remarkable. It doesn't look like the situation here is going to change for the better in the near future."

"That's not all," Fletcher said. He nodded toward Bowman. "Paul, would you care to apprise Captain Jones about the ozone?"

"Yes, sir," Bowman said, a glum look on his face. "The ozone situation is not good, Captain," Bowman said dejectedly. "Our spectrometer readings indicate that the ozone hole has become virtually permanent. We've suffered total depletion of the ozone layer over Antarctica."

"You have data confirming that?" Jones asked, frowning.

Bowman nodded, referring to a piece of paper in front of him. "This is something you probably haven't been made aware of, Captain, but the most recent passes by TOMS indicates an ozone level of one part per billion parts of air at between fifteen to thirty miles altitude in most areas below thirty degrees south latitude. Except that, directly over Antarctica, it's one part per one hundred billion."

Jones stared at Bowman. He didn't know the ozone layer was totally gone. The normal historical level of ozone in the stratosphere was about six parts per million. At one part per hundred billion, there may as well no longer be an ozone layer. If the data came from TOMS, it had to be considered accurate. TOMS was the acronym for a NASA satellite orbiting 596 miles above the earth, the Total Ozone Mapping Spectrometer.

"Starting two years ago, sir," Bowman explained, "DOD classified all data coming out of TOMS as ultra top secret, need to know only. About three dozen top NASA scientists were made to take an oath of secrecy and a special group within the Pentagon took over the program. Admiral Hart wanted you briefed because this information may have something to do with the ice cap melting. You may need the information for your analysis."

"I had no idea it was this bad. I'm sorry," Jones mouthed the words, suddenly feeling ashamed. How could we have let this happen? he asked himself.

"Yes," Fletcher said. "We're all sorry. Now you know why I was concerned they didn't give you a hat for your trip here. You can no longer go out in the sun here unless you're protected."

Jones nodded his understanding. The South Pole was being bombarded with the sun's rays, and there was nothing anyone could do about it. The infrared rays were being trapped in the atmosphere, and the ultraviolet rays were coming through. "Is the increase in ultraviolet contributing to the loss of ice?" Jones asked.

"It could be," Van Horne answered. "But I simply don't know. The water temperatures in the ocean are abnormally high, but it's very difficult to tell if that's because of atmospheric temperatures or due in part to shortwave radiation."

"What is the ocean temperature right now?" Jones asked.

"Right off the coast it's twenty-nine degrees at the surface," Van Horne replied. "But two miles out it quickly rises to thirty-three degrees. At fifty miles out it's forty-seven degrees. We've never recorded a water temperature that high in the Antarctic Ocean. My theory is that the UV is helping to warm the water. I don't think it's a neutral factor."

"Yes," Bowman concurred. "Without cloud cover here, we're getting hit with everything the sun can hit us with, and I mean everything. Right now, we may as well be on the surface of the moon. The short wave radiation striking the South Pole is the highest it's ever been."

"The band of warmth extends to a depth of just over five feet," Van Horne continued. "At depths below five feet, the water temperatures are still high, all the way down to one hundred feet, where they go back to normal. We know that UV penetrates the sea to a depth of at least ninety feet, so it is possible that there's a cause and effect relationship between UV and the abnormally high water temperature. I've got some experiments set up over on Ferrar Glacier, just across the Sound, but I've had to order more equipment. At this time, I've only got a theory."

"It's worth following up on," Jones said. "In fact, the data may be invaluable. Pursue your theory. Maybe you'll come up with something."

Admiral Fletcher looked around the table. "Does anybody have anything else?" he asked.

Thorson, Bowman, and Van Horne all shook their heads. They had nothing else to report. The three naval scientists looked at Jones, as if seeking help with a vexing problem. They were looking up to him for some answers.

What could he tell them? Jones asked himself. Everything seemed to indicate the situation was worsening. It wasn't getting any better.

"I'm sorry this has happened," Jones finally said, "but you're doing excellent work under the most difficult circumstances. Your information has been most helpful, and I'll make damn sure the Pentagon understands the seriousness of this. The data will be put to good use."

"What are you going to do?" Bowman asked.

"There isn't much we can do, except continue to make forecasts and try to establish a timetable as to how fast the ice will melt, if it's going to continue or suddenly stop. If it doesn't stop, if this weather persists, then the Navy needs to know exactly how fast and how much the oceans are going to rise. The lives of millions of people will be depending on us. We're going to have to evacuate millions of people who live in the affected areas. Operation Safeharbor is already underway. The Navy will do everything possible." He paused and looked around to see if his words had any positive effect, but he saw only a resigned hopelessness on their faces, all except Fletcher, who seemed to be in good spirits. Jones' impression was that Fletcher relished having a command under these near-wartime conditions. The others, all scientists, realized the world was in serious trouble. They couldn't care less about the challenge and about their careers.

Just then, Fletcher's driver walked in with two plates full of sandwiches. "Thanks, Todd," Fletcher said. "Just set them here on the table."

"Yes, sir," Todd replied, placing both plates squarely in the middle of the conference table. As he left the room, Jones noticed his rank, seaman first class, and Jones wondered how the enlisted men were handling this crisis. They were so far from home, and their communications were completely shut off.

"Well," Fletcher said, "why don't we break for lunch? Captain, we need to get a hat and some skin cream for you. After lunch, you're scheduled for a tour of some of the glaciers across the Sound. There's a chopper waiting. Commander Thorson will accompany you." Fletcher smiled and picked up one of the plates, holding it up in front of Jones. "Does that sound okay?"

"Yes, sir," Jones replied, as he selected one of the sandwiches. "I'm anxious to see what it's like out there."

Ninety minutes later, Thorson and Jones boarded a Light Observation Helicopter (LOH) and they flew off directly across McMurdo Sound. Jones was wearing the same skin cream as everyone else, and Admiral Fletcher had given him a cowboy hat, ordering him to wear it all times while outside. Attired like everybody else, Jones felt like part of the Antarctic team.

As the chopper gained altitude, Jones saw Mount Erebus, the huge towering volcano on the far end of the island that completely dominated the landscape. It was the only part of Ross Island that was completely covered with snow. Looking down, Jones saw that there were large patches of black ground all over Ross Island, areas where the snow had melted. His mind began to wander. He was witnessing the first dire effects of global warming. Should he feel privileged, or should he feel something else?

The chopper turned slightly and headed out across the water, which was littered with floating icebergs.

"They're melting fast," Thorson shouted, pointing downward.

"What is?" Jones asked, his mind still wandering.

"The icebergs! Because of the sun and the high water temperatures, they're not getting as far as they normally do. Most of them just sweep up the coast to the west, and they get trapped in bays and inlets. Those that head out to sea, unless they're really big, don't make it past sixty-five degrees south latitude."

"Is that unusual?" Jones asked.

"Yes. At the rate the ice is melting, you should be seeing the ocean level increase any day now up in Fiji!"

Jones nodded, his jaw set in a grimace. It was something he really didn't want to have to see. Thorson was right. The icebergs were adhering to an age-old cycle. The glaciers of Antarctica flowed to the sea, the ice broke off into bergs, and these floated out to sea to eventually melt. In the winter, gigantic blizzards ranging over the entire continent replaced the ice.

What would happen here this winter? Jones wondered. Would there even *be* an Antarctic winter?

The LOH crossed over the coast and made a climbing turn, heading up the mouth of the Ferrar Glacier. Below, Jones saw that the glacier was glistening brightly beneath the sun. Even from high above, Jones could see streams flowing on the glacier, water flowing freely toward the ocean.

"Wow!" Thorson exclaimed. "She's really coming apart!"

The chopper continued up the glacier for another thirty miles, then Thorson tapped the pilot on the shoulder, gesturing for him to take them down and land. The pilot nodded and began a descent. A minute later, he landed carefully on a relatively flat part of the glacier, looking back at Thorson for direction.

"Shut her down," Thorson shouted. "We'll be at least ten or twenty minutes on the ice." The pilot nodded and shut down the chopper's turbine engine.

Thorson waited until the rotors stopped. "Come on," he said to Jones. "Let's go." He opened the door and hopped out of the chopper, Jones following. Thorson began a slow walk away from the chopper. After only a few yards, Jones' feet went out from under him and he crashed flat onto his back.

Thorson reached down to pull him up. "You okay?" he asked.

Embarrassed by his clumsiness, Jones smiled. "Yeah, I think so. There's nothing broken."

Thorson, hearing this, hauled him to his feet. "The glacier has very little snow covering, Captain," he warned. "It's got some real slick ice in places. Be careful!"

Jones shook off the fall, and they went on. After walking a hundred yards, they came upon a stream running through the glacier, cutting a canyon deep into the ice. Thorson held up his hand, signaling Jones not to get too close to the edge of the ice.

"This is what I wanted to show you," he said, pointing to the moving water below them. "We're finding these streams all over the glaciers. You see how it's cutting down through the ice, building upon itself?"

"I see it," Jones nodded. The surface of the stream was at least thirty feet below the surface of the glacier. The stream was nearly twenty feet wide and flowing strongly. It appeared to be several feet deep.

"This is really amazing." Thorson said. "Pretty soon, this will join up with some other stream and they'll cut down all the way through the ice, right to bedrock. Then it'll become a damned river. Unless this weather reverses, Ferrar Glacier will be history. *All* the glaciers will be history."

Rob Jones watched the stream, transfixed. The water looked sparkling clear and inviting. But he knew the stream represented a threat to the world. Here was *prima facie* evidence that the earth was experiencing a runaway greenhouse effect. The ice that had been locked up at world's end for hundreds of thousands of years was coming apart, turning into water and flowing out to sea. He realized he was seeing only one stream. Certainly, what he was witnessing was happening elsewhere too. The importance of it all suddenly hit home, and Jones' heart began pounding. He felt his face flush. The South Pole was melting right before his eyes, and he was here to see it.

"It's kind of beautiful, huh?" Thorson stated. "Strange, but beautiful."

"I don't know what to say," Jones replied. "This is incredible."

"You don't have to say anything. I know how you feel. I had the same reaction the first time I saw it."

Jones stepped back from the edge of the ice and looked around the glacier. He took a deep breath and felt his body begin to relax. After a moment, he felt the blood leave his face, and he was back to normal.

The air at this place was pristine, and he realized he'd never breathed air this pure in his entire life. In the distance, dark brown peaks of the nearby mountains rose against the velvet soft hue of a majestic blue sky. Jones wondered if there could be any place more magnificent on earth.

"You okay?" Thorson asked.

"Yeah," Jones replied. "I'm fine. It's just hard to believe this is really happening."

"I know. But it is happening. The world is changing and there's nothing we can do about it. It makes you feel helpless."

"At least I'll make damn sure the people in Washington know what's going on down here. Maybe they'll come up with something, an idea."

"I doubt it," Thorson said skeptically. "No power on earth is going to reverse this. This is the result of a century of abuse. We assaulted the earth in the most perverse way, and now it's turning on us." He laughed harshly. "No," he said, shaking his head. "This will not be undone."

Rob Jones did not respond, but he hoped Thorson was wrong. There *had* to be something they could do — there *had* to be a way to fix this.

He and Thorson stood there for several minutes, neither saying anything more, both of them taking in the full spectacle of the Antarctic landscape. Watching a scene of such beautiful serenity, Jones now felt totally calm, the tranquility broken only by the sound of the running water.

TWELVE

Jake Jurado lay flat on his belly and peered into the night. A light fog had crept in near the Los Angeles coast, making this place eerie and surreal. For just a brief moment, Jake wondered what he was doing here. He took a deep breath through his nostrils to gather his courage, smelling the ocean and the refinery, exhaling out his mouth. His heart was pounding. Relax, Jake, he told himself. It will be all right. He checked his watch one more time. It read eleven, and it was December thirty-first.

Nearby, a chainlink fence ran for several hundred meters in both directions, lit at intervals by security lamps. Jake looked up and down its length. Seeing no one, he quickly crawled forward, a pair of bolt cutters in his hands.

On the other side of the fence lay the Six Star Oil Refinery of San Pedro, adjacent to the main channel of Los Angeles harbor. Six Star Oil was a California corporation, wholly owned by Stellar Marketing Enterprises, a New Jersey corporation which was completely controlled by Saudi Arabia.

Tonight, the Los Angeles units of the Defenders of the Planet were going to attack the Six Star refinery, and four other major Southern California refineries.

Tonight's fog had been unexpected. The weather forecast had called for clear weather. Jake thought it augured trouble. He took another deep breath, his adrenaline flowing strongly and, as he approached the fence, his stomach filled with butterflies. From his present perspective, the Six Star refinery appeared to be an omnipotent fortress. The terminal and refinery completely dominated the skyline, a myriad of security lights and running lights outlining the pipes, towers and various structures of the giant installation.

In spite of modern pollution controls, the area smelled of hydrocarbons offgassing from all the dark, viscous liquid being processed into gasoline and other petroleum products. Even with the constant ocean breezes, the place was a perpetual haze of molecules of hydrocarbons drifting about in the air.

Jake took one last look around, then raised the bolt cutters and began cutting the chainlink fence, making a hole in the wire big enough for a man wearing a backpack to go through. He slithered into the opening, got up and ran forward. The rest of his group, fourteen in all, quickly followed him through, crawling on their bellies one by one just as Jake had.

Once inside the giant refinery, they ran forward, regrouping near the outer wall of a trench surrounding a large storage tank, the trench designed to contain any spill. John Haney knelt down next to Jake.

"We're in," Haney said. "Nice going, Jake!"

"Yeah, now all we've got to do is blow this place up!"

"Piece of cake!" said Linda Ramirez, Jake's girlfriend and his top lieutenant within their unit. Her long black hair was pulled into a tight ponytail, and her face blackened with greasepaint. Like all the others, she wore a black sweater, black pants and heavy black boots. On her back was a pack filled with plastic explosives, and she carried an assault rifle firmly in both hands. To Jake, she seemed calm and at ease.

"I'm glad you're not nervous," he commented.

"This is going to be fun," she replied, smiling.

"We'll see how much fun it is," he said sardonically. "Anyway, stay close to me. I don't want to lose you in this place."

"Don't worry, Jake. I'll be right behind you."

"Okay, everybody," Jake said. "You all know the plan of attack. Stay with your teams. If anyone is injured or wounded, we don't leave anyone behind. Okay, let's go. Let's do it!"

The fifteen Defenders of the Planet split into five three-person teams and began moving through the refinery at a slow trot, just as they had practiced in recent night exercises. Each team had a two-way radio and everybody carried first aid kits, water, candy bars, a hundred rounds of ammunition and, most important of all, five bundles of plastic explosives with electronic detonators, which they would time to explode at midnight.

Jake, Linda, and John Haney headed toward their specific target, the heart of the refinery — the fractional distillation plant. If they could destroy this plant, the oil refinery would be incapable of refining oil into gasoline and other products.

At the distillation plant, the crude oil was heated by a furnace to 700 degrees. The resulting vapors and gases condensed inside a high bubble tower, then were siphoned off and converted into different petroleum products. The heaviest matter condensed at the bottom of the bubble tower, this to be converted into products such as asphalt and grease, while the lighter gas rose to the top of the tower, to be converted into jet fuel and high octane gas. Since the whole system was under pressure, at any given time the fractional distillation plant was one gigantic bomb ready to explode, a very complex and dangerous piece of engineering.

Jake Jurado's unit was fully aware of the layout of the Six Star refinery. Several months before, they had taken aerial photographs of the entire area, and Jake had required each member of his team to memorize the entire complex, not just their individual targets, in case the plan went awry.

Besides the fractional distillation plant, they had targeted the refinery's control room, the blending plants, storage tanks, and the loading site for the tanker trucks. In its entirety, the plan of attack would probably render the refinery useless for quite a long time. All they had to do was place the plastic explosives, set the detonators, then get out fast.

As they got closer to their intended target, Jake held up a clenched fist and knelt down. Linda and John knelt down beside him. The area ahead was well lit.

"They'll probably have cameras covering all the approaches," Jake said. "If we're challenged, try to avoid contact. Avoid shooting unless it's absolutely necessary. Remember, we can throw our diversionary explosives if we have to." He patted the small square of plastic explosive which clung to the front of his backpack's shoulder strap. It was a special package, with a detonator which had a six second delay. Everybody was carrying one, but they were only to be used in case they ran into security forces.

"I'm not going to let them stop me," John Haney said.

"No," Linda agreed. "We're going to blow this place or die trying."

Inside the office complex at Six Star, two security guards sat in front of a panel of twenty-four closed circuit television monitors, carefully watching for movement on any screen. When Jake cut the hole in the fence, an alarm had sounded within the security center, alerting the guards that somebody had penetrated the refinery. In spite of what the Defenders of the Planet had hoped for, these two security guards were all business, not caring in the least that this was supposed to be a night of revelry. After a few minutes, one of the monitors came to life and three figures dressed in dark clothes and obviously carrying rifles were seen moving through the refinery.

"We've got trouble," said one of the security men. His name was Jack Sawyer, a young man of thirty-three, and he had spent ten years in the LAPD before coming to this job, which paid him twice as much as he had earned working for the city of Los Angeles.

"Looks like we've got big trouble," agreed the man sitting next to him. Tom Hess, also a former LAPD officer, pointed to a different monitor. "There's another group, and they've got weapons, too!"

Sawyer nodded to still another screen. "There's more of them! Christ! It's a damned army!" He picked up a telephone and dialed 911.

"You have reached the 911 Operator," a recorded female voice said. "All lines are temporarily busy. Please stay on the line and your call will be handled..." In disgust, Sawyer hung up the phone.

"The 911 lines are busy," he told Hess. "I should have known."

"New Year's Eve," Hess grunted. As former policemen, they both knew that for the emergency services, this night was traditionally the busiest of the year, with more traffic accidents and more fatalities than on any other night.

"We'd better not take any chances," Sawyer said. "We'd better declare an emergency," and with that he dialed a special direct line to the nearest Los Angeles central dispatch station.

"LAPD," a female voice answered. "What is the nature of your emergency?" Her computer screen told her that it was Six Star calling on a special emergency line.

"I'm Jack Sawyer, head of security here. I want to report a large group of armed intruders who have just entered the refinery. They are in a restricted area and they shouldn't be here. They look like terrorists. They could be the Defenders of the Planet."

"What kind of weapons do they have?" she asked.

"They're definitely carrying assault rifles. God knows what else they've got."

"How many are there?"

"We've counted nine of them so far, but this is a big refinery. There are probably more of them," Sawyer said.

"Okay," she said. "I'm rolling units now to your front gate. They'll be there in a few minutes."

"Send your SWAT team," Sawyer urged.

"Only my supervisor can request SWAT," she said. "I'll notify him of the situation and we'll get back to you. As of now, I am declaring an emergency."

Sawyer then called Pete Morris, the guard on duty at the front gate, notifying him that LAPD units would be entering the refinery.

"What's going on?" Morris asked.

"We've got armed intruders inside the plant. They came in through the fence at sector nineteen."

"You've got to be kidding," Morris said.

"No, this is on the level," Sawyer said seriously. "There are at least nine of them, maybe more. Stay alert. It looks like they're carrying automatic weapons. I'm sending our alert team to sweep from the control room toward you."

"Roger," Morris said, his heart suddenly beating fast. He put down the phone and immediately turned off the light inside his booth, to make sure he wasn't an easy target for a sniper. Then he put on his armored vest, grabbed a shotgun hanging against a wall, and chambered a shell. Taking the shotgun in both hands, he crouched near a window and began scanning the interior of the refinery, looking for any movement.

Within the security complex, Sawyer set off an alarm to wake up his alert response team, two security men who were sound asleep in an adjacent room. Both of them quickly came running out, boots, bulletproof vests, and weapons in hand.

"What's up?" Jay Reynolds asked, a look of concern on his face. His partner, Ronald Shokowski, wore a similar expression. Both were like Sawyer and Hess — young, intelligent and with excellent records as former police officers.

Not immediately answering, Sawyer pointed to a TV monitor. Reynolds and Shokowski came around the console to get a better look, and they both spotted the black figures moving on four different monitors.

"Damn!" Reynolds exclaimed. "I bet it's the Defenders of the Planet. How many of them do you count?" He immediately dropped to the floor and began pulling on his boots. "Did you call the police?" he asked, not waiting to hear the answer to his first question.

"Yes, the police are on the way... and there are twelve of them." Sawyer carefully watched all the monitors. "Wait! There's three more. Fifteen, so far."

"Have you notified Holmgren?" Reynolds asked.

"No," Sawyer responded. "Been too busy, but I will now." He dialed Six Star's main control room and told the refinery's night operations manager, Jim Holmgren, that the oil refinery was under terrorist attack.

"Is this your idea of a joke?" Holmgren asked seriously. "Because if it is, it's not very funny."

"No joke, sir," Sawyer said. "This is on the level. I've already called the police. I've requested the SWAT team. We'll send the first police units to the control room, to make sure it's safe, but I strongly advise that you close the refinery down."

Holmgren swore violently, then said. "This is incredible. I don't want to do this, and it's a damn shame, but I'm going to start shutting down now." He swore again, a long string of harsh expletives. "Sawyer, you'd better get them. Kill those bastards!"

"Roger, sir," Sawyer said. "I'll keep you apprised of the situation."

When Reynolds and Shokowski were fully dressed, Sawyer pointed toward the exit. "I want you to sweep to the front gate," Sawyer ordered. "Clear a route for the police from the gate back to here."

"Okay, boss," Reynolds smiled, his adrenaline beginning to flow. He and Shokowski trotted toward the exit. Both men carried nine millimeter handguns and heavy caliber assault rifles capable of fully automatic fire.

"And be careful!" Sawyer shouted after them.

When they got to the outer door of the office complex, Reynolds pulled out his two-way radio. "We're at the exit. Is the door outside clear?" Reynolds asked.

"You're clear," Sawyer answered, as he looked at the monitor which covered the area just outside the offices.

Reynolds put the radio back into its pouch and nodded at Shokowski. They burst through the door and began a fast, crouched run down the main road toward the front gate. After going only fifty meters, they spotted movement to their left, and they both rolled into the ground, coming to a stop in a prone position, weapons at the ready.

Both of them scanned the area but the intruders had disappeared into the shadows. Reynolds strained to detect any sign of the terrorists.

"You see anything?" he whispered to Shokowski.

"No, nothing," Shokowski replied.

Suddenly, there was a deafening explosion twenty meters to their front. The concussion was so great it knocked Shokowski momentarily unconscious and broke Reynold's left eardrum. Stunned and deaf, Reynolds instinctively fired his weapon on full automatic into the dark toward his attackers. Then he rolled to his right, loaded another magazine and fired again. In response, three assault rifles opened up on him, the rounds striking perilously close to the ground on either side of him. He shouted to his partner.

"Shokowski! Shokowski! Are you okay? Shokowski!" Dazed, Reynolds was quite surprised that although he was shouting, he couldn't hear his own voice. He felt the blood dripping from his ear, but his adrenaline was pumping so hard he couldn't feel any pain. He rolled toward his left and came within reach of Shokowski, grabbing his chest and shaking him violently.

At this, Shokowski came to, and both men got to their knees, then retreated from their attackers. Reynolds pulled out his radio. "We're under fire!" he shouted. "They've got explosives. We need assistance out here!"

Inside, Sawyer had heard the explosion and the staccato bursts of gunfire over one of his monitors and quickly redialed central dispatch.

"This is Sawyer again," he shouted hoarsely into the phone. "Our security officers are under attack. There are explosions within the refinery."

"Okay, stay calm," the female officer responded. "I have notified my supervisor of your emergency and he has authorized SWAT. They have been called and they are on the way. And our first black-and-whites should be arriving at your location any second now. Stay cool, gentlemen. The cavalry is on the way."

"Outstanding," Sawyer said, putting down the phone. "Watch the desk," he told Hess. "I'm going out to help Reynolds and Shokowski."

Jake, Linda, and John reached the fractional distillation plant just as the fighting started within the refinery. The gunfire seemed far away, yet also strangely close, and the sound of it suddenly struck home to Jake. The gunshots were powerful and deadly. Nearby, he realized, people were trying to kill each other.

"We've been made!" he told Linda and John, as they knelt next to him. He looked at his watch. It was only eleven fifteen.

"This isn't good," Jake said. "It's still too early."

"Better switch to our Delta plan," Linda advised.

"I know," Jake agreed. "We don't have any choice." He pulled out his radio and spoke into it. "This is Lobo, switch to plan Delta. I repeat, switch to Delta!"

The Delta plan called for hitting targets of choice by using detonator settings of just seconds or minutes, depending on the target. It was a plan of last resort, for the team members would have to escape from the refinery through a raging inferno caused by their own explosives.

"Come on!" Jake said, looking up at the distillation plant. "Let's get up there and set our explosives, and then get the hell out of here." He ran over to a nearby ladderwell and looked up, hesitating.

"What's wrong?" Linda asked.

"Our rifles don't have slings," he said. "We can't carry them and climb at the same time." He swore, angry with himself for his lack of foresight. He set his rifle down. "Leave them here," he said. "They'll just be in the way." And with that, he started climbing, Linda and John right behind him. After going straight up thirty feet, the ladderwell opened up onto a platform and series of stairs. All around them was a maze of pipes and towers, stairs and platforms going in all directions. It would be easy to get lost up here.

"I can't see which is the bubble tower," said John Haney.

"Damn, neither can I," Jake said. "Let's just go for broke. Place your explosives on anything that looks good."

"What setting?" Linda asked.

"Ten minutes on the first ones, down to six minutes." Jake said. "Meet back here in five minutes. That won't give us much time, so we'll have to work fast. Spread out and let's go."

The three of them scurried off in different directions and they began pulling plastic explosive bundles out of their backpacks and placing them against key points on the distillation plant. Each bundle weighed ten pounds and was the equivalent of thirty sticks of dynamite, capable of causing a tremendous blast.

Jake set two of the explosive devices and moved onto a higher platform, then found another ladderwell that went up sixty feet. He climbed up as fast as he could and came out onto another platform that led to a large cylindrical tower. He paused to catch his breath, studying the silhouette of the tower. From this high vantage point, he could clearly see that it was the largest tower from among all the others. That has to be it! he decided.

Suddenly, there was a deep, booming explosion far off in the distance. Jake wheeled around just as a huge flash of light engulfed the entire horizon. Amazed by the scene, he watched as a large storage tank rose nearly a hundred feet straight up into the air. It looked like a rocket, trailing a tail of fire and smoke. The sight of it was the strangest, most spectacular sight Jake had ever seen in his life. The tank fell back to the ground, creating a secondary explosion and a huge fireball. Even at this distance, he could hear the roar of the fire.

In quick succession, four more storage tanks exploded. None of them rose high into the air like the first had, but one blew sideways into yet another tank, causing it to also explode in flames. Within seconds, an eerie, bright glow filled the night sky.

He walked forward on the platform, taking off his backpack and reaching inside it for an explosive bundle. It would only take one to blow the tower, and he wanted to place it as high as he could. The platform around the bubble tower gave way to a series of catwalks. Jake climbed out onto the catwalk and gingerly walked around to the far side of the tower, placing the bundle of plastic explosive right next to the side of the tower, setting the electronic detonator to explode in six minutes. Then he climbed down, running back on the platform to the sixty-foot ladderwell, placing his last two bundles of explosives and eventually finding his way back to the lower ladderwell.

Linda was there waiting for him. She handed him his rifle. In the half light, Jake could see that she was smiling.

"Did you see that storage tank?" she asked, her eyes wide.

"Sure did!" Jake said. "I felt like cheering, except I knew better."

"Me, too," she said. "Did you place all your explosives?"

"Yeah!" he said excitedly. "And I found the bubble tower, too. When that sucker blows we'd better be far away!" He stopped talking and quickly looked all around. "Where's John?" he asked.

"I don't know," she said, looking at her watch. "But he'd better get his butt down here. My first explosive will go off in about three minutes."

"John!" Jake yelled as loud as he could. "John!"

"Up here," he yelled from high above. A full minute later, they finally saw him coming down the ladderwell. When he reached the bottom, Jake patted him on the shoulder and handed him his rifle.

"Nice going. Now let's get the hell out of here. This place is about to blow sky high!"

The three of them began running at full speed through the refinery. After a minute, they heard gunshots echoing far off in the distance. Then there were more gunshots, this time from automatic weapons that fired in rapid bursts. These were followed by explosions and return gunfire. Shortly, they heard more gunfire from a totally different direction.

Linda yelled over to Jake. "Maybe we should go help."

"No way!" Jake said. "Each team is on its own. Those are the orders! Besides, the Delta Plan is in effect. No telling what is going to be blown up next."

Just then, there was a loud explosion very close by, followed by a dozen more, and a gigantic fireball began to engulf the area just ahead of them. The fireball rose nearly two hundred feet into the air and began to plume sideways. They stopped dead in their tracks, realizing their path was blocked.

"This way!" Jake pointed.

"No!" shouted Linda. "This way!" Without hesitation, she began running in the opposite direction from that which Jake wanted to go. John began to follow her.

Jake watched them take off, hesitating for just a second. Then he shrugged. "What the hell?" he said, and began sprinting after them. He let out a loud warhoop as he caught up to them. He felt like a kid again. In response, John Haney let out his own warhoop.

Suddenly, there were three deafening explosions behind them, and they stopped and turned to watch, knowing it was the fractional distillation plant. Three separate fireballs rose into the night sky. There was a fourth explosion, and another fireball began to rise up. In the next several minutes, there was a series of blasts. All of them were devastating. Transfixed by the scene, Jake froze in place, astonished at the destruction he had caused.

"There she goes!" John shouted over the roar.

"We got it!" Jake yelled. They began slapping each other on the back, and Linda hugged both of them. Then a tremendous explosion shook the entire refinery, throwing the three of them violently to the ground. Pieces of metal and shrapnel began to rain down all around them, many of them red hot and trailing smoke. There were several secondary explosions, and the ground rolled as if an earthquake had struck. A blast of heat surged against their bodies and the entire area around them erupted in flames.

Jake got to his feet and he pulled Linda up. "We've got to get out of here!" he shouted. Linda and John, their faces filled with fear, needed no further urging. They sprinted as fast as they could away from the distillation plant. Suddenly, something exploded right in front of them, and a tube of fire shot out at them, as if being directed by a giant flamethrower. Jake and Linda threw themselves to the ground, but John didn't react quickly enough. Although the tube of fire only lasted for a few seconds, it hit him directly in the face and chest and, as he tried to turn away, his whole body caught fire. In panic, he began to run.

"Hit the ground and roll! John! Hit the ground!" Jake shouted futilely. His body on fire, Haney continued to run. Jake got to his feet to go after him, but it was too late. From beneath a group of large pipes, a lake of liquid fire began to spread across the ground and John, totally blind, ran right into it. He sank to his knees and uttered an ear-piercing scream, then fell to the ground, disappearing beneath the flames.

Linda screamed, knowing John was dead, but there was nothing they could do for him now. Jake grabbed her shoulder and hauled her to her feet. He looked closely into her face and saw that the fire had singed her eyebrows off. His own face had a stinging sensation all around it, and he realized that he too had been burned.

"Come on! Let's go!" he shouted at her, but she was in shock, unwilling to move. He looked back, seeing that the lake of fire was coming close. Taking her by the arm, he led her away from the fire, just as more explosions shook the area around them.

There was only one way out, one area where the fire had not yet reached, and he moved in that direction. Linda pulled away from his arm and began running on her own.

"I'm all right!" she shouted angrily.

"Okay, then! Keep moving!" Jake shouted back. "Don't stop!"

They ran and ran, weaving through obstacles, jumping over pipelines, climbing walls and eventually reaching the outer perimeter of the refinery, close to the place where they had entered. Behind them, the refinery was exploding and burning.

Jake and Linda realized that they had accomplished their mission. They had destroyed the Six Star refinery, though at great cost. There was no telling how many others besides John had been killed. The question nagged at Jake as he and Linda escaped from the inferno they had created. The acrid smell of burning oil and gasoline was everywhere.

When they got close to the perimeter fence, Jake saw that all the security lights were out and he realized that the refinery must have lost its electrical power. It didn't matter, though, because the whole area was lit by flames shooting hundreds of feet into the night sky.

They walked slowly and carefully through the smoke and the fog. Jake felt like he was in a war zone, and his survival instincts were in full control. Suddenly, he stopped and grabbed Linda.

"Get down!" he whispered, throwing himself to the ground.

Linda plopped down beside him. "What is it?" she asked in a low voice. "I don't see anything."

"There's somebody out there," Jake responded. "I know there is. Start crawling," he said to her. "And keep your head down." He began crawling toward the chainlink fence, his body hugging the ground. Linda was right next to him, also crawling low. Seconds later, they heard two near-simultaneous shots and heard the bullets whiz right over their heads.

"Keep down," Jake urged Linda. "They've spotted us."

"Did you see where it came from?" she whispered.

"The other side of the fence. They must be patrolling, looking for us." Jake looked around, searching for a way out. To his right, he saw nothing that would be of help, but to his left, there was a slight depression in the ground.

"Over there," he pointed. "Follow me."

The two snipers who had fired the shots were from the L.A.P.D.'s 12th SWAT Team. They were sitting on a low knoll seventy meters on the other side of the chainlink fence, close to the sector where the Defenders of the Planet had first penetrated the refinery. Their commander had placed them here to kill any terrorist stragglers.

Both of them were armed with nine millimeter automatic pistols and long-barrel seven point six two millimeter sniper rifles with infrared scopes. The knoll gave them enough height to look down over the fence.

"I can't see a damned thing," said Billy Ray Travis, as he peered through the infrared sniperscope from a prone position. "We must have missed them. The heat from the fires is throwing my scope off," he complained.

His partner, who was lying right beside him, Nick Warnick, was having no better luck. He had seen the two figures out in the open for just a few seconds, but he had lost them in the smoke. A moment later he noticed movement on the ground, and Travis saw it at the same time. Both had fired, but whoever they had seen had vanished. Several minutes went by, and they saw nothing else out there.

"Maybe we should shift our position," Warnick suggested.

"No way," Billy Ray said. "The captain said to dig in here, and this is where we stay." As a sergeant, he outranked Warnick, and so they remained in their spot.

In the distance, the roar of the burning refinery, punctuated by gunshots and explosions and the shrill sirens of responding fire trucks drowned out any nearby sounds, and so the two SWAT police didn't hear Jake and Linda come up from behind.

"Don't move," Jake said in a loud voice. "You're covered."

"Drop your weapons," Linda ordered, "and put your hands up in the air!"

Travis and Warnick froze, not responding to Linda's commands. The two policemen lay there for just a split second, both of them prepared to whirl around and fire. Suddenly, two gunshots rang out and the bullets struck between them, kicking up the earth next to their heads.

"I said drop them!" Linda shouted.

At this, they let go of their rifles and raised their hands.

"Watch them!" Jake commanded, and he stepped forward and took away their automatic pistols. He patted them down, and found they were also both carrying .38 snubnose revolvers in boot holsters. He pulled out the .38s and tossed them aside.

"Are there any more of you out here?" he asked in a low growl, but he got no answer. He waited for a few seconds, then stepped forward and forcefully stuck the tip of his rifle barrel deeply into the crack of Billy Ray's butt.

"I said, are there any more of you out here?" he repeated. "You better tell me or I'll blow your balls clean off!"

"No!" Travis said excitedly. "We're the only ones! I swear it!"

"Good," Jake said. "Now, get up and take your clothes off. And don't turn around and look at us. If you look at us, we'll be forced to kill you. Do you understand?"

Both officers nodded, then got up and began to undress, removing their armored vests first. Soon they were both buck naked.

"Now, go straight ahead and climb over that chainlink fence in front of us. Walk directly toward the refinery and don't even think about coming back here, 'cause we'll be waiting for you. You got it?" Without waiting for an answer, he prodded them in the lower back with his rifle barrel, forcing them down the knoll.

Travis and Warnick walked to the fence and quickly climbed over, then started walking toward the burning refinery. Warnick, the younger of the two, began to tremble, convinced he was about to be shot in the back. After going twenty meters, the two SWAT team members broke into a full sprint, hoping they could outrun the bullets they were sure were about to be fired.

"There go two of LA's finest," Linda said quietly, lowering her weapon.

"Yeah," Jake agreed. "We really scared the piss out of them, huh?" He laughed softly. "They probably thought we were going to shoot them in the back!"

"Probably," Linda said. She sighed deeply, a scowl upon her face. "There's been enough death for one night. I hope nobody else dies."

"Me too," Jake nodded. He sat down amid the clothes discarded by Travis and Warnick. "Let's wait here for a while," he said, "To see how many of our team get away. And we can keep this area secured in case there are any more snipers."

Linda sat beside him, taking off her backpack. Both of them were dead tired, and she pulled out a water bottle and a couple of candy bars, handing one to Jake. He took it, unwrapped it, and began to chew.

On the horizon before them, the Six Star refinery was burning furiously. They were more than a half mile from its center, yet they could feel the heat and smell the burning oil and gasoline. Occasionally, a fireball erupted upward, sending plumes of yellow and blue flames and sparks arcing out across the sky. For Jake and Linda, silently watching the scene beyond, it was the most dazzling display of fireworks they had ever seen.

THIRTEEN

The next morning, a stony-faced President sat in the Oval Office, copies of the big two Washington papers laying on his desk. "THE DEFENDERS OF THE PLANET STRIKE!" read one headline. "OIL REFINERIES ATTACKED!" read the other.

The articles went on to say that the Defenders of the Planet had struck in six cities on New Year's Eve: Los Angeles, New Orleans, Baton Rouge, Philadelphia, Baytown, and Galveston. Five oil refineries had been destroyed, eleven others seriously damaged. Gasoline production in Los Angeles had been severely crippled, and rationing would have to be implemented immediately. New Orleans, Baton Rouge and Philadelphia had fared only slightly better, while gasoline production in Texas was expected to be only thirty percent below normal.

Casualties were numerous: five police officers were dead, nine firemen had been killed trying to fight the fires, and seventeen refinery employees had died in the infernos. Several hundred emergency service personnel had been injured, some of them wounded by gunfire. Eleven of the terrorists had been killed, and seven had been captured.

A related article on the front pages concerned a communique from the Defenders of the Planet sent directly to a dozen major newspapers in America. It demanded that the government start telling the people the truth about the weather. The communique also demanded that the burning of fossil fuels must be stopped immediately.

The President had spent the past hour discussing his options with Malcolm Teale, James Sisk, and Jack Roper. They had all agreed that the events of New Year's Eve amounted to sedition. They were angry, and determined to exact revenge. They felt as if war had been declared.

Thirty minutes into their conversation, the President summoned Chester Kelton, the Director of the FBI, to the Oval Office. The FBI was the one government organization which could quickly strike back at the Defenders, and President Rawlings hoped that the FBI's top man would have some answers for him. When the Director arrived, he exchanged solemn formalities with everyone present. Kelton was an imposing man, standing six feet six, weighing two hundred forty-five pounds. He had a prominent chin and jaw line, was well groomed, and carried himself with an air of total self-confidence.

The President offered Kelton coffee and then they all sat down.

"Any leads yet?" asked President Rawlings.

"Mr. President, as you know," began Kelton, "we captured some of their people last night, and we are interrogating them. I've sent special agents to each city involved. According to the last reports I've received, none of the terrorists are talking. They appear to be extremely disciplined. They won't even identify themselves. We're running fingerprint checks on all of them, including the dead."

"I see," said the President. "Chet, how in the hell did they do it? This situation is... devastating."

"Plastic explosives," Kelton answered. "Large amounts of the stuff were involved. We believe it was purchased from Bulgarian agents and smuggled into the country through New York five months ago. We knew about it, and I assigned a special group to track it, but it was an impossible job. If you recall, all intelligence agencies were alerted back in August."

"Yes," James Sisk said. "I do remember. The alert was based on information provided by a European informant for the CIA."

"That's right," Kelton nodded. "That informant was found a few days later with his throat slashed. We knew we had a solid lead, but whoever was selling the stuff covered their tracks very well. They were undoubtedly professionals. In Europe, the CIA had every station working on the case, but they all came up empty. Now we know where that plastic explosive went and what it was going to be used for."

The President glared in the direction of James Sisk, his National Security Advisor. "This is embarrassing," Rawlings stated. "These Defenders of the Planet have outwitted our best intelligence agencies! How in the hell could they have gotten away with it?"

"They're good, Mr. President," Kelton answered. "They're very good. What they did last night proves it."

"What about the Bureau's overall involvement in this case?" Rawlings asked. "Can you bring me up to date?"

Kelton nodded. "As of today," he answered, "we've got over five hundred agents working on it. I can assure you, Mr. President, the FBI will get these little piss-ants. It's just a matter of time."

The President frowned. He wasn't in the mood for such a pat answer. "Chet," he said seriously, "we don't have much time. Because of this weather situation, the Navy has begun Operation Safeharbor. During this operation, we must have law and order within our borders. We have to set an example for the rest of the world.

"If the Navy experts are right, it will only be a matter of time before the oceans start to noticeably rise. Once that happens, there may be panic here in the United States. Any day now, I'm going to have to come clean with the American people and tell them what we're doing. I'm going to have to tell them about the problem in Antarctica.

"Meanwhile, we have to keep the situation under control. These goddamned environmental terrorists running around is only going to complicate the situation. I can't emphasize enough how critical this is." The President was visibly upset, and he rose from his desk, pacing about the Oval Office.

"Now, despite the circumstances concerning this weather, we cannot have anarchy in the United States. I simply cannot allow that to happen. I don't care what you have to do, Chet. Take shortcuts! Bend the rules if you have to. I want these people under lock and key. You need to find out who is responsible for these acts of terrorism." President Rawlings sat back down, glancing briefly toward Malcolm Teale, his Chief of Staff. Teale took the cue and looked over at Kelton.

"Chet, what about penetrating their organization?" Teale asked. "Have you had any luck there?"

"Quite candidly, Malcolm, the answer is no. We have ninety special agents in twenty-two different cities, all undercover, all using aliases and pretending to be fervent environmentalists. But the Defenders of the Planet are very careful about whom they recruit. It appears they are getting advice from experts about this."

"What do you mean?" asked James Sisk, the President's National Security Advisor.

"Now, Jim, you know damn well what I mean!" Kelton said, obviously piqued by Sisk's question. "I have written at least four different memos to your people about this situation. Where the hell have you been for the last two years?"

"Now, Chet," soothed Jack Roper. "Let's not get upset."

"I'm sorry! But I've been sending up warning flags about the danger of this organization for a long time. Now they've done something really serious and I'm being held accountable. I asked for special funds, and I was turned down. I repeatedly asked for NSA's experts and computers to try to find and decode any computer encrypted messages, and I've been denied access."

"And with good reason," replied Sisk. "We couldn't have the FBI and NSA doing such widespread spying on our citizens. It simply wouldn't look good."

"Obviously, Chet," said Malcolm Teale, "the situation has changed. Now we're willing to take more extreme action."

"Well," Kelton stated, "you can be assured we're doing all we can, but the Defenders of the Planet are sophisticated in their methods of operation. As I was saying, we think they are getting expert advice, possibly from former intelligence agents."

"Are you sure about that?" asked Teale.

Kelton nodded. "It's the only plausible reason why we can't penetrate them."

"Maybe," suggested Jack Roper, "they've penetrated you. Have you thought of that?"

"Of course we've thought of that," snapped Kelton, his voice full of asperity, his face turning red. "We're working on that possibility also."

"What about Jonathan Holmes?" Sisk asked. "Could he have engineered this whole thing? Is he responsible for this?"

"We have him under constant surveillance," Kelton replied. "The hotel room where he is staying is completely wired. I don't think he was directly involved in the refinery attacks. For the forty-eight hours prior to last night, nothing unusual was reported concerning his activities."

"What has he been doing since his release from jail?" asked Sisk.

"He hasn't been doing anything, really. After he made bail, he's been staying within the county border, just like the court ordered."

At this, Sisk looked perturbed. "The man is some kind of guru to the environmentalists. They look up to him, like the man can walk on water or something. I quite frankly don't understand it. In the current situation, Holmes is nothing but a menace. Is there any way we can get him back in jail?" asked Sisk.

"I don't think so. The case is being closely monitored in the Phoenix press. The prosecutor cooperated with us and asked for no bail, but a federal judge saw things differently. The man is very popular. Besides, I have to admit, we have very little evidence against him. The judge is no dummy."

"We need to keep him quiet," Sisk said flatly. "His ideas are dangerous. I don't think it's any coincidence that he gave a speech calling for attacks on oil refineries, and then a week later, we have attacks on sixteen oil refineries. Sixteen!" Sisk said, obviously irritated.

"We've exhausted all legal means. Short of killing him, I don't know what else we can do," replied Kelton.

"That would only make a martyr out of him," Sisk stated. There was a moment of silence as they all reflected on this possibility.

"Let's get back to the Defenders of the Planet," Rawlings said. "What about their organization? What do you have so far?" he asked.

"Well," Kelton said, "we know it's a national organization. They appear to be operating in individual cells with a strict top-to-bottom chain of command. The people at the bottom do not have any clue who the main people in the organization are. We know they are using computers to send their communications back and forth. We believe these communications are coded.

"This kind of operation is very difficult to penetrate. To make matters worse, they have a lot of support out there. Because of this weather situation, the environmentalists are gaining a great deal of sympathy. As of now, the quickest answer in terms of getting to the heart of this organization is probably going to be with the ones we captured last night."

"Can you make them talk?" asked Jack Roper.

Kelton thought for a moment. Then he said, "If we are allowed to use special procedures, you're damned right we can make them talk. The question is, are we willing to totally suspend all their civil liberties and take extreme measures?" Kelton made sure to emphasize the word *extreme*.

The President got up again, walking over to the windows and gazing outward. Only he could authorize this. As they all waited for his answer, the silence in the Oval Office became pronounced.

"During the Civil War, President Lincoln had to suspend certain civil liberties," the President finally said, turning to face them with a somber expression. "We all agree that this is an extraordinary situation, like a war. Unfortunately, we must resort to extraordinary measures." The President shot a penetrating glance at Kelton. "Do whatever you feel is necessary, Chet. We have to find out who's leading this organization, because whoever he is, he's a very dangerous man. These people have to be stopped."

"May I get that in writing?" asked Kelton.

The President, as well as the others, realized Kelton was only trying to cover himself. It was a natural request. Again, the President glanced toward Malcolm Teale.

"Chet," Teale explained. "We feel that this conversation is highly sensitive. We cannot put anything in writing. This is a tenuous situation. Right now, we face a national crisis, but if the weather suddenly goes back to normal, people may wonder why we ever resorted to such extreme actions. You see the dilemma we have?"

Kelton nodded, realizing the President and his advisors had already decided upon a course of action. His presence was just a formality. Nothing had been said over a phone, nothing was going to be put into writing. And now they were asking him to come up with some answers, any way he could.

Kelton rose from his chair. "Mr. President, I'll do whatever it takes. You'll have the full cooperation of the FBI."

The President came forward and shook his hand. "Chet, I'm sorry it has to be this way, but we can't let this country be torn apart."

"Don't worry, Mr. President. We'll get these bastards."

FOURTEEN

On New Year's Day, Jonathan Holmes and Jamie were having breakfast in the coffeeshop of the Phoenix Hilton when suddenly a newspaper was tossed onto their table. It was the morning edition of the *Arizona Daily Times.*

"Have you seen this?" a male voice asked.

Holmes looked up to see Mike Allen standing next to the table. Allen was the *Times* reporter who had taken a keen interest in his case. He had called Holmes several times for an interview, but since Martin Sherman had advised him not to talk to anyone about his upcoming hearing, especially members of the press, Holmes had been putting him off. This tactic had only made Allen more persistent.

Jamie picked up the paper that had been tossed down and read the headlines aloud: "AMERICAN OIL REFINERIES ATTACKED BY TERRORISTS." She scowled at Allen. "You don't think my father had anything to do with this, do you?"

"You tell me," Allen responded. "Is your father a member of the Defenders of the Planet?"

"You had better sit down, Mr. Allen," Holmes said.

As he did so, a waitress came over and poured the reporter a cup of coffee. "Would you like to order?" she asked.

"No, thank you," Allen replied. "Coffee will do."

She nodded curtly and walked away. Allen waited until she was out of earshot, then leaned over and spoke in a low voice to Holmes. "In your speech at ASU, you called for attacks upon the oil industry. And now we've got this!" Allen nodded toward the newspaper. "There are rumors that you are somehow connected to these environmental radicals. Are you their leader?"

Holmes looked at him evenly. "No," he said. "I am not their leader. I have nothing to do with the Defenders of the Planet."

He picked up the newspaper and quickly read the first several hundred words, then he dropped the paper back onto the table.

"Any comment?" Allen asked.

"This is amazing," Holmes said, shaking his head in bemusement.

"What do mean?" Allen asked.

"Just this. These people who attacked the oil refineries have a great deal of courage," he said. "I can't imagine going into a dangerous place like an oil refinery in the dead of night with the intention of blowing it up. They must have done it because they fervently believe in their cause."

"So you think it was a courageous act?" Allen appeared skeptical, and his expression said so.

"Yes, very courageous." Holmes replied.

"And you had nothing to do with it?"

"I was here in Phoenix last night, at a dinner party at the home of Bill and Maggie Roosevelt. In fact, I'm leaving this hotel thanks to them. They've invited us to stay at their home. You can ask them. They will tell you where we were last night. Both Jamie and I were there until nearly one in the morning."

"That's right," Jamie said. "It was a good dinner party and lots of people saw us there! You're barking up the wrong tree."

Allen nodded and said, "Look, I know you weren't directly involved in these attacks. I happen to know you were in Phoenix last night. I've already done some checking. But you've got to admit, it's a strange coincidence. Some people are beginning to think you give the orders to these people."

Hearing this, Holmes couldn't help but chuckle. Then his face grew serious. "I'm sorry people got killed or hurt last night," he said. "A lot more will get hurt if global warming is beginning, and I believe that it is. People must stop burning fossil fuels! Therefore, I believe the attack on the refineries was the correct course of action."

"Can I quote you on that?" Allen asked.

Holmes thought for a moment, then decided to ignore Sherman's advice. This newspaperman was giving him a voice to the world, and Holmes decided to take advantage of it. "You're damned right you can quote me," he said. "I want the whole world to know how I feel, and what I believe. The world is in crisis, Mr. Allen, and..."

"Then you won't mind if I record this, just to make sure I get it right. Hold on." Allen pulled a small tape recorder out of his suit jacket and set it on the table facing toward Holmes. As he switched on the record button, he said, "Go on... you were saying the world is in crisis."

"Mr. Allen, people are living in some kind of fantasy world. With the carbon dioxide levels rising as they are, there can be no escape from the inevitable. Why do you think the planet is warming up the way it is? People have to realize that this is a life and death matter. The criminals aren't the ones who blew up the oil refineries. Indeed, it should be a criminal act to allow the refining of oil into gasoline."

"Dr. Holmes, will the attacks on the oil refineries help the global warming crisis?"

"Yes, of course they will," Holmes answered. "The less carbon dioxide that goes up into the atmosphere, the better the chance that the atmosphere will stabilize itself."

"Then you agree with the methods of the Defenders of the Planet? Do you believe in violence?"

Holmes stared at the newspaperman. "Listen, I've never espoused the use of violence to achieve an objective. But this is a very special moment in the history of the world. Our climate is on the brink of rapid change. Once it goes over the edge, there will be no turning back. It will take many years for the atmosphere to cleanse itself, and by then we'll all be dead. So I ask you, which is the lesser crime? To try to stop the global warming, or to let it happen?"

"But some people think that global warming is a myth, that it's not really going to happen. What do you say to them?"

"This heat wave we've been having is not normal. I'm sure it marks the beginning of drastic climactic changes. As I said in my speech, the temperatures in the Southern Hemisphere have reached all-time record highs. We cannot ignore the evidence."

"But here in America the heat wave is over. Today, Phoenix is only going to be about seventy-six degrees, and it's going to get cooler over the next week. It snowed in Montana and North Dakota last night and today, and the storm is expected to move into the Midwest tomorrow. In other words, it's getting back to normal around here."

"It's not getting back to normal," Holmes insisted. "This cooling trend was to be expected in the Northern Hemisphere. After all, everything is relative. It should have snowed in Montana several months ago. How can you explain the delay?"

"A temporary heat wave," Allen offered. "Now it's over."

"No," Holmes said. "It's not over. I predict the winter here will be much shorter than normal. In March, April at the latest, it will start getting very hot again. This summer will be the hottest ever in the Northern Hemisphere. And again, you're ignoring what is happening in the Southern Hemisphere. I called my friends in Australia yesterday. The temperatures in the interior deserts are approaching one hundred and fifty degrees. Sydney was one hundred and twenty-four degrees."

"That's pretty far removed from what's happening here in the United States, Dr. Holmes. Wouldn't you agree?"

"No, I wouldn't, Mr. Allen. In reality, we all live on a very small planet. It's hot down under. It's rare for Sydney, which is on the coast, to see temperatures over one hundred degrees. The thing I'm most concerned about is the ice cap on the Antarctic continent, which isn't that far away from the Australian coast. If it melts, which I believe it is doing, you Americans will find out just how small the world really is."

"Do you have any evidence that it is melting?" Allen asked.

"I'm doing some checking. But I have no firm evidence. It's difficult to work when you are living out of a strange hotel room in a strange city. But, you see, everything is relative. If it's one hundred and twenty-four degrees on the coast of Australia, it's probably in the seventies or eighties in Antarctica, warm enough to cause the ice to melt rapidly."

"What would that mean?"

"Simply this. Every coastal city in the world will be inundated by the oceans. It will be a worldwide catastrophe. And that might only be the beginning. If the mean global temperature hits one hundred and thirty degrees, all life on the planet will die."

"Okay, Dr. Holmes. If your theory about global warming is correct, what started it? Why is it so hot in the Southern Hemisphere right now?"

"Several things started it, I'm afraid. Man has continued to burn fossil fuels over the years, in spite of evidence that atmospheric carbon dioxide levels are increasing. At the same time, the world's rain forests have almost disappeared. In the past, large trees absorbed carbon dioxide and helped mitigate the effect of global warming. But the world is losing its large trees. Most of them have been destroyed.

"As of last year, more than seventy percent of the Amazon has been burned to make way for cattle ranches. In Indonesia and New Guinea, one hundred percent of the forests have been cut down. They're completely gone. Here in the United States, most of your forests have been cut down to provide logs for the timber and paper industries, and the young trees planted to replace them haven't matured yet. And they won't mature for another thirty to seventy years, depending. It's been proven that young trees are not capable of absorbing much carbon dioxide. Since you've logged most of your old growth forests, you Americans have done more than your share in contributing to global warming. In the northeast part of America and Ontario and Quebec, the hardwood trees and pines have suffered severe damage due to acid rain. Many of these forests are in the process of dying. They are very sick trees, and there's simply no way of knowing precisely how little carbon dioxide they are absorbing due to their weak condition.

"Finally, the oceans have lost much of their ability to produce oxygen and ozone. I believe this is due to damage from ultraviolet rays because of ozone layer depletion. UV rays are capable of penetrating over ninety feet below the surface of the ocean, killing oxygen-producing plankton. The damage to the ocean is particularly disturbing, because it may be thousands of years before it can be reversed. Maybe tens of thousands of years.

"I believe we're witnessing a runaway greenhouse effect over the entire planet. All of our major ecosystems are out of balance: the atmosphere, the oceans, and the forests. It's all due to the pollution created by mankind. Unless we take severe and stringent measures, we may very well lose this planet.

"So there you have it, Mr. Allen. I ask you again, who are the greater criminals, the commercial interests who have all but destroyed our ecosystems, or the young people who call themselves the Defenders of the Planet? Who has the purest motives — businessmen who thrive on greed and profit, or people acting upon their ideals to help their fellow man, the earth, and other living beings?"

Allen sat there staring at Jonathan Holmes. He couldn't exactly respond to the question. "Dr. Holmes, if everything you say is true, then what should Americans be doing right now?"

Holmes smiled and sipped his tea. "That's easy," he said bitterly. "They should do what they should have been doing for the past thirty or forty years!"

"We have passed many laws preventing pollution, especially air pollution."

Holmes looked into Allen's eyes, his face contorted into a pronounced frown. "Your attempts at stopping pollution have been halfhearted at best," Holmes said. "For instance, your Congress has never passed a law which stopped pollution. It's because of the way they approach the problem. It's their attitude."

Hearing this, Allen looked chagrined. "Can you explain what you mean by that?" he asked.

Holmes smiled. "Let me give you an analogy. Suppose there is an apartment building housing several hundred people, including lots of children. Next door to the apartment building is a big swimming pool where all the children swim. Now, next to the swimming pool is a bar where men go and drink. Let's say for the sake of argument there are one hundred men. After they have plenty to drink, all one hundred go over to the swimming pool and urinate in it." Holmes grinned broadly. "Preposterous idea, isn't it? But, that's what the polluters do in real life. They piss on everything, except it isn't just urine, it's chemicals, pesticides, heavy metals, radiation, or whatever! Now then, back to my analogy.

"Along comes the U.S. Congress and they decide this urinating in the swimming pool isn't healthy. After all, it might make the children sick. So, they pass a law to alleviate the situation. But they don't want to hurt the bar business next door, so the law is written so that not all one hundred men can still urinate in the swimming pool, but instead, only fifty are allowed to continue to urinate. They'll just add lots of chlorine to take away the smell. They don't bother stopping the pissing in the swimming pool. Ridiculous isn't it? I mean, everyone ought to be able to see that no one should be allowed to urinate in that swimming pool. But, that's the way the U.S. Congress operates.

"You see, the lawmaker's approach is to compromise. In real life, they compromise with everybody to make everybody happy, the oil and chemical companies, big business, utilities, environmentalists and everybody else.

"Do you see the danger in that approach, Mr. Allen? Because the earth is a small, fragile planet, there can be no compromise. All this compromising over the years has caught up to us. The earth is just like that swimming pool, only it's obviously much bigger. But then again, the relative pollution is also greater. We don't have one hundred men pissing on the earth. We have hundreds of countries and hundreds of industries all spitting out several hundred billion tons of pollutants each and every year. And the earth can't take it any more."

"Your argument seems farfetched," Allen said.

"Does it?" Holmes asked. "Do you realize that tens of millions of people have died in the past fifty years from cancer, a direct result of the chemicals being poured into the environment? To put it succinctly, your U.S. chemical companies have poisoned and killed more people than the Nazis did during World War II."

"So what do you recommend?" Allen asked, ignoring the implications of what Holmes had just said.

Holmes was getting tired of Allen's questions. He looked at his daughter, who had thus far stayed out of the conversation. "Jamie knows the answer to that. Why not ask her?"

Allen looked at Jamie. "Okay, I will." He turned the tape recorder to face her. "What should Americans do?" he asked.

"Well," she began, "it's pretty well known what we should be doing. I'm sometimes amazed that people don't want to try because, after all, every little bit will help." She paused and looked at Allen, a sad expression on her face. "The most important thing is using alternate fuels, especially exotic fuels like liquid hydrogen. If we had been burning it instead of petrol, we wouldn't be in the fix we're in now. It's not too late to switch over now. All governments could begin a crash program, as if we're at war. And you know, we *are* at war — with Mother Nature, and she is the most powerful enemy you can ever have against you."

"Go on," Allen urged her.

"The next best thing would be to save what is left of the world's forests. We need a complete ban on cutting down and burning trees. And people can immediately voice their opinion by doing other things."

"What things?" Allen urged.

"Well, for one thing, don't eat hamburgers at fast food restaurants anymore. Boycott them. Just think of it this way: for every hamburger or cheeseburger that gets eaten, another tree gets cut down. If the market for fast food meat evaporates, the

Brazilians won't burn down any more of the Amazon rain forests. Maybe we can save what little is left.

"Also, we are wasting too much paper. Especially you Americans. Bill Roosevelt showed me the junk mail he's received in just the past few days. I was amazed! Pounds of it!"

"So what about junk mail?"

"Well, I think people should take the time to write back to the companies who provide these mailing lists, and order them to take their names off. That way they'll stop receiving it. And I know a simple way to do it," she said.

"What's that?" Allen asked.

"You send it back yourself. Just take whatever piece of this mail has your name on it, and you write a brief note near where your name is located on the piece, and you tell them to take your name off their list. Then you mail the entire thing back in their return envelope. Normally, this envelope is prepaid postage, which they only have to pay for if it's returned by you. So you send back their junk mail and they have to pay for the postage. That will send them a message. And I'm sure that will keep their employees quite busy."

"And what if they don't have a return envelope?"

"You can still send it back, except you'll have to pay the postage. Another alternative is to just refuse receipt of the junk mail in the first place," she said.

"The United States Postal Service wouldn't appreciate that," Allen said. "Besides, they make a lot of money off junk mail."

"Then the postal service and the U.S. Government are contributing to the problem. Junk mail! Why?" Her eyes grew wide. "Why on earth do you allow it to continue? It's sheer nonsense! No one ever reads all of it. Studies show that less than ten percent of junk mail is even read by anyone, so why should you cut down trees so that they can be turned into junk mail? And why should you let your Postal Service condone this unethical situation? After all, they are just public servants and they work for the people." She looked at Allen skeptically.

"What else should people be doing?" Allen asked.

"We should not allow trees to be turned into paper. It's time we grew other crops to provide paper. There's far too much wasted paper in the western world. It just winds up in landfills."

"We are recycling paper."

"Oh, hogwash!" Jamie said. "They are still cutting down entire forests every year to make paper. If the paper is being recycled, then why are they still cutting down trees?"

"I'm not sure if that's correct," Allen said.

"Oh, believe me, it's true," Jamie said. "The world's forests are getting smaller, not larger. All that wood must be going somewhere."

"Wood is part of the international economy. Tens of thousands of people depend on logging and forest products."

"People who cut down trees for a living are shitheads!"

"I see," Allen said, wondering if he would later edit that statement from his article. "What other crops are you referring to, in terms of making paper?" he asked.

"Many years ago, society used hemp to provide fiber for paper. Hemp is an excellent cash crop and could be grown by your farmers. If it weren't for your government's paranoid views about it, hemp could once again become the valuable paper source it used to be."

"That would be very controversial. I doubt if you could get Congress to go along with it."

"Congress needs to rethink its priorities, especially in view of the probable change in the earth's climate."

"Even so, you can't build a house from hemp. They build homes from trees," Allen countered.

"You raise a good point, and that's another thing," Jamie said. "Why must we build homes out of wood? There are plenty of other building materials available. Save Our World believes that wood is an obsolete building material. The world needs its forests. The governments of the planet should pass laws prohibiting the building of homes with wood. They should be built with concrete blocks, with metal studs and joists and concrete roofs and such. There's no need anymore to use wood to build a shelter.

"People who believe in the environment need to become politically active. They must get involved in the day-to-day decisions concerning the environment. Otherwise, their voices will never be heard. There are so many things we should be doing, Mr. Allen. But we're not. The leaders of government have no vision, and they haven't had any vision for the past fifty years. I think it's up to the people to start doing what's right for the earth, and for themselves. That's all." She stopped talking and sat back in her chair, folding her arms on her chest.

Allen turned to Holmes. "Is there anything you would like to add to that, Dr. Holmes?" he asked.

"I think Jamie covered the most important aspects. If people can't do a simple thing such as switching over to alternate fuels, why even try to do anything else? It would be futile."

Allen turned off the tape recorder. "Thanks for the interview, Dr. Holmes. You can look forward to it being placed into tomorrow's edition, and we'll probably put it out on the newswires so other papers will pick it up."

"Good. Thank you, Mr. Allen," Holmes said.

"No, I'm the one who should thank you, Dr. Holmes," Allen said, pulling a dollar from his wallet and leaving it on the table. "It was nice of you to finally talk to me." He got up and strode quickly away.

When he had gone, Jamie looked questioningly at her father. "Father!" she protested. "I thought you weren't supposed to talk to the press. What do you call that?"

"Just a bit of inspiration, my dear daughter. And after all, I didn't know about those attacks upon the oil industry. He caught me by surprise, but I think we did the right thing by talking to him. Don't you? Somebody should defend the Defenders of the Planet."

Jamie frowned. "Bloody good, Father! Now, people really *will* think that you have something to do with them."

FIFTEEN

Two days after the attacks on the oil refineries, a coded message was transmitted among the corporate headquarters of the major oil companies in the United States. Using longstanding procedures, the encrypted communication could be deciphered only within the chief executive's office in each of the companies.

The message was short, but its meaning was clear:

MEETING: THE RANCH: JAN 4 1300: JET ONLY
ALPHA ONLY: SECURITY LEVEL ONE
MANY THANKS, PXL

The Chairman and Chief Executive Officer of Texex, Paul Xavier Lowe, had decided it was time for a powwow, and had elected to invoke the procedure for calling the meeting, which would be held at Lowe's sprawling cattle ranch in West Texas, right on the Pecos River. Smack in the middle of the 60,000-acre ranch was a mini airport which included a 4,000-foot all-weather runway, a manned flight tower, and an instrument landing system which included state-of-the-art Doppler radar, capable of detecting a micro-burst during a heavy thunderstorm.

Level One meant that the meeting would be held in secrecy. Total secrecy. No one in the outside world would ever know the meeting took place. The CEOs would jet in and jet out.

Given the present circumstances, Lowe knew none of the others would refuse the meeting, and he was absolutely right. At the appointed time, the heads of Arxon, Global Oil, and Calrev flew into West Texas. Three corporate jets landed within twenty minutes of each other, taxiing to a parking area where two other jets already sat.

The oilmen who flew into the ranch on the Pecos River were among the most powerful in the world. There was John P. Solomon, head of Arxon, Grant Thomas Wingate, Chairman and CEO of Calrev and Richard Ripley McCoy, top man at Global Oil. Individually, these men headed huge international corporations. Collectively, they represented the most powerful monopoly ever to exist on earth. Together with Texex, their corporations' total annual sales were more than one thousand billion dollars.

The multinational's control over governments and politicians was legend, and for good reason. Nearly every industry and machine in the world ran on oil, including the ships, planes, and trucks of the world's armed forces. Throughout the world, the oil companies were free to do whatever they wanted. As a group, they had more cash than most governments and over the decades, they had used that cash freely to buy off politicians everywhere.

The security at the airport was heavy and the CEOs, accompanied by two dozen bodyguards, were brought in a convoy of five armored limousines to the main ranchhouse where thirty more men, all of them ex-FBI or former police officers, were on guard. They were armed with Uzi automatics or shotguns with special armor piercing loads. As an added touch, a two-man team sat back to back on the roof of the house, each holding a Stinger IV surface-to-air missile.

As the oilmen entered the house, they were brought to the library, a windowless, soundproof room of immense proportions, nearly twenty-four hundred square feet large, with thirty foot high ceilings. One by one, as they entered the library they were greeted by Paul Xavier Lowe and by Prince Abdul Shalid, the oil minister of Saudi Arabia. The oilmen were not surprised he was there; all of them had recognized his personal jet parked at the airport. He graciously shook hands with them, a broad confident smile on his face. In the background, three of Shalid's men stood ready to attend the Prince.

Lowe ushered them to five high-back leather chairs that had been arranged in a circle. Out of deference to the Prince, no alcohol was served. If the oilmen wanted to drink, it would have to be coffee and tea. The meeting began immediately and no words were wasted.

"We have a problem," Lowe said. "It must be dealt with immediately and we must leave nothing to chance. The attack on our refineries signals a new era in our worldwide operations. If we let this get out of hand, we'll end up the losers. We all recognize the seriousness of this situation." He paused, nodding to the Prince. "Prince Shalid has something to say."

"Thank you, Paul," said Shalid. "I have been sent here to relay a message to you from my brother. First, he sends all of you his best wishes and highest personal regards. He has the utmost respect and admiration for all of you." The prince smiled benignly, but slowly the smile turned into a frown. "My brother is very concerned about these terrorist attacks, as I'm sure you are. The question is, what are we going to do about it?"

"Prince Shalid," soothed Solomon, "of course we're all concerned. Otherwise we wouldn't have dropped everything and flown to the ranch. I want to get these bastards as much as anyone else does. And we will get them! I can promise you that."

"How?" asked Shalid. "What plans have you made?"

There was silence, then Lowe spoke up. "That's why I called this meeting. We've got to use whatever assets we have available. We can't wait for government inaction," he stressed the word *inaction*. Lowe's face developed a dark scowl.

"This son of a bitch, Jonathan Holmes, gave a speech urging people to blow up oil refineries. Some of our people have done some checking, and they found that the government hasn't done a damned thing to him. In fact, he's out on bail!"

"Yes," said Shalid, seriously. "This man is a great worry to our government. We recognize that in your country you have the Constitution, and freedom of speech, but there are limits. You cannot cry *fire* in a crowded theater. People would be hurt. For the same reason, you cannot say *blow up oil refineries*. Again, people would be hurt. Such a thing cannot be tolerated." Shalid stopped talking, his jaws clenched. Then he said, "We feel that

Jonathan Holmes might be the head of the Defenders of the Planet."

"That's right," Lowe added. "All this bullshit he's spouting about global warming is keeping our P.R. departments busy as hell countering his propaganda. We don't need that kind of adverse publicity. He must be stopped."

"So let's get rid of him," Solomon said simply. "Paul, you must have already thought about it."

"Yes, I have," Lowe said. "We have contacts with a certain group of people in Chicago. You all know who they are. They are professionals, but they command a high price. These men can easily take care of Holmes. My idea would be a contract of, shall we say, ten million dollars? I've already done some checking, and I've been assured that it would happen very quickly, and then he'd be gone. Is this okay with you?"

Solomon, Wingate, and McCoy said nothing, merely nodding their agreement with the briefest tilt of their heads. Though barely noticeable, the nods were an affirmation of Lowe's "idea."

It was decided. The oil companies were willing to pay a huge price to get Jonathan Holmes out of the way. Their contacts in the Mafia would take care of it. For all intents and purposes, Holmes was a dead man.

"Good," Lowe stated. "Now, there's just one other matter. The Defenders of the Planet. Our people in Washington have assured me that the FBI has not had any luck in getting them. Prince Shalid has suggested that we use our own resources to track them down. Any thoughts?"

"We have contacts within Washington," said McCoy. "We need to use them to our fullest capability. We should know whatever the FBI knows, and damned quickly, too. Once we have the information, we can act upon it in the most expeditious manner."

"Agreed," said Solomon.

"Yes," said Wingate.

"Using what assets?" asked Prince Shalid.

"We'll bring in special mercenaries from all around the world," replied Lowe. "If they know who to go after, they'll have no problem in taking them out."

"Good," smiled Shalid. "They have worked out well in the past whenever there has been a problem."

"Okay," said Lowe. "We now have a plan. We'll coordinate the entire operation though my office. That way there won't be any screwups. As you all know, my chief of security is a former CIA man. He's very discreet and quite good." Lowe allowed himself a little chuckle. "I'm sure he can work out the details. We'll communicate through our usual secret channels."

"I want you to know that my brother and I will render whatever assistance you require," Shalid said. "We want everything to get back to normal as quickly as possible." He smiled at them all, happy that they had selected the proper course of action.

"Anybody have any questions?" Lowe asked. There were none. "Okay, then," he said. "If there is nothing else, I suggest we adjourn. I've got to get back to my office."

The others nodded and stood up. The meeting was over.

SIXTEEN

Carrie Cameron had finished DSN's eleven a.m. weather report and had returned to her office when she received a telephone call from Christchurch, New Zealand. The switchboard operator said the caller had something "urgent" to discuss, that it had to do with global warming. Carrie quickly reached into her desk and pulled out a mini tape recorder, sticking its mike onto her phone.

"Please put him through," Carrie said, and a moment later, she heard the slight hollow static of a very long distance call.

"Carrie Cameron," she said.

"Hello, Carrie? Carrie Cameron?" a male voice asked, in a near-English accent, though with a rough singsong quality.

"Yes, this is Carrie Cameron," she said. "Who's this?"

"My name is John Ritchie, and I'm calling from Christchurch, South Island, New Zealand. I've just returned from Antarctica," he went on, "and I was wondering if you knew how hot it is down there?"

"No, I don't," she said. Carrie tried to sound calm as she asked, "How hot is it?"

"Yesterday, it was seventy-seven degrees. I was at Scott Base on Ross Island, very close to the big Yank base at McMurdo. I flew back to New Zealand today, courtesy of the Yanks, and I wanted to call you."

"Seventy-seven degrees in Antarctica? What does that mean?" Carrie asked, playing dumb. She already knew what it meant, but she just wanted to hear him say it.

"It means that the bloody place is melting like crazy!" he said excitedly. "It also means that nobody in the whole world really gives a damn, that's what."

"What do you mean?"

"It's not being reported, that's what I mean. I just watched your newscast, you know, we get DSN here on South Island, and I didn't see one thing about the situation at the South Pole. Don't you people realize what will happen if this continues?"

"Yes, I think I do. But what you're telling me is unconfirmed. I have no official reports about any seventy-plus degree temperatures in Antarctica."

"Look, Carrie! I'm a scientist and I know what's going on down there. You people just can't suppress this information. The world must know about this. You have to tell them. I mean, it's the decent thing to do, don't you think?"

"What kind of scientist?" she asked, trying to elicit more information from him.

"I'm a paleontologist," he replied. "I study fossils."

"I see."

"Look, I know how to read a bloody, friggin' thermometer, all right? And I happened to be with scientists whose specialty is meteorology and atmospherics and so on, so believe me, the temperature down there really is what I say it is."

"Why did you leave?"

"My particular assignment was finished, and I was scheduled to come back, that's all. Scott Base isn't that big, and it simply doesn't have the right facilities, so my assignment didn't call for staying for the whole summer. But listen to this. When I got back to Christchurch, I was visited by a member of our government. He made me swear an oath of silence about what's going on down there. He said I might create a panic if I told anyone. Naturally, as soon as he left, I turned on the telly, and there you were. I made up my mind right then and there to tell you. The world must know about this. Carrie, you've got to do something!"

"Have you noticed anything else unusual? Can you tell me about any unusual activity in Antarctica?"

"Yes, McMurdo Station has been placed off-limits to New Zealand personnel, except that they're flying us in and out. I happen to know they've lost Williams Field, and they've brought in U.S. Navy Seabees to build a new runway right on Ross Island. They had to come in by parachute, because there was no place to land. We saw four of your large transports come in and drop off several hundred men, and then these huge parachutes dropped some large equipment, bulldozers and the like. The whole thing was utterly fantastic.

"Also, Scott Base has been unable to communicate with our home base here in New Zealand. We think the Yanks have been jamming all communications, although they told us it was due to increased solar activity, which you may know automatically prevents radio communications."

"Yes, I know," Carrie said. "But I don't understand. If the base is off limits, why are they allowing you to go back and forth to your native country? Can you explain that?"

"Not really. It's just that we're not in prison or anything, so they have to let us come and go. Also, New Zealand has an established right to Ross Island, where the Yanks have built their base. With Williams Field gone, they have to fly us in and out. I suspect that there's cooperation at the highest level of government. Otherwise, why would someone from my own government come and visit me, to make sure I keep my mouth shut?"

"It sounds complicated. It's very difficult to believe."

"You've got to believe me! I was there. I know! All the snow around Ross Island is melting. Around McMurdo Sound, the glaciers are melting like crazy. You should see it. In fact, DSN should go down there. Yes, you should see it for yourself. Send a news crew down there. Look, I'm a reputable scientist. What would I have to gain by lying about this?"

"I don't know," Carrie replied.

"Goddamn! You Yanks are something!" And Ritchie hung up in disgust.

Carrie heard the phone being slammed down. She set her own phone down and turned off the tape recorder. Then, she replayed the whole tape to make sure it had been properly recorded. Listening to it again, she knew the man had not been lying. He was telling the truth.

Carrie turned on her main computer and began typing a message. It read:

Have received definite confirmation from scientist who was at Scott Base. Antarctic ice cap is melting rapidly. Government is attempting to cover-up situation. Birddog.

She encrypted the message using her special encoding software and sent it out to the electronic bulletin board in New York City.

She turned off her computer, got up from her desk and walked over to Susan Dahlman's office. "I've got something you need to hear," she announced as she walked in. "You'll find this very interesting."

Susan looked up from her paperwork, removing her glasses. Carrie pulled the tape out of her skirt pocket and set it on her desk.

"What is it?" Susan asked.

"It's a tape of a phone call I just got from New Zealand. Play it. It's self-explanatory."

Susan smiled and shrugged, then inserted the tape into the recorder at her desk and pressed the play button. Together, she and Carrie listened to the entire conversation.

"Hmmmmm," Susan mused, frowning, as she hit the rewind button. "I've been around you and the weather long enough to know that this is extraordinary. It never gets that hot at the South Pole, does it?"

"Never!" Carrie emphasized. "It's summer there, but even in summer it rarely gets above thirty-two degrees. Mark my word, seventy-seven is incredibly hot for Antarctica. But it fits. The Southern Hemisphere is still having a heat wave. Why shouldn't the South Pole?"

"He said the place is melting," Susan said. "Should we take that literally?"

"I think so, but that's why I came over. I think we should get a news team down there right away. If we can confirm this man's story, it will be the biggest breaking news event since World War II, the biggest story in the last hundred years!"

"But why are they trying to cover this up?" Susan asked.

"It's too big, Susan. Washington is probably trying to figure out a way to present this to the public. Put yourself in their shoes. What do they tell the public? And after they tell them, what if the weather goes back to normal? Then they look very foolish, which is the last thing a politician wants."

"You're right about that! Tell me, is there any other ammunition you can give me before I go see Jim?"

"Some scientist friends of mine have heard reports of abnormally high temperatures in Antarctica. Also, I believe the government has purposely shut down Nimbus IV, the satellite which can give us direct data about Antarctica. It all points to a cover-up, Susan."

"This could explain the news blackout from the Pentagon," Susan said. "It certainly fits the scenario. It is beginning to smell like a cover-up. And you're right — this could be the biggest story since World War II." Susan picked up her phone and rang Jim Gabriel, DSN's vice-president of News.

"Jim, this is Susan. I think we have a major story in the making. I think we should meet right away."

"How major?" Gabriel asked nonchalantly.

"It's big, Jim. The biggest, most important story we'll probably ever cover!" Her excited tone of voice indicated she was deadly serious.

"I see. Uh... I've got meetings the rest of the morning. How about if we meet after lunch?"

"This is too big to wait, Jim. We need to start moving on this right away."

"I've heard that one before. And I really am very busy."

"Just give me five minutes. If I can't convince you after that, we'll talk again after lunch."

"Five minutes?"

"Yes, five minutes. Believe me, this is very big!"

Gabriel frowned. There was something in her voice, an earnestness he hadn't heard lately that told him she was on the level. "Okay," he said. "Come on over right now. Let's see what you've got."

"Thanks, Jim." Susan immediately got up from her desk and pulled the tape out of her recorder. "You had better come along, Carrie. He's only giving us five minutes and two heads are better than one, although I'm sure we can stretch five minutes into ten. Besides, this is your story. You'll need to be in on this from the very beginning."

"But... I'm a weather reporter."

"Well," Susan smiled, "this is about the weather. I couldn't think of a better person than you to cover this. I think I'll try to convince the powers that be around here that you are the best person for this assignment. Come on, let's go see Jim."

They walked down the corridor to the elevator, taking it up five floors to the sixteenth floor. Jim Gabriel's office was a suite on one end of the DSN building overlooking the northwest part of Denver and the Rockies beyond. Jim's secretary, Jackie, smiled at them as they approached her desk. "Go on in," she said. "He's expecting you."

When they entered his office, Jim was on the phone, and he waved both of them into the chairs facing his desk. This was only the second time Carrie had been in his office, the first when she was originally hired by DSN. The view out the wall of windows was breathtaking.

After a minute, Jim put the phone down. "Now, what is this about the biggest story in history?" he asked.

"Carrie got a call from New Zealand a short while ago," Susan explained. She pulled the tape from her jacket pocket. "I think you should listen to this," and she handed over the tape.

Gabriel frowned, not liking mysteries, but he pulled out a tape recorder, inserted the tape, pressed the play button and began to hear Carrie's conversation with John Ritchie. Afterward, Gabriel looked confused. "I thought the weather was cooling down," he said to Carrie.

"It's cooling here in the United States and other parts of the Northern Hemisphere," she said. "But south of the equator it's hotter than blazes. The heat wave there isn't merely continuing, it's getting worse."

"It is?" he asked innocently. "Have we been reporting that?"

"No, Jim," Susan said. "It's not our policy to routinely report the weather for the entire globe. We do North America and Europe, but that's about it."

"I did recently report that a new world high temperature was recorded in Australia," Carrie quickly added.

"I didn't see that. How hot was it?"

"One hundred forty-five degrees Fahrenheit."

"Jesus Christ! A hundred forty-five!" Gabriel exclaimed, a puzzled expression on his face. He leaned forward and pressed one of the buttons on his phone. "Jackie," he spoke into the intercom line, "hold my calls."

"Okay, Jim, will do," came her voice through the phone.

Gabriel turned his attention to Carrie. "If Antarctica is melting, as this individual says it is, then maybe it's a disaster about to happen. Do you think his story is on the level? Is he telling the truth?"

"Yes," Carrie said. "It makes sense. Something tells me he's not lying. Also, I know that it is very hot right now in the Southern Hemisphere, not just in Australia. The heat wave is also hitting South America, New Zealand, and southern Africa. It's only logical that it's affecting Antarctica."

"I see what you meant, Susan. This is big, very big!" He sat back in his chair, and turned to look out the windows at the view beyond. He pursed his lips, frowning. "Those bureaucratic dimwits in Washington said this wouldn't happen. I smell a cover-up. We should have been onto them long ago."

"That's what I think," Susan agreed, smiling at Carrie.

He turned back to them. "Okay, I guess the logical thing to do would be to send a news crew to the South Pole and see what is going on. We need to get a firsthand look."

"That won't be easy," Carrie said.

"Why not?"

"Antarctica is basically a military operation. Civilians go there only at the discretion of the government and it's very difficult to get a clearance to go. A lot of good scientists are routinely rejected to go and do studies down there. Anyway, for us to get permission would take weeks, if not months, and since the government is probably covering this whole thing up, I doubt they'd ever let us go down there."

"Nothing is going to hold us back from covering this story," Gabriel said, emphasizing the word *nothing*.

"We can cover it, we just can't get directly to the American base in Antarctica," Carrie said.

"So what do we do to get this story out?" Gabriel asked. "Do you have any ideas?"

"Well, my idea would be to go first to Punta Arenas at the tip of South America. It's very close to Antarctica and from there we might get some more leads. You know, interview different people. From Punta Arenas we could probably charter a plane and at least fly over parts of Antarctica."

"Dynamite!" Gabriel said. "I'll get a news crew down there right away. This is too important to screw around with!"

"Jim," Susan spoke up. "I think the best person for this assignment is Carrie."

"Carrie?" Jim asked. "But she's a weather reporter."

"And this is a weather story. Of all our reporters, Carrie is the most qualified to report this. She is a meteorologist, and she has the educational background to report this in the most technical manner possible. Also, she can evaluate information being given to her and decide what needs to be said and what doesn't. Besides, we're all agreed that she has a special ability to communicate. I really believe the best person DSN has to cover this assignment is Carrie. We should send her to Chile."

"I see," Gabriel mused. "And naturally, since you two work together so well, you'd be the best person to produce the story. I assume you'd have to go along."

"That's right," Susan smiled.

Gabriel nodded, and immediately reached a decision. "Okay, then. You've got the assignment. Carrie will report and you will be the producer in the field. Both of you go home and start packing. We'll book you on the first available plane to Punta Arenas."

"The nearest major airports are either Santiago, Chile or Buenos Aires in Argentina. From either of those cities, we can fly to Punta Arenas," Carrie said.

"Okay. I'll have Jackie check with our travel agent. She can call you at home and tell you which airline to go to at Stapleton. I'll have a camera crew meet you there. We're gonna get moving on this ASAP."

Susan stood up, and so did Carrie. "Thanks, Jim. I guarantee this is going to be one hell of a story."

Gabriel got up from his chair and walked around to the front of his desk. "Susan, before you leave, go down to accounting and draw out some cash. Say, five thousand. And get a DSN company credit card, one with no limit. I'll tell Ron to expect you. Now, both of you better get going. This story can't wait."

He shook hands with both of them, and walked them to the door. Then he went back to his desk and started making phone calls, the first to Ron Hornung, DSN's controller. After he gave precise instructions to Hornung about the money and credit card, Gabriel called Laurie Hill on his production staff. "Laurie," he said. "I'm sending Susan Dahlman and Carrie Cameron to South America to do a story."

"You are?" Laurie asked.

"Yes. It looks like a really big story is breaking. I want to give them one of our best camera operators. Who's available to go with them?"

"Al Hollings is here," Laurie replied.

"Great!" Gabriel exclaimed, knowing Al was one of the best in the business. "Tell him he's going to South America, to a place called Punta Arenas."

SEVENTEEN

Punta Arenas is located near the tip of South America on the coast of the Straits of Magellan, which separate the mainland from the island of Tierra del Fuego, half which belongs to Chile and half to Argentina. From Cape Horn, at the southern tip of Tierra del Fuego, it is over six hundred miles across the Drake Passage to Antarctica.

This region of the world is known for its strange winds and difficult ocean currents. At Cape Horn, the cool waters of the South Atlantic meet the warm waters of the South Pacific, the powerful, almost vortexlike ocean currents tossing ships about at will. For centuries before the opening of the Panama Canal, sailors feared having to round the dreaded Cape Horn.

The tip of South America is normally cool year-round and even in the summer the temperature normally doesn't get much higher than fifty degrees. Because of the chilly winds, the people of the region wear sweaters even in January and February, their summer months.

This summer, no one was wearing sweaters. Punta Arenas was experiencing hot weather for the first time since anyone could remember. When the crew from DSN arrived by plane over the Punta Arenas area, the pilot informed them that the temperature below was ninety degrees and there was little wind. As the plane approached for landing, they noticed that the countryside was covered with vast rolling moors, perfect for the region's main industry, raising sheep.

As Carrie, Susan, and Al walked off the plane and into the small terminal, they noticed that the obviously aged air-conditioning system was noisily churning at full speed, yet the building was hot and stuffy. It took half an hour to gather their luggage and equipment, and when they left the terminal they were all soaking in perspiration.

"This place is unusually hot," Carrie remarked.

"It is? But shouldn't it be? It is summer here," Susan said.

"Yes, but we're far south of the Tropic of Capricorn. The summers this far south are very mild. I think this proves that John Ritchie was telling the truth. If it's this hot here, it could easily be in the seventies at the South Pole."

"How far away is Antarctica?" Susan asked, not familiar with the geography of the region.

"From here, it's only about seven hundred miles to the Antarctic Peninsula."

"It isn't far, then."

"No, not that far at all." Carrie said, her eyes studying the sky. "That gives me an idea."

"What?" Susan asked.

"There's going to be plenty of daylight, so why don't we charter a plane and fly down over Antarctica right now? It'll make a great visual piece for our first report."

Susan frowned, pursing her lips. They had just spent the better part of a twenty-four-hour day on planes and in airports to get here, and now Carrie wanted to hop on another plane and fly seven hundred miles to Antarctica.

Carrie could see that Susan wasn't too keen on the idea. She quickly said, "Look, Susan, we shouldn't waste any time. And we're already right here at the airport. If we can get some shots of hot weather in Antarctica, it'll lend credence to our story. You don't have to go. I can go with Al," she said.

"Yes, you're right. Okay, you can go, if Al is willing. Personally, I'm exhausted. I'll stay here in Punta Arenas and see to our hotel rooms."

"Thanks, Susan," Carrie beamed. "I know this will be a good way to start our assignment."

Susan smiled, surprised at Carrie's enthusiasm. "Go get 'em, tiger," she said.

They discussed it with Al Hollings, who immediately said, "Let's do it." He nodded approvingly at Carrie, sensing she had the killer instinct found only in the best reporters.

The three of them checked around the airport and soon located a local charter service that specialized in tours to Antarctica, but the desk was closed and no one was to be seen. Brochures lying about on the counter advertised two night, three day backpacking and ski trips to the "land of perpetual ice."

"I'm going to look around," Carrie said. "There must be somebody around here." She walked across the terminal area and tried a closed, though unlocked door, and saw that there were some men working in the adjacent hangar. She closed the door and waved at Susan and Al.

"Over here!" she said.

Susan and Al hurriedly walked over, and Carrie pointed to the door, opening it just enough so they could all peer through.

"I think that's one of their planes," Carrie said.

"You're right," Susan agreed. "Come on. Let's go see if we can charter it."

They walked into the hangar and approached the plane, a large Twin Otter. A man standing near one of the engines saw them coming and walked out to meet them.

"Sorry, folks, but we're closed," he said in perfect English.

"Let me handle this," Susan whispered to the others, and she gave the man her best smile. "Hi. I'm Susan Dahlman, and this is Carrie Cameron and Al Hollings. We're Americans with Direct Satellite Network. We'd like to charter your plane. We want to fly to Antarctica." She held out her hand.

The man took her hand and briefly shook hands with her. "I'm Ivan Baldrich," he said, a broad smile on his face. He looked carefully at Carrie Cameron, recognizing her face from television.

"Yes, I know Carrie. We get DSN down here in Punta Arenas." Baldrich's expression became serious. "I'm sorry you came all this way for nothing. Antarctica is off limits at the present time. No flying right now."

"Why?" Susan asked.

"Hot weather," Baldrich announced. "The snow and ice down there is too mushy. We can't land. I've never seen anything like it in all my twenty-six years of flying."

"And that's the only reason?" Susan asked.

"Not exactly," Baldrich said. "The Chilean government has banned all civilian flights over the continent."

"Really? But why?"

"I suspect they're worried that the public will get excited about all that ice melting. But what are we going to do, anyway? This is our home. We can't just leave, even if Antarctica is melting."

"You're sure it's melting?" Carrie asked.

"Positive. Every pilot in the area knows what's going on. We've been told to keep our mouths shut or they'd confiscate our planes. Lousy bastards!"

"How hot is it down there?" Carrie asked.

"I heard it was up around seventy or so."

"Look, Mr. Baldrich. This is an important story for our viewers, millions of people all around the world. They should know the truth, and that's what we're here to find out. What if we pay you to just fly over Antarctica," Susan suggested. "We'll pay you double your normal rate just to let us get some camera shots of the continent."

Baldrich thought about how much trouble he would get into if he did this woman's bidding, but he was low on funds, and he could use the money. Besides, he liked the idea of getting the truth out to the world. I might become famous, he thought.

"Double?" he asked.

"Yes, and we'll pay you in cash."

He frowned, wondering if he should do it. Finally, he said "Okay, but my plane won't be ready for an hour. We're putting the finishing touches on some routine maintenance. By the way, this is my co-pilot, Steve Kerzich," and he pointed to the man lying on the wing, working on the engine. Kerzich grinned at them from above. "Hi, folks," he said.

"Nice to meet you," Susan smiled. Both Carrie and Al waved at Kerzich and smiled. Carrie started to get butterflies in her stomach, realizing she was about to go to Antarctica, the world's most distant place. What was happening down there would affect the entire planet.

"If we leave in an hour, Mr. Baldrich, will there be any daylight left by the time we get there?" Susan asked.

"Lots of it," Baldrich stated. "Down here, we're presently getting over twenty hours of daylight every day. There will be plenty of light when we get there. I can fly you as far south as Palmer Land, but then we'll have to turn around and head straight back. You can expect we'll be in the air for nine or ten hours."

"Can your plane fly that long?" Susan wondered.

"No problem. She's outfitted with special fuel tanks. Now, let me help finish with this work. Be back here in an hour. By the way, my normal charter fee is twenty-five hundred dollars per trip, but that includes a two-night stay in Antarctica. Since we're just going down for the day, I'll only charge you three thousand."

"It's a deal," Susan said. "We'll go get our camera and sound equipment, and we'll be back in about an hour."

As they left the hangar, Susan tugged at Carrie's arm and said. "I've changed my mind. I'm going along, no matter how tired I am. This is too good to pass up."

"Great, Susan!" Carrie said. "What's another ten hours in the air, right?" They both laughed.

An hour later, Carrie, Susan, and Al Hollings boarded the Twin Otter. The plane taxied out of the hangar and onto the taxiway. A minute later, as the aircraft sat at the head of the main runway, Baldrich received clearance for takeoff. He gunned the engines and the big twin engine plane raced down the runway and was airborne.

The flight to Antarctica took over four hours, Susan and Al sleeping most of the way, both tired from the trip from the U.S. to Punta Arenas. Carrie stayed awake, drinking coffee and thinking about what she should say about the climactic change taking place in Antarctica. She wanted to be factual yet dramatic, revealing to the world the truth about the situation and the possible dire consequences that would follow. She penciled notes on a notepad, constantly crossing out and revising as she wrote.

Baldrich hailed them just before they crossed the coast of the Antarctic Peninsula.

"We're over Antarctica!" his voice boomed over the plane's loudspeakers.

Carrie blinked and pressed her face against the nearest window. Yes, there it was. Antarctica was below! "Antarctica!" she exclaimed. "Susan, Al, it's Antarctica!"

Susan shook the cobwebs out of her head, and stared out the window. "I'll be damned," she said. "Antarctica. It even looks hot down there. Carrie, we're witnessing history in the making."

"Yes," Carrie agreed. "Isn't it exciting?"

Al held up his camera and checked the light settings. "We can get good tape," he soon announced. "The light is tremendous. No problem shooting right out of the plane."

"Oh, great!" Carrie said. "Excuse me, Al, but I'm going to freshen my makeup. Then you can shoot me. Okay?"

"Sounds good," Al replied. "You'll have to sit right next to the window and we'll turn on all the overhead lights, just in case. Do you know what you're going to say?"

"You bet," she said. "I've been thinking about it ever since we left Punta Arenas."

"You'll be great, Carrie," Susan said.

Then Baldrich came back into the cabin. "We can't stay too long," he said, "but long enough to fly over Palmer Land and the Ronne Ice Shelf. We'll cross the ice shelf, fly out over the Weddell Sea, and then come back up the other side of the Antarctic Peninsula. You'll see what I mean about the ice melting, believe me." Baldrich looked out of the window and pointed with his right index finger. "Do you see those mountains over there at two o'clock?" he asked.

"Yes, I see them," Carrie replied.

"Well, those babies are normally covered with snow and ice all year. Look at them right now. Their north faces are completely barren of snow, almost right up to the tops." Baldrich scowled as he gazed out the window. "It must be getting hotter," he stated. "There aren't many clouds over the continent right now. Normally, even in the summer, it's overcast down here."

"Really?" Carrie asked excitedly. "Then you would say this is very abnormal?"

"It's abnormal as can be. I've never seen anything like it."

"How hot do you think it is down there?"

"Probably around seventy-six or more. The interior of the plane is eighty, and our air conditioning and heating systems are all off. We'd be a little warmer because of our windows. Yeah, I'd say seventy-six is a good guess." He turned to Susan and Al. "Would you like something to eat and some coffee?" he asked.

"Yes," Susan said. "That sounds wonderful."

"Sounds good to me," Al said.

"Good. I've brought some roast beef sandwiches, on sour dough bread. My wife made them and brought them over to the hangar before you got back. I'll go get them." He went forward to the tiny galley just behind the cockpit and set out some plates, bringing the sandwiches out from a small refrigerator. Then he poured three cups of coffee, setting the cups in the built-in holders on the plates, coming back into the cabin while deftly balancing the plates in his hands and on his left forearm.

"Here you go," he said. "Nothing like homemade food." He handed each of them a plate, and they all began eating.

"This is great," Al said, chewing voraciously. "Thank you very much."

"Yes, thank you," Susan and Carrie both said.

"No problem," Baldrich smiled. "Service is our business."

"Where did you learn to speak English so well? Are you from Europe originally?"

"No, born and raised in southern Chile. We speak mostly Serbian-Croatian, though English is our second language. My grandparents came here from Croatia back in 1914. There's lots of Croatians here. Lots of blue-eyed blondes." Suddenly, he looked sad. "That's why the skin cancer rate here is so high."

"It is?" Susan asked.

"Yes. It's the damned ozone hole. It's been really bad lately. We're getting tons of ultraviolet."

"It's bad everywhere," Carrie said.

"Not as bad as here," Baldrich stated flatly. "Half of our sheep population is blind from ultraviolet caused cataracts. And rabbits and birds have been found blind. I'm glad you people from DSN are here. The world needs to know what's going on down here."

"Don't worry," Susan said. "We'll get this story out, come hell or high water!"

"High water, it sounds like to me," Baldrich said. "Look, we've flown farther to the west than we normally would have, so we've crossed the peninsula pretty far down. We'll spend another hour flying down the peninsula and then we'll cross over Palmer Land. Then, we'll make a big turn back north and to home. I suggest you save your film for Palmer Land. The scenery is much better than around this area."

Susan nodded. "Okay, Mr. Baldrich. I think we'll take your advice. You must know the terrain."

He smiled. "Call me Ivan," he said. "No need to be formal."

"Okay, Ivan."

"Well," he said, turning to go back to the cockpit. "I'll notify you when we cross into Palmer Land. Enjoy your food."

Exactly an hour later, Baldrich told them over the intercom that they were crossing that part of the Antarctic Peninsula known as Palmer Land. In the distance, they saw a snowcapped mountain range, and Al began shooting videotape from out of the plane's windows.

"How does it look?" Susan asked.

"Good," Al replied. "It definitely looks like Antarctica."

"Look," Carrie said, pointing out the right side of the plane. "There's an interesting mountain range right over there."

Just then, Baldrich came back into the cabin. "Yes," he said. "That's Vinson Massif, Carrie. One of the peaks in that range is the highest point in Antarctica. Over sixteen thousand feet tall."

Al went over to a window on the right side of the Twin Otter and began shooting Vinson Massif. "Yes," he said. "That does look more interesting. And the light is better."

"It will just take twenty minutes or so to cross Palmer Land," Baldrich said. "Then we'll be over the Ronne Ice Shelf and starting to head north. You'll see some interesting glaciers on the east side of the peninsula. I'll be hugging the coast and flying low so you can get some good shots."

"Excellent," Susan said. "Thank you so much, Ivan. This is really quite an experience."

"You're welcome," he said, and he disappeared back into the cockpit.

"Are you ready, Carrie?" Susan asked.

"As ready as I'll ever be," she replied.

"Okay, then. We'll have Al shoot you with that mountain range in the background. Then, Al, just after she's finished speaking, zoom in on the background."

"No problem," he said, pulling back from the window. He set the camera on a seat and began setting up a microphone.

"Hold the mike about four inches from your mouth, Carrie," Susan said. "And don't pop your P's."

"I won't," she said.

"Also, remember, we're doing the lead in to this piece back in Punta Arenas, so you don't have to introduce yourself."

"Got it," Carrie said.

"Okay, here you go," Al said, handing her the mike, then he turned on all the overhead lights near Carrie's seat, picked up the camera and started shooting. "Looks okay," he said. "We've got good light. Carrie, let's test the mike level Go ahead and speak into the microphone."

"Testing, one, two, three, four, five, six..."

"It's good," Al said. "Okay, anytime you're ready."

She nodded and looked directly into the camera. "Antarctica is known as the frozen continent, the coldest place on earth. It was here that the coldest temperature ever recorded was made, back in 1983, at minus one hundred and twenty-eight point six degrees Fahrenheit.

"Well, today it looks as if Antarctica is unfreezing, and it's happening very rapidly. Right now, temperatures on the continent are reported to be in the mid-seventies. DSN has learned that the United States government, in concert with other nations who have bases here, is attempting to hide this information from the public, fearing widespread panic.

"But DSN has learned from reliable sources that the temperatures here have been steadily increasing over the past month or so, and this has caused alarm in capitals all around the world. Temperatures of seventy-five degrees or more are the highest ever recorded here, and many fear that if these high temperatures continue, they are sufficient to completely melt the ice cap over the South Pole. Now, the ice cap of Antarctica is about two miles thick, with enough water locked up in the ice to raise the world's oceans by two hundred feet if it should completely melt, inundating many of the earth's largest cities. In the United States, low-lying areas such as Florida and the Gulf States will be especially hard hit."

"We are currently flying over Palmer Land. Behind me is the Vinson Massif, the highest elevation in Antarctica. In a moment, we'll be crossing over the Ronne Ice Shelf and then heading north up the east side of the Antarctic Peninsula and back to our base at Punta Arenas. Many of the mountains below us have lost much of their snow due to the record high temperatures. It should be overcast here, but right now, outside our plane, the sun is shining brightly and there are few clouds in the area, confirming everything we've heard about this situation.

"Across the continent, at America's Antarctic base, McMurdo Station, the primary airfield is no longer capable of landing aircraft. Williams Field was built right on the ice, but because the ice has shifted, it is too dangerous to land on the ice runway. The

U.S. Navy has brought in a contingent of Seabees to construct a new runway on Ross Island, a volcanic island located in McMurdo Sound, where the United States base is located.

"Our own pilot, who is in the business of bringing tourists to Antarctica on three-day excursions, where they would normally ski and do some backpacking, has told us that he can longer land this plane on the normally hard ice surface. It has melted to the point of becoming mushy.

"And so, as we fly over the world's southernmost continent, it would appear that Antarctica is in trouble, in danger of melting away, and there is little if anything the rest of the world can do about it."

Carrie stared into the camera for a few more seconds, then lowered her microphone. Al took his camera off her and zoomed in on the mountain range in the distance, shooting for nearly a minute before turning the camera off.

"How did I do?" Carrie asked.

"You did wonderfully," Susan exclaimed. "You got it on the first take. And you covered everything that needed to be said. When we get back to Punta Arenas, we'll set up our transmitter and do a live lead-in and ending for the first piece and get it off to Denver right away. This is going to hit hard back home, Carrie. You'll knock their socks off!"

Carrie smiled. She had purposely used a serious, yet matter-of-fact tone that would only emphasize the enormity of the problem in the eyes of the viewers.

Later, Carrie made her first broadcast from the town plaza of Punta Arenas, a bronze statue of Ferdinand Magellan in the background. The story was beamed up to DSN's satellite and fed live to America, where DSN interrupted its normally scheduled program to announce a "DSN SPECIAL REPORT."

Within hours, most Americans had heard the disturbing news of the Antarctic situation, though many had trouble believing it. How could the South Pole be melting? And what did it mean for America?

EIGHTEEN

On Wednesday, January 10, Jonathan Holmes awoke to another hot, humid day. His bedroom windows were open, and outside his room he heard the chirping of dozens of birds, all intent on singing their morning songs. He lay there for awhile, listening to them, and it made his heart glad. Thank God for birds, he thought. They always seem so happy. Perhaps the weather is going to reverse itself, he mused, and the birds can sense the change.

Holmes sighed, realizing he shouldn't indulge in such a fantasy, not after what he now knew. Not after the storms he had seen on the mesa near Yuma and the one east of Phoenix, the memories of which were still clear in his mind. Since he had been freed from jail, Holmes had been in contact with scientists from around the world. All reports suggested that the planet's atmosphere was in a state of flux. There were strange storms striking all over the globe.

Holmes knew that the reason for these powerful and unusual winter storms was because of excess water vapor in the atmosphere, so much that the atmosphere couldn't hold onto it. And there could only be one reason why there was excess water vapor present. It was due to atmospheric heat.

The heat from the atmosphere was causing more water to evaporate from the world's oceans. As the water vapor rose into the upper reaches of the atmosphere, it condensed in the cooler air and formed raindrops, trillions of them, which eventually responded to the laws of gravity. The water droplets were being dumped back to earth in an unusually severe fashion.

As he thought about it, Holmes suddenly shivered beneath his sheets. The storms could only be a harbinger of things to come.

If the heat continues, he thought, the violent storms will get worse. The earth is, after all, a water planet.

He threw back his covers, sprang out of bed and pulled on a pair of pants. God! he thought, I've got to get out of Arizona. I've got so much work to do.

He opened the screen of the sliding glass door and went outside, eager to see what the sky looked like. He walked out into the backyard and stood facing the east. The sun had just come up over the horizon, and it looked to be a clear day.

A week ago, he and Jamie had moved from the Phoenix Hilton to the Roosevelt's home in the suburbs of north Phoenix. Their home was spacious and well laid out, and they had made him feel welcome and comfortable. But he longed to be moving on so he could work on the SOW project.

Holmes went back inside and, after showering and shaving, dressed in his only suit, recently dry-cleaned and pressed, making especially sure he did not have his usual rumpled look. He combed his hair neatly and gave himself the once-over in front of the bathroom mirror. Not bad, he decided, for an old man. Hopefully, he might make a good impression on the judge.

Today he was to go to court for his preliminary hearing. According to Martin Sherman, there was a chance the judge would see through the government's case and simply let him free, not letting it go to trial. The prosecution had no evidence.

Holmes went to the kitchen, where he found the Roosevelts and Jamie sitting in the breakfast nook, all drinking coffee.

"Ready for the big day?" Bill Roosevelt asked.

Jonathan Holmes smiled broadly. "I'm as ready as a man could be," he said. "A little nervous, though," he admitted. He walked over and joined them. The nook adjoined the kitchen and it had a large bay window that overlooked the rugged mountains and foothills to the northeast. The view was harshly beautiful.

"You'll do just fine," Maggie said confidently.

"I hope so," he said. "I've got to get on with my work."

"Would you like some coffee?" Maggie asked.

"Sure, why not?" he replied.

She got up and poured him a cup, bringing it over and setting it in front of him. He thanked her and took the little pitcher of cream sitting in the middle of the table and added some to his coffee, taking a sip. It was good and strong.

"How is it?" Bill asked.

"It's excellent," Holmes replied sincerely.

"It's from Hawaii, from the Kona coast," Bill said. "Grown in the U.S.A. and subject to our agricultural and EPA rules, unlike all that Third World stuff. Do you know that they still use DDT in parts of the world? And God knows what else. American coffee is the safest."

"Yes, I'm aware of that. I normally drink tea," Holmes said. "But when in Rome..."

Maggie laughed. "Careful, Jonathan. It's habit-forming."

"Yes, I'm sure. But so is tea. At any rate, it is good, and I could use the caffeine. Martin said I need to be on my toes today."

"He called while you were in the shower," Bill said. "He's on his way over to pick you up. He should be here any minute."

Holmes nodded. "Look, Bill... Maggie. Whatever happens, I want to thank you for letting us stay here. It has meant a lot to me, and I'm sure to Jamie also." Then, seeing the expression on his daughter's face, he reached over and patted her arm. "Don't worry, Jamie," he said. "Martin has promised to take care of this whole matter. I think everything will be okay."

"I'm not worried, Father," Jamie said. "It's just that this whole thing is so... unnecessary."

"Yes," he said. "I couldn't agree with you more. Cheer up, my dear. There are better days ahead. I'm sure of it."

Outside the Roosevelt's home, three different carloads of men were watching the house. Parked on an adjacent cross street with a clear view of the house sat a black van with dark windows. Inside, Special Agent Mark Kessler and two other FBI agents were monitoring every word that was uttered within the house.

"Holmes hasn't said anything about blowing up the oil refineries!" Kessler said bitterly. "Like he's completely innocent or something." He was sitting in front of a large tape deck, its reels spinning slowly as it recorded the conversation in the Roosevelt's kitchen. Days earlier, agents had placed hidden miniature microphones throughout the home.

Kessler was under orders to maintain maximum surveillance on Holmes because the government needed more evidence in order to go to trial. Eventually, they figured, Holmes would say something incriminating, and then they'd have something that they could pin on him. So far, the agents knew their case against him was weak.

"It could be they're highly disciplined," agent Ed Baker remarked. "The last memo from Washington indicated that they may have received highly specialized training."

"He'll slip up," Kessler said. "It's just a matter of time."

"Mark," said Mike Lacy, "we've been on this guy for over a week. He hasn't said anything that says he's guilty. Not one shred of evidence. Maybe he's on the level, and his speech about blowing up oil refineries was just a coincidence."

"No way," Kessler retorted. "It couldn't be just a coincidence. He's just very clever, that's all. He's got to be part of the Defenders group. It wouldn't surprise me if he's their leader. We're going to get this guy!"

"If we don't, someone else intends to," Lacy said, referring to a recent law enforcement intelligence bulletin which said that there was a ten million dollar contract out on Jonathan Holmes.

"Just keep your eyes peeled," Kessler said. "As long as we're here, I don't think anything will happen," he said, telling a half-lie to his fellow agents. Kessler pursed his lips into a half-smile, knowing that the contract on Holmes wasn't really a concern of his. He had already been in contact with the Director on the matter of the intelligence bulletin and Kelton's direct orders were not to protect Holmes. "If they get him, then they get him," the Director had said. Kessler's mission was to maintain surveillance on Holmes and nothing more.

In yet another van, this one gray and parked far down the street the Roosevelt's house was on, sat four men, all professional killers. Three of them had just flown in from Chicago the night before. They were aware of the FBI's presence, but this didn't concern them. They were pros and they had already decided that they must make their move this morning before the court had a chance to revoke Holmes' bail, or before anyone else could do the job. They would make the hit when he exited the house.

These four men did not talk to each other, for there was nothing to be said. They all knew what Jonathan Holmes looked like, and when they saw him they were going to shoot him. If anybody got in the way, they would shoot them, too. It was that simple. Using the tactic of surprise, they would hit quickly and with maximum firepower, and then they'd be gone before the FBI could do anything about it. If the Feds were able to react quickly, there would probably be a gunfight, and somebody might get killed, or worse, get caught and go to prison. But that was a chance the four men were willing to take. For two and a half million each, it was worth the risk.

Far down the street in the opposite direction, James Flynn and Jeff Walker were sitting in Jeff's beat-up 1999 Pontiac. Flynn was watching through powerful binoculars. He knew they were being totally indiscreet, but it was the best they could do on short notice.

Flynn, routinely checking through his police intelligence files, had only learned last night that there was a ten million dollar contract out on Jonathan Holmes. He had a gut feeling they would hit him right away.

He also knew that the FBI was keeping a surveillance on the Roosevelt house. All Phoenix law enforcement had been ordered by the Feds to stay out of the neighborhood. This was an FBI operation and they didn't need or want interference. Flynn wondered if the FBI was aware of the recent bulletin about the contract that had been put out on Holmes. Or did they care?

Earlier that morning, Flynn had called Jeff, knowing he would be off duty, and they armed themselves and drove over to the expensive neighborhood. They were taking a big gamble, but they thought it was worth it. If the FBI caught them there, Flynn figured he could always flash his badge, though he'd have a lot of explaining to do. As he spied through the binoculars, Flynn saw Martin Sherman pull into the Roosevelt's driveway.

"There's a Ford coming in," he said softly. He glanced at the clock in the Pontiac. It read 9:06 a.m. "That must be his attorney. Shouldn't be much longer. The hearing is scheduled for ten o'clock."

Jeff let out a deep breath. He felt uncomfortable in the suit and tie, and he didn't like carrying a large revolver beneath his jacket. "I never thought I'd have to protect Jonathan Holmes, all because of something I, I mean we, did," he said.

"What we did was good for the planet," Flynn stated. "And I'd do it again any day. If we save the earth, then we save lives, and that's what it's all about. What Jonathan Holmes did, however, is different. He had the audacity to take on the whole establishment. To become a spokesman. A leader. Now, they want to kill him, even though he's just a scientist."

"The pen is mightier than the sword," Jeff quoted. The two of them sat there, watching a man get out of the Ford and walk toward the front door.

Martin Sherman had arrived to take Holmes and Jamie downtown for their preliminary hearing. He had flown back to Phoenix early this morning, having spent the last week at his ranch in Idaho. He knew that nothing could be gained by waiting around in Phoenix. Hopefully, he thought, the matter will be ended this very day. He had credible witnesses lined up who could prove that Jonathan Holmes was nowhere near Winslow when the power line had been damaged.

He walked up to the front door and rang the doorbell. A few seconds went by, and then Maggie Roosevelt answered the door.

"Good morning!" Sherman said.

"Good morning. Come in, Martin. We're just having coffee. Would you like a cup?"

"Yes, I'd love a good cup of coffee," he replied, following her through the house and into the kitchen.

He walked into the breakfast nook, and was glad Holmes appeared to be in good spirits. "How are you doing, Jonathan?" Sherman asked.

"I'm fine," Holmes replied. "How was your trip?"

"It was good, though it rained a lot in the northwest. But it's a wonderful morning here in Phoenix," Sherman smiled. He was wearing a cowboy hat and a western-style suit, and he looked the part of a successful lawyer/rancher. He sat down as Maggie handed him a cup of coffee. "Thank you, ma'am," he said, smiling. "Did you all hear this morning's news?" he asked.

"No," Bill Roosevelt shook his head.

"Nor I," said Holmes.

"It's incredible! For the first time that I've heard, they're reporting the situation in Antarctica. On DSN, the weather reporter said that she has information that Antarctica has air temperatures in the high seventies. She talked about global warming, the South Pole melting, and the oceans rising. She had pictures of Antarctica."

"High seventies?" Holmes asked, his eyes widening.

"Yes, Jonathan." Martin said. "She was in a plane flying over Antarctica. They talked at length about the ramifications of the South Pole's ice cap melting."

"That is remarkable! So my suspicions are confirmed!" Holmes looked solemnly around the table. "The world is in great danger. All governments everywhere must begin a crash program to stop burning fossil fuels. It might be our only hope at this point. Martin, you must get me out of this ridiculous situation. I need to get to my headquarters in New York."

"Relax, Jonathan," Sherman said. "I feel confident that the government's case is weak. You should be free by this afternoon if all goes well. But, I've told you, I can't control what the judge will or will not do."

"I should have known that this was happening," Holmes lamented. "It's all beginning to make sense now. Come on," he said, rising from the table. "Let's get to the court and get this over with. I want to get to New York by this evening."

Seeing that he was visibly upset, the others all immediately decided it was no use arguing the matter, and they followed him toward the front door.

"Here they come!" Flynn said, seeing that Jonathan Holmes and a group of people had come out of the house. He quickly scanned up and down the street with his binoculars and noticed the tiniest of movements far down the street, a slight puff of white smoke.

"Uh, oh," he said softly.

"What is it?" Jeff asked.

"A van just started its engine. Way down the street."

"Maybe it's the FBI," Jeff suggested.

"No. I happen to know that they're driving a black van. These guys are somebody else. You better lock and load. I've got a feeling about this. Come on, start your engine."

"Damn!" Jeff protested, turning the ignition key. "I can't believe we're taking on the goddamned Mafia." He pulled his assault rifle up from beside his seat and chambered a round.

"We're the Defenders of the Planet," Flynn said. "We took an oath to lay down our lives if we have to. This could be one of those times." He pulled his rifle up from beside him, inserting a thirty-round magazine into it. He chambered a round and set the safety to the off position, gently cradling the gun in his lap.

Seconds later, the gray van pulled away from the curb and started down the street. "Goddamn it. Here they come!" Flynn motioned with his left hand and said, "Move out, and drive slowly. Try to arrive in front of the house just as they do. They're going to hit him. I can feel it."

Jeff pulled out and began driving the Pontiac down the street at twenty miles an hour, both he and Flynn staring at the van as the two vehicles approached each other. When they were within twenty yards of the gray van, it suddenly stopped in the middle of the street, and four men jumped out, weapons in their hands.

"I knew it!" Flynn said. Without waiting for the car to stop, he opened his door and jumped out, knowing he should warn Holmes and his friends.

"Get down!" he shouted forcefully and in the same instant he fired a volley at the four men who had exited the car, all of whom were carrying shotguns or automatic weapons. Flynn thought he might have hit one of them, but the others quickly turned on him and fired, so quickly that Flynn was forced to find cover behind the Pontiac.

Jeff barely had time to slam his car into park and jump out the driver's side before a blast from a shotgun blew out the windshield. He dove to the ground and scrambled for cover. As he did so, a bullet tore cleanly through his left calf muscle, causing intense pain in his leg. Jeff swore violently and quickly crawled beneath a car parked on the opposite side of the street. Fortunately, Flynn had kept firing, providing him with the opportunity to get to cover. Jeff looked up and saw he was safe for the moment. The four Mafia killers were concentrating on Flynn. He examined his leg and, seeing the blood oozing from his pants, tore off his tie and used it as a bandage. What, he thought, have I got myself into? The hit men were quick, and they were very good. When he had tied off his wound, he raised his weapon and began firing at the closest assailant he could see. He was sure he shot the man in the arm, though the gunman quickly backed out of view behind the gray van.

On the adjacent street, the FBI agents did not see the gray van until it stopped in front of the house and the four armed men jumped out. Kessler was surprised to see Flynn and Walker suddenly come out of nowhere and start shooting toward the killers who were trying to assassinate Holmes. The sharp reports of their assault rifles immediately caused Kessler's adrenaline to begin flowing strongly.

"Who are those guys in the Pontiac?" Baker asked excitedly.

"They both look like cops," Kessler answered angrily, jumping into the front seat. "Must be Phoenix undercover. Goddamn it, they're not supposed to be out here."

"Those guys," Baker said, pointing toward the gray van, "look like pros. Are we going to help the locals?"

Kessler was irritated. They couldn't just sit there and watch. They would have to help the Phoenix cops.

"Get moving!" he shouted.

Baker, sitting in the driver's seat, started the engine and gunned it. The van raced toward the intersection. Kessler, sitting next to Baker, pulled out his nine millimeter.

"Faster!" he shouted at Baker. He turned back toward Lacy. "Felony stop procedure!" he said. "Lacy, go out the back. We'll take either door. Shoot to kill!" When they were within twenty yards of the gunfight that had erupted in the quiet Phoenix suburb, the three FBI agents jumped out and began firing toward the men who were now clustered around the gray van. The agents only had their nine millimeter automatics, but to a man they were expert shots. They immediately wounded two of the gunmen.

Unwittingly, Jeff and Flynn and the three FBI agents had achieved a crossfire and for a minute they pinned down the Mafia killers. The ugly sound of gunfire reverberated throughout the area. With a firefight erupting in this posh, normally quiet neighborhood, people started dialing 911 and in a matter of minutes, sirens began to wail in the distance.

Flynn was the first to hear the sirens, and he decided he'd better make a move toward Holmes. The killers would make their move while there was still time, before the whole area was flooded with cops. He dashed across the street to the car underneath which Jeff lay.

"They'll be going for Dr. Holmes," he said. "I've got to get up there. Get behind this car so you can keep me covered."

Jeff hesitated, not wanting to get shot again, then he gritted his teeth, rose up and got behind the car, firing as he did so.

"You're hit!" Flynn exclaimed, noticing his leg.

"I'll be all right," Jeff said. "I don't think it hit bone."

"Bastards!" Flynn said. Then he noticed one of the hit men running toward the house. The man was carrying a shotgun. Flynn saw that Holmes and the others had taken cover behind the Ford in the driveway. They didn't have a chance.

"Cover me!" he shouted and, as Jeff began to fire a volley from his rifle, Flynn sprinted across the sidewalk and over a neighbor's lawn toward the Roosevelt house. But he was too late and he saw he wasn't going to make it in time. The man with the shotgun raised his weapon and fired at the group of people hiding behind the Ford.

Flynn yelled and fired his rifle from the hip, one round after another, and on his third shot, the killer went down. Flynn ran forward, thinking he had saved them, but to his horror the man got up and fired his shotgun again at the group of people clustered near the Ford. Flynn swore, then stopped dead in his tracks and knelt down, taking careful aim at the man's head. He squeezed off a shot and there was a violent spray of blood as the bullet went into the man's left temple. The man fell to the ground, and his body began to jerk spasmodically. Flynn ran toward the group of people the gunman had been firing at. He looked with dismay at the scene. There was blood everywhere.

The first shotgun blast had hit Bill Roosevelt in the upper chest, killing him almost instantly. The man with the shotgun was firing "shredders," armor piercing loads which were incredibly lethal. Maggie, crouching next to her husband, was splattered with his blood when the shredder struck him down. She screamed and fell to the ground next to him, hugging him, trying to stop the bleeding with her own body.

Seeing this, Jonathan Holmes was infuriated. This violence was so senseless. Why are they trying to kill us? he asked himself in vain. He crouched next to Jamie behind Martin's rented Ford with his left arm around his daughter, trying to protect her from the gunfire. When the shotgun blast hit Bill, both he and Jamie were splashed with his blood.

"God!" Jamie screamed. "They're going to shoot us!"

"Stay down," Holmes told her and rose to go to Maggie's aid. He felt he had to do something instead of just cowering there. He reached down and pulled Bill's body by the armpits, not realizing he was already dead, and began to drag him to better cover.

"Come on, Maggie," he urged. "Let's move him behind the car. We must stop the bleeding."

"Keep down!" Martin Sherman shouted. "He's still coming!" Sherman watched as Flynn shot the gunman in his left arm, the energy of the bullet spinning him to the ground. But, then the man got up and once again came toward them, bringing his shotgun to bear on them. Sherman, who had been lying face down on the ground, sprang up to protect Maggie and Jonathan, both of whom were completely exposed. As he turned to help them, the gunman's second blast caught him squarely in the back.

The shredder tore through his entire upper body, ejecting blood and tissue forward onto Holmes and Maggie. Aghast, Holmes looked up and helplessly watched as Sherman fell to the ground, his body torn apart by the shotgun.

"God!" Holmes cried aloud, thinking he was about to die. He saw the gunman load another round, then aim the shotgun toward him. An instant later, the gunman's head exploded in a bloody mess.

Then James Flynn was there pressing Holmes back behind the Ford. "Stay here!" he commanded. "You're in great danger, Dr. Holmes. Those men have a contract to kill you!"

"A contract?" Holmes shouted.

"Yeah, ten million bucks' worth!"

"Who are they?"

"Professional killers! Don't ask me from where, but I've got to get you out of here. Now!"

"This is diabolical," Holmes stated. He was confused and his mind was racing. "How do I know who you are?"

"My name is... unimportant. I'm a member of the Defenders of the Planet, here to protect you. Now, come on! We've got to get you out of here. There are more of them."

"How can I believe you?"

"He just saved your life, Jonathan," Maggie sobbed. "Go with him. You must go!"

"What about my daughter?" Holmes protested.

"It's not her they're after," Flynn shouted. "They want you! If you come with me, they'll just ignore her. Come on!"

Holmes nodded. If they were trying to kill just him, then what Flynn said made sense. And there was no doubt somebody was trying to kill him. He decided to place his trust in this young man who had just shot the gunman who had killed his two friends. He turned to Jamie. "Stay with Maggie, Jamie. You'll be all right here. I love you, dear."

"No, Father!" Jamie shouted hoarsely, trying to choke back her tears. "I'm going with you!"

"No, you're not," Flynn shouted, pressing her back with his free arm. "It's too dangerous! You have to stay here."

Holmes looked at Jamie sadly. "Look after Maggie," he said. Then, he took Maggie's hand in his own. "I'm so sorry..."

Before he could say anything else, Flynn roughly hauled him up and forced him to begin running. As they made their way back to Jeff's position, Jeff covered them with a volley of gunfire. Flynn fired from the hip as he ran.

"Come on, Jeff!" Flynn shouted. "I've got Dr. Holmes. Let's get out of here. Pronto!" He took hold of Holmes' arm and guided him toward Walker's car. The three of them jumped into the Pontiac, which still had its engine running. Flynn pressed Holmes into the back seat and jumped in on top of him, telling him to stay down, while Jeff dove into the front seat and threw the car into reverse. He slammed his foot down on the pedal, forcing it to the floor. The Pontiac screeched away from the scene backwards. A hundred yards down the street, Jeff turned the car around, and they sped out of the neighborhood. Flynn quickly jumped into the front seat and, several blocks later, Jeff slowed down, just as two patrol cars turned from a side street and headed toward the scene of the gunfire.

"That's it for the bad guys," Flynn said. "They're going to be boxed in." He turned to his friend. "How's your leg?" he asked.

"I've felt better, but I'll make it," Jeff replied. "I hope I never have to do this again. I think we got all four of them. Did you see those FBI guys?"

"Yeah, kind of, but I was too busy shooting. I went through forty or fifty rounds."

"Goddamn!" Jeff said. "I shot off three magazines. Those guys never knew what hit them!"

"You did good, my friend!" said Flynn, suddenly smiling. "We pulled it off! We saved him from cold-blooded contract killers."

Holmes rose up from the backseat. "Who are you?" he asked. "What in God's name is this all about?"

"I told you... we're Defenders of the Planet. I'm James Flynn and this is Jeff Walker. In my everyday life I'm a police officer. Jeff is a fireman."

"Police officer? Fireman? This is crazy." Holmes sank back into the backseat, his eyes wandering about, looking for a way out of this. This can't be happening! he thought.

"That's right, Dr. Holmes," Flynn said. "We're just ordinary people. But, we believe in what we're doing. We help the earth wherever we can. Despite what you think, we want to help you. You've got to be protected."

"Where are you taking me?" Holmes asked.

"You'll have to get out of Arizona, and fast," Flynn answered seriously. "I'm afraid you're a wanted man, Dr. Holmes. Somebody has put out a contract on your life. They want you killed. They'll have people at the airports looking for you, but there are ways to avoid them. We need to get you out of harm's way."

"Where to?" Holmes asked.

"I'm not sure, but probably Mexico for the time being. Jeff, head for my house. Marty can fix your leg up. We'll stash your car in my garage, since I'm sure the FBI got a good description of it."

"Sounds good," Jeff said. Flynn's wife, Marty, was a nurse, and he definitely needed some medical care. The wound in his leg was throbbing, but he knew it wasn't life threatening.

"Tonight we'll call our contact and see what they want us to do," Flynn said. "Later on, we'll most likely head south for Mexico."

"Mexico, huh? What about our jobs? I've got to report to my station at eight in the morning."

Flynn thought for a minute. "I can take you home, later. As for me, I'm going to help Dr. Holmes get to a place of relative safety. I'll call my department and tell them I've got a family emergency, that I'm flying back to see my mother... that she had a stroke. It'll probably work. You'll be out of commission for awhile with that bullet wound."

"I wish I could help, too," Jeff said.

"Don't worry about it, Jeff," Flynn said. "It might be best if you went to work as soon as possible. I can always get Stu to help me with Dr. Holmes."

From the backseat, Holmes had been listening and the realization set in that these two young men were on the level. After what had just happened, they were his only hope. "We don't have much time," Holmes said.

"We can afford to wait," Flynn responded. "We'll hide you at my house until I get further orders."

"That is not what I meant," Holmes stated. "I meant the earth does not have much time. If Antarctica is experiencing air temperatures in the high seventies, then the entire world is going to suffer, and suffer tremendously. I would say the ocean will begin to rise quite soon. Millions of people will lose everything."

Flynn and Jeff looked at each other, not sure how to react to Holmes' statement. Holmes, seeing their expressions, realized they were perplexed by his words. "If that ice melts," he said, "there will be utter chaos everywhere in the world. Millions displaced, their homes gone, their jobs lost, and I'm sure casualties will be many. It's no wonder that the U.S. government doesn't want to admit what is happening. But this cannot wait. It's too big."

"Antarctica is a long way away," Jeff said.

"Perhaps so, but in reality we live on a very small world," Holmes said. "I've learned a lot in my life. Probably, the most important lesson I've ever learned is that you can't run from your problems. You must stand there and squarely face up to them. Sticking your head in the sand, drowning yourself in a bottle, running away from reality... these are just forms of defeatism and won't help. The earth is in serious trouble. I can't tell you just how serious it is. We must not run away."

"What can we do?" Jeff asked, implying that the situation might be futile.

"I can't think any more," Holmes said plaintively. He sat back into his seat. The adrenaline rush had finally started to slow down, and he realized just how close to death he had come. He thought about Martin Sherman and Bill Roosevelt, and he began to quiver. Two of his best friends were dead. He crossed his arms on his chest, his face in a tight grimace. It had been a long time since he had seen anyone die a violent death. Why did it have to be them?

When they got to Flynn's house, Flynn got them both out, showing Holmes to a bathroom so he could clean up, taking Jeff directly to his bedroom. Marty, Flynn's wife, immediately saw that something bad had happened. Jeff was limping and was obviously injured. When she cut his bloody pants off, she saw a bullet wound. As she began treating him, Flynn called Stu, who immediately left his office and came over, medical kit in hand.

Jeff was lying in bed and, when he saw Stu walk in, he grinned and waved at him. "How you doing, Doc?" he smiled.

"I should ask you that question," Stu replied. "How do you feel?" he asked, as he made a quick examination of the cleaning and bandaging done by Marty.

"I'll live," Jeff said. "I don't think I lost too much blood. It's really starting to hurt, though."

"Good work, Marty," Stu told her. "There's not much more I can do, except give him some medication for the pain, and antibiotics to prevent infection." Stu looked at Jeff. "You were lucky," he said. "The bullet went right through your leg. Another half-inch and it would have shattered your tibia."

Jeff had taken enough paramedic classes to know what that would have meant. In spite of the pain he was in, he laughed out loud. There is a God! he thought.

Flynn laughed too. "If you're gonna get shot," he said. "there's nothing like a good clean wound."

"You'll need to take it easy for a couple of days," Stu advised. "At least, until it scabs over. Otherwise, it could start bleeding on you, and then people might wonder what you've been up to. I suggest you call in sick tomorrow, and explain that you fell on a nail."

"Good idea," Jeff agreed.

Flynn looked at his wife. "Honey, would you mind fixing Dr. Holmes something to eat? He's sitting in the kitchen, drinking a beer. He's had a rough time and, right now, I think he could use a feminine touch."

"Sure, I'd be glad to," she said. She smiled at all of them and left the bedroom.

After she left, Stu looked at Flynn. "Does she know anything?"

"Probably," Flynn said. "She's not stupid."

Stu nodded, taking a hypodermic out of his medical bag. "Well, he said, "we'll just have to trust her. There's really nothing else we can do, is there?" He filled the needle with an anesthetic.

"What is that?" Jeff asked.

"Morphine. This will completely kill the pain for the next four hours. After that, you'll have to rely on your pain pills. More than one of these shots and you'll be too groggy to function. Roll over and pull your shorts down."

Jeff nodded and did as he was told. He grimaced as the needle went in, but within seconds, his body began to feel as if it were floating on air. "Thanks, Doc. I needed that," he said.

"Yeah, I can imagine. You'll be all right, though." He put his medical supplies back into his bag.

"Stu," Flynn said, "I called our contact before you got here. We're going to take Dr. Holmes into Mexico. They don't want us to make an immediate run for the border, so we'll keep him here for a day or two. They'll get back to me tomorrow, after they've figured out the gameplan."

"What happened out there?" Stu asked.

"We got ourselves into a firefight," Jeff said. "There were bullets flying everywhere. You ought to go see my Pontiac. It's a complete wreck."

Flynn laughed. "It's got a few holes all right. Nothing that can't be fixed." He told Stu everything that had happened, starting with the intelligence bulletin about the contract on Holmes. Stu listened intently to the whole story. Afterwards, he could only smile in complete amazement. His friends had been very lucky. Undoubtedly, if it hadn't been for their initiative, Dr. Holmes would be dead right now.

"James, my friend," he said, looking at Flynn, "I think you're going to need some help getting Dr. Holmes down to Mexico. I'll go with you. Besides," he said, "I could use a few days off from work. I'll just refer my scheduled patients to my associates."

"That's great!" Flynn said enthusiastically. "I can use your help. But I should warn you, there's no telling what we'll run into down around the border, you know?"

"It shouldn't be too bad," Stu remarked. He lowered his voice so only the three of them could hear. "It sounds like somebody really wants Dr. Holmes dead."

"These were definitely professionals," Flynn said. "And there will be more of them coming after him, not to mention the Feds. Getting Dr. Holmes safely across the border could be a very dangerous mission," he said.

Stu smiled. "Danger is my middle name," he said.

NINETEEN

A day later, Flynn and Stu began their trek to Mexico, taking with them Dr. Holmes, who in effect had become a hostage of circumstance. In the time spent at Flynn's house, Holmes had not been allowed to make any phone calls, and he couldn't go outside the house, so he was virtually confined to the living room, where he passed the hours watching television. His face was being shown on nearly every newscast he watched. The gunfight in Phoenix, coupled with his recent remarks about the environment, had made him a notorious figure. Now that he was on the run, the media had taken a keen interest in him, especially since the situation in Antarctica had become public information. Holmes had no choice but to resign himself to the fact that his life and his future were completely in the hands of James Flynn and his friends.

"Cheer up, Dr. Holmes," Flynn had said. "Things could be worse. You could be dead right now."

James Flynn had more important things on his mind than trying to boost Holmes' morale. When he received word from his contact within the Defenders that they should make their move, Flynn stole a car from the police impound yard. It was a double oh five Cadillac, and it would be several days before anyone noticed it was missing, giving them plenty of time to get deep into Mexico. The owner of the Cad had recently been arrested for drunk driving, his third offense, so Flynn knew the man wouldn't be needing his car for quite a long time.

When he got the Cadillac home, he found his wife waiting for him in the driveway. She was standing near the garage door as he opened it by remote and drove the Cadillac in.

"Nice car," Marty smiled as she walked around the driver's side. "I didn't know they sold Cadillacs around here at three in the morning."

Flynn grimaced, a tight smile on his face. He had been found out, and he knew it. He quickly closed the garage door. "Come on, Marty" he said. "We need to talk. Where's Dr. Holmes?"

"In his room, sound asleep... I made some coffee."

"Good," he said. "I'll need some." They went into the kitchen, which was just off the garage, and Flynn poured himself a cup. He sat down at the kitchen table and Marty sat down across from him, staring placidly into his eyes.

"Stu and I have to take Dr. Holmes to Mexico," he began. "We have to get him out of the country. The Mafia has a contract to kill him. An informant in Chicago told a Chicago detective about it. The contract is for ten million dollars. Anyway, Chicago spread the word via our special law enforcement network. So Jeff and I went to where he was staying to try and protect him."

"Jeff is a fireman," Marty replied.

"Yes, well, he's not your ordinary fireman..."

"He's not?"

"No... we're both in the Defenders of the Planet." He paused and looked directly into her eyes. "We were the ones who blew up the power line near Winslow. And the coal train."

Marty shook her head. "So it wasn't just a weekend camping trip? Goddamn it, James! Why haven't you told me this before?"

"It's against our rules. Neither Stu's wife nor Jeff's girlfriend know anything about us, about any of this."

"You could have trusted me," Marty said. "It's not like I would be against you. I'm your wife!"

"It's more complicated than that, Marty. What if someday we got divorced? Then you'd always know about me. You could hurt us very badly. Try to understand. We have to be careful. The Defenders are extremely meticulous in their methods."

"How long have you been doing this?" she asked.

"A long time. Stu recruited me. He joined because he got sick and tired of seeing kids, young kids getting skin cancer because we've screwed up the ozone layer. Because we're friends, and because they need police officers in the organization, he recruited me. And eventually I became the leader of the Phoenix unit. It was the natural thing to do, because I had access to information Stu didn't have and I was always in a position to react more quickly."

"The Phoenix unit?" Marty inquired.

"Yes. There are only the three of us in the whole state."

"But in Los Angeles...."

"Los Angeles has a lot more of us because we do different things over there."

"Like blow up oil refineries."

"Look, Marty. You've heard the news. Antarctica is melting." He looked at her questioningly, then he recalled Holmes' words. "The entire world is going to suffer because of what's happening down there. What we were trying to do was stop the world from using fossil fuels. That's what caused this problem. Now, it may be too late."

Suddenly, she looked sad. "I know," she said. "We've really messed things up, haven't we?"

"Yes."

"James, I want to help," she stated.

Flynn smiled gratefully. "We could use your help," he said.

"What do I have to do?"

"Just cover for us while we take Dr. Holmes to Mexico. We can't let him be killed by the goddamned Mafia. Those sleazebags have been dumping toxic waste up and down the East Coast for decades. Now they want to kill a man who's just trying to do the right thing. Lousy bastards!"

"Who do you think put out the contract on him?"

"I'd bet it was the oil companies. When we hit their refineries, we must have hurt them badly. It was just a stupid coincidence about Holmes saying we should attack them. Because of the government accusing him of blowing up the power lines and arresting him, and because of what he said in his speech, the oil companies think he's our leader. So they want to kill him before he does something else radical. But he's not part of the Defenders. He had nothing to do with any of this. Do you understand? I feel responsible for what's happened."

"Don't worry, James. I'll cover for you," Marty said. "I just hope you don't get hurt. You and Jeff could have been killed the other day."

"Before this is over, I think many people will be hurt. I can't believe the government is covering this whole thing up. I've found out that the FBI has definitely identified those hit men. They are known Mafioso, and they've all got previous records, two of them for attempted murder, one of them for second degree murder. And yet the FBI hasn't released that information to the press. It's like they don't want to say anything that might make Jonathan Holmes look good. Goddamned Feds!"

"When are you leaving?" Marty asked.

"First thing this morning. Stu's coming over in a couple of hours."

"Good," she said. "Then we've got time to go back to bed." She got up and took his hands, pulling him up toward her. She kissed him softly, then said, "I'm sure you could use a little more sleep."

"Sounds good to me," Flynn said, and then, still holding hands, he led her back toward their bedroom. He suddenly felt bad about lying to her over the years. He realized he could have trusted her. As they walked down the hall, he took a deep, forceful breath. Someday, he thought, I'll make it up to her. Someday, when the world isn't in such a mess, maybe we'll go to Hawaii.

He suddenly stopped and took her shoulders in his hands, turning her toward him. "Marty..." he started to say, but he couldn't find the right words.

"Yes, James," she said, looking at him questioningly in the dark.

"I'm sorry," he said. "I didn't mean to drag you into all this."

"Don't feel badly about it. You're doing what's right. I'm proud of you."

"You are?"

"Yes." She suddenly laughed. "I'm glad you told me. Now it all makes sense. You see, all this time I thought you might be having an affair."

"Me? Cheat on you? You mean, you really didn't believe those times when I told you we were going on camping and fishing trips?"

"Not really," she replied. "I knew something was going on, I just didn't know what."

"You're a smart woman," he said, and he laughed. "We could use someone like you in our unit."

"Try me," she said. "I'm pretty tough."

"Well, let's see," he said, and he led her into the bedroom.

They left Phoenix in the Cadillac at six and headed south for Mexico, Stu driving, Flynn sitting in the passenger seat and Holmes lying in the back seat, completely out of view from other cars, a necessary precaution since his face had recently become so recognizable.

Flynn and Stu were heavily armed, both carrying snub-nosed .38s beneath their shirts. Several Uzi automatic rifles were hidden in the trunk.

Their intention was to get to Nogales, check into a motel, reconnoiter the border area, then decide how to get Holmes across the line and on his way into the interior of Mexico. If everything went well, the entire mission would only take a few days. If it didn't go well, then anything was possible.

"It's been awhile since I've been down to Nogales," Stu said. "Remember those times in college?"

"Sure do," Flynn smiled. "We were wild and crazy."

"We're still wild and crazy," Stu laughed. "Otherwise we wouldn't be doing this."

"Don't worry, Stu. We're not going to be completely alone. Headquarters is sending us some help."

"They are? Who?"

"I don't know. We'll meet them in Nogales. I was told that once we get the motel room, we're not to cross Holmes until we get further word."

"Nogales!" Stu shook his head. "Hey, you remember that one time back in '92 when we went down there and those four Mexican women were buying us drinks?"

Flynn laughed. "Yeah, I remember, and they were arguing about who was gonna get who."

"Yeah! Man, those were the days..."

Holmes lay on his back, listening to their conversation. He heard them reminisce about their college days and weekend drinking sprees across the border, where the age limit for drinking wasn't enforced. The talk reminded Holmes of his own youth and his own college days so many years ago.

Yes, he thought, so many years ago. And now here I am, lying on my back like a bloody old fool, being spirited away to Mexico by these young men who called themselves Defenders of the Planet. He recalled his recent words to Mike Allen, when he had said that the Defenders were courageous in their deeds to protect the planet. Now he was with them. He almost felt like he was part of them.

Holmes wasn't afraid, but he was apprehensive, feeling somehow that he must remain alive during this world crisis. He knew it would become far worse. More than anything else, the continued silence of the world's governments bothered him. Stupid men were becoming even more stupid.

Once they were well beyond the outskirts of Phoenix, Flynn tapped Holmes on the shoulder. "It's okay, Dr. Holmes. I think you can sit up now."

Holmes immediately sat up and looked around at his surroundings. They were in a desolate area, and the road was flat and long, stretching and narrowing toward a distant southern horizon.

"Where are we?" he asked.

"On the road to Tucson," Flynn replied. "It's a couple of hours from here. After Tucson, it's another hour to Nogales and the Mexican border. My orders are to hole up there and wait for reinforcements. My guess is the FBI and the Mafia will be waiting for us."

"What do you propose to do?" Holmes asked.

"I don't know yet," Flynn said sincerely. He added, "Just get across the border and stay alive."

"Will you kill more people if you have to?"

"If we have to," Flynn replied. "Are you opposed to violence, Dr. Holmes?"

Holmes nodded. "No," he said seriously, "but only if it's absolutely necessary. The universe is a violent place, and so is the earth. If you think about it, violence is all around us. Mother Nature uses violence to achieve her goals. We experience earthquakes, volcanoes, hurricanes, tornadoes, and lightning. We can't control any of them. Every year they kill people, and yet they're part of our world, part of us. On this planet, by the very nature of it, people are subconsciously used to violent death because they've been exposed to it since the beginning."

"What about men killing other men?" Stu asked.

"That's different," Holmes said. "When men kill other men, it's usually unnecessary. I firmly believe that most wars could have been prevented if men had only listened to reason."

"What about what we've been doing? What about all those people who died when we blew up the oil refineries?"

Holmes thought for a moment. Then he said, "There are times when men must kill for a just cause. I think that this is one of those times. I believe that you are fighting for a just cause."

Stu and Flynn looked at each other. They were glad that Holmes believed in them, that he was on their side, but neither one of them could quite figure him out.

"Dr. Holmes," Flynn wondered, "if you believe in our cause, why did you ask if we were going to kill people, and make it sound like maybe we were wrong?"

"I asked that because I wanted to make sure you knew what you were doing," he answered. "And that you are fully aware of the path you're on. I have a feeling we're taking a very dangerous journey. Only God knows where it will end."

Stu and Flynn looked at each other again. Of course, they already knew that, but having it said to them didn't make them feel any better about it.

Stu drove on, and soon they were through the city of Tucson and heading due south for the Mexican border. Twenty minutes south of Tucson, they passed a convoy of motor homes.

"Who are these people?" Holmes asked.

"They're heading to Mexico for the winter," Flynn replied. "Here in Arizona, we call them snowbirds."

"Snowbirds?"

"Yes, they're probably all from the Midwest or northern states. They're going to be wintering in Mexico, where the weather is warmer."

"The bloody fools!" Holmes said vehemently. "Don't they know they're contributing to the crisis? Those bloody motor homes only get about four or five miles to the gallon!"

"That's right," Stu agreed. "Plus, it's not even cold where they all came from. This trip was probably planned a long time ago, so they're going to Mexico regardless of the hot weather back home."

"Goddamned bloody fools!" Holmes raged. "How can we fight this kind of mentality?" he asked the question rhetorically, not expecting Stu or Flynn to answer him.

"We could kill them all," Stu suggested, a smile on his face.

Holmes shook his head in disgust. "It's things like this that make it all seem so hopeless." He sat back in his seat, dejected by the sight of the large motor homes cruising south toward Mexico. To him, they were nothing but gas-guzzling monsters. "This must cease!" Holmes said firmly. "Antarctica is melting, and no one seems to even care!"

"It's a sad situation," Stu agreed.

Later, as they reached the outskirts of Nogales, Holmes spied something else that caused him anguish. "Look at that!" he suddenly said.

"What?" Stu and Flynn excitedly chorused.

"Those!" Holmes said, pointing out the window. "Those highway signs. They're all built using trees! See the poles they're built upon? What a waste of good trees, just so some greedy businessman can advertise his cheescburgers or some motel. No wonder America's forests have been depleted." Holmes looked angrily at the signs as they whizzed by on either side of the road.

"You're right," Stu said. "It's too bad. This is really pretty country. I hate to see these signs clutter it up any more than you do. Unfortunately, capitalism puts a small premium on the environment. Here in America, business comes first."

"Yes, and I hope America's businessmen are the first to suffer," Holmes said coldly. He was slowly becoming disgusted with Americans. What a bunch of bloody idiots, he thought to himself, not wanting to offend Flynn or Stu, who were opposed to such nonsense.

"You had better get down now, Dr. Holmes," Flynn advised. "We're coming into Nogales. They might be on the lookout for you."

Holmes nodded and lay down across the back seat. He took a deep breath and let it out slowly, trying to relax. No wonder, he thought, the world is in such a mess. But, at this late date, was there anything he could really do to make a difference?

TWENTY

At two forty-five in the afternoon, Jack Feldman's blood was boiling over. He had waited in line for over four hours for his ration of gasoline, and his car was on dead empty. For the hundredth time, he counted the number of cars ahead of him. There were eighteen. Would he get to the pumps before he ran out?

Feldman was fifty-five years old, and he knew he could never push his four door, late model double oh six Mercedes the necessary fifty or so yards to reach the gas station. And in Los Angeles now, he didn't expect anyone to help him, not with emotions running feverishly high. He was trying to get to the Arxon station on the corner of La Brea and Olympic, which he had been assured had recently taken a delivery of 20,000 gallons of unleaded gas. Was he to get so close for nothing? He swore several times, then slammed his palm down on the steering wheel. He swore again. "Jesus Christ! This is ridiculous!" he ranted. "All because of those goddamned Defenders of the Planet!" He felt a slight twinge of pain in his chest.

Calm down, he told himself. Just cool it. You don't need another heart attack. He breathed deeply to try to relax, then he reached for another antacid tablet and popped it into his mouth, chewing evenly and slowly. Calm down, he thought again. Just calm down.

The air temperature was over ninety degrees outside, and the humidity in L.A. was nearly eighty percent, totally unreal for January. Inside his Mercedes, though, Feldman couldn't feel the heat. He had his air conditioning set on maximum cool.

Suddenly, two cars ahead of him, a black BMW swerved into the line, forcing its way in. Feldman swore violently again. His expression of complete calmness turned into vicious rage.

"Those assholes!" he screamed. Something snapped inside him. He wanted to kill them, and that's just what he was going to do. He reached under his seat for the .357 magnum he kept there, sticking it into his belt and hiding it beneath his shirt. He shoved his transmission into park and flung open the door of his car, stomping over to the BMW.

He banged on the driver's window. "Get out of there!" he shouted. There was no reaction from within, and since the windows were darkly tinted, Feldman couldn't see inside, which only made him angrier. "Get out of there!" he shouted again.

The BMW edged forward about twelve feet, the line moving ahead, and Feldman ran to catch up. He viciously kicked the driver's door with his heel, putting a dent in it. At this, the driver's door flew open, and a young black male jumped out.

"Man!" he yelled. "What do think you're doing?" The man turned and inspected the damage to his door. "Man, look what you did! You crazy, ugly son of a bitch!" He pulled a switchblade from his pocket and clicked it open and started forward toward Feldman.

Feldman didn't hesitate. He whipped out his revolver, took aim, and pulled the trigger. He shot the man in the face, killing him instantly. "Stupid asshole!" he shouted. Then, Feldman looked inside the open door of the BMW. A young boy of about fourteen sat in the passenger's seat, his face frozen with fear. The boy started to escape out his door, but he was too late. Feldman shot him in the head from less than ten feet away. The bullet went right through him, breaking through the passenger's side window.

"Goddamned idiots!" Feldman screamed, and then several cars behind the BMW peeled out of the line and screeched from the scene as fast as they could, fearing they would be next. Feldman slammed the door of the BMW shut.

Nobody can mess with me! he thought triumphantly. Stepping over the body of the man he had just shot in the face, he walked back to his Mercedes and got in. That'll teach those assholes, he thought. Nobody's going to pull that shit on me!

Feldman's heart was pounding, and he could feel the flush of blood all around his face. Suddenly, he felt a sharp pain in his chest and in both of his arms. The pain became acute and he grimaced, biting his tongue in the process. Blood began to trickle from his lip. He grabbed the steering wheel with his free hand to brace himself, trying to catch a breath, but it was impossible. He began to gag. "Oh God!" he whispered in agony. A few seconds later, he suffered a massive coronary and died instantly. A large accumulation of gas and fecal matter immediately passed through his lower intestine, filling the Mercedes with a foul odor. Feldman fell forward, his body slumped over the steering wheel, his right hand still clutching his .357 magnum, his eyes staring lifelessly at the dashboard.

"L.A. is a real mess!" Jake Jurado said, taking another sip of wine. "It's complete bedlam out there."

"Thanks to us," Linda Ramirez said, a wry grin on her face.

"Do you think we did the right thing?" Jake asked, his expression serious.

Linda looked at him and nodded. "You're not having doubts about it, are you?" There was scorn in her voice.

"Yes," he admitted. "I'm having doubts! People are dying out there because of what we did." Jake gestured toward the big screen TV in the living room. They were sitting on the sofa, watching the six o'clock local news, and it wasn't good. Los Angeles was not readily adapting to gas rationing. On this one day alone, eighteen people had died fighting over gasoline.

"Jake," Linda said, "we can't have any doubts. If you think this is bad, what will happen to these people when the Pacific Ocean starts knocking on their front door?"

"They'll have to evacuate most of L.A." Jake replied. "But, because of what we did, they won't have enough gas to get out of here. Then what?"

"Then they walk," Linda replied. "It might be good for them. Especially all those fat asses who live in Beverly Hills."

"We may be walking ourselves."

"If we have to," she said. "I'll walk to San Bernardino. I've got an aunt there. She lives in the foothills. You can come, too. We'll backpack it."

"Yeah, sounds like fun." Jake took another swallow of wine. "It might be safer to walk. They'll probably be carjacking anything on wheels that's moving."

"It's their own fault," Linda said. "They should have switched to alternate fuels a long time ago. Then this wouldn't have happened."

There was a knock on the door, and Linda got up to answer it. Tom Ramsey stood on the porch.

He came in and joined them in the living room. Linda offered him a glass of wine, which he readily accepted. As Ramsey sat down, Jake reached for his remote and turned off the TV. "What's it like out there?" he asked, knowing that Ramsey must have just driven across the city.

"It's insane," Ramsey replied. "I rode over on my neighbor's Harley. I can't believe they're killing each other over gasoline. About two miles back, twenty cop cars were at a gas station, trying to maintain some order. The line of cars must have been three miles long. These people are panicking. They ought to just stay put and relax." He nodded gratefully as Linda handed him his wine. "Thanks," he said.

"Los Angeles depends on cars. Without them, everybody's lost," Linda said. "It's too bad they had no vision."

"Screw Los Angeles," Ramsey said. "They had plenty of chances to do the right thing. These selfish idiots are getting exactly what they deserve. They had plenty of chances to bring in rapid transit."

"Yeah," Jake agreed. "And now to top it off, the media is finally reporting that Antarctica is melting, that the Southern California coast is going to move inland about twenty miles or so. I'm sure these people are starting to think they may have to get out of Dodge fast."

"I'm not so sure," Ramsey said. "A lot of people don't even believe it. Some people I work with think this whole thing is a joke. They want to see it happen before they start packing. Their attitude is crazy."

"Man, everything is going crazy," Jake said.

"How's Sharon doing?" Linda asked.

"She'll be all right," Ramsey said. "We've hired a retired nurse to look after her. I believe the nurse will keep her mouth shut, but we've got the house bugged just in case."

Sharon Holt had suffered second degree burns on her arms and back on New Year's Eve, and she was still experiencing considerable pain. But, they all considered her lucky. Both of her team members had been killed that night.

"Any word on Lewis?" Jake asked.

Ramsey nodded. "No, Kathy can't find out anything. We only know the FBI has taken him back to Washington. We suspect they'll somehow make him talk."

"Oh, man!" Jake moaned. "We're screwed!"

"That's why I came over. My contact in Washington thinks it would be best if you both got out of here for awhile. If Lewis talks, you'll both probably be compromised. For all I know, he may have already spilled his guts."

Both of them nodded their understanding. Lewis was part of Jake's unit, captured by the police during their attack on the Six Star Refinery. Lewis could identify Jake. Since Linda lived with Jake, she too would probably be arrested if Lewis talked.

"So what do we do?" Linda asked.

"Leave town. That's why I came over on the Harley. I want you to take it. It gets just over seventy miles a gallon." Ramsey smiled, seeing the surprise on their faces.

"And this is okay with your neighbor?" Linda wondered aloud.

"He doesn't exactly know about it. You see, I stole it from out of his garage this afternoon." He smiled again, dangling a key in front of them. "I even got his extra ignition key. I know where he keeps it in his garage." Ramsey shrugged, as if to say, sorry, but these are desperate times.

"After I took his Harley, I drove over here, but first I stopped and filled the tank. It took nearly three hours, but from what I hear, I was lucky it didn't take any longer." He tossed the key over to Jake. "Here you go, buddy."

Jake caught it easily in his right hand, examining it carefully. He suddenly realized that the key represented more than just a mere piece of metal. It was the key to his future.

"How will you get back?" Linda asked.

"I can walk home. It's only twenty-two miles from here. The important thing is you. You both have to pack and leave here ASAP. We've got to get you out of the state before the Feds have a chance to make Lewis talk."

"But where?" Jake asked.

"We've got something happening in Arizona," Ramsey replied. He eyed Jake appreciatively. "You and Linda are needed there. You heard what happened to Jonathan Holmes day before yesterday, about the shootout?"

"Yeah," Jake said. "It was on the news today, again. But they didn't seem to know much about the shooting, just that he is hiding out somewhere. Those were very prominent people who got murdered. Shotgun style."

Ramsey nodded. "It turns out it was some of our people who saved him. They're hiding him in Phoenix. My contact wanted me to ask if you'd go to Arizona. They need to get Holmes out of the country, and Mexico is the best way out. Since you both speak Spanish, you can be a great help. If you go along, we can kill two birds with one stone. You escape from L.A. to Mexico and help Dr. Holmes escape, too."

Linda and Jake looked at each other, and they both shrugged. To them, fate was now dealing the cards, and all they could do was play along and see what came up.

"I have to forewarn you," Ramsey said, "the FBI aren't the only ones after Holmes. I was informed that the Mafia has a contract to kill him, so they're after him, too. It was their hit men who killed the ASU professor and the attorney. This could be very risky. Do you want to do it?"

"Yes," Linda said without hesitation. "I'll go. I'm not afraid of them, any of them."

"Sounds like we don't have much of a choice," Jake said, not thrilled with the idea that at any moment the FBI could come busting down his front door, though taking on the Mafia didn't sound like a good alternative. He nodded. "Okay. If Linda goes, I go, too. I'm not afraid of them, either."

"Good," Ramsey said. "Here's the plan. Tonight, you head for Mexico, to a place called Nogales, Arizona. You'll meet our people and Holmes in the morning in Nogales. From there, all of you will cross the border and head into Mexico. You'll need to take your weapons, so I suggest you disassemble your rifles and put them inside a bedroll on the back of the bike."

"And from there?"

"I don't know," Ramsey said. "My contact didn't tell me. All I know is you're to get Holmes and yourselves into Mexico. After that, you're on your own." He reached into his pocket and pulled out a large wad of bills. "Here's ten thousand dollars, in fifties and twenties. It's an emergency fund I've had for an occasion just like this." He handed the money over to Jake.

"We've got another ten thousand we've been keeping here," Jake said. "This should be enough to last us quite awhile down there."

"We'll try to wire you some more once you're established in Mexico. You are to both follow escape and evade procedures. You'll have to pack your laptop computer with its modem so you can communicate. We'll leave messages here for you on our local bulletin board. If I were you, I wouldn't exactly depend on our people in Phoenix. I have no idea who they are.

"Tomorrow, I'll call your offices and tell them I'm your father, that your mother died and you're going to Madrid, Spain, which is where I'm going to tell them I live. That should cover you for a few weeks anyway." Ramsey frowned, knowing that his words were small comfort, knowing he was asking them to give up their lives and go on the run.

"Don't worry," Linda said. "We both knew this might happen. If worse comes to worst, we can stay in Mexico for the rest of our lives. I'm getting tired of L.A. anyway."

"Yeah," Jake agreed. "Me, too. It sounds like everyone around here is going to kill each other, anyway." He smiled, and finished his glass of wine with a long swallow. "But how and where exactly do we meet our people who have Dr. Holmes?"

"Get a motel in Nogales and call in tomorrow on the bulletin board. There'll be a message telling you where to go to find them. They'll be staying at another motel. Then you simply go over there and introduce yourself. We'll have a password set up for you. Got it?" Ramsey asked.

"Got it," Jake replied. "Piece of cake."

Instinctively, Linda got up and parted the curtain to the window that overlooked the street. A blue van was parked across the street. "Tom," she asked, "was that van there when you got here?"

Ramsey got up and walked over to the window. Linda stepped aside, and he peered through the crack between the curtain and the window frame. "No," he said. "It must have just pulled up."

"I don't recognize it," Linda said. "It's never been in the neighborhood before." She looked directly into Ramsey's eyes, a stoic expression on her face.

"Damn it, Linda!" Ramsey said. "You'd better start packing right away. That could be the FBI."

"I think you're right," she said.

Jake came over to the window and peered out. The sudden appearance of the blue van seemed ominous. "Lewis must have talked," he said. "Where did you park the Harley?"

"I brought it into your side yard, just in case."

"Good thing," Jake said. "We can get out the back gate and into the alley without being seen. I suggest you leave the same way, my friend."

Ramsey nodded. "You two get moving. I'll keep an eye on them. You'd better hurry. We may not have much time."

TWENTY-ONE

The Harley was the big touring model, and Linda and Jake crammed as much of the most necessary items as they could into each rear side compartment. They couldn't pack much, so it only took them about ten minutes to gather up the few belongings they would need for the trip to Arizona. Jake packed their weapons, ammunition, and food, while Linda packed their money, clothing and personal hygiene supplies, and their laptop computer with its built-in modem.

When they were ready, Jake and Ramsey pushed the bike through the small back yard and through the gate and out into the alley. Jake jumped on, inserted the ignition key and started the engine. It fired up immediately.

Jake grinned at Ramsey and gave him a thumbs up. "Haven't ridden one of these in years. This is gonna be fun!"

Linda hugged Ramsey, then gave him a quick kiss. "Take care of yourself, Ramsey. Come visit us in Mexico."

"I will," he said. "You two take care of yourselves."

She got on the bike and put her arms around Jake's waist.

"Ready?" Jake asked, looking back at her over his shoulder.

She nodded. Jake waved at Ramsey and started down the alley. Ramsey watched as they drove away. Jake made a right turn out onto the street and they were gone.

"So long," Ramsey said softly, wondering if he'd ever see them again. He went back into their house and into the living room, parting the curtains and peering outside.

A gray sedan had pulled up in front of the house, and it was evident the men sitting in the front seat were Feds. They wore suits and dark sunglasses, although it was nearing dusk.

"Goddamned jerks!" Ramsey said aloud. His mind began to race. Quickly, he formulated a plan of attack. It was evident to him that the Feds were about to raid Jake and Linda's house. No telling what evidence they might find. He had to destroy everything, and he knew he mustn't leave anything to chance.

He walked back into the house and took one of Linda's candles from the dining room table. He quickly made a tour of the house, making sure all the windows were shut, then he set the candle on the floor in a corner of the living room and lit it. This should provide them with quite a surprise, he thought. He went into the kitchen and blew out the pilot lights on the gas stove. He took a deep breath and held it, and turned all the range and oven settings to maximum. The obnoxious odor of the gas began to fill the room. He let out his breath and backed away.

Ramsey went back into the living room and pushed the entertainment unit and big screen TV in front of the door. He began to pile sofas and chairs around it, making a strong barrier to any forced entry from the front. Satisfied he had done a good job, he left via the backdoor, locking it behind him. He went out into the alley and sprinted in the same direction that Jake had taken.

Once out on the street, he looked around. Seeing nothing suspicious, he innocently sauntered down the sidewalk to the intersection, then turned left in the direction of the blue van and the gray sedan. The van was on the other side of the street, but the sedan was parked almost directly in front of Jake and Linda's house. As Ramsey walked by it, he looked carefully at the two agents sitting in the front seat. They both looked straight ahead, pretending not to notice him.

Ramsey couldn't help but crack a smile. You shitheads! he thought. He kept walking, not breaking his stride. When he was fifty yards down the street, he looked back, just in time to see two more sedans pull up in front of the house.

Linda had been right about the blue van when she first spotted it. Ramsey could only wonder about her, knowing her instincts were rarely wrong. Lewis talked, he thought. He wondered what they had done to him. According to Jake, Lewis was one of the toughest men he had ever met. Had they used drugs on him, torture, or a combination of both? Ramsey knew that he didn't have to worry about Lewis talking. He had not personally recruited him. Jake had.

Ramsey crossed the street and walked another thirty yards, then ducked behind a large bush. He positioned himself so he couldn't be seen from the street or from the area in front of Jake's house. From behind the bush, he could safely watch as events unfolded.

Five minutes later, two more sedans drove down the street from opposite directions. Ramsey could see that they were filled with FBI agents. Both cars turned at their respective intersections and drove out of his sight. Probably heading into the alley to cover the back, Ramsey figured.

A few more minutes went by, then all the Feds sitting in front of the house began to file out of their cars. Ramsey counted twelve agents heading for the front door, all of them weaving and ducking, making a military style approach. Two of them were carrying a battering ram, the rest were armed with small automatic weapons. They ducked all along the front wall, then the two who were carrying the battering ram dashed toward the front door, bashing the ram squarely against it. The door held firm, not budging an inch. They pulled back and rammed the door again, and again it held.

Come on! Ramsey thought. Blow, you son of a bitch! Come on! he silently urged. If it blew now, no one would get killed. He watched as they battered the front door several more times. Finally, they began to push it open, enough so that they could squeeze through. Four more agents followed the first two in. A second later, the house blew up.

Ramsey saw a bright flash of light, and a split second later a deafening explosion rocked the whole neighborhood. Those agents standing on the porch were blown clear out to the street. One of the men who had entered the house came running out, his body engulfed in flames. His screams could be heard over the now-roaring inferno that once had been Jake and Linda's house. The rest of the agents who had gone in, Ramsey assumed, must have been killed. He watched in horror as what was left of the house began to viciously burn up, the fire and smoke rising high into the air.

Jesus Christ! Ramsey thought. I've just killed them! He began to tremble, and he turned away and began a fast walk down the street, turning right at the first intersection. The sight of the burning, screaming man was imprinted upon his mind, a sight he would never forget. As the realization hit home that he had violently killed other men, he began to walk faster, trying to get away from the scene. He heard sirens coming from all directions.

For the next ten minutes, his mind was numb, and he walked along in the right direction by instinct alone. Slowly, the shock of what he had done wore off and he began to analyze what had just happened.

He decided that they must have used drugs on Lewis — or torture. How else could they have found Jake and Linda? And if they had tortured him, he wondered what they might have done to Lewis, if he had done any screaming, if he might even still be alive. Ramsey shook his head. This was a nasty business and there was no telling where it would all end. For the first time, he no longer felt like an environmentalist — he felt like a revolutionary.

Jake and Linda rode east on Interstate 10, not aware that their house had been destroyed, nor that they were now wanted for first degree murder in addition to all the crimes listed against them for the attack upon the Six Star Oil Refinery. Just after three a.m. they reached the outskirts of Phoenix, where they stopped to eat at a large truck stop.

Jake parked the bike where it could be easily seen from inside the truck stop's restaurant, and the two of them walked in, taking a booth along the wall of windows that looked out upon the parking lot. The Harley was in plain view.

"I wonder if Ramsey made it back to his house okay," was the first thing Jake said to Linda.

"Probably," she said. "Ramsey is one smart hombre. I wouldn't worry about him if I were you."

"Yeah," Jake agreed. "I should probably worry about us. It's not that much further to Nogales."

Linda smiled at Jake, revealing her even, bright white teeth. "I'm glad this all happened, Jake," she said. "We've got a new life ahead of us now."

He smiled back. "I know. We can get false IDs and blend into Mexico with no problem. I think we should head for the other side of the mainland, a place like Veracruz. What do you think?"

"Veracruz sounds lovely," she said. "Maybe we can open up a cantina, or something."

Jake nodded. "Or maybe we can get some recruits and form a unit. Mexico, you know, has serious environmental problems."

Linda laughed. "I know," she said. "Wouldn't that be something?"

TWENTY-TWO

Flynn and Stu drove around downtown Nogales for half an hour before they decided that none of the motels looked right. They were looking for a hiding place, and they wanted privacy. The motels they saw were easily observable from the streets and parking lots, or they looked cheap.

"Man," Stu noted as he drove along, "this is one ugly town. It's changed a lot from what I remember."

Flynn laughed. "We were always here at night, never during the day, so we couldn't see everything."

"Not too much to see. Nogales needs a town beautification committee or something. Look at all that trash on the ground."

They drove around for a few more minutes, looking the town over, then Stu said, "Why don't we go back to that place we saw coming in? It looked decent."

"Yeah, but I was hoping to get something close to the border." He thought for a few seconds, then said, "Well, okay. Let's try it. It couldn't be any worse than what we've seen so far. At least it was set back in the hills."

"Yeah, I noticed that, too. We probably should have gone directly there." Stu got back on the freeway and they headed north, driving fifteen minutes and then getting off at the Rio Rico offramp, turning left toward a hotel complex that was half a mile west of the interstate. It was called the Rio Rico Resort.

Stu drove up a winding road and pulled into the main parking lot. The hotel looked well maintained, and it appeared that they would have maximum privacy.

"This is it," Stu stated. "The Rio Rico Resort. It looks good to me. What do you think?"

"Okay," Flynn nodded. "I'll check us in. I'll get two rooms somewhere in the back. You two wait here." He got out and walked up the steps to the resort office.

Stu watched as Flynn went into the building, then he looked over his shoulder at the still form of Jonathan Holmes lying in the back seat. Holmes had remained quiet since they had entered Nogales. "You okay, Dr. Holmes?" he asked.

Holmes looked up at him and nodded, smiling for the first time in several days. "I'm okay, Stu," he said. "I was just doing some thinking. I'm getting used to being in this silly position. I feel ridiculous."

"Won't be much longer and you can stretch your legs."

"I'm looking forward to that. Do you think we'll be safe here?" Holmes asked.

"As safe as anywhere else around here. Probably much safer, I'd say." Stu squinted and looked around the parking lot, his right hand brushing the .38 pistol in his belt. He didn't see anything even remotely suspicious. Realizing the interior of the car was becoming hot, he turned the key just enough so that he could lower the windows. Immediately, fresh air entered the car, and it began to cool off.

"Greenhouse effect," Holmes said. "It's especially pronounced in an automobile."

"I know," Stu said. "That's why I lowered the windows."

"The rapid increase in interior temperature is due to the fact that there is very little thermal mass inside an auto," Holmes explained. "The sun comes in, is trapped by the glass, and the infrared energy has nowhere to go. There's no storage medium, so it gets hot rapidly."

Stu thought about this, then decided to ask a question. "The earth is suffering from the greenhouse effect, and it has plenty of mass. Why is it getting so hot?"

"It's the same basic principle. Yes, the earth has great thermal mass, especially when considering the oceans, but the planet is getting a stronger greenhouse effect, and it's been creeping up on us for the past year now. Last August, several scientists reported unusually high water temperatures in the Atlantic and the Pacific. But did anyone care?"

Stu nodded sadly. "Of course not," he said.

"Exactly. People paid no attention to this warning sign. It was just more of the same. Nothing happened! It received a slight mention in the press and was quickly forgotten. Everyone continued on their merry way, burning fossil fuels and polluting the earth! We at SOW tried to alert humankind that the planet was out of kilter, but to no avail. So we sped up our research to prove irrefutably that something abnormal was occurring, but we were too late. Now we're witnessing the beginning of global warming. The planet is acting just like this car. Unfortunately, with the earth, we can't simply open the windows and put everything back to normal."

"Where's it all going to end?" Stu wondered.

"I really don't know. The planet might be all right if we can convince everyone to immediately stop using fossil fuels. But, even then, the odds will be against us. There are other factors at work. For instance, we have greatly damaged the ozone layer. At our current level of technology, the effect of ozone depletion is impossible to assess in terms of total atmosphere dynamics as it pertains to the greenhouse effect."

"Yes, except I've seen the results up close. Skin cancer is not a pretty thing."

Holmes nodded his agreement. "No, it isn't."

Then, Flynn came back out, room keys in hand. He got in the car and pointed to his left. "That way, Dr. Smith. We've got two rooms in the very back of this place. Rooms F262 and F263."

Stu smiled. "Excellent," he said, starting the engine and backing up. "How did you pay for them?"

"False ID and credit cards. We are registered under the name of Robert Weaver. I told them we're real estate investors, down here to look over some property."

"Sounds good to me," Stu said. He backed out and turned the big Cadillac to the left, proceeding slowly along the curving driveway. On the right stood individual three-story buildings, each marked with big letters. To the left, the high desert country of Southern Arizona encroached right up to the edge of the resort.

They drove around to the very rear of the complex and Stu parked in front of a set of stairways built into the slope leading to the three-story F building, a big red F painted on the side of it.

"It looks like it might be okay," Stu said.

"Yeah, looks clear," Flynn agreed. "Let's all quickly get inside. Dr. Holmes, you can get up now. Let's go."

"Thank heavens," Holmes said, sitting up straight in the back seat. He didn't have time to gather in his surroundings.

"Let's move!" Flynn commanded, and he and Stu got out of the car and ushered Jonathan Holmes into room F-262 as quickly as they could. Once inside, the three of them stood there in the middle of the room. There was a momentary awkward silence.

"What happens now?" Holmes asked Flynn.

"We'll get our stuff out of the Cadillac, then check in with the laptop and modem and see if there's a message for us on our electronic bulletin board. Then we sit tight and wait."

Later that morning, Jake and Linda rode into Nogales on the big Harley and checked into a downtown motel. They had ridden all night, and they were both tired. Jake unpacked the bike and immediately hooked their laptop computer and modem up to the room phone. He dialed their bulletin board in Los Angeles, and with Linda looking over his shoulder, together they viewed the message displayed on the laptop's screen. It read:

"Friends at Rio Rico Resort, approx. twelve miles north of Nogales. Contact four p.m. at resort bar. Sit at the bar. Your contact will approach you and say 'the weather seems to be getting hotter, doesn't it?' and you will say 'the weather is very unpredictable. Perhaps there will be an earthquake.' Precise response important. Go there fully packed. Stay there tonight. Bad guys everywhere. Get into Mexico as fast as you can. FBI is looking for you. Your house in LA was blown up. Many casualties. Be careful. Foghorn."

"Our house has been blown up!" Linda exclaimed.

"What the hell happened?" Jake asked, knowing Linda didn't know any more than he did. Then he said, "Ramsey must have done it! He must have set off some kind of a bomb. And now they're looking for us. Jesus!"

"Don't worry," Linda said coolly. "If our house has been blown up, they won't have our current pictures, at least, the way we look right now. That will give us more time."

"Yeah, that's true, but eventually they'll come up with something. They're smart bastards!" Jake turned off the computer and looked at his watch. It was eleven-thirty a.m. They had plenty of time to rest before going out to meet their friends.

"I wonder what he meant by bad guys?" Linda asked. "How does he know there are bad guys down here? I didn't see any feds or mafioso types when we rode in here."

"Neither did I," Jake said. "But he must know something."

"We'll have to be very careful, Jake. It looks like we've ridden into a hornet's nest."

Jake looked at her with hard eyes. "If I go," he said, "I'm taking as many of them with me as I can!"

She immediately laughed. "Don't be so melodramatic." She turned away and began to undress. "I'm going to take a shower and get cleaned up. Why don't you go get us some food?"

He nodded. "Some burritos okay?" he asked.

"Yes, and some coffee, too," and she disappeared into the bath room. Jake picked up the room key and left, locking the door behind him. He walked out to the Harley, started it and drove out onto the main street of Nogales, heading north. After a minute, he saw a restaurant off to his right, a place called Zula's, and he pulled in to the parking lot.

He walked in, looked around and saw that the restaurant was empty except for six men sitting at two different tables. Jake instinctively knew they weren't locals. Whoever they were, they looked like tough hombres. One of them turned and eyed him suspiciously. Jake quickly looked away.

He sauntered all the way through the restaurant, taking a seat at a table near the back. From there, he could discreetly watch the entrance and keep an eye on the six suspicious-looking men. Out of the corner of his eye, he saw one of them staring at him. He tried to act as if he didn't notice anything, but he knew their guard was up. Did they know him? Was Linda wrong and was his picture in the news? Doubts filled Jake's mind.

A waitress soon came over and handed him a menu. "Don't leave," Jake commanded. "I'm ready to order." He quickly looked over the menu and made a fast decision. "I'd like two carne asada burritos to go, and also two large coffees with cream and sugar. And I'm in a hurry. Okay?" He gave her a big grin.

"Would you like some coffee while you wait?" she asked.

"Please," he said, leaning back into his chair as she poured him a cup. She left, then came right back with some cream. Jake began adding cream and sugar to his cup of coffee, hoping he wouldn't have to wait too long. He took a sip. It tasted very good.

Jake sat there, noticing the decor of the restaurant. The building was obviously old, but they had done their best to dress it up, and the place was conspicuously clean. Must be a family operation, he thought. As he looked about, he was aware that the man who had been eyeing him was no longer interested. None of the others were staring at him, either. They must think I'm a Latino local, Jake figured.

He sat there for ten minutes, and then his waitress brought his order in two white paper bags. She set them on the table and handed him his check. "You can pay up front," she said.

Jake nodded, downed his cup of coffee, and headed for the front cash register. As he was paying for the food, he saw that the six men had finished their meal and were getting up. He also noticed that one of them tossed a hundred dollar bill into the middle of his table. All six of them were wearing short-sleeved shirts and slacks, and Jake thought he noticed bulges under their shirts. Who are these guys? he asked himself.

The lady at the cash register handed him his change, and he turned to leave just as the six men were walking by. He did some quick thinking, then made his move, forcibly bumping into one of the six, his hand touching the man's waist.

"Watch it, asshole!" the man said sternly, giving Jake a nasty look.

"Oh, excuse me. Sorry, man." Jake said, a feeble grin on his face. He stepped back against the counter and let the six pass by. He had taken a risk, but it was worth it. He had definitely felt a hard metal object under the shirt. After they left, Jake turned to the waitress at the cash register. "Are those men from around here?" he asked in Spanish.

"No. They're new," she answered, also speaking Spanish. "They came today for the first time."

"Thanks." He walked outside, just in time to see two rental cars start to pull out of the parking lot.

Jake realized he was standing there in the open, and again they'd have a clear view of him, when he saw some newspaper racks just outside the entrance. He quickly turned his back on the two cars, walked over and glanced at the newspapers displayed inside the racks. One of the papers was a daily out of Tucson. Its bold headlines read: FBI MANHUNT! A subheadline read: Feds Launch Nationwide Search For Terrorists. His picture and Linda's were prominently displayed beneath the headline. The pictures had come right out of California's Department of Motor Vehicles computer.

Jake began reading the story and, in the first paragraph saw his and Linda's name in print. Jesus Christ! he thought. Now we're in it! He waited until he knew the cars behind him had pulled out into the street, took a deep breath and turned away from the newspaper rack, and strode over to the Harley. He tried to concentrate on the task at hand, and he was determined to not worry about the incident in California.

Those men he had just seen inside the restaurant were definitely not Feds. Must be Mafioso, here to find Jonathan Holmes and kill him. He set the bags of food and coffee into the side pouch, got onto the Harley and gunned the engine, driving out to the edge of the main street. He looked both ways, then pulled out and turned left. Ahead of him, he could see one of the rental cars, a shiny green four-door Buick. He decided to follow it.

The Buick drove at precisely the thirty-five mile per hour speed limit, and after a minute it turned right into the parking lot of the Americana Hotel. Jake pulled over next to the curb, in a position to observe. Leaving the Harley's engine running, he watched as three men filed out of the Buick and walked into the hotel. He glanced around the parking lot, but the other rental car was nowhere to be seen. His focus shifted back to the three men who were going into the hotel. He noticed that all three of them walked on the balls of their feet, like cats. They were obviously in excellent physical condition. Real bad guys, Jake thought.

When they were gone, he pulled away from the curb and went back to his motel. Linda was sitting on the bed, a towel wrapped around her, brushing her long black hair, which was dripping wet.

"Guess what I just saw?" Jake exclaimed.

"What?" she asked, her eyes widening.

"I just spotted a group of contract killers. Pros! Ramsey was right. The bad guys are here!"

"Are you sure?" she asked.

"Yes, I'm sure," he said, and he told her what he had seen, emphasizing the part about feeling the man's gun. Linda listened raptly to the entire story. When Jake was finished, she frowned, pursing her lips.

"This isn't good, Jake. Even if we get into Mexico okay, I don't think these guys will stop," she said. "Not if they're professionals. They'll probably follow us right across the border. They're paid killers. They've got a job to do, and they'll do it."

"What are you getting at?" Jake asked, seeing that her mind was working in high gear.

"We're going to have to get them, before they get us."

Jake looked at her harshly. "You want to take them on? Like in the gunfight at the OK Corral? Have you gone loco?"

Linda didn't immediately respond. She sat there looking at him. Finally, she said, "We could set them up for an ambush. They don't know that you and I are here. We could surprise them."

"I think we'll have to see what the others have to say about that," Jake said calmly. "They may not like your idea."

"We'll see about that," Linda said, her eyes flashing.

"There's something else you should know about," Jake said matter-of-factly. "Our pictures are all over the front pages. We're wanted for what happened in L.A. The Feds are looking for us everywhere. A nationwide manhunt!"

Linda simply shrugged. "It was to be expected," she said.

Jake nodded and said, "Yeah, I guess so." He reached into the bags and pulled out the two burritos and the coffee. "For now, let's eat and then get some rest. I'm dead tired."

Linda sat down and began to unwrap a burrito. She smiled demurely at him, letting the towel fall away from her breasts. "Too tired for some fun?" she asked as she bit into the end of the burrito, smiling and chewing at the same time.

"You know I'm never that tired," Jake smiled back at her.

Later, they rode out to the Rio Rico Resort, arriving and entering the bar at precisely four o'clock. Other than the female bartender, there were only two couples sitting at tables near the windows. No one else was there.

Jake and Linda sat down squarely in the middle of the long section of a U-shaped bar.

"What would you like?" the lady tending the bar asked.

"Wine, please," Linda said. "Chablis."

"I'll have the same," Jake said. He looked around the room, then glanced at his watch. "Whoever they are," he said quietly, "they're late. It's four oh two."

Linda shrugged. "Maybe they've been delayed."

The bartender came back with their wine, setting two glasses in front of them. "That'll be eight dollars," she said, wearing a pleasant smile on her face. Jake took out his wallet, handing her a ten dollar bill, and she promptly turned away to go ring up the sale. Jake noticed that she didn't appear to recognize them. So far, so good, he thought.

They sat there for several minutes, sipping their wine, and then James Flynn walked in and sat on a barstool next to Linda's. He ordered a soft drink and, when it was served to him, he glanced over at Linda and said, "The weather seems to be getting hotter, doesn't it?"

Linda immediately responded by looking directly at him and saying, "The weather is very unpredictable... perhaps there will be an earthquake."

Flynn nodded and smiled. "I'm James Flynn, from Phoenix, and I'm really glad to see both of you."

Linda smiled. "It's nice to meet you," and she shook hands with Flynn. Jake extended his hand, too. "Nice to meet you, James."

Flynn looked at the bartender, realizing she could probably hear every word they said, though she appeared not to be listening. "Why don't we sit at a table?" he said softly. "We'd be more comfortable."

Jake and Linda nodded, and they all got up from the bar and walked over to a table where they could talk in privacy. Flynn waited until they sat down, and then sat across from them, his back to the wall. For a brief moment, he looked them over, appraising both of them. They calmly stared back at him.

"Are there any more of you?" Flynn asked.

"No," Jake replied. "We're it. How many are with you?"

"Just one, so I guess that makes four of us. It'll have to do. We're really outnumbered."

"Yeah," Jake said, "I counted six professional hit men this afternoon at a local restaurant in Nogales. And there could be more of them around here."

"How do you know they were hit men?" Flynn asked, his eyes narrowing. "What made you think that?"

"Because they were carrying guns and flashing hundred dollar bills. I don't think Feds would carry hundreds. They don't make that kind of money. And besides, these guys looked like killers. Nasty types."

"What were they wearing?"

"Short-sleeved shirts, expensive-looking slacks, expensive-looking shoes."

"And the shirts weren't tucked in?"

"No," Jake said. "I purposely brushed up against one of them, and that's when I felt his gun. I think it was an automatic of some kind, maybe a small nine millimeter."

"Probably," Flynn said. "That's everybody's favorite gun. With six of them, it would mean they've got lots of firepower."

"There may be more," Jake suggested. "With shotguns and everything else."

"You could be right," Flynn agreed.

"The question is, why are they here?" Jake wondered aloud. "How did they know we were all coming to Nogales?"

"Easy," Flynn said. "It's the logical thing for us to do, especially since our gunfight in Phoenix. They know Holmes is on the run, and they know that he's got friends. Deadly friends."

"Were you in that gunfight?" Jake asked.

"Yes. I know I killed one of them. We might have wounded some, too. One of our people got shot, but he'll be okay. Anyway, they were definitely pros. Real killer types."

"And now they're down here," Linda said.

"Yes," Flynn nodded. "Looking for Dr. Holmes."

"James, I've been doing some thinking. I have a plan. I think we've got to hit them before they hit us," Linda said. "I know they'll follow us into Mexico. They won't give up just because we've crossed the border. We could ambush them somehow. You know, set them up."

Flynn looked circumspectly at Linda, then he couldn't help but grin broadly. For a woman, he thought, she's got balls. "That's not a good idea, Linda. If we get into a gunfight, every killer in the world will know we've crossed into Mexico from Nogales." Flynn shook his head. "I'm sorry, but it won't work. There's a ten million dollar contract out on Dr. Holmes, so even if we got all six of the men Jake saw, we'd only draw dozens more to our trail. Our best bet is to sneak across into Mexico unobserved and then try to get as far south of here as possible. That way, no one will ever know which way we went."

Jake smiled. "I agree with you, James. No need for violence if we can avoid it. I like the idea of just sneaking across."

"Yes," Flynn went on, "especially after what happened in Los Angeles. I think the two of you would be better off trying to be as discreet as possible. You know what I mean?"

"You heard about what happened?" Jake asked.

"Have you seen this morning's papers?"

"Yes," Jake said blandly. "We know all about it."

"You killed five FBI agents making your getaway from L.A. A sixth agent is on life support not expected to live. In its entire history, the FBI has never taken a hit like that. I have to give you credit. When you do something, you do it big!"

"We didn't kill anybody," Linda said. "We think one of our members in L.A. did it, to cover for us."

"That's right," Jake added. "We left quietly, without any trouble. Whatever happened, happened after we left."

"I see," Flynn said, seeing the dismay on their faces. "Regardless, it's you they want. That's why you're going to have to get across the border fast and assume new identities. Right now, you don't have any other choice. I'm a cop, and I should know."

"You're a cop?" Jake's jaw nearly dropped.

Flynn smiled. "Yes. A detective. Phoenix PD. But don't worry. I'm a Defender first, a cop second. Besides, I know enough about the FBI not to feel sorry for them."

"Oh," Jake said meekly. "I see."

"This is new ground for us... we're not sure who we can trust," Linda said, looking over at Jake with a puzzled expression. She suddenly wondered who this James Flynn was.

"You can trust me," Flynn said firmly. He looked at them carefully, and he saw that they appeared skeptical. "Look, we're in a war. The Defenders know that. Most people are apathetic, but we're not. We've been called to action, and I know which side I'm on. And it seems like you know which side you're on. Right now, our primary objective is to get Dr. Holmes heading south out of harm's way. Those idiots you saw want to kill him. And obviously, the two of you also have to leave the country. It's going to be up to you to get Dr. Holmes deep into Mexico. Then my partner and I can get back to Phoenix. You won't need us down there. For now, you're going to have to trust us."

Jake said, "I trust you."

"And you?"

"Yes," Linda sighed. "I trust you."

"Good. Now, I need to know everything about your escape from Los Angeles. Tell me every detail, starting with when you first realized the Feds were onto you."

"Why?" Jake asked.

"Because it's important," Flynn said simply.

"Okay," Linda agreed, and she began the story of their getaway, Jake occasionally adding his own comments.

When they were through, Flynn nodded his approval. "It doesn't sound like you would have been tracked down here. I'd say you and your friend Ramsey were very thorough. Do you have any idea about what part of Mexico you'd like to go to?"

"Maybe Veracruz," Jake said. "We've got enough money to start a little business down there."

"What kind of work do you do?" Flynn asked.

"I'm an accountant," Jake said. "CPA."

"I'm a legal secretary," Linda said. "I work for a large law firm downtown... I mean I worked for a law firm."

Flynn suddenly felt sorry for them. "It's not going to be easy for you," he said. "I know a lot has happened. I'm sorry."

"Don't be sorry," Jake said. "We were getting sick of L.A. anyway. Besides, the whole place is about to go ballistic. I see bad things happening there, and soon."

"Yes," Linda agreed. "We feel good about leaving. We have a whole new life ahead of us. All we have to do is get across the border."

"You'll have to be careful for a long time," Flynn said. "The FBI will never let this one go. Believe me."

"And what about Dr. Holmes?" Linda asked. "How long do we keep him with us?"

"I don't know. Maybe for a long time. First things first, however. We have to get all of you across the border. It's not going to be easy. I happen to know that every U.S. Customs agent in Nogales is on the lookout for Dr. Holmes. The FBI has sent forty agents down here on a special detail. They're inspecting all cars going into Mexico. They've got all the likely border crossings covered. Also, the U.S. Border Patrol has special foot patrols out in the hills to the west and east, complemented by the U.S. Army. They've brought in several hundred soldiers from Fort Huachuca. They're members of elite units. Rangers."

"U.S. Army Rangers? How do you know all this?" Linda asked.

"Back in Phoenix, I have access to the Law Enforcement Computer Network. I know everything the Feds are doing before they do it. I checked up on them before we left Phoenix."

"They really want this Dr. Holmes, don't they?"

"Yes," Flynn answered. "You see, they probably believe he's the leader of the Defenders of the Planet."

"Do you think he's one of us?" Linda asked.

"No, I'm sure he's not," Flynn smiled. "I don't think he really knows anything about the Defenders."

"Then why is he so important to them?"

"Because when we attacked the oil refineries, we attacked America itself. We may as well have bombed the Capitol. Oil is the lifeblood of this country. The way the system is set up, America can't run without oil. That's just the way it is."

"I'm glad we blew up their damned refineries," Linda said bitterly. "Burning oil is what got the world into this mess. And all those bigshots in Washington don't even care."

"It seems that way," Flynn said. "I figure most of the politicians in this country have been bought off with oil money, one way or another. Anyway, the government and big oil have a stake in getting Dr. Holmes out of the way. To them, he's a very dangerous man. He does with words what we do with guns. I think everyone in the establishment wants him dead, or permanently put away in some prison hole."

"So how do we get him across the border?" Linda asked.

"Yeah," Jake added, "with all these big guns down here?"

"I have a plan," Flynn replied. "I think we can pull it off, but it's going to be risky."

"Just tell us what you want us to do," Linda said.

"Look," Flynn said earnestly, "it would be best if we went back to my room." He looked around suspiciously. "You're taking a risk being out in public like this. Did you bring all your equipment with you?"

"We've got everything, just like we were told."

"Good, I don't want you going back to your motel tonight, just in case someone spotted you. You can stay with us. We've got two rooms. Let's go back and I'll explain my plan, and you can meet Dr. Holmes. Okay?"

"Sounds good," Jake agreed.

"Okay," Flynn said. "I'll leave first. You leave a minute or two after me. We'll be in room F-262. It's toward the very back of this place. Just walk right in. I'll leave the door unlocked."

"F-262," Jake repeated. "Got it."

Flynn got up and walked out of the bar, and a minute later, Jake and Linda followed him. They walked through the middle of the resort and a few minutes later found room F-262.

They entered the room and saw two men sitting at a table playing cards. Flynn immediately came out from behind the door, a pistol in his hand, and locked the door behind them.

"Did anyone spot you?" Flynn asked. "Were you followed?"

"No," Jake answered. "I don't think so."

Flynn nodded and waved toward the table. "This is my partner, Stu Smith, who is a medical doctor, and this is Dr. Jonathan Holmes."

Jonathan Holmes rose up from the table, extending his hand in Linda's direction, shaking hands with her and then with Jake.

"Pleasure to meet you," Holmes said. "Thank you for coming to help me." He smiled graciously at both of them.

"Well, sir," Linda began, "after what happened in California, it looks like we don't have much choice. We're all in this together. I'm Linda Ramirez, and this is Jake Jurado."

"Hello, Dr. Holmes," Jake said. "Nice to meet you. We're looking forward to taking you into Mexico," he added. "And just so you know, we're glad to be out of L.A."

Stu then came forward and also shook hands with both of them. "Hi," he said. "Glad to meet fellow Defenders under any circumstances. Congratulations on Operation Red Sky. I thought it was brilliantly executed."

"You think so?" Jake asked.

"Absolutely," Stu said. "You guys took out the biggest source of air pollution in the world. Too bad the people couldn't handle it. What's it like in Los Angeles right now? Is it as bad as we hear?"

"Worse," replied Linda. "The city is going crazy. Los Angeles is on the verge of a major riot. There are gas lines everywhere, and people are very frustrated, fighting over gas, killing each other. It's a bad situation."

"In a way, I'm sorry we blew up the refineries," Jake said. "When we did it, we didn't know it would be a national operation. We thought we'd just be attacking Los Angeles. Now, the bullshit is really starting to fly. It's like we've started a war. They've probably got the CIA after us."

"Our Phoenix unit wasn't told about Red Sky in advance, either," Flynn said. "Headquarters sent a memo to our bulletin board well after the fact. That's the way it has to be."

"Even if the CIA is after us," Stu said calmly, "they won't get us. We're too spread out and we're too careful. Besides, they'll never be able to break our codes or trace our electronic bulletin boards," he added. "The codes are too complex, they're changed often, and the bulletin boards move around too much. If they haven't tracked us down by now, they probably never will."

"And if they do find us, so be it," Linda said, her voice filled with resolve. "Then we all go to prison for the rest of our lives, or maybe we'll die, but I'll die knowing I did something good. The planet earth is worth dying for."

"Good for you, young lady!" Holmes suddenly exclaimed. "I like your spirit!"

Flynn waved toward the beds. "Come on, everyone. Sit down, and I'll tell you my plan for getting across the border. Dr. Holmes, why don't you join us? Any ideas you have would be welcome."

The five of them all sat huddled on the edges of the two beds. Then Flynn began to tell them his plan. It was simple. He and Jake would create a diversion in the rail yard near the border. A few minutes later, Dr. Holmes, wearing a disguise, would simply walk across the international line at the main border crossing, Linda walking close to him and pretending to be a close relative. Stu would drive across by himself in the Cadillac, pick up both Holmes and Linda and then drive south to Magdalena, a little town about sixty miles south of Nogales. Flynn and Jake would follow them down to Magdalena later on the Harley. All their weapons and special gear would be carefully hidden in the trunk of the Cadillac.

"It sounds like it will work," Jake said. "But what kind of diversion did you have in mind?"

"High explosives," Flynn said casually. "Stu and I brought several pounds of plastic explosive with us. And we've got four digital detonators. We can use two of them and blow up two rail tank cars. Hopefully, we'll find some tank cars filled with something which will make lots of noise or smoke, but not anything toxic."

"I thought you wanted to sneak across discreetly," Linda reminded Flynn. "Blowing up railroad tankcars loaded with chemicals is not my idea of being discreet."

"Hopefully, everyone will think it was an accident," Flynn said seriously. "Tank cars blow up all the time. Trust me, Linda. We need a diversion. The Feds have the border crossings covered to the max. We blow some tank cars and get them out of our way."

"If you must do that, then I suggest you locate a car containing methyl ethyl ketone," Holmes advised. "It's highly flammable but will burn without creating a toxic gas."

"Methyl ethyl ketone?" Flynn asked.

"Yes, it's a solvent that's widely shipped by rail. Compared to some of the chemicals the railroads transport, it's an innocuous substance when it's burned. Just don't drink it."

"Thanks, Dr. Holmes," Flynn said. "I'll try to put that information to good use."

"I feel like I'm becoming part of this conspiracy," Holmes chuckled. "After this, they really will be after me."

"Dr. Holmes," Stu laughed, "they already really are after you. There's a ten million dollar contract out on you. That's why you're going to have to wear a disguise."

"But what disguise shall I wear?" Holmes asked.

Stu grinned. "I went out a few hours ago. Shopping. And I bought a few ingredients guaranteed to make you a new man; dark hair dye, an instant tanning solution for your skin, and a fake mustache. I'll fix you up later tonight. Tomorrow morning, when you wake up, you won't recognize yourself. You won't be a blonde anymore. You'll be a Latino!"

Holmes frowned, and everyone laughed at his discomfort with the idea of wearing a disguise.

"Dr. Holmes," Flynn explained. "It's a necessary precaution. I happen to know that your picture is in the hands of every lawman on the border. And you are readily recognizable. When Stu went out earlier to buy groceries, his main mission was to get the supplies for your disguise. We weren't sure if you'd like the idea, so we didn't tell you. But now we have to. I hope you understand. This is for your own good."

Holmes nodded, and finally smiled. "Oh well," he sighed. "If I have to, I will. After all, how can I argue with the Defenders of the Planet?"

"Our objective is to get you into Mexico discreetly," Flynn said. "I think this is the best way."

"Will they check for ID at the border?" Linda asked.

"Probably not," Flynn said. "Not if you're on foot. But if anyone does stop you, tell them you're from Tucson and you're going across the line to do some shopping for the day. Tell them you're separated from your party, you didn't drive, and therefore you didn't bring any identification with you. But I don't think you'll have any problems."

"It sounds pretty simple," Jake agreed.

"Yes, it is, and that's why it'll work. Just remember, Linda. Don't try to cross until after you hear the initial explosions. The diversion should draw most of the FBI agents away from the border crossing. They're the ones I'm most worried about. If anyone will see through the disguise, it'll be one of them."

"What about you, Stu?" Linda asked him. "What if your car is stopped and checked and they find all our gear and weapons?"

"I don't think they'll check me out," he answered. "I'm not the suspicious type. But, if they do, I'll cross that bridge when I come to it. Don't worry about me. I have the easiest part to perform." He smiled broadly, displaying a smile that could disarm anyone.

"Any other questions?" Flynn asked. No one spoke up, so Flynn said, "That's it, then. We'll go over this one more time in the morning. Tonight," he said to Jake and Linda, "you'll sleep in the next room. Room F-263. Dr. Holmes, Stu, and I will stay here. Just in case of trouble tonight, you'd better bring your weapons inside with you."

Jake nodded. "I'd better go get the Harley and bring it around. All our belongings are packed in it."

"No, you stay here," Flynn ordered. "I'll go get it. You've already taken too many chances for one day. One more thing. Don't go out tonight. You'll have to stay in your room. We'll order room service. We can't take the chance of someone recognizing you, not with your pictures plastered in the national media."

Jake shrugged, reached into his pocket and pulled out the motorcycle's key, tossing it over to Flynn. "Whatever you say, James. You're in charge of this operation."

Linda smiled at Holmes. "Why don't you let me dye your hair tonight, Dr. Holmes? I think you'll find I have the right touch."

Holmes smiled at her. "I couldn't think of a better person to turn me into a Latino," he said.

Stu said, "I'll get the supplies and we can get to work."

"OK, then," Flynn said. "I'll go get the motorcycle. I'll be right back."

It was dark outside, and Flynn detected a slight chill in the air. Still, he knew, it was far too warm for the month of January in the high desert. It should have been thirty or forty degrees colder.

As he walked down the steps leading to the drive, Flynn paused and looked up. The stars were shining brightly against a deep black sky. They'll never change, he thought. The world is changing, but the stars would never change. Flynn swallowed hard, feeling puny as he gazed upward into the heavens, and he realized that perhaps nothing that happened here on earth really mattered, at least not in universal terms. Does anyone up there know what is happening to the earth? he wondered.

Suddenly, bright headlights came into view, and to his left a recreational vehicle drove into the parking area and parked at an angle, taking four parking spaces. For a brief moment, its lights overwhelmed the darkness. The vehicle was large, at least forty feet long, and Flynn watched as its engine noise shattered an otherwise peaceful evening. After nearly a minute, the driver of the vehicle turned the engine off.

Flynn shook his head, and then he remembered the question Holmes had posed about these monstrosities. "How can we fight this kind of mentality?" The words had stuck in Flynn's mind. He quietly moved into the shadows and watched as an elderly couple eventually exited the RV and walked up into the resort. Flynn observed them carefully, deciding that both had been drinking, both talking a bit too loud, their stride not quite normal.

Flynn wanted to blow up their vehicle, but he knew it would do no good. He figured there were probably more than a million such RVs in use on the highways just in America and Canada. What good would it do to blow up this one? He walked off down the drive toward Jake's motorcycle, taking one last look at the monstrosity on wheels. It reminded him of a dinosaur, and probably soon to be just as extinct.

The next morning, the five packed their belongings and left the Rio Rico Resort, driving directly into Nogales. As planned, they drove into the parking lot of the U.S. Post Office several hundred yards north of the border. From there, the railroad yards were in clear view. Jake parked the Harley next to the Cad and Linda quickly got off and went into the post office. Holmes got out of the back seat of the Cadillac and followed her into the post office. A minute later, they both came out and began walking south toward the border.

Flynn took hold of the straps of a small duffel bag sitting on the floor by his feet and started to get out of the Cad. He hesitated momentarily, then looked at Stu and said, "I guess it's showtime. Don't worry. This will be a piece of cake."

Stu looked at him seriously. "You take care, now, James. I wouldn't want anything bad happening to you, okay?"

"I'll be all right," Flynn said. "You be careful, too. I'll see you in Magdalena!" and with that he got out of the Cad. Stu put the car in reverse, backed up, then pulled forward and out onto Morley Avenue, turning left toward the border.

Jake came over, and he and Flynn stood and watched as the Cadillac drove off.

"It's just going to be you and me, Jake," Flynn said.

"Yeah," Jake responded, suddenly feeling alone now that Linda was gone. He had Stu's .38 revolver tucked beneath his shirt, but it didn't make him feel any better.

Inside the duffel bag, Flynn carried the plastic explosives and detonators, and two Uzi submachine guns with eight fully-loaded magazines. He hoped this wouldn't get messy, and that the weapons would not be necessary. What would they encounter in the train yard?

"Let's get going," Flynn said, nodding in the direction of the nearest group of boxcars, and the two men crossed Morley Avenue, heading for the railroad yard. Flynn looked up and down the length of the street, but he saw nothing suspicious.

"You okay?" he asked Jake.

"Yeah," Jake laughed. "What's a tank car or two, compared to an oil refinery?"

Nearby, at Nine North Grand, Special Agent Mark Kessler stood in a second story office of the U.S. Customs Building overlooking the International Port-of-Entry into Mexico. A half-dozen other agents were busy in the office, coordinating the Federal net that had been put in place around Nogales. If Jonathan Holmes attempted to escape into Mexico, the FBI would catch him. It has to be here, and it has to be soon, Kessler figured.

Elsewhere in the state, in addition to his regular contingent of nearly sixty agents, one hundred seventy-five more agents had been flown in from around the country, on the lookout for Holmes at every airport, bus station, and train station in Arizona. Also, every road out of Arizona had a roadblock of law enforcement officers searching vehicles. So far, the man had not surfaced.

Kessler's gut feeling told him that whoever had rescued Holmes would try to get him out of the country through the nearest possible port-of-entry. And that was here, in Nogales, and that was why he was here, too. I'm going to get him, he thought.

Agent Ed Baker came over to Kessler and stood by him, the two looking down at the border crossing. There was a steady flow of people coming and going but, in the morning sunlight, everybody on the street was clearly visible to them.

"Anything?" Kessler asked.

"Nothing yet," Baker replied.

"He's coming through here. I can feel it," Kessler said.

"I've got four people up on the roof with high-powered binoculars. A blue-eyed blond shouldn't be too hard to spot in that crowd."

"What have we got out on the street right now?"

"We've got ten of our people checking the cars as they approach the border. U.S. Customs and the Nogales City Police have a border checkpoint set up and are checking every vehicle that crosses into Mexico. We've got several agents working with them. The border is completely covered."

"Good," Kessler grunted. "I want that son-of-a-bitch!"

"We'll get him," Baker said. "I don't see how he can possibly escape us."

"He could try to cross by going overland, east or west of here."

"The Border Patrol is watching all the passes and canyons, and they've got four companies of U.S. Army Rangers with them. They're spread out twenty-five miles to the east and nearly thirty miles to the west. Nothing moves out there without them knowing about it."

"Anything from Douglas?" Kessler asked.

"No, it's completely quiet there. I just spoke to Lacy on the phone. It sounds like he's doing it by the book."

"It'll be here in Nogales," Kessler said confidently.

"Yeah, I think you're right, Mark," Baker agreed. "It'll probably go down right here."

Kessler sighed wearily. He'd been up since two, and he'd had precious little sleep during the night. "Let's grab some coffee," he said. "I could use another cup."

"Yeah, good idea," Baker said. He'd been up since three, and he, too, was tired. The agents headed for the break room, unaware that Jonathan Holmes would be coming into view in just a matter of minutes, though they wouldn't have recognized him anyway. No one would recognize him.

As he left the office, Kessler hesitated, turned and looked back toward the window. He wanted to stay there watching, but right now a cup of coffee sounded awfully good. He turned back and followed Baker toward the break room.

As Flynn and Jake walked south down Morley Avenue, Jake saw something he recognized out of the corner of his eye, and he turned to take a more careful look.

"Damn!" he suddenly swore.

"What is it?" Flynn asked.

"Look!" Jake nodded in the direction of a Buick that had just pulled over next to the curb across the street. The car had four men in it, all looking directly at Jake. "Those are some of the men I saw yesterday. They're looking right at me! Do you think they spotted me?"

"They're not dummies," Flynn said. He took a quick look at the car, realizing they had been made. "Okay, come on," he said earnestly. "Let's head for the railyard. We can take them on there."

"So much for discretion," Jake wisecracked as the two of them began a brisk stride down the sidewalk to the south.

Flynn looked over at Jake and grinned. "Yeah, oh well, as the saying goes... the best-laid plans of mice and men..." he laughed harshly.

"This isn't funny," Jake said. "Those guys are pros! And all I've got is a lousy .38 and six stinking bullets. Now, I'm definitely pissed. If I have to die, I'm taking at least one of those jerks with me!"

"I've got an Uzi for you, with plenty of ammo," Flynn explained. "Inside the bag. I packed two of them. One for you and one for me."

"Why didn't you tell me?"

"I *am* telling you," Flynn said. He looked back over his shoulder to see that the car with the four men was moving again, and definitely following them. Another car had come up behind it. It too had four men in it. Down the road, yet another car was speeding toward them. They must have radios, he figured. Flynn decided they weren't Feds. These guys were Mafia.

"There are two more cars coming up," he said. "Eight or nine more men. They're all over the place."

"Jesus Christ!" Jake swore. "We're really outnumbered."

"Don't worry, we've got an advantage," Flynn explained. "They don't know that we've got plastic explosives. They're going to be very surprised when those tank cars blow up! Maybe we can lure them close in to the blast radius."

"Blast radius?"

"Yeah, that's right," Flynn said.

Jake suddenly laughed. "Man, you are one cool dude." He laughed again. "Blast radius!" he repeated. "Yeah, that'd be good. That'd be really good!"

Flynn looked back again. The cars were getting closer, and it looked like they were getting ready to make a move. Flynn knew they'd better move first. "Can you run?" he asked.

"Of course I can run," Jake said.

"I mean can you run fast?"

"Linda and I were running ten miles a day in preparation for Operation Red Sky. You bet I can run."

"Good," Flynn said. "Then let's move out! Muy pronto!"

"I'm ready," Jake said.

"Now!" Flynn shouted, and they both broke into a sprint toward the railyard. They dashed across the open ground and easily covered the distance to the first group of cars. They rounded them and kept running into the middle of the yard.

Flynn grabbed Jake by the shoulder and pointed ahead, guiding him toward several tankcars in the distance. "We have to set these explosives fast," he yelled. "They'll be after us."

"Understood," Jake gasped, slightly out of breath.

Flynn reached into the duffel bag and pulled out an Uzi, handing it to Jake as they ran. He quickly pulled out four magazines and handed them over, too. Jake stuffed three of them into his belt, one into the Uzi.

"At the next boxcar," Flynn shouted, "you break off and cover me. Try to hold them off for a minute or two, then come and get me. Got it?"

"Okay," Jake said, and ran toward the nearest boxcar, disappearing from Flynn's sight.

Flynn kept running and, after another hundred yards, he came to the first tank car. He slowed to a jog, scanning it carefully. The letters PROPYLENE GLYCOL were stenciled on the side of the car. The next car was also labeled PROPYLENE GLYCOL. Suddenly, he heard a burst of an automatic weapon in the distance. He recognized the staccato burst of an Uzi. Jake must have found a target.

Flynn kept moving down the track. None of the cars seemed to be carrying anything flammable. Finally, Flynn spotted a car carrying METHYL ETHYL ETHER. It was marked with the warning DANGER: HIGHLY FLAMMABLE MATERIAL. The car next to it also carried the same chemical.

It isn't methyl ethyl ketone, he thought, but it will have to do. He was running out of time. He stepped between the two cars and pulled out his bundles of plastic explosives. He took both detonators in his hands and simultaneously set both of them to hit zero in three minutes, then inserted each electronic detonator into the claylike material. He placed a bundle against the end of each of the tank cars and stepped away.

The plastic explosive was extremely powerful, a modern type developed around the turn of the century. Each bundle had the equivalent explosive energy of a thousand-pound bomb. Flynn looked at the digital readout on the nearest bundle, then set the stopwatch feature on his watch. It began counting upward, exactly ten seconds behind the digital readout of the detonator. In two minutes, forty-five seconds, this area would be one big smoking hole.

He pulled his Uzi from the duffel bag and began running toward Jake, ducking next to a boxcar as another burst of fire echoed through the railyard.

"Jake!" he shouted. "Come on!"

There was no answer. He edged around the corner of the boxcar. He saw several figures approaching, weapons at the ready, firing as they walked forward. Jake must be pinned down, he figured. He peered around the boxcar again, counting three men moving against Jake. Where were the others?

Flynn sprinted across the yard to the next track full of cars, jumping between two of them, stopping to look cautiously around the edge. Two men were moving toward him about forty yards away. Both were carrying assault-style shotguns. To Flynn, it looked like they were trying to sneak up on Jake's backside.

He released the safety from the Uzi and chambered a round. He looked around the edge of the boxcar again, then stepped out and pointed the weapon, carefully squeezing the trigger in three and four shot bursts.

The first burst hit the closest man squarely in the inner part of his left leg, throwing him violently to the ground. The man began to scream out in pain. Flynn quickly shifted his fire toward the second man. His first two bursts missed completely, but the third burst was lethal, one round striking his forehead, killing him instantly.

Flynn sprinted forward. "Jake," he called out loudly, but he got no answer. Damn it! he muttered to himself. Where did Jake go? He suddenly felt exposed running through the middle of the railyard, so he cut back to the right, then back toward the tank cars where he had placed the plastic explosive. He ran about forty yards, then jumped between two boxcars and almost ran into a big man carrying a shotgun. In an instant, Flynn raised the Uzi and fired, putting five rounds into the man's lower torso. The man fell to the ground, his shotgun falling to his side. As he lay there moaning, Flynn kicked the shotgun away.

Flynn knelt down beside the wounded man, his eyes wary for any movement from his peripheral field of vision. The two of them were alone in this area of the train yard. Flynn looked down at his adversary. Blood had started to trickle from his mouth. He was dying.

"You're hit bad," Flynn said. "You're not going to make it."

"Go to hell," the man said weakly.

"Who are you? Who hired you to come here?"

"You'll never know," he said. This time his words were accompanied by bubbles of bloody foam spurting from his mouth. Flynn guessed that one or more of the bullets had hit a rib and ricocheted up into his lungs. He leaned closer.

"Tell me," he said. "Who do you work for?"

The man shook his head and smiled. "You can go fuhhh..." he started to say, then his eyes rolled backwards. He was dead.

Flynn stood up. He stared at his watch, seeing he only had forty-five seconds until the detonators blew. He had to get out of here. Where, he wondered, was Jake?

His ears gave him the answer. In the distance, he heard the roar of a motorcycle and gunshots. After a moment, he saw the silhouette of a man on the cycle coming in his direction. As the cycle got closer, Flynn smiled. It was Jake on the Harley, running a gauntlet of shotgun fire. The guy has nerve, Flynn thought, and pelotas made of steel.

As Jake got closer, Flynn ran forward, calmly inserting a new magazine into the Uzi. He knelt down and took careful aim, firing long bursts of covering fire at several figures who were shooting at Jake. As dozens of bullets kicked up the dust around them, the figures began to run for cover.

Jake roared up to Flynn's position, driving another twenty yards before skidding to a complete stop. "Come on!" he shouted. "Let's get the hell out of here!"

Flynn needed no further prompting. He sprang forward and jumped on the back of the Harley. Jake sped off, and Flynn looked back to see at least ten men chasing them. As they rode right by the tank cars full of methyl ethyl ether, Flynn checked his watch again. It read 2:35, 2:36, 2:37...

"Faster!" Flynn shouted. "Faster!"

Jake gunned the motorcycle and sped up to nearly sixty miles an hour. Flynn took one last look behind. The men chasing them were getting very close to the tank cars. Flynn leaned forward and grabbed Jake's waist. "Hold on!" he shouted.

A second later, the explosion sent a huge fireball three hundred feet into the air, and a powerful circular shockwave went out in all directions, breaking windows up to a mile away. Both tank cars were instantly vaporized, and the railyard nearby was turned into a twisted mass of smoldering metal. The blast dug a crater nearly twenty feet deep and a hundred feet in diameter. A giant mushroom cloud began to rise up into the sky.

Standing near the pedestrian crossing into Nogales, Sonora, Jonathan Holmes and Linda took cover as red hot shrapnel began to rain down. They watched as people began running away from the border. The scene was one of complete chaos.

Flynn's diversion worked exactly as he had predicted, drawing away all the FBI agents and most of the other law enforcement officials. Holmes turned to Linda and said, "It looks like they're leaving as planned. They did it! Incredible!"

"I knew they would," Linda said, taking him by the arm. "Now, Dr. Holmes, let's get across the border while there's lots of confusion around here."

"More like total panic, I'd say," Holmes added.

They walked across the international line and into Mexico. A few minutes later, they saw the big white Cadillac driving down the main street. They waved at Stu and, as he slowed to a stop, they both jumped into the front seat.

"Any trouble?" Linda asked him, sliding over next to Stu.

"None," Stu said. "It was fantastic! The police at the roadblock started running around at the first sound of gunfire. They were really caught by surprise. After the explosion, everybody was too busy ducking for cover because of the shrapnel that was coming down everywhere. So I just drove right through, and there you were."

"Well," Linda said, "let's get the hell out of here!"

"Right on!" Stu smiled. He pressed down on the pedal and the car sped south, well beyond the speed limit, but no one paid much attention. The Mexicans on either side of the street were gawking at the giant mushroom cloud to the north.

"That was a very big explosion," Holmes said, obviously worried. "I hope our friends are okay."

"Don't worry about Flynn," Stu said. "That guy has nine lives. If anybody could survive that explosion, he could."

Just then, the Harley roared past them, Jake and Flynn waving at them. Flynn pointed to the south, signalling Stu to keep driving. Stu waved back at them.

Linda laughed excitedly. "They did it!" she exclaimed.

"I knew they would," Stu said. "Flynn is too damned good."

"Remarkable," Holmes said. "It looks like we're on our way to Magdalena. The danger has passed."

"Yeah," Stu agreed. "For now, we'll be okay. Just sit back, Dr. Holmes, and enjoy the drive. Tonight we'll be drinking tequila."

"To be honest with you," Holmes said, "right now, I could use a drink. I haven't had this much excitement in years."

Stu laughed. "You hang around us long enough, and you'll have plenty of excitement. More than you'll ever need."

"Yes," Holmes chuckled. "That's what I'm afraid of."

TWENTY-THREE

"The ocean is rising," Kristin Yates said excitedly.

"It's risen forty-three point two centimeters in the past four days," Bruce Pike told Rob Jones. "It's really happening!"

Jones frowned at hearing the bad news. He had just arrived back on Matuku Island after his trip to McMurdo to find Kristin and Pike waiting on the beach as his chopper landed. He hopped off the Sea Stallion and headed for the camp, Kristin and Pike at his side. The chopper had brought fresh supplies, and the flight crew began to haul them to the campsite. On this trip, they didn't wear flight suits. Everyone in the islands was wearing tropical clothes, preferably as loose as possible. Jones noticed that both pilots wore tank-top shirts, shorts, and sandals, keeping their boots and socks behind their seats. Nobody seemed to care. The Fiji Islands had become very hot, and everyone was having to adapt as best as possible.

"Is this based on your last reading?" Jones asked. He walked between them, carrying his duffle bag. Kristin was on his left and Pike on his right. Both were in an agitated state.

"Yes, as of yesterday afternoon," Kristin replied. "The water is coming up fast, Rob. Real fast."

"It's definitely rising," Pike said. "The speed of it is incredible. You were right. This place could be underwater in just a few months, especially if it gets much hotter."

When they got to the camp, Jones went to his tent and stowed his bag, then walked over to their beach chairs and sat down, Pike and Kristin doing the same. Dawn was just breaking, yet it was already over ninety-five degrees on the island.

Jones sat quietly, thinking through all the recent events and his own eyewitness experiences. Of course it was happening, he realized. He had no reason to doubt their numbers. He had seen the ice melting in Antarctica. He did some quick mental arithmetic: forty-three point two centimeters was more than seventeen inches. It represented a tremendous displacement of water.

"With that kind of rise," he said, "they should be noticing it all over the world. Have you notified the Pentagon?"

"No," Pike said. "We thought you would want to. We didn't know if they'd really believe us."

Jones nodded understandingly. It was unbelievable. But it was real, and it was happening. "Okay," he said. "I'll call Washington after we do the next reading and verify the data with the others on Moala and Totoya." He looked at the two of them very carefully, noticing that they seemed different. Kristin was sunburned and Pike looked totally frazzled. The mission was obviously wearing on them.

"You both look tired. Have you been drinking lots of water?" he asked them.

"Yes, tons," Kristin replied. "It seems to perspire out my system as soon as I drink it. But I'm getting kind of used to the heat, though it's been getting hotter. Yesterday, it hit one hundred and thirty in the afternoon."

"One thirty?" Jones exclaimed.

"Yes, one thirty."

"It's torture," Pike said. "Pure torture! Even the nights are roasting and humid. I haven't had a good night's sleep since we landed on this damned island!"

"Going in the ocean helps," Kristin said. "The water temperature is much lower than the air temperature. Yesterday, during the afternoon, I went snorkeling for three hours. But just after you get out, you start sweating all over again. I've never experienced anything like this." Jones noticed she was wearing a frown, and he felt sorry for both of them. Their mission had turned into a bitch of an assignment.

"Kristin," Jones said, "you're going to have to start wearing more sunblock. You're sunburned. I found out that the ozone layer is almost completely gone. They told me in Antarctica that there is no ozone layer any longer over the South Pole. It's vanished. And it isn't much better anywhere else."

"Why haven't we been told?" she asked.

"I don't know. I suppose nobody wants to admit to it. We're going to have to start protecting ourselves from the sun better. That's an order."

"Yes, sir," she said glumly.

"Well," he consoled them. "We shouldn't be here too much longer. I think Washington will pull us out of here sooner rather than later. Our only job was to confirm that the ocean level is rising. I think we've accomplished that."

"The sooner I get out of this place, the better," Pike said angrily. "I don't see how we can survive this for much longer. "

"Relax, Pike. You'll survive. And you're not dead yet. Just keep drinking lots of fluids. Start doing what Kristin has been doing. During the afternoon, go snorkeling." Jones looked around the camp. By now, their marine guard should have arrived. "Where are the marines?" he asked.

Kristin shrugged. "We haven't been told exactly why they're not here, only that they're very busy on the main islands of Fiji. Some of the islanders on the big island were upset when they heard rumors they were going to be evacuated off the islands. Some of them went to the Nandi airport and caused a ruckus."

"I heard about that when I landed from Christchurch," Jones said. "But I assumed we'd still be getting our contingent of marines. I guess I thought wrong. I'll check into it. The marines really should be here, especially when we notify the islanders that they're going to lose most of their islands."

"The locals haven't hassled us at all," Kristin said. "A few of them came by and watched us for awhile, but for the most part, they don't seem to be too interested."

Jones nodded. The foot trail was several hundred meters inland, not visible through the jungle, and there was really no reason for the local villagers to come to this particular beach. They would probably be safe, though if there was any trouble the three of them would be totally defenseless.

"Have you eaten breakfast yet?" Jones asked.

Both of them nodded negatively. "Good. I'm starving," Jones said. "Let's eat, and then we'll worry about getting another reading and calling Washington. Okay?"

"Sounds good," Kristin said. "I'll heat some water."

A few minutes later, the chopper's crew finished unloading the supplies, and Jones invited them to stay for breakfast, an invitation they respectfully declined, knowing that there was a full-fledged cafeteria back at Nandi. Jones really couldn't blame them. He walked the crew back to the beach to see them off. The pilot started up, the whine of the big chopper's powerful engines violently disturbing the morning sounds of the jungle. As the Sea Stallion lifted off and flew out over the water, the aircraft's rotors beat furiously against the air, as if the big helicopter was urgently needed elsewhere. Eventually, the rapid staccato pulsebeat of the chopper faded into the distance.

Jones walked back to the camp, to the crate containing dehydrated meals, and pulled a bag out of an open case. It read *Turkey Stew With Rice.* Good enough for breakfast, he decided. All he had to do was add boiling water and stir it for a minute. Kristin searched through the case for a real breakfast, one that said *Ham & Eggs,* while Pike used the same method Jones had, just picking a meal at random. He got *Spaghetti With Meat Balls.* They added water and began stirring. Their coffee was instant, and it came in individual packets that they poured into their canteen cups, adding hot water. All three of them used cream and sugar, again from individual packets. Food and coffee in hand, they sat down in their beach chairs to eat. It was instant food, but it was good.

After they ate, they sat drinking coffee for nearly half an hour. Jones noticed that Kristin's description of liquid going right through them was accurate. Just sitting there, he began to perspire, and the day was going to get much hotter. He realized that Kristin and Pike had become acclimated to this place with its unrelenting heat and humidity, at least, as much as humanly possible. Because of his trip to McMurdo, he would have to start the acclimation process all over again.

The sun had come up and was quickly rising high into the sky. It fairly flooded the jungle with its light, the rays penetrating through the foliage in bright yellow beams that contrasted sharply with the surrounding shadows. The jungle was teeming with thousands of different birds, some calling, some chirping, some hooting. Jones suddenly had the impression they might be cries for help, that the birds were distressed by the heat, not used to the hundred degree plus temperatures. In the past, the Fiji Islands hardly ever got above eighty or ninety degrees.

"It's almost oh seven hundred," Kristin announced. "Low tide this morning is at 0713."

"Whose turn is it to man the transit?" Jones asked.

"It's mine," Kristin said.

"Okay. I'll carry the radio. Bruce, you get the generator started. Let's head for the platform."

Pike went ahead to start the generator, and Jones and Kristin went to the command tent, Jones taking their portable radio out of its waterproof case, Kristin grabbing the transit in its shockproof carrying case. Together they walked out to the platform on the beach, which had been placed away from the water, close to the jungle.

The platform was galvanized steel, painted dark blue, and served the same purpose as a surveyor's tripod, except the platform was on four thick tubular legs which they had sunk in concrete so that it couldn't move. The base of the platform was perfectly level, eight feet off the ground and just big enough for two people to stand on. Horizontal bars between two of the platform's legs served as a ladder. From the base, an adjustable post came up another five feet. The transit attached to the top of the post.

Kristin climbed up to the platform first, followed by Jones. Pike handed them the transit and carrying case, which weighed nearly forty-five pounds. They took the transit out of its case and quickly mounted it on top of the post, checking all the settings to make sure nothing had changed. She read them off to Pike, who stood below and gave her confirmation.

At precisely 0700 hours, Jones called the other teams on Moala and Totoya to make sure that they were on line for the low tide reading.

"This is Albatross calling Seagull and Gooney Bird. Do you read? Over."

"Roger," came the response from both teams.

"We will sight in at precisely 0713. Are you ready?"

"We're ready, Albatross," said Seagull.

"Roger that," Gooney Bird responded.

"Albatross out." Jones switched off the radio. Both the other teams had identical platforms on their respective beaches, their transits pointed toward the ocean in the direction of the middle of the triangle formed by the three islands. There, a computerized measuring buoy had been placed. It was a buoy of a special design, not anchored in one position.

Since this measuring buoy could freely move, a nuclear submarine had been placed on station to keep track of it, and just before the designated time for the reading, the submarine surfaced, placing the buoy in its proper position, at exactly 179 degrees, 55 minutes east longitude, 18 degrees, 40 minutes south latitude. Using the Global Positioning Satellite, the sub was able to return the buoy to within a foot of its designated spot.

Kristin sighted through the transit and immediately spotted the measuring buoy, right where it was supposed to be. "I've got it," she said.

"Okay, let's hook up," Jones said, dropping the transit's power cord to Pike below, who plugged it into the generator.

The transit needed power because it used a laser beam to mark a spot on a tall column in the center of the buoy which could be easily seen by the crew of the submarine, on station around the buoy in inflatable craft, who could then transmit the data back to the oceanographers. The column was marked in centimeters. The buoy was of special construction, nearly twenty feet high, designed with a large tripod base to keep its bobbing motion to a minimum.

Kristin put on a headset and plugged it into the transit, then squinted her right eye into the eyepiece. After a moment, she heard a tone in her headset.

"Bingo! I'm on the mark," she said. Then, she heard a call from one of the inflatable boats, on a special frequency which could only be heard through the transit's headset.

"Albatross, this is Sea Lion. Do you read? Over."

"Sea Lion, Albatross reads you loud and clear. What have you got for me? Over."

"It's hitting at mark 224.58. I repeat mark 224.58. Over."

"224.58," Kristin repeated, loud enough for Bruce to hear.

"224.58," Bruce called out from below, recording the information onto his clipboard.

"Thank you Sea Lion," Kristin said. "We've got it down. See you boys at high tide, over."

"Okay, Albatross. Say, when are you going to come out and visit? We're dying to see what you look like. Over."

"Sorry guys, but it's not in the program."

"Stay cool, Albatross. Sea Lion out."

At this, Kristin smiled. The men from the submarine were probably eating their hearts out every time she talked to them through the transit's radio. They were getting to be notorious flirts.

"What did they want?" Jones asked.

"They want me to come out and visit them," Kristin replied. She looked wistfully out toward the ocean.

"Yeah, I'll bet," Jones smiled. In a way, they all envied the men on the sub. The submarine had air conditioning on board.

Jones waited a few minutes, then switched on the portable radio. He decided to call the team on Moala Island first. "Seagull, this is Albatross, do you read, over?"

"Roger, Albatross. Got you five by five, over."

"Seagull, what have you got? Over."

"Roger Seagull, wait one. Over....Seagull, we've got 224.59, but we just spent the morning recalibrating the settings on our platform. Is that what you got? Over."

"You're very close, Seagull. We hit it at 224.58. Over."

"We must have screwed up. Do you want us to recalibrate and take another reading? Over."

"You're close enough, Seagull. Leave your settings as they are for the rest of the day. You can recalibrate tonight. Over."

"Roger, Albatross. Anything else?"

"No thanks, guys. Albatross out."

"Take care, Albatross. Seagull out."

Next, Jones called the team on Totoya Island. "Gooney Bird, this is Albatross. Do you read me? Over."

"Roger, Albatross. We read you clearly, over."

Jones recognized the voice of Lieutenant Jan Perrine, the leader of the team on Totoya. "Gooney Bird, what was your reading, over?"

"224.58. Are we in the ballpark? Over."

"You're right on the money, Gooney Bird. 224.58 is what we've got. Over."

"Damn!" Perrine said into her radio. "It's really coming up, sir. It's really starting to happen!"

"Roger that," Jones said. "Next reading at high tide. See you in about six hours. Albatross out."

Immediately Pike called from below. "It's risen over eight inches in twelve hours, Rob. It's getting worse! The rate of rise is increasing."

Jones helped Kristin take the laser transit off its post, securing it in its case. They handed it to Pike and climbed down off the platform, turned off the generator, and walked back to camp.

"I'll call the Pentagon right away," Jones told them. "They need to know about this."

"What will they do?" Kristin asked.

"Probably go through the chain of command, right up to the commander-in-chief. But this should prove once and for all that we've got serious trouble ahead."

"What will the President do about it?" Pike asked.

"I'm not sure. Maybe a public announcement," Jones replied. "Other than that, there isn't much he can do except make the right decisions. The Navy and Air Force have the responsibility for the dirty work."

"What if they don't believe us?" Kristin asked.

"Don't worry, Kristin. Admiral Hart will believe us."

When they arrived back in camp, they stowed the equipment in the command tent, then spent twenty minutes going over all the data, using a laptop computer. Jones sat down in front of their main radio, hooked up to a satellite dish linked to the MILSTAR system. MILSTAR was an extremely high-frequency satellite communications system. It was a secure system that could not be jammed and was capable of sending voice or data transmissions. Jones turned on the radio and entered a code. A minute later, he was in contact with Admiral Hart.

"Sir, I've got very bad news," he began.

"Give it to me straight, Rob," Hart said evenly.

"Our latest reading indicates the Pacific Ocean has risen eight point three inches in the last twelve hours. In the past four days, the water has risen twenty-five point seven inches. All teams confirm the data, and there is no doubt about this. Sir, the Pacific Ocean has risen and will continue to rise. It's happening just as we thought. By now, the rise should have been noticed on both coasts, sir."

"Yes, we've seen it, but as of yet, we're not sure the civilian population is aware of it. Here in Washington, it's not as great as where you are."

"You'll be seeing the same thing in twelve to sixteen hours, sir. Within a few days, everybody will know what's going on. Believe me, sir. It will be public information."

"I believe you, Rob. I was waiting for your report before I tell the Secretary of Defense and he notifies the President. Have you been in touch with McMurdo?"

"No, sir. Not since I left yesterday. But, as I told you before I left the station, the ice there is definitely melting and very rapidly. I don't think it will stop. We were right, Admiral, to begin Operation Safeharbor. You made the right decision, sir."

"Thanks, though that's little consolation right now. We've got big trouble on the horizon. This afternoon, a riot started in Los Angeles. They're reporting that several hundred people have been killed already."

"Several hundred? How did it start?"

"At a gas station in South Central Los Angeles. There was another shooting over gas and the police were called. It turned into a major gunfight. I saw some of the news footage. It's pretty ugly. They gunned down about twenty police officers, and the police retaliated. They're expecting a very bad night there. The governor has called out the national guard. The President is sending an army unit from Fort Irwin."

"I'm sorry to hear that, Admiral. It doesn't sound good."

"It could be the tip of the iceberg. We're anticipating a great deal of civilian unrest when we go public with this whole thing. People aren't going to want to leave their homes. We've seen this kind of thing before, though on a much smaller scale. This is a major friggin' tragedy in the making."

"Yes, sir," Jones said. "I know. I can empathize with people not wanting to give up their homes. Unfortunately, pretty soon they won't have any choice. Admiral, may I speak freely?"

"Go ahead, Captain. This is no time for protocol."

"I suggest they go public right away, sir. I'm worried about all those people in Florida. They're going to take this on the chin, sir. In two more weeks, Florida's coast is going to be one big swampland. In five or six weeks, most of the state will be completely underwater, sir. We've got to give them as much notice as possible, especially considering Florida's large population."

"I'll convey your opinion directly to the President, Rob. I'm sure Secretary Wilson and the President will do the right thing. You shouldn't worry. Now, then, are your people okay?"

"They're surviving, sir. Yesterday, the temperature here hit one hundred thirty degrees. The humidity is quite high. Today looks like more of the same, if not worse."

"Yes, I'm afraid it will get worse. I called Admiral Fletcher an hour ago. Just so you know, they're anticipating it will hit eighty there today. The high pressure system over Antarctica is continuing to build."

"Yes, sir. I was kind of expecting that."

"I'll pull you and your team out of there when I can. Keep up the good work, Rob. I'm proud of you."

"Thank you, sir. We'll do the best we can."

"Take care, Rob. I'll be in touch." And Admiral Hart ended the transmission.

"What did he say?" Kristin asked.

Rob Jones shook his head negatively. "There's a riot in Los Angeles, and the temperature at McMurdo has increased to eighty degrees."

"Jesus!" Pike exclaimed. "Then the water will be coming up even faster."

"Yeah," Jones agreed. "No telling what's going to happen next, but things are definitely getting hotter."

TWENTY-FOUR

It was just after three in the afternoon in Washington when Admiral Hart received Rob Jones' report, and he immediately took the information to the Secretary of Defense, including Jones' recommendation that the public be warned about the impending disaster. William Wilson glumly accepted his report.

"This is a goddamned disaster!" a haggard Wilson said.

"Yes, sir," Hart replied. "But at least we have the satisfaction of knowing that we made the right decision in the first place. We were right to move on Operation Safeharbor."

Secretary Wilson, a pronounced frown on his face, reached for his phone and called the President on his direct line. After a brief conversation, the President agreed to meet Wilson immediately at the White House. The Secretary of Defense hung up the phone, switched on his intercom and ordered his secretary to get his car ready, then he switched it back off and looked up at Hart. "I want you to come with me, Admiral. I'd like you to brief the President about this. Afterwards, I'll suggest to him that it's time to go public."

"I don't think he'll have much choice," Hart said. "We've got to give the people some warning. The situation is rapidly worsening. Admiral Fletcher reports that Antarctic temperatures have hit eighty degrees and will continue to climb. The ice down there is melting faster than ever. Between his reports and the data Rob Jones is sending, we have absolute confirmation that the ocean level is rising. We will all notice the change very soon. I am sure I can make that clear to the President."

"I want you to know that Captain Jones and his group are to be commended," Wilson said. "I can't imagine having to work in one hundred and thirty degree weather. Humid weather at that.

It must be awful down there. How are the rest of your people doing?"

"Not too good, I'm afraid. Our ships are having a hard time of it. I'm getting reports that in some of the engine rooms, temperatures are reaching one hundred fifty degrees. One ship reported an interior temperature of one hundred sixty. They had no choice but to stand down because the entire engine room crew suffered heat stroke."

"Jesus Christ!" Wilson swore. "That is incredible. How much higher can the temperature go?" he asked plaintively.

"I don't know," Hart responded. "But I'd like to get this evacuation process going so I can pull my men out of the South Pacific as quickly as possible. We can't operate much longer in those conditions."

Wilson nodded. "We're completely ready to enlist the merchant marine and all the airlines. We're going to have to start moving millions of people off all those islands." Wilson stared out into his office, his eyes weary and somewhat out of focus. "I don't know how people are going to react to this," he said, mouthing the words slowly. "Even I am having trouble accepting it." He took a deep breath, refocusing his mind, and he rose up from his highly polished cherrywood desk. "Let's go, Admiral. My limousine is waiting."

The two of them made the short drive over to the White House, and a marine escort took them up into the Oval Office, where President Rawlings and his top advisors were awaiting them.

Admiral Hart made a brief but dramatic report to the President that the Navy had confirmed that the ocean was rising — and rising very quickly. Hart finished by saying that in his opinion, the weather would not soon reverse itself but, if anything, would continue to worsen. When he finished, there was an eerie silence within the room. They all realized that the worst was upon them. The situation had become urgent.

"Mr. President," Wilson spoke up, "I recommend that you go before the public and make an announcement. This operation is too big and too complicated to keep secret any longer. Besides, the media is pretty well onto the problem in Antarctica. It will serve no useful purpose to try to maintain further secrecy. Also, in order to evacuate people in the numbers involved, we will need to enlist all the airlines and the entire merchant marine, beginning immediately."

President Rawlings nodded. There could be no argument on this and everyone there knew it. "You're right, William." He looked over at Malcolm Teale. "Malcolm, set up a television announcement for this evening. I intend to tell the American people the truth."

"Yes, sir," Teale said. "I'll set it up for nine o'clock Eastern Standard Time. Shall I get the staff to work up a draft?"

"No," the President intoned. "I'll write the first draft myself. You can look it over and tell me if you see any problems." The President turned and looked at Hart. "Admiral, just how much time do we have before the people who are living on the coast see that the ocean is starting to rise?"

"Some of them have probably already noticed it, Mr. President. But we will see a very significant change within the next twelve to twenty-four hours. We need to start planning the evacuation of areas that fall within the flood plain."

James Sisk looked at the President and said, "I would advise that you immediately call up all military reserve units in case of civil strife. What is happening in Los Angeles will probably be repeated in other parts of the country. Also, I suggest we place our remaining quick response military units on full alert."

"William, what is the status of those units?" the President asked.

"They've been ready now for such an order for over two weeks, Mr. President. All commanders have been notified that such an order is imminent. The level two units have also been notified. I can move fifty thousand heavily armed troops into our cities within twenty-four hours. Within forty-eight hours, we can send in another fifty thousand."

"Mr. President," said Sisk, "I think it's time we consider invoking the Internal Security Act. These people who are causing these riots need to be put away so the rest of us can get on with solving this problem. I need an executive order to begin building the camps. The locations are ready."

At hearing this, the President became noticeably saddened at the prospect of giving such an order. "This is a most unfortunate situation," he said to no one in particular. "Go ahead, James," the President said. "Do whatever is necessary. I'll sign the order after I give the speech tonight." He looked around at his assembled advisors. "Is there anything else?" he asked.

Everyone nodded in the negative. The mood within the Oval Office was one of urgency and despair. No one envied the President's momentous responsibility of informing the American people that a global catastrophe was about to befall them. Even more ominous, they all knew that the very welfare of the country was in jeopardy. If Los Angeles was any precursor, violence and death would become the order of the day, and the military would be required to use deadly force to maintain civil order.

That night, the President went on national television, and every network in the country carried his address. President Rawlings began solemnly, his face wearing a stern frown.

"My fellow Americans, it is with a heavy heart that I come before you this evening. It's time I tell you what we know about the developing situation that is occurring so many thousands of miles away on the continent of Antarctica.

"Many of you have heard the rumors that the South Pole is melting due to the unprecedented hot weather the earth has been having over the past months. It is true that there is a very unusual high pressure system over the South Pole. The latest temperature readings there have been in the high seventies. Today, the temperature reached eighty degrees. These temperatures are high enough to warrant great concern here in the White House.

"We have been carefully monitoring all this, and we have determined that the ice in Antarctica is beginning to melt." The

President paused, taking a breath, looking directly into the camera with a pained expression.

"Now, we have been carefully studying all aspects of this situation and, for some time, we've hoped that things would cool down and go back to normal. Unfortunately, this has not happened. We have been informed that, because of the amount of ice that is melting, the oceans are beginning to rise. There is nothing we can do to prevent this.

"Tonight, it is my responsibility to tell you the absolute truth as we know it, so I must inform you that we are facing a very grave crisis. We need to begin evacuating some of our low-lying coastal areas. The federal government will work side-by-side with state and local governments to carry out these evacuations, and we will help protect lives and property to the maximum extent possible.

"I wish I could tell you differently, but I'm confident that we can face this crisis together. Throughout its great history, the United States of America has endured the most trying of times. We have faced wars, natural disasters and economic downturns. I'm sure we will survive this coming crisis. If any of our cities do become flooded, we will rebuild them. We must remember that America is a vast land. We have unlimited resources at our disposal, and together we can overcome any natural disaster. If the oceans continue to rise, there is no reason to panic or to be afraid. We can cope with any natural disaster, and we will cope with this one.

"In the near future, I will be addressing the nation again, to keep you informed of the situation as events warrant. I urge you to be courageous, and to be strong.

"To those out there who see this as an opportunity to commit crimes of violence, I say to you that we will not tolerate such behavior. We must maintain law and order, and so we shall. The evacuation process must be peaceful and orderly.

"I urge all of you to do the right thing. Let's commit ourselves to helping each other during this crisis. In times like this, we have a history of working together. Now, more than ever before, we must work together. We are a great nation, and no matter what nature has in store for us, we will survive this. So, as we evacuate from those regions hit by coastal flooding, I want you to treat your fellow Americans as you would any member of your family. Remember how they must feel, having been displaced from their homes and their property. We must all stay together, work together, and help one another."

Then, with sad, almost desperate eyes, the President bid farewell to the American people. "Thank you, God bless you, and God bless America."

TWENTY-FIVE

Seven hours after the President's address, night fell on the Fiji Islands. Just after dark, a full moon began to rise over the calm, dark waters of the Pacific Ocean. As the earth rotated, the moon cleared the eastern horizon, an eerily beautiful, pinkish-orange luminescent sphere that seemed double its normal size. In the pristine atmosphere of the South Pacific, the moon's features were starkly visible and, as it rose higher in the night sky, its reflected light shone brightly down upon Matuku Island. The features of the beach became recognizable and the water regained some of its lost color.

Rob Jones and Kristin Yates were sitting on the beach, each drinking from a plastic bottle of mineral water and soaking their feet in the ocean, both fatigued from the heat. Even after the sun had set and it became dark, the temperature was one hundred and ten degrees, with eighty percent humidity. They sat watching the ocean as one by one, several large waves broke over the outer reef. The sound of the water falling on itself in a steady lulling rhythm was almost hypnotic.

"Must be a storm out there somewhere," Kristen said. "We haven't had waves like this since we've arrived here."

"There are storms all over the place," Jones agreed. "From the way those waves are breaking, I'd say it's to the east of us. Maybe to the northeast."

"Yes, probably," Kristen said. "I hope it comes this way. We could use a nice, cool rain."

Jones sighed. "It's too bad this had to happen," he said listlessly. He was worn down by the hot weather and, though he'd drunk four cups of strong coffee on this day, taken his salt tablets and drunk plenty of other fluids, the heat had drained his energy. Moving around had become an effort. He was glad the day's work was over, and he was content to just sit there and watch the moon over the water and listen to the sounds of the pounding surf.

"Yes," Kristin agreed, "It's too bad."

Jones took a long swallow of mineral water. "We've really screwed up the planet," he said. "Now, no power on earth can make the process stop. The oceans will continue to rise."

"It's not our fault this happened," Kristin said. "You shouldn't blame yourself, Rob."

"But I do blame myself, and everyone else. We created the problem, and we failed to act. Once Antarctica completely melts, the world will never be the same, not in my lifetime, not in the next generation's lifetime. This is more serious than anyone cares to admit."

"I know," Kristin agreed. "It's going to be terrible."

"Yes," Jones said. "I'm glad I'm in the Navy."

"Me, too," she agreed. "And I'm glad I'm an oceanographer. At least I understand the oceans. I don't consider them our enemy."

Jones looked at her in the moonlight, suddenly appreciating her feminine logic. She said it in a way that only a woman could have. "I don't consider them our enemy" was something he, as a man, would never have thought of.

"The oceans are a very powerful force," Kristin went on. "Perhaps we were wrong to build cities right next to them. Now, we're going to lose all of them, and a lot more besides."

"You're looking at it in very philosophical terms. We weren't wrong to build cities next to the oceans. We had to build around our harbors. Oceans have historically been the primary means of transportation for international commerce. A ship can haul thousands of tons of cargo at one time. Nothing else can do that. But you're right about the oceans not being our enemy. I suppose we were our own worst enemy."

Kristin didn't reply immediately, thinking about what he had just said. A minute later, she responded. "It's true," she said with finality. "We were our own worst enemy. We should have come up with alternate fuels when we had the chance." She laughed. "The funny thing is, now we're still going to have to come up with alternate fuels. We can't just let the planet keep heating up. Gasoline will probably be banned pretty soon."

"The sooner the better," Jones said. "People can't live in this kind of weather for very long. It's awful. If the heat gets this bad in the United States, they won't be able to grow food. We'll all starve to death."

"I hadn't thought of that," Kristin said. "But I guess most crops would wither in one hundred and thirty degree weather. I'm surprised I'm able to handle it."

"How's Bruce doing?" Jones asked.

"I checked on him an hour ago. He's sleeping like a baby. He took two sleeping pills after dinner and they really knocked him out. He was very tired."

"I know. I can't say I blame him. I'd take them, except I don't like to use drugs."

"Me neither," she agreed. "But it is difficult to sleep. I think I'm getting somewhat used to it, though. I do like it here. It's so beautiful. If it weren't for this heat, I'd say this is paradise."

Jones had to admit she was right. The moon looked more spectacular than he'd ever seen it. The sound of the ocean was powerfully serene. It seemed as if the world was at peace. But he knew it wasn't so. He suddenly wondered what the moon looked like from Ross Island.

"What was Antarctica like?" Kristin asked, as if reading his mind. "Was it really strange?"

"Kind of," he said, gathering his thoughts. "It was beautiful, too, in its own way. It's getting a tremendous amount of sunlight right now, nearly twenty-four hours a day. To sleep, you have to draw the curtains in your room.

"McMurdo Station itself is a drab little base, but once you get away from it, you realize how beautiful Antarctica is. I went on a helicopter to the dry valleys west of McMurdo Sound. We flew over a glacier, then landed. The ice was melting fast, and the streams inside the glaciers were getting bigger and bigger.

When I saw that, I realized just what was going on down there. Then we took off and flew up to the dry valleys. We were surrounded by mountain ranges, and you could tell you were in Antarctica because there was absolutely nothing growing anywhere. No trees or anything. It was total desolation, just rocks, some snow, and that velvet blue sky. The sky was different there. It looks so different from anywhere else."

"It sounds incredible," Kristin said. "I wish I were there right now. It would be so much cooler."

"Yes, about fifty degrees cooler."

"You sound like you really liked it."

"Yes, I did like it. I'll never forget it. Antarctica," he breathed out the word. "That continent will have a big effect upon the rest of us. I wish it would go back to normal."

"It doesn't seem like it will," she said.

"No, I suppose not... Whatever happens, I want you to know that I think you and Bruce have done a hell of a job. Admiral Hart is very proud of you, too."

"He is?"

"Yes, he told me so in our last radio conversation. The work we've done here helped convince the President to make his announcement, I think sooner than they would have otherwise. You did good, Kristin."

"Thanks, Rob," she said, looking at him impishly, leaning over and kissing his cheek.

"Hey, what was that for?" he asked.

"I just felt like it," she replied. She remained close to him, looking deeply into his eyes.

Jones gazed back at her, not able to take his eyes away from hers. He edged closer to her face and kissed her fully on her lips. She responded by putting her arm around him and kissing him passionately, her tongue probing deeply into his mouth. It was as if a dam had burst, and neither of them held back. They hugged each other, deep-kissing for several minutes.

Suddenly Kristin pulled away from him, got up and took off her clothes. "I'm going swimming," she announced. "Care to join me?" and with that she ran out into the water.

Jones watched as she swam away from the beach. In the moonlight, her body looked supple and terribly inviting. Maybe it's the full moon, he decided, or maybe it's just that we're in this impossible situation. He gazed at her figure for several seconds more, wondering if he should go after her.

What the hell? he thought, starting to take his clothes off. He was only wearing shorts and a T-shirt, and he undressed in seconds and walked out into the water, plunging in waist deep, then leaning forward into a fast crawl.

He caught up to her in less than a minute, swimming up from behind and grabbing her around the waist. She immediately stopped swimming and they went into each other's arms, treading water and kissing at the same time. After a minute, Kristin backed away.

"We should have done this sooner," she said. "I couldn't think of a better way to spend an evening."

"It's totally against regulations."

"Don't worry, I won't turn you in," she said, a big smile on her face. "Besides, I kissed you first, didn't I?"

"Yes, but I should have known better."

"What does the Navy expect?" she asked. "We're not priests and nuns, after all." She swam toward him, kissed him lightly, then swam by and continued on, gracefully pulling herself through the water with a breast stroke. Jones laughed and followed her. He caught up to her and they swam side by side, paralleling the nearby reef. Each time a wave came in, they both turned into it and after it passed over them, they turned again and swam on.

He felt lightheaded. It had been years since he had swum naked with a woman, and that had been when he was in college at USC. He and his first wife had swum together off the beach of Malibu just before they got married. It, too, had been a moonlight swim, and it had led to a night of intense pleasure. He had never forgotten it, and he wondered if this evening would turn out the same way.

The water was much cooler than the air, and it felt good to be out in it, naked and free. For the first time since his return from Antarctica, he felt cool and relaxed. They swam together for nearly ten minutes, so close that they continually brushed against each other in the water. As if on cue, they both turned and headed for shore. They had swum several hundred yards and, as they walked out of the water, they found they were far down the beach in a remote part of the shoreline. Suddenly she stopped, turned and put her arms around him, kissing him gently.

"No matter what tomorrow brings," she said. "I'll have no regrets about this evening."

"Neither will I," he said, and they sank down on the wet sand together, their bodies locked in a tight embrace.

TWENTY-SIX

The water from the melted ice of the continent of Antarctica flowed simultaneously into the South Pacific Ocean, the South Atlantic Ocean, and the Indian Ocean. Molecule by molecule, the melted ice water displaced the water it flowed into, forcing it to move north and completely disrupting the normal ocean currents. Since water always takes the path of least resistance, the oceans began to force themselves into the most likely places along the coastlines of the continents, estuaries, wetlands, rivers, and natural harbors. Slowly yet steadily, the rising water probed the other areas of the coastlines, advancing inexorably up onto dry land.

The fishermen around the world noticed it first. Within a week, their boats were riding two feet higher against the docks. And they could see it elsewhere, their sharp eyes noticing that coastal landmarks were slowly sinking into the ocean. Ominously, the water continued to rise, the oceans and seas changing right before their eyes.

To them, such a change was utterly fantastic, for they knew how massive the oceans were, they knew that this huge displacement of water would not be readily reversed. Worse, the water kept rising and showed no signs of stopping. It made them terribly afraid.

The fear of the fishermen was a prelude to a world panic. In the South Pacific, low-lying atolls simply disappeared, and the beaches on the bigger islands began to erode. Waves began to wash over Kwajalein Atoll in the Marshall Islands, and the entire island was evacuated. In the Federated States of Micronesia, on the island of Kosrae, a multimillion dollar large-jet runway built on an atoll right on the coast was lost to the ocean, and lost, too, was any hope of rescuing the people of Kosrae by airlift.

On Tierra del Fuego, at the very tip of South America, the roads in the town of Ushuaia began to wash out and people realized they were going to lose their homes. Up the coast, at the mouth of the Rio de la Plata, in the cities of Montevideo and Buenos Aires the roads also began to wash out, and the sewer systems started to overflow. At Punta del Este, Uruguay's best coastal resort, the entire beach vanished in a week and, at high tide, the waves lapped against the first floor of those posh hotels built right on the ocean. As the water flowed north, other coastal resorts in South America began to lose their beaches. In Brazil, most of the beaches of Guanabara Bay began to go underwater, and the residents of Rio realized they were about to lose their favorite playground.

In New Zealand, citizens of Auckland, Wellington, and Christchurch, the largest cities in the country and all ports built very close to the water, realized their cities were fated for a tragic ending. At the present rate of rise, the city streets would be underwater within another month.

In Australia, the situation was bleaker simply because there were more people involved. The major cities of Australia were all low-lying ports: Sydney, Melbourne, Brisbane, Darwin, Perth, and Hobart on the island of Tasmania. Word quickly spread throughout Australia that the ocean was rising and that in another month their biggest cities would be need to be evacuated.

In the Phillippines and Japan, the situation was much the same as in Australia. Most of the major cities were port cities, teeming with millions of human beings. In Manila, the largest port in the South China Sea, people saw the water rise and began to leave the city, heading inland to higher ground. Within days, Manila became a ghost town.

In Japan, the people also noticed the ocean rising higher but, with defiant tenacity, they refused to leave their home towns, though it was obvious they would eventually be forced to. Perhaps, they reckoned, things would go back to normal. Every hour, the Japanese news media broadcast the slightest change in the rise of water, and all of Japan watched with stoic fascination. They would not leave until the last possible minute.

In China, the sense of loyalty to the cities in which they lived did not enter the people's decision to flee. They owned little to begin with, so packing up and leaving was not deemed a sign of cowardice, but the only rational course of action. In dozens of port cities, including Hong Kong, Macao, and Shanghai, tens of millions of Chinese left their homes and began to move inland.

In the Indian Ocean, thousands of atolls known as the Maldive Islands began to disappear beneath the surface of the water. A little further south, the Chagos Archipelago began to sink, and the island of Diego Garcia had to be evacuated. The Seychelles Islands lost most of their beaches, and the tourists began to flee back to Europe, bringing with them tales of an impending catastrophe.

In the Bay of Bengal, the water surged northward, and rivers like the Ganges, the Hooghly, and the Brahmaputra began to overflow their banks. The onslaught of water was unrelenting, and tens of millions of people began to think about moving north. This would be difficult because heavy rains throughout the area had turned the roads into saturated bogs, making a trek north a life or death matter. The astute and wealthy Indians of Calcutta began to fly to inland cities, to places like Delhi, where they immediately began purchasing new property.

In the Arabian Sea, the people of the island city of Bombay on India's west coast saw that the ocean was rising and demanded that the government protect them. A large protest numbering nearly a million people turned into a riot, and thousands were killed. Half the population fled the city in panic, jamming the bridges that led to the mainland and, in a sign of what the future would hold, over a thousand people were trampled to death in the rush to escape. In Karachi, Pakistan's most populous city and built right on the coast, millions of people also began to flee inland, though the swollen banks of the Indus River made their progress extremely difficult.

On the other side of the Arabian Sea, the rising waters of the Indian Ocean pushed into the Gulf of Oman, through the Straits of Hormuz and into the Persian Gulf where, in the confines of the narrow waterway, it was noticed in a matter of hours. Within a week, beaches began to erode and a great debate raged in the capitals of the Gulf nations.

Their livelihood was in great jeopardy. The threat from the ocean would inevitably shut down the economies of all the Gulf countries because their offshore loading facilities for oil were built along the coasts. At Saudi Arabia's Sea Island loading terminal, where a million barrels of oil a day were being pumped, the water had already covered some of the lower pipelines at high tide. The handwriting was on the wall: in less than a month, the entire facility would be lost to the Gulf and then no more oil would be pumped from Sea Island. The situation was much the same at all the other loading terminals.

At the port of Ras Tanura, the site of Saudi Arabia's largest petroleum exporting facility, most of the storage tanks had been constructed just a few feet above sea level. Given the rapid rise in the ocean, Ras Tanura would be lost in another three weeks. The King of Saudi Arabia was enraged, knowing it would cost billions of dollars to replace the facility, not to mention the daily loss in revenues.

Further up the Gulf, the sheiks of Kuwait began leaving the country, flying to their summer homes in Europe. To them, it was evident that Kuwait was fated for a tragic ending and, since they really had no allegiance to the barren, sandy patch of ground and the people who lived there, why stay? Besides, ninety-nine percent of their money was in European bank accounts, and most of their property was also in Europe.

On the continent of Africa, the first major city to witness the change in the ocean was the port city of Cape Town at the southernmost tip of the continent. The entire population began to evacuate the area, leaving Africa's biggest and most beautiful city to the mercy of the ocean. At Port Elizabeth and Durban, also large cities on the coast, nearly everyone started moving their belongings inland and away from the potential flooding. The evacuation began in relative calm. In Africa's other major port cities, the populations also began to flee but, with plenty of room in the interior of the continent, the process was mostly orderly.

In Europe, the one country most susceptible to flooding was the Netherlands. The Dutch had invested billions of dollars into sea barriers such as the Oosterschelde Barrier in the southwest corner of the country, and in dikes. The Netherland's biggest and longest dike, the Afsluitdjik, separated the bay the Dutch called IJsselmeer from the North Sea. For awhile, the people of the Netherlands knew that their barriers and dikes would hold. They were engineering marvels that had been designed to withstand everything the sea could throw at them. Everything except the predicted two hundred foot displacement of the earth's oceans caused by the melting of the ice cap at the South Pole. A worried Queen Beatrix went to the Afsluitdjik, government engineers pointing out to her the extent of the sudden rise in the North Sea, their party followed by nearly two hundred reporters. The image of the elderly queen standing atop the dike staring out at the sea was imprinted on the minds of all Europeans.

Just across the North Sea, in London, people began to wonder if they, too, should consider an evacuation. Already, the Thames River was rising, and inevitably it would back up into London proper, overflowing its banks and flooding the city. For the English, losing London would be a major catastrophe. Like Australia and New Zealand, most of Great Britain's major cities were ports: Southampton, Portsmouth, Plymouth, Liverpool, Glasgow, Edinburgh, and dozens of others. And many suburbs of these cities were within the coastal plain that would eventually lie underneath the surface of the ocean. Across St. George's Channel, the citizens of Dublin in Ireland were angry over the impending calamity. To the north, the people of Belfast reacted similarly.

Across the English Channel, the coastal cities of northern France would suffer a similar fate. Indeed, nearly every country in Europe had large coastal cities: Helsinki, Stockholm,

Copenhagen, Oslo, Gdansk, Lisbon, Barcelona, Marseilles, Nice, Naples, Palermo, Venice, Athens, and more. The people of Italy were especially aghast at news of the impending calamity. Millions of Italians lived in small coastal towns and villages, and the experts were saying that the Mediterranean Sea would claim every one of them. The people of Greece wouldn't fare any better, nor would those on the islands of Sardinia, Sicily, and Crete.

Europe was in an uproar. As word spread about how bad it would get, an oil refinery was blown up, as were several dozen gas stations. In London, an oil company executive was kidnapped, his body found a day later, hanging from a light pole.

There were riots in Berlin, Amsterdam, Rome, and Athens. The riot in Berlin turned into a pitched battle between police and citizens. At least four hundred people were killed. In Spain, they immediately passed a law making all use of automobiles and trucks forbidden, except by the authorities. Police were ordered to shoot anyone who broke the new law. This action only enraged the Spanish, some of whom began carrying guns and shooting back.

The industrial nations, which had created most of the gases involved in global warming, were the very countries who couldn't cope with the present crisis.

The situation in America was far worse than in Europe. Just as the President and his advisors had feared, widespread unrest broke out simultaneously in twenty-two American cities, while in nearby Cuba and Puerto Rico there were riots in Havana and San Juan, making any kind of orderly evacuation impossible. There were also riots in Kingston, Port au Prince, and Santo Domingo. All of this was an exercise in futility, for Mother Nature paid no attention to the ravings of man, and the oceans continued their advance up onto land, all along the shores of the North American continent and the Caribbean islands.

In America, the tip of Florida saw it first. The beaches of Key West and the Florida Keys were inundated by an ocean so vast, the people who lived there realized they were going to lose their precious islands and never see them again. The hundred thousand plus residents of Key West Island, the other key islands, and Key Largo began a hurried evacuation on the overseas highway to the mainland of Florida.

Just up the coast from Key Largo, Miami was the first big metropolitan area to be noticeably affected by the rise in the Atlantic Ocean. Within the week, it became evident that several hundred billion dollars of prime real estate was going to go underwater. The communities of Coral Gables, Coconut Grove, Key Biscayne, South Beach, Surfside, Bal Harbour, Golden Beach and, of course, the famous Miami Beach, all knew they were doomed. At the end of the week, at high tide, the ocean began to lap up onto the concrete patios of the posh hotels lining Miami Beach. The residents were dismayed and astounded that the ocean could change so drastically and in such a short period of time. How could this happen? they kept asking themselves.

Not only were most of Florida's major cities right on the coast — Miami, Fort Lauderdale, Tampa, St. Petersburg, Daytona Beach, Pensacola, and Jacksonville but, even worse, the entire Florida peninsula was barely above sea level. When it became evident that the ocean would eventually cover Florida, the governor decided to declare the entire state a disaster area and he ordered all residents to begin evacuating north into Georgia and Alabama. Of all the states, Florida would suffer the worst.

The entire nation watched the beginning of the Florida evacuation with agonized consternation. Suddenly, in the eyes of many, the actions of the Defenders of the Planet didn't seem so radical after all, for Mother Nature was proving to be more terrible than any group of humans ever could be. Adults became afraid, and their children, sensing their fear, also became afraid. The world was changing right before their eyes, and there wasn't anything anyone could do about it.

Elsewhere along the Atlantic seaboard, entire communities were uprooted and forced to begin moving inland. At the time the evacuation began in Florida, those who lived on the barrier islands of Georgia, South Carolina, and North Carolina were also forced to leave their homes to the fury of the Atlantic Ocean, leaving behind forever everything that was dear to them, their homes, most of their belongings, and the islands they loved.

All along the east coast, the great cities of America began to contemplate the catastrophe that was about to befall them. Even cities like Washington and Philadelphia weren't safe from the rising oceans, for there was no doubt that the rivers that emptied into Chesapeake Bay and the Atlantic Ocean would eventually begin to back up and overflow their banks. With each high tide, this became more and more evident as the banks of rivers like the Potomac and the Delaware began to disappear.

In Virginia, the James River began to back up as far inland as Richmond. The cities clustered around the mouth of the James River, including Hampton, Norfolk, Chesapeake, Portsmouth, and Newport News began drawing up plans for a complete evacuation. Farther east, Virginia Beach residents wondered about moving inland, asking themselves the same nagging question that plagued millions of other human beings whose communities faced the Atlantic Ocean: where would they go?

In Maryland, all the rivers that emptied into Chesapeake Bay began a steady and constant rise against their banks. Sewers and storm drains began backing up, and in many low-lying areas toilets began spilling water out onto bathroom floors. The overflowing toilets could not be fixed, and people, even those who didn't want to believe it, finally began to realize the crux of the problem: the Atlantic Ocean was preparing to move inland, it was going to move soon, and nothing could stop it.

Delaware residents were informed that they would eventually become part of an island with Maryland, the island bordered by Chesapeake Bay on the west, Delaware Bay and the Atlantic on the east, and an enlarged Delaware Canal to the north.

In New Jersey, the governor was told by scientists that the entire lower half of the state would eventually be lost to the ocean or become uninhabitable. Drawing a line from the city of Trenton all the way east to Asbury Park on the coast, it appeared that most of the land south of such a line would be inundated or else become completely surrounded by sea water. Next to Florida, it seemed that the people of New Jersey would suffer the most from the anticipated rise in the Atlantic. Much of the state would simply disappear beneath the ocean.

The residents of the barrier islands along the east coast of Maryland, Delaware, and New Jersey began an evacuation to higher ground to the north and west, mostly into neighboring Pennsylvania, where entire tent cities began springing up on high ground around places like Allentown, Lancaster, York, and smaller cities like Hanover, Waynesboro, Greencastle, and Uniontown, sorely taxing the ability of these communities to provide aid and shelter to the influx of American refugees.

In some areas the evacuations were orderly, but mostly it was disorganized mayhem. People were easily angered, and it seemed that everyone was taking their guns with them. Shootings became prevalent, often over the slightest irritant.

One of the worst areas for violence was New York City and nearby Newark. The homicide rate, especially by handguns, tripled within days of the President's address to the nation. What was already an intolerable murder rate became an obscene murder rate, and bodies littered the streets of the giant metropolis.

New Yorkers quickly came to realize that their great city was changing right before their eyes. The level of water in New York Harbor steadily rose against the concrete seawalls and at high tide crashed over the walls. Worse, and even more ominous, the subway tunnels began to fill with seawater, and pumps operating twenty-four hours a day couldn't stop the influx. Eventually, the subway trains had to stop running altogether and for New Yorkers this was particularly disturbing news. Hundreds of thousands of people began to flee the city.

This was just the beginning. The citizens of New York really started to panic when it was announced that La Guardia Airport would be closed permanently because waves were lapping over the runways at high tide. With frenzied activity, people prepared to leave New York, and with every day that went by, the killings and the violence within the city increased.

Northeast of New York, tens of millions of other Americans also realized that they would soon have to leave their homes. All along the coasts of Connecticut, Rhode Island, Massachusetts, New Hampshire and Maine, people started packing and preparing to move inland. The cities and towns along the New England coast were some of the oldest and most developed communities in the United States, including Greenwich, Stamford, Norwalk, Fairfield, Bridgeport, Milford, New Haven, New London, Norwich, Providence, Pawtucket, East Providence, New Bedford, Plymouth, Boston, Portland, and hundreds of smaller towns built right on the ocean. The millions who lived here had great difficulty accepting the catastrophe that was about to befall them.

Up in Canada, even citizens of Montreal and Quebec were affected by the rising oceans. At high tide, the St. Lawrence River backed up and began rising against its banks all along the river, as far inland as Montreal. The people of Montreal were told that they had a grace period, but at the current rate of ice melt in Antarctica, that would only be for another four or five weeks.

Across the continent, in the Pacific Northwest, millions more Canadians and Americans prepared to leave their homes and move inland, people from Vancouver, Victoria, Seattle, and Tacoma. In Portland, Oregon and many smaller cities, hundreds of thousands of people who lived in low-lying areas along the banks of the Columbia River also decided that they would have to leave. With each successive high tide, the Columbia rose higher and higher against its banks, flooding over in several places.

Most of the those living in the hills surrounding San Francisco Bay realized they would be safe for the time being, but some of the city's most famous landmarks began to suffer almost immediately from the rising Pacific Ocean. Candlestick Park lost its entire parking lot and, hours later, Candlestick's playing field was several feet under water. Farther south, San Francisco

International Airport had to be closed because of water on the runways. Across the bay in Oakland, the situation was far worse, for much of the built-up areas were right on the water at perilously low elevations. Within a week, many of Oakland's streets were awash in water, and the sewer system backed up in all the low-lying parts of the city.

All along the coast of California, the beaches began to erode away into the rising Pacific Ocean, and millions who lived near the water began to think about fleeing inland. The change in the coastline was real, and it was scary. In many areas, the ocean at high tide caused lagoons and coastal flood plains to spill over into adjacent developed land. Near San Diego, the famous Del Mar racetrack parking lot and surrounding area became a bog. Just to the south, the grounds of the resplendent Hotel Del Coronado became a mushy swamp smelling of seawater, and all the lush gardens of flowers and plants began to die a slow death.

Near San Clemente, the San Onofre nuclear power plant was built right on the beach, fully exposed to the overwhelming force of the ocean. Utility officials began toiling day and night to shut the plant down safely and remove all the stored irradiated waste and materials, but it seemed utterly hopeless. There was simply no way to do it quickly without great hazard. And when Orange County residents were told that the plant was to be taken off-line, with subsequent loss of electric power, they bitterly realized that what was happening in Antarctica would pervade into their lives as nothing else had ever done. The melting ice was causing tremendous displacement, not just of water, but of the very fabric of American society.

This realization hit hardest at the wealthy elite of Orange County. With each succeeding high tide, their yachts and sail boats harbored at any of the prestigious Newport Beach marinas rose higher and higher against their moorings. The rising ocean would soon render the flotation marinas useless, and the owners of these boats all faced the same dilemma. They either had to move the vessels out into the harbor and anchor them there, or take them out to sea. Even worse, many of the boats' owners had their homes right on the edges of Newport Bay. These million dollar houses were filled with expensive art and furniture, and so these people, the wealthiest in Orange County, actually faced multiple dilemmas. Which of their prized possessions would they tend to first? Where would they take them?

Their problems were compounded by what was happening to the north. In Los Angeles, the violence was getting especially ugly, even to city residents who had become inured to death by guns. It was estimated that, since the riot had started, over a thousand people had been killed. Fighting spread outside the city limits to other areas of Southern California, subjecting the population to night after night of abject terror, people killing each other with slightest provocation.

Americans, never having to face a crisis of this magnitude, were unable to overcome their fears. America began to fall apart. Entire regions became splintered and factionalized, and the military and government authorities began to lose control. Guns were everywhere, and people used them promiscuously.

Eventually, the President declared Marshal Law to be in effect across the entire nation, ordering federal troops into the worst hotspots. Deadly force became the only sense of order people respected. Although no one had an accurate count, it was estimated that within the first days after the President's initial address, troops and police shot more than twelve thousand people.

This all happened before any large city had sunk beneath the waves of the oceans, before any entire region had been made uninhabitable. And, though no one wanted to admit it, everyone knew that the worst was still to come.

EPILOGUE

The five of them were sitting at a table in the bar of the Algonquin Hotel, drinking tequila. It was past ten in the evening, and the bar was sparsely filled with people, mostly locals from Magdalena who were talking about the weather and the rising ocean and how it might affect Mexico.

They had tarried in Magdalena for nearly three days, but they knew it was time to be moving on. After eating a late dinner, they'd gone into the bar for a drink, each instinctively knowing that tonight would be their last night together. They made small talk for awhile, but then Jonathan Holmes looked around the table, his expression becoming serious.

"What next?" he asked.

"Stu and I need to get back to Phoenix," Flynn said.

Stu nodded. "Yes. I've got children to look after... my patients."

"Don't worry, Dr. Holmes," Flynn said, "you'll be okay now. I think you're out of danger, at least for the time being. Mexico is a big country. You should be able to hide out here." Flynn looked fondly at Jake and Linda. "And you'll be in good hands."

"Jake and I thought about going to Veracruz," Linda said.

"Veracruz is right on the coast," Holmes said. "I don't think we should go there."

"God!" Linda frowned. "I forgot. You're right, Dr. Holmes. Veracruz will be in turmoil, like every other coastal city on earth."

"No problem," Jake said. "We'll go into the interior."

"Well," Holmes said, "I was studying a map earlier today. There is a place to the east of here. It's called Chihuahua, and it has mountains. It seems like it would be a good area."

"Take the car," Flynn offered. "We can take the Harley back to the border. From there, we'll be able to get back to Phoenix muy pronto."

"You're sure?" Jake asked.

"Yes," Flynn said. "It'll be all right. You should leave first thing in the morning. We've all got work to do. We can't let our planet go down."

"That's the right spirit!" Holmes said. "If we're going to save this planet, we'd better get moving."

Stu pulled out a business card and wrote a phone number on it. He handed the card to Holmes. "Memorize this phone number, then destroy the card. It's our local electronic bulletin board in Phoenix. I'll pass along any messages you send us. It's important that you stay in touch with us. We can help you."

"I'm sure you can," Holmes said. "But I can't stay in hiding for very long. With the oceans rising as they are, it's vital that I convince the leaders of the world that quick action must be taken, possibly extreme measures. The world is changing rapidly now, and mankind must change with it."

"How will you convince them?" Stu asked.

"I'm not sure, but if I could get to Washington, I could meet with President Rawlings. He has to understand that this is not going to be the end of it. The very future of the planet is at stake."

Linda looked at him with wide eyes. "What do you mean when you say that this is not going to be the end of it?" she asked.

"The melting of the ice caps and the rising of the oceans will not be the only weather-related phenomenon that is going to occur due to this greenhouse effect. There's no doubt we're going to lose our coasts, but the conditions within the continental land masses will become absolutely miserable. It's important that people understand that."

"Miserable?" Jake asked. "What's going to happen?"

"It won't be good, Jake," Holmes said. "The hydrologic cycle of the earth will be greatly affected by a warming atmosphere.

As more water evaporates in the oceans due to the increased atmospheric heat, there will be large low pressure systems developing all around the globe: hurricanes, typhoons, and cyclones. We'll have increased storms and heavy rains everywhere because of this warming. Torrential rain will persist in some areas for weeks on end. That alone will make things miserable due to localized flooding and erosion. That's not all, however. I'm afraid these rainstorms will be accompanied by strange winds... tornadoes and water spouts in areas where we've never seen them before."

"It doesn't sound too cool," Jake said.

Holmes nodded. "No," he said. "But, even worse, I fear that with the big low pressure systems, it's possible we could see super hurricanes, with wind speeds of three to four hundred miles per hour."

"My God!" Linda exclaimed.

"That couldn't be possible," Stu stated. "Could it?"

"I believe it could. A hurricane develops when air starts flowing in vertical currents due to high air temperatures. If these air temperatures are increased because of the greenhouse effect, then the airflows will more than likely be stronger. Much stronger. Also, the size of hurricanes will probably become much larger than normal. We could have hurricanes with eyes that are hundreds of miles wide, with hurricane force winds over an area a thousand miles in diameter, or more.

"You see, a hurricane is nature's way of dissipating the enormous heat that builds up in the equatorial regions of the planet. As this heat increases, as I'm sure it will, the hurricanes forming in the future will be real monsters. I suspect if one of these super hurricanes hit the east coast of America, it could level an entire state before it dies out. It could kill hundreds of thousands of people."

"What about typhoons and cyclones?" Stu asked.

"They are nothing more than hurricanes. The only reason they have a different name is because they occur in different oceans. A similar storm system in the Pacific is called a typhoon.

In the Indian Ocean, they're called cyclones. Under conditions of global warming, the Pacific Ocean can breed a super typhoon just as easily as the Atlantic can breed a super hurricane. Unfortunately, in the Far East they'll be much more vulnerable. In Japan they just wouldn't have anywhere to hide. A super typhoon would completely cross any one of their islands before it died out, and in a heavily populated area like Tokyo, such a storm could kill a million or more people. Their houses are poorly constructed, though a three or four hundred-mile-per-hour wind would take down even the strongest buildings."

"Dr. Holmes, even if you told the President that this would happen, would he believe it?" Flynn asked.

"I think I could convince him. After all, not too long ago who would have believed that Antarctica would melt? But it's much more serious. What I just described is the short-term forecast. In the long-term, growing crops on a wet, hot planet may become impossible. If we don't have food, eventually nothing else will really matter, will it?" Holmes looked at them with a sad expression, and then he said, "We are running out of time."

"Is there any hope for us?" Linda asked.

"I don't know the answer to that," he responded. "But I'm not going to sit around and wait for the end. We must act, and we must be strong. But whatever the future holds, I'm glad to be in the company of people like yourself. I almost feel like I'm becoming a member of the Defenders of the Planet."

"I think maybe you already have," Flynn suggested.

Holmes raised an eyebrow but said nothing. Flynn's words were closer to the truth than he dared to admit.

"Dr. Holmes, if we get you to Washington, what will you say to convince the President?" Linda asked. "What can you say that would do any good?"

Holmes thought for a moment, then said, "I'd say that it's not too late to try to rectify the wrongs of the past. We may be too late to prevent the melting of Antarctica's ice, but we aren't too late to save this planet. If we act aggressively, we'll probably be okay. We human beings are, after all, rugged and adaptable creatures. And we will adapt to the changing world. I'm afraid we won't have much choice. If we don't adapt, we will become extinct."

Linda looked at him with a blank expression. "I hope it's not too late, Dr. Holmes," she said. "For our own sake, and for the sake of the earth. I'm so sorry that this has all happened."

Holmes' face became grim. He drank his remaining tequila, setting the empty glass down heavily onto the table, gazing into it as if he were staring into a crystal ball. Frowning, Holmes searched for the right words. Then, he said, "People are in for a period of terrible suffering. It's the price we're going to pay... for burning billions of barrels of oil over all these years, for sending millions of tons of ozone-depleting chemicals high into the atmosphere, and for worldwide deforestation. We've totally screwed up this planet. If only people had listened... if only we had done things differently."

"Do you think it's too late for us, then?" Jake asked.

"No," he answered. "It's never too late, not as long as we remain committed to doing what is right."

"And as long as we fight," Linda added.

Holmes looked up from his glass, directly into her eyes. "Yes," he said. "We must fight, and we must keep on fighting."

3